SELECTED STORIES OF
EUDORA WELTY

SELECTED STORIES OF
EUDORA WELTY

A CURTAIN OF GREEN AND OTHER STORIES

WITH AN INTRODUCTION BY
KATHERINE ANNE PORTER

THE WIDE NET AND OTHER STORIES

THE MODERN LIBRARY
NEW YORK

Welty, Eudora
[Selections. 1992]
Selected Stories of Eudora Welty/Introduction by Katherine Anne
Porter.—Modern Library Ed.
p.   cm.
ISBN 0–679–60002–7
I. Title.
PS3545.E6A6 1992   813'.52—dc20   92–50232

Manufactured in the United States of America
2 4 6 8 9 7 5 3 1

EUDORA WELTY

Eudora Welty was born in Jackson, Mississippi, on April 13, 1909. Of her tranquil childhood she wrote: "I am a writer who came of a sheltered life. A sheltered life can be a daring life as well. For all serious daring starts from within." She studied at Mississippi State College for Women, the University of Wisconsin, and Columbia University, intending on a career in advertising, an idea abandoned in favor of writing after her stories began to be published regularly in the mid-1930s. The appearance of her work in *The New Yorker* and *The Atlantic Monthly* established a reputation that was furthered by the publication of her first story collection, *A Curtain of Green,* in 1941. After her college days she had returned to Jackson, where she would live permanently.

Further stories were collected in *The Wide Net* (1943), *The Golden Apples* (1949), *The Bride of the Innisfallen* (1955), and a book of stories for children, *The Shoe Bird* (1964). Another collection, *Moon Lake,* appeared in 1980 along with *The Collected Stories.* The novella *The Robber Bridegroom* was published in 1942 and was followed by other longer works of fiction: *Delta Wedding* (1946), *The Ponder Heart* (1954), and, after a hiatus of several years, *Losing Battles* (1970), which focused new attention on her work. Her next book, *The Optimist's Daughter* (1972), won the Pulitzer Prize. A collection of essays, *The Eye of the Story* (1978), was followed by the memoir *One Writer's Beginnings,* which in 1984 became an unexpected best-seller.

In addition to her work as a writer, Welty has published a book of photographs, *One Time, One Place* (1971), recording her visual impressions of Mississippi in the early thirties. Two of her books, *The Ponder Heart* and *The Robber Bridegroom,* have been adapted for the stage. This Modern Library edition contains the first two volumes of Welty's books of stories, *A Curtain of Green* and *The Wide Net.* The original edition of *A Curtain of Green* was published with an introduction by her mentor Katherine Anne Porter, and it is included here.

CONTENTS

A CURTAIN OF GREEN

CONTENTS

THE WIDE NET

A CURTAIN
OF GREEN
AND OTHER
STORIES

———◆———

INTRODUCTION TO THE ORIGINAL EDITION OF
A CURTAIN OF GREEN
by Katherine Anne Porter

Friends of us both first brought Eudora Welty to visit me three years ago in Louisiana. It was hot midsummer, they had driven over from Mississippi, her home state, and we spent a pleasant evening together talking in the cool old house with all the windows open. Miss Welty sat listening, as she must have done a great deal of listening on many such occasions. She was and is a quiet, tranquil-looking, modest girl, and unlike the young Englishman of the story, she has something to be modest about, as this collection of short stories proves.

She considers her personal history as hardly worth mentioning, a fact in itself surprising enough, since a vivid personal career of fabulous ups and downs, hardships and strokes of luck, travels in far countries, spiritual and intellectual exile, defensive flight, homesick return with a determined groping for native roots, and a confusion of contradictory jobs have long been the mere conventions of an American author's life. Miss Welty was born and brought up in Jackson, Mississippi, where her father, now dead, was president of a Southern insurance company. Family life was cheerful and thriving; she seems to have got on excellently with both her parents and her two brothers. Education, in the Southern manner with daughters, was continuous, indulgent, and precisely as serious as she chose to make it. She went from school in Mississippi to the University of Wisconsin, thence to Columbia, New York, and so home again where she lives with her mother, among her lifelong friends and acquaintances, quite simply and amiably. She tried a job or two because that seemed the next thing, and did some publicity and newspaper work; but as she had no real need of a job, she gave up the notion and settled down to writing.

She loves music, listens to a great deal of it, all kinds; grows flowers very successfully, and remarks that she is "underfoot locally," meaning that she has a normal amount of social life. Normal social life in a medium-sized Southern town can become a pretty absorbing occupation, and the only comment her friends make when a new story appears is, "Why, Eudora, when did you write that?" Not how, or even why, just when. They see her about so much, what time has she for writing? Yet she spends an immense amount of time at it. "I haven't a literary life at all," she wrote once, "not much of a confession, maybe. But I do feel that the people and things I love are of a true and human world, and there is no clutter about them. . . . I would not understand a literary life."

We can do no less than dismiss that topic as casually as she does. Being the child of her place and time, profiting perhaps without being aware of it by the cluttered experiences, foreign travels, and disorders of the generation immediately preceding her, she will never have to go away and live among the Eskimos, or Mexican Indians; she need not follow a war and smell death to feel herself alive: she knows about death already. She shall not need even to live in New York in order to feel that she is having the kind of experience, the sense of "life" proper to a serious author. She gets her right nourishment from the source natural to her—her experience so far has been quite enough for her and of precisely the right kind. She began writing spontaneously when she was a child, being a born writer; she continued without any plan for a profession, without any particular encouragement, and, as it proved, not needing any. For a good number of years she believed she was going to be a painter, and painted quite earnestly while she wrote without much effort.

Nearly all the Southern writers I know were early, omnivorous, insatiable readers, and Miss Welty runs reassuringly true to this pattern. She had at arm's reach the typical collection of books which existed as a matter of course in a certain kind of Southern family, so that she had read the ancient Greek and Roman poetry, history and fable, Shakespeare, Milton, Dante, the eighteenth-century English and the nineteenth-century French novelists, with a dash of Tolstoy and Dostoievsky, before she realized what she was reading. When she first discovered contemporary literature, she was just the right age to find first W. B. Yeats and Virginia Woolf in the air around her; but always, from the beginning until now, she loved folk tales, fairy tales, old legends, and she likes to listen to the songs and stories of people who live in old communities whose culture is recollected and bequeathed orally.

She has never studied the writing craft in any college. She has never belonged to a literary group, and until after her first collection was ready to be published she had never discussed with any colleague or older artist any problem of her craft. Nothing else that I know about her could be more satisfactory to me than this; it seems to me immensely right, the very way a young artist should grow, with pride and independence and the courage really to face out the individual struggle; to make and correct mistakes and take the consequences of them, to stand firmly on his own feet in the end. I believe in the rightness of Miss Welty's instinctive knowledge that writing cannot be taught, but only learned, and learned by the individual in his own way, at his own pace and in his own time, for the process of mastering the medium is part of a cellular growth in a most complex organism; it is a way of life and a mode of being which cannot be divided from the kind of human creature you were the day you were born, and only in obeying the law of this singular being can the artist know his true directions and the right ends for him.

Miss Welty escaped, by miracle, the whole corrupting and destructive influence of the contemporary, organized tampering with young and promising talents by professional teachers who are rather monotonously divided into two major sorts: those theorists who are incapable of producing one passable specimen of the art they profess to teach; or good, sometimes first-rate, artists who are humanly unable to resist forming disciples and imitators among their students. It is all well enough to say that, of this second class, the able talent will throw off the master's influence and strike out for himself. Such influence has merely added new obstacles to an already difficult road. Miss Welty escaped also a militant social consciousness, in the current radical-intellectual sense, she never professed Communism, and she has not expressed, except implicitly, any attitude at all on the state of politics or the condition of society. But there is an ancient system of ethics, an unanswerable, indispensable moral law, on which she is grounded firmly, and this, it would seem to me, is ample domain enough; these laws have never been the peculiar property of any party or creed or nation, they relate to that true and human world of which the artist is a living part; and when he dissociates himself from it in favor of a set of political, which is to say, inhuman, rules, he cuts himself away from his proper society—living men.

There exist documents of political and social theory which belong, if not to poetry, certainly to the department of humane letters. They are reassuring statements of the great hopes and dearest faiths of mankind and they are acts of high imagination. But all working, practical political systems, even those professing to originate in moral grandeur, are based upon and operate by contempt of human life and the individual fate; in accepting any one of them and shaping his mind and work to that mold, the artist dehumanizes himself, unfits himself for the practise of any art.

Not being in a hurry, Miss Welty was past twenty-six years when she offered her first story, "The Death of a Traveling Salesman," to the editor of a little magazine unable to pay, for she could not believe that anyone would buy a story from her; the magazine was *Manuscript*, the editor John Rood, and he accepted it gladly. Rather surprised, Miss Welty next tried the *Southern Review*, where she met with a great welcome and the enduring partisanship of Albert Erskine, who regarded her as his personal discovery. The story was "A Piece of News" and it was followed by others published in the *Southern Review,* the *Atlantic Monthly,* and *Harper's Bazaar.*

She has, then, never been neglected, never unappreciated, and she feels simply lucky about it. She wrote to a friend: "When I think of Ford Madox Ford! You remember how you gave him my name and how he tried his best to find a publisher for my book of stories all that last year of his life; and he wrote me so many charming notes, all of his time going to his little brood of promising writers, the kind of thing that could have gone on forever. Once I read in the *Saturday Review* an article of his on the species and the way they were neglected by publishers, and he used me as the example chosen at random. He ended his cry with 'What is to become of both branches of Anglo-Saxondom if this state of things continues?' Wasn't that wonderful, really, and typical? I may have been more impressed by that than would other readers who knew him. I did not know him, but I knew it was typical. And here I myself have turned out to be not at all the martyred promising writer, but have had all the good luck and all the good things Ford chided the world for withholding from me and my kind."

But there is a trap lying just ahead, and all short-story writers know what it is—The Novel. That novel which every publisher hopes to obtain from every short-story writer of any gifts at all, and who finally does obtain it, nine times out of ten. Already publishers have told her, "Give us first a novel, and then we will publish your short stories." It is a special sort of trap for poets, too, though quite often a good poet can and does write a good novel.

Miss Welty has tried her hand at novels, laboriously, duti-
fully, youthfully thinking herself perhaps in the wrong to
refuse, since so many authoritarians have told her that
was the next step. It is by no means the next step. She
can very well become a master of the short story, there
are almost perfect stories in this book. It is quite possible
she can never write a novel, and there is no reason why she
should. The short story is a special and difficult medium,
and contrary to a widely spread popular superstition it
has no formula that can be taught by correspondence
school. There is nothing to hinder her from writing novels if she wishes or believes she can. I only say that her
good gift, just as it is now, alive and flourishing, should
not be retarded by a perfectly artificial demand upon her
to do the conventional thing. It is a fact that the public
for short stories is smaller than the public for novels; this
seems to me no good reason for depriving that minority.
I remember a reader writing to an editor, complaining
that he did not like collections of short stories because, just
as he had got himself worked into one mood or frame of
mind, he was called upon to change to another. If that is
an important objection, we might also apply it to music.
We might compare the novel to a symphony, and a collection of short stories to a good concert recital. In any
case, this complainant is not our reader, yet our reader
does exist, and there would be more of him if more and
better short stories were offered.

These stories offer an extraordinary range of mood,
pace, tone, and variety of material. The scene is limited
to a town the author knows well; the farthest reaches of

that scene never go beyond the boundaries of her own state, and many of the characters are of the sort that caused a Bostonian to remark that he would not care to meet them socially. Lily Daw is a half-witted girl in the grip of social forces represented by a group of earnest ladies bent on doing the best thing for her, no matter what the consequences. Keela, the Outcast Indian Maid, is a crippled little Negro who represents a type of man considered most unfortunate by W. B. Yeats: one whose experience was more important than he, and completely beyond his powers of absorption. But the really unfortunate man in this story is the ignorant young white boy, who had innocently assisted at a wrong done the little Negro, and for a most complex reason, finds that no reparation is possible, or even desirable to the victim. . . . The heroine of "Why I Live at the P.O." is a terrifying case of dementia praecox. In this first group—for the stories may be loosely classified on three separate levels—the spirit is satire and the key grim comedy. Of these, "The Petrified Man" offers a fine clinical study of vulgarity— vulgarity absolute, chemically pure, exposed mercilessly to its final subhuman depths. Dullness, bitterness, rancor, self-pity, baseness of all kinds, can be most interesting material for a story provided these are not also the main elements in the mind of the author. There is nothing in the least vulgar or frustrated in Miss Welty's mind. She has simply an eye and an ear sharp, shrewd, and true as a tuning fork. She has given to this little story all her wit and observation, her blistering humor and her just cruelty; for she has none of that slack tolerance or sentimental tenderness toward symptomatic evils that amounts to criminal collusion between author and character. Her use of this material raises the quite awfully sordid little tale to a level above its natural habitat, and its realism seems almost to have the quality of caricature, as complete realism so often does. Yet, as painters of the grotesque make only detailed reports of actual living types observed more keenly than the average eye is capable of observing, so Miss Welty's little human monsters are not really caricatures at all, but individuals exactly and clearly presented: which is perhaps a case against realism, if we cared to go into it. She does better on another level—for the important reason that the themes are richer—in such beautiful stories as "Death of a Traveling Salesman," "A Memory," "A Worn Path." Let me admit a deeply personal preference for this particular kind of story, where external act and the internal voiceless life of the human imagination almost meet and mingle on the mysterious threshold between dream and waking, one reality refusing to admit or confirm the existence of the other, yet both conspiring toward the same end. This is not easy to accomplish, but it is always worth trying, and Miss Welty is so successful at it, it would seem her most familiar territory. There is no blurring at the edges, but evidences of an active and disciplined imagination working firmly in a strong line of continuity, the waking faculty of daylight reason recollecting and recording the crazy logic of the dream. There is in none of these stories any trace of autobiography in the prime sense, except as the author is omnipresent, and knows each character she writes about as only the artist knows the thing he has made, by first experiencing it in imagination. But perhaps in "A Memory," one of the best stories, there might be something of early personal history in the story of the child on the beach, alienated from the world of adult knowledge by her state of childhood, who hoped to learn the secrets of life by looking at everything, squaring her hands before her eyes to bring the observed thing into a frame—the gesture of one born to select, to arrange, to bring apparently disparate elements into harmony within deliberately fixed boundaries. But the author is freed already in her youth from self-love, self-pity, self-preoccupation, that triple damnation of too many of the young and gifted, and has reached an admirable objectivity. In such stories as "Old Mr. Marblehall," "Powerhouse," "The Hitch-Hikers," she combines an objective reporting with great perception of mental or emotional states, and in "Clytie" the very shape of madness takes place before your eyes in a straight account of actions and speech, the personal appearance and habits of dress of the main character and her family.

In all of these stories, varying as they do in excellence, I find nothing false or labored, no diffusion of interest, no wavering of mood—the approach is direct and simple in method, though the themes and moods are anything but simple, and there is even in the smallest story a sense of power in reserve which makes me believe firmly that, splendid beginning that this is, it is only the beginning.

"But now that so much is being changed, is it not time that we should change? Could we not try to develop ourselves

a little, slowly and gradually take upon ourselves our share in the labor of love? We have been spared all its hardship . . . we have been spoiled by easy enjoyment. . . . But what if we despised our successes, what if we began from the beginning to learn the work of love which has always been done for us? What if we were to go and become neophytes, now that so much is changing?" *

KATHERINE ANNE PORTER
August 19, 1941

The Journal of My Other Self, by Rainer Maria Rilke. Translated by M. D. Herter Norton and John Linton. Published by W. W. Norton & Company, Inc.

TO
DIARMUID RUSSELL

LILY DAW
AND THE
THREE LADIES

———————◆———————

MRS. WATTS AND MRS. CARSON were both in the post office in Victory when the letter came from the Ellisville Institute for the Feeble-Minded of Mississippi. Aimee Slocum, with her hand still full of mail, ran out in front and handed it straight to Mrs. Watts, and they all three read it together. Mrs. Watts held it taut between her pink hands, and Mrs. Carson underscored each line slowly with her thimbled finger. Everybody else in the post office wondered what was up now.

"What will Lily say," beamed Mrs. Carson at last, "when we tell her we're sending her to Ellisville!"

"She'll be tickled to death," said Mrs. Watts, and added in a guttural voice to a deaf lady, "Lily Daw's getting in at Ellisville!"

"Don't you all dare go off and tell Lily without me!" called Aimee Slocum, trotting back to finish putting up the mail.

"Do you suppose they'll look after her down there?"

Mrs. Carson began to carry on a conversation with a group of Baptist ladies waiting in the post office. She was the Baptist preacher's wife.

"I've always heard it was lovely down there, but crowded," said one.

"Lily lets people walk over her so," said another.

"Last night at the tent show—" said another, and then popped her hand over her mouth.

"Don't mind me, I know there are such things in the world," said Mrs. Carson, looking down and fingering the tape measure which hung over her bosom.

"Oh, Mrs. Carson. Well, anyway, last night at the tent show, why, the man was just before making Lily buy a ticket to get in."

"A ticket!"

"Till my husband went up and explained she wasn't bright, and so did everybody else."

The ladies all clucked their tongues.

"Oh, it was a very nice show," said the lady who had gone. "And Lily acted so nice. She was a perfect lady—just set in her seat and stared."

"Oh, she can be a lady—she can be," said Mrs. Carson, shaking her head and turning her eyes up. "That's just what breaks your heart."

"Yes'm, she kept her eyes on—what's that thing makes all the commotion?—the xylophone," said the lady. "Didn't turn her head to the right or to the left the whole time. Set in front of me."

"The point is, what did she do after the show?" asked Mrs. Watts practically. "Lily has gotten so she is very mature for her age."

"Oh, Etta!" protested Mrs. Carson, looking at her wildly for a moment.

"And that's how come we are sending her to Ellisville," finished Mrs. Watts.

"I'm ready, you all," said Aimee Slocum, running out with white powder all over her face. "Mail's up. I don't know how good it's up."

"Well, of course, I do hope it's for the best," said several of the other ladies. They did not go at once to take their mail out of their boxes; they felt a little left out.

The three women stood at the foot of the water tank.

"To find Lily is a different thing," said Aimee Slocum.

"Where in the wide world do you suppose she'd be?" It was Mrs. Watts who was carrying the letter.

"I don't see a sign of her either on this side of the street or on the other side," Mrs. Carson declared as they walked along.

Ed Newton was stringing Redbird school tablets on the wire across the store.

"If you're after Lily, she come in here while ago and tole me she was fixin' to git married," he said.

"Ed Newton!" cried the ladies all together, clutching one another. Mrs. Watts began to fan herself at once with the letter from Ellisville. She wore widow's black, and the least thing made her hot.

"Why she is not. She's going to Ellisville, Ed," said Mrs. Carson gently. "Mrs. Watts and I and Aimee Slocum are paying her way out of our own pockets. Besides, the boys of Victory are on their honor. Lily's not going to get married, that's just an idea she's got in her head."

"More power to you, ladies," said Ed Newton, spanking himself with a tablet.

When they came to the bridge over the railroad tracks, there was Estelle Mabers, sitting on a rail. She was slowly drinking an orange Ne-Hi.

"Have you seen Lily?" they asked her.

"I'm supposed to be out here watching for her now," said the Mabers girl, as though she weren't there yet. "But for Jewel—Jewel says Lily come in the store while ago and picked out a two-ninety-eight hat and wore it off. Jewel wants to swap her something else for it."

"Oh, Estelle, Lily says she's going to get married!" cried Aimee Slocum.

"Well, I declare," said Estelle; she never understood anything.

Loralee Adkins came riding by in her Willys-Knight, tooting the horn to find out what they were talking about.

Aimee threw up her hands and ran out into the street. "Loralee, Loralee, you got to ride us up to Lily Daw's. She's up yonder fixing to get married!"

"Hop in, my land!"

"Well, that just goes to show you right now," said Mrs. Watts, groaning as she was helped into the back seat. "What we've got to do is persuade Lily it will be nicer to go to Ellisville."

"Just to think!"

While they rode around the corner Mrs. Carson was

going on in her sad voice, sad as the soft noises in the hen house at twilight. "We buried Lily's poor defenseless mother. We gave Lily all her food and kindling and every stitch she had on. Sent her to Sunday school to learn the Lord's teachings, had her baptized a Baptist. And when her old father commenced beating her and tried to cut her head off with the butcher knife, why, we went and took her away from him and gave her a place to stay."

The paintless frame house with all the weather vanes was three stories high in places and had yellow and violet stained-glass windows in front and gingerbread around the porch. It leaned steeply to one side, toward the railroad, and the front steps were gone. The car full of ladies drew up under the cedar tree.

"Now Lily's almost grown up," Mrs. Carson continued. "In fact, she's grown," she concluded, getting out.

"Talking about getting married," said Mrs. Watts disgustedly. "Thanks, Loralee, you run on home."

They climbed over the dusty zinnias onto the porch and walked through the open door without knocking.

"There certainly is always a funny smell in this house. I say it every time I come," said Aimee Slocum.

Lily was there, in the dark of the hall, kneeling on the floor by a small open trunk.

When she saw them she put a zinnia in her mouth, and held still.

"Hello, Lily," said Mrs. Carson reproachfully.

"Hello," said Lily. In a minute she gave a suck on the zinnia stem that sounded exactly like a jay bird. There she sat, wearing a petticoat for a dress, one of the things

Mrs. Carson kept after her about. Her milky-yellow hair streamed freely down from under a new hat. You could see the wavy scar on her throat if you knew it was there.

Mrs. Carson and Mrs. Watts, the two fattest, sat in the double rocker. Aimee Slocum sat on the wire chair donated from the drugstore that burned.

"Well, what are you doing, Lily?" asked Mrs. Watts, who led the rocking.

Lily smiled.

The trunk was old and lined with yellow and brown paper, with an asterisk pattern showing in darker circles and rings. Mutely the ladies indicated to each other that they did not know where in the world it had come from. It was empty except for two bars of soap and a green washcloth, which Lily was now trying to arrange in the bottom.

"Go on and tell us what you're doing, Lily," said Aimee Slocum.

"Packing, silly," said Lily.

"Where are you going?"

"Going to get married, and I bet you wish you was me now," said Lily. But shyness overcame her suddenly, and she popped the zinnia back into her mouth.

"Talk to me, dear," said Mrs. Carson. "Tell old Mrs. Carson why you want to get married."

"No," said Lily, after a moment's hesitation.

"Well, we've thought of something that will be so much nicer," said Mrs. Carson. "Why don't you go to Ellisville!"

"Won't that be lovely?" said Mrs. Watts. "Goodness, yes."

"It's a lovely place," said Aimee Slocum uncertainly.

"You've got bumps on your face," said Lily.

"Aimee, dear, you stay out of this, if you don't mind," said Mrs. Carson anxiously. "I don't know what it is comes over Lily when you come around her."

Lily stared at Aimee Slocum meditatively.

"There! Wouldn't you like to go to Ellisville now?" asked Mrs. Carson.

"No'm," said Lily.

"Why not?" All the ladies leaned down toward her in impressive astonishment.

" 'Cause I'm goin' to get married," said Lily.

"Well, and who are you going to marry, dear?" asked Mrs. Watts. She knew how to pin people down and make them deny what they'd already said.

Lily bit her lip and began to smile. She reached into the trunk and held up both cakes of soap and wagged them.

"Tell us," challenged Mrs. Watts. "Who you're going to marry, now."

"A man last night."

There was a gasp from each lady. The possible reality of a lover descended suddenly like a summer hail over their heads. Mrs. Watts stood up and balanced herself.

"One of those show fellows! A musician!" she cried.

Lily looked up in admiration.

"Did he—did he do anything to you?" In the long run, it was still only Mrs. Watts who could take charge.

"Oh, yes'm," said Lily. She patted the cakes of soap fastidiously with the tips of her small fingers and tucked them in with the washcloth

"What?" demanded Aimee Slocum, rising up and tottering before her scream. "What?" she called out in the hall.

23

"Don't ask her what," said Mrs. Carson, coming up behind. "Tell me, Lily—just yes or no— are you the same as you were?"

"He had a red coat," said Lily graciously. "He took little sticks and went *ping-pong! ding-dong!*"

"Oh, I think I'm going to faint," said Aimee Slocum, but they said, "No, you're not."

"The xylophone!" cried Mrs. Watts. "The xylophone player! Why, the coward, he ought to be run out of town on a rail!"

"Out of town? He is out of town, by now," cried Aimee. "Can't you read?—the sign in the café—Victory on the ninth, Como on the tenth? He's in Como. Como!"

"All right! We'll bring him back!" cried Mrs. Watts. "He can't get away from me!"

"Hush," said Mrs. Carson. "I don't think it's any use following that line of reasoning at all. It's better in the long run for him to be gone out of our lives for good and all. That kind of a man. He was after Lily's body alone and he wouldn't ever in this world make the poor little thing happy, even if we went out and forced him to marry her like he ought—at the point of a gun."

"Still—" began Aimee, her eyes widening.

"Shut up," said Mrs. Watts. "Mrs. Carson, you're right, I expect."

"This is my hope chest—see?" said Lily politely in the pause that followed. "You haven't even looked at it. I've already got soap and a washrag. And I have my hat— on. What are you all going to give me?"

"Lily," said Mrs. Watts, starting over, "we'll give you

24

lots of gorgeous things if you'll only go to Ellisville instead of getting married."

"What will you give me?" asked Lily.

"I'll give you a pair of hemstitched pillowcases," said Mrs. Carson.

"I'll give you a big caramel cake," said Mrs. Watts.

"I'll give you a souvenir from Jackson—a little toy bank," said Aimee Slocum. "Now will you go?"

"No," said Lily.

"I'll give you a pretty little Bible with your name on it in real gold," said Mrs. Carson.

"What if I was to give you a pink crêpe de Chine brassière with adjustable shoulder straps?" asked Mrs. Watts grimly.

"Oh, Etta."

"Well, she needs it," said Mrs. Watts. "What would they think if she ran all over Ellisville in a petticoat looking like a Fiji?"

"I wish *I* could go to Ellisville," said Aimee Slocum luringly.

"What will they have for me down there?" asked Lily softly.

"Oh! lots of things. You'll have baskets to weave, I expect. . . ." Mrs. Carson looked vaguely at the others.

"Oh, yes indeed, they will let you make all sorts of baskets," said Mrs. Watts; then her voice too trailed off.

"No'm, I'd rather get married," said Lily.

"Lily Daw! Now that's just plain stubbornness!" cried Mrs. Watts. "You almost said you'd go and then you took it back!"

"We've all asked God, Lily," said Mrs. Carson finally, "and God seemed to tell us—Mr. Carson, too—that the place where you ought to be, so as to be happy, was Ellisville."

Lily looked reverent, but still stubborn.

"We've really just got to get her there—now!" screamed Aimee Slocum all at once. "Suppose—! She can't stay here!"

"Oh, no, no, no," said Mrs. Carson hurriedly. "We mustn't think that."

They sat sunken in despair.

"Could I take my hope chest—to go to Ellisville?" asked Lily shyly, looking at them sidewise.

"Why, yes," said Mrs. Carson blankly.

Silently they rose once more to their feet.

"Oh, if I could just take my hope chest!"

"All the time it was just her hope chest," Aimee whispered.

Mrs. Watts struck her palms together. "It's settled!"

"Praise the fathers," murmured Mrs. Carson.

Lily looked up at them, and her eyes gleamed. She cocked her head and spoke out in a proud imitation of someone—someone utterly unknown.

"O.K.—Toots!"

The ladies had been nodding and smiling and backing away toward the door.

"I think I'd better stay," said Mrs. Carson, stopping in her tracks. "Where—where could she have learned that terrible expression?"

"Pack up," said Mrs. Watts. "Lily Daw is leaving for Ellisville on Number One."

In the station the train was puffing. Nearly everyone in Victory was hanging around waiting for it to leave. The Victory Civic Band had assembled without any orders and was scattered through the crowd. Ed Newton gave false signals to start on his bass horn. A crate full of baby chickens got loose on the platform. Everybody wanted to see Lily all dressed up, but Mrs. Carson and Mrs. Watts had sneaked her into the train from the other side of the tracks.

The two ladies were going to travel as far as Jackson to help Lily change trains and be sure she went in the right direction.

Lily sat between them on the plush seat with her hair combed and pinned up into a knot under a small blue hat which was Jewel's exchange for the pretty one. She wore a traveling dress made out of part of Mrs. Watts' last summer's mourning. Pink straps glowed through. She had a purse and a Bible and a warm cake in a box, all in her lap.

Aimee Slocum had been getting the outgoing mail stamped and bundled. She stood in the aisle of the coach now, tears shaking from her eyes.

"Good-bye, Lily," she said. She was the one who felt things.

"Good-bye, silly," said Lily.

"Oh, dear, I hope they get our telegram to meet her in Ellisville!" Aimee cried sorrowfully, as she thought how far away it was. "And it was so hard to get it all in ten words, too."

"Get off, Aimee, before the train starts and you break your neck," said Mrs. Watts, all settled and waving her dressy fan gaily. "I declare, it's so hot, as soon as we get a few miles out of town I'm going to slip my corset down."

"Oh, Lily, don't cry down there. Just be good, and do what they tell you—it's all because they love you." Aimee drew her mouth down. She was backing away, down the aisle.

Lily laughed. She pointed across Mrs. Carson's bosom out the window toward a man. He had stepped off the train and just stood there, by himself. He was a stranger and wore a cap.

"Look," she said, laughing softly through her fingers.

"Don't—look," said Mrs. Carson very distinctly, as if, out of all she had ever spoken, she would impress these two solemn words upon Lily's soft little brain. She added, "Don't look at anything till you get to Ellisville."

Outside, Aimee Slocum was crying so hard she almost ran into the stranger. He wore a cap and was short and seemed to have on perfume, if such a thing could be.

"Could you tell me, madam," he said, "where a little lady lives in this burg name of Miss Lily Daw?" He lifted his cap—and he had red hair.

"What do you want to know for?" Aimee asked before she knew it.

"Talk louder," said the stranger. He almost whispered, himself.

"She's gone away—she's gone to Ellisville!"

"Gone?"

"Gone to Ellisville!"

"Well, I like that!" The man stuck out his bottom lip and puffed till his hair jumped.

"What business did you have with Lily?" cried Aimee suddenly.

"We was only going to get married, that's all," said the man.

Aimee Slocum started to scream in front of all those people. She almost pointed to the long black box she saw lying on the ground at the man's feet. Then she jumped back in fright.

"The xylophone! The xylophone!" she cried, looking back and forth from the man to the hissing train. Which was more terrible? The bell began to ring hollowly, and the man was talking.

"Did you say Ellisville? That in the state of Mississippi?" Like lightning he had pulled out a red notebook entitled, "Permanent Facts & Data." He wrote down something. "I don't hear well."

Aimee nodded her head up and down, and circled around him.

Under "Ellis-Ville Miss" he was drawing a line; now he was flicking it with two little marks. "Maybe she didn't say she would. Maybe she said she wouldn't." He suddenly laughed very loudly, after the way he had whispered. Aimee jumped back. "Women!—Well, if we play anywheres near Ellisville, Miss., in the future I may look her up and I may not," he said.

The bass horn sounded the true signal for the band to begin. White steam rushed out of the engine. Usually the train stopped for only a minute in Victory, but the engineer knew Lily from waving at her, and he knew this was her big day.

"Wait!" Aimee Slocum did scream. "Wait, mister! I can get her for you. Wait, Mister Engineer! Don't go!"

Then there she was back on the train, screaming in Mrs. Carson's and Mrs. Watts's faces.

"The xylophone player! The xylophone player to marry her! Yonder he is!"

"Nonsense," murmured Mrs. Watts, peering over the others to look where Aimee pointed. "If he's there I don't see him. Where is he? You're looking at One-Eye Beasley."

"The little man with the cap—no, with the red hair! Hurry!"

"Is that really him?" Mrs. Carson asked Mrs. Watts in wonder. "Mercy! He's small, isn't he?"

"Never saw him before in my life!" cried Mrs. Watts. But suddenly she shut up her fan.

"Come on! This is a train we're on!" cried Aimee Slocum. Her nerves were all unstrung.

"All right, don't have a conniption fit, girl," said Mrs. Watts. "Come on," she said thickly to Mrs. Carson.

"Where are we going now?" asked Lily as they struggled down the aisle.

"We're taking you to get married," said Mrs. Watts. "Mrs. Carson, you'd better phone up your husband right there in the station."

"But I don't want to git married," said Lily, beginning to whimper. "I'm going to Ellisville."

"Hush, and we'll all have some ice-cream cones later," whispered Mrs. Carson.

Just as they climbed down the steps at the back end of the train, the band went into "Independence March."

The xylophone player was still there, patting his foot. He came up and said, "Hello, Toots. What's up—tricks?" and kissed Lily with a smack, after which she hung her head.

"So you're the young man we've heard so much about," said Mrs. Watts. Her smile was brilliant. "Here's your little Lily."

"What say?" asked the xylophone player.

"My husband happens to be the Baptist preacher of Victory," said Mrs. Carson in a loud, clear voice. "Isn't that lucky? I can get him here in five minutes: I know exactly where he is."

They were in a circle around the xylophone player, all going into the white waiting room.

"Oh, I feel just like crying, at a time like this," said Aimee Slocum. She looked back and saw the train moving slowly away, going under the bridge at Main Street. Then it disappeared around the curve.

"Oh, the hope chest!" Aimee cried in a stricken voice.

"And whom have we the pleasure of addressing?" Mrs. Watts was shouting, while Mrs. Carson was ringing up the telephone.

The band went on playing. Some of the people thought Lily was on the train, and some swore she wasn't. Everybody cheered, though, and a straw hat was thrown into the telephone wires.

A PIECE
OF NEWS

———◆———

SHE HAD BEEN out in the rain. She stood in front of the
cabin fireplace, her legs wide apart, bending over, shaking her wet yellow head crossly, like a cat reproaching
itself for not knowing better. She was talking to herself—
only a small fluttering sound, hard to lay hold of in the
sparsity of the room.

"The pouring-down rain, the pouring-down rain"—
was that what she was saying over and over, like a song?
She stood turning in little quarter turns to dry herself, her
head bent forward and the yellow hair hanging out streaming and tangled. She was holding her skirt primly out to
draw the warmth in.

Then, quite rosy, she walked over to the table and
picked up a little bundle. It was a sack of coffee, marked
"Sample" in red letters, which she unwrapped from a wet
newspaper. But she handled it tenderly.

"Why, how come he wrapped it in a newspaper!" she
said, catching her breath, looking from one hand to the
other. She must have been lonesome and slow all her life,
the way things would take her by surprise.

She set the coffee on the table, just in the center. Then she dragged the newspaper by one corner in a dreamy walk across the floor, spread it all out, and lay down full length on top of it in front of the fire. Her little song about the rain, her cries of surprise, had been only a preliminary, only playful pouting with which she amused herself when she was alone. She was pleased with herself now. As she sprawled close to the fire, her hair began to slide out of its damp tangles and hung all displayed down her back like a piece of bargain silk. She closed her eyes. Her mouth fell into a deepness, into a look of unconscious cunning. Yet in her very stillness and pleasure she seemed to be hiding there, all alone. And at moments when the fire stirred and tumbled in the grate, she would tremble, and her hand would start out as if in impatience or despair.

Presently she stirred and reached under her back for the newspaper. Then she squatted there, touching the printed page as if it were fragile. She did not merely look at it—she watched it, as if it were unpredictable, like a young girl watching a baby. The paper was still wet in places where her body had lain. Crouching tensely and patting the creases away with small cracked red fingers, she frowned now and then at the blotched drawing of something and big letters that spelled a word underneath. Her lips trembled, as if looking and spelling so slowly had stirred her heart.

All at once she laughed.

She looked up.

"Ruby Fisher!" she whispered.

An expression of utter timidity came over her flat blue eyes and her soft mouth. Then a look of fright. She stared

33

about. . . . What eye in the world did she feel looking in on her? She pulled her dress down tightly and began to spell through a dozen words in the newspaper.

The little item said:

"Mrs. Ruby Fisher had the misfortune to be shot in the leg by her husband this week."

As she passed from one word to the next she only whispered; she left the long word, "misfortune," until the last, and came back to it, then she said it all over out loud, like conversation.

"That's me," she said softly, with deference, very formally.

The fire slipped and suddenly roared in the house already deafening with the rain which beat upon the roof and hung full of lightning and thunder outside.

"You Clyde!" screamed Ruby Fisher at last, jumping to her feet. "Where are you, Clyde Fisher?"

She ran straight to the door and pulled it open. A shudder of cold brushed over her in the heat, and she seemed striped with anger and bewilderment. There was a flash of lightning, and she stood waiting, as if she half thought that would bring him in, a gun leveled in his hand.

She said nothing more and, backing against the door, pushed it closed with her hip. Her anger passed like a remote flare of elation. Neatly avoiding the table where the bag of coffee stood, she began to walk nervously about the room, as if a teasing indecision, an untouched mystery, led her by the hand. There was one window, and she paused now and then, waiting, looking out at the rain. When she was still, there was a passivity about her, or a

34

deception of passivity, that was not really passive at all. There was something in her that never stopped.

At last she flung herself onto the floor, back across the newspaper, and looked at length into the fire. It might have been a mirror in the cabin, into which she could look deeper and deeper as she pulled her fingers through her hair, trying to see herself and Clyde coming up behind her.

"Clyde?"

But of course her husband, Clyde, was still in the woods. He kept a thick brushwood roof over his whisky still, and he was mortally afraid of lightning like this, and would never go out in it for anything.

And then, almost in amazement, she began to comprehend her predicament: it was unlike Clyde to take up a gun and shoot her.

She bowed her head toward the heat, onto her rosy arms, and began to talk and talk to herself. She grew voluble. Even if he heard about the coffee man, with a Pontiac car, she did not think he would shoot her. When Clyde would make her blue, she would go out onto the road, some car would slow down, and if it had a Tennessee license, the lucky kind, the chances were that she would spend the afternoon in the shed of the empty gin. (Here she rolled her head about on her arms and stretched her legs tiredly behind her, like a cat.) And if Clyde got word, he would slap her. But the account in the paper was wrong. Clyde had never shot her, even once. There had been a mistake made.

A spark flew out and nearly caught the paper on fire. Almost in fright she beat it out with her fingers. Then she murmured and lay back more firmly upon the pages.

There she stretched, growing warmer and warmer, sleepier and sleepier. She began to wonder out loud how it would be if Clyde shot her in the leg. . . . If he were truly angry, might he shoot her through the heart?

At once she was imagining herself dying. She would have a nightgown to lie in, and a bullet in her heart. Anyone could tell, to see her lying there with that deep expression about her mouth, how strange and terrible that would be. Underneath a brand-new nightgown her heart would be hurting with every beat, many times more than her toughened skin when Clyde slapped at her. Ruby began to cry softly, the way she would be crying from the extremity of pain; tears would run down in a little stream over the quilt. Clyde would be standing there above her, as he once looked, with his wild black hair hanging to his shoulders. He used to be very handsome and strong!

He would say, "Ruby, I done this to you."

She would say—only a whisper—"That is the truth, Clyde—you done this to me."

Then she would die; her life would stop right there.

She lay silently for a moment, composing her face into a look which would be beautiful, desirable, and dead.

Clyde would have to buy her a dress to bury her in. He would have to dig a deep hole behind the house, under the cedar, a grave. He would have to nail her up a pine coffin and lay her inside. Then he would have to carry her to the grave, lay her down and cover her up. All the time he would be wild, shouting, and all distracted, to think he could never touch her one more time.

She moved slightly, and her eyes turned toward the window. The white rain splashed down. She could hardly

36

breathe, for thinking that this was the way it was to fall on her grave, where Clyde would come and stand, looking down in the tears of some repentance.

A whole tree of lightning stood in the sky. She kept looking out the window, suffused with the warmth from the fire and with the pity and beauty and power of her death. The thunder rolled.

Then Clyde was standing there, with dark streams flowing over the floor where he had walked. He poked at Ruby with the butt of his gun, as if she were asleep.

"What's keepin' supper?" he growled.

She jumped up and darted away from him. Then, quicker than lightning, she put away the paper. The room was dark, except for the firelight. From the long shadow of his steamy presence she spoke to him glibly and lighted the lamp.

He stood there with a stunned, yet rather good-humored look of delay and patience in his face, and kept on standing there. He stamped his mud-red boots, and his enormous hands seemed weighted with the rain that fell from him and dripped down the barrel of the gun. Presently he sat down with dignity in the chair at the table, making a little tumult of his rightful wetness and hunger. Small streams began to flow from him everywhere.

Ruby was going through the preparations for the meal gently. She stood almost on tiptoe in her bare, warm feet. Once as she knelt at the safe, getting out the biscuits, she saw Clyde looking at her and she smiled and bent her head tenderly. There was some way she began to move her

arms that was mysteriously sweet and yet abrupt and ten-
tative, a delicate and vulnerable manner, as though her
breasts gave her pain. She made many unnecessary trips
back and forth across the floor, circling Clyde where he sat
in his steamy silence, a knife and fork in his fists.

"Well, where you been, anyway?" he grumbled at last,
as she set the first dish on the table.

"Nowheres special."

"Don't you talk back to me. You been hitch-hikin'
again, ain't you?" He almost chuckled.

She gave him a quick look straight into his eyes. She
had not even heard him. She was filled with happiness.
Her hand trembled when she poured the coffee. Some of it
splashed on his wrist.

At that he let his hand drop heavily down upon the
table and made the plates jump.

"Some day I'm goin' to smack the livin' devil outa
you," he said.

Ruby dodged mechanically. She let him eat. Then,
when he had crossed his knife and fork over his plate, she
brought him the newspaper. Again she looked at him in
delight. It excited her even to touch the paper with her
hand, to hear its quiet secret noise when she carried it,
the rustle of surprise.

"A newspaper!" Clyde snatched it roughly and with
a grabbing disparagement. "Where 'd you git that?
Hussy."

"Look at this-here," said Ruby in her small singsong
voice. She opened the paper while he held it and pointed
gravely to the paragraph.

Reluctantly, Clyde began to read it. She watched his damp bald head slowly bend and turn.

Then he made a sound in his throat and said, "It's a lie."

"That's what's in the newspaper about me," said Ruby, standing up straight. She took up his plate and gave him that look of joy.

He put his big crooked finger on the paragraph and poked at it.

"Well, I'd just like to see the place I shot you!" he cried explosively. He looked up, his face blank and bold.

But she drew herself in, still holding the empty plate, faced him straightened and hard, and they looked at each other. The moment filled full with their helplessness. Slowly they both flushed, as though with a double shame and a double pleasure. It was as though Clyde might really have killed Ruby, and as though Ruby might really have been dead at his hand. Rare and wavering, some possibility stood timidly like a stranger between them and made them hang their heads.

Then Clyde walked over in his water-soaked boots and laid the paper on the dying fire. It floated there a moment and then burst into flame. They stood still and watched it burn. The whole room was bright.

"Look," said Clyde suddenly. "It's a Tennessee paper. See 'Tennessee'? That wasn't none of you it wrote about." He laughed, to show that he had been right all the time.

"It was Ruby Fisher!" cried Ruby. "My name is Ruby Fisher!" she declared passionately to Clyde.

"Oho, it was another Ruby Fisher—in Tennessee,"

cried her husband. "Fool me, huh? Where 'd you get that paper?" He spanked her good-humoredly across her back-side.

Ruby folded her still trembling hands into her skirt. She stood stooping by the window until everything, out-side and in, was quieted before she went to her supper.

It was dark and vague outside. The storm had rolled away to faintness like a wagon crossing a bridge.

PETRIFIED
MAN

"REACH IN MY PURSE and git me a cigarette without no powder in it if you kin, Mrs. Fletcher, honey," said Leota to her ten o'clock shampoo-and-set customer. "I don't like no perfumed cigarettes."

Mrs. Fletcher gladly reached over to the lavender shelf under the lavender-framed mirror, shook a hair net loose from the clasp of the patent-leather bag, and slapped her hand down quickly on a powder puff which burst out when the purse was opened.

"Why, look at the peanuts, Leota!" said Mrs. Fletcher in her marvelling voice.

"Honey, them goobers has been in my purse a week if they's been in it a day. Mrs. Pike bought them peanuts."

"Who's Mrs. Pike?" asked Mrs. Fletcher, settling back. Hidden in this dell of curling fluid and henna packs, separated by a lavender swing-door from the other customers, who were being gratified in other booths, she could give her curiosity its freedom. She looked expectantly at the black part in Leota's yellow curls as she bent to light the cigarette.

41

"Mrs. Pike is this lady from New Orleans," said Leota, puffing, and pressing into Mrs. Fletcher's scalp with strong red-nailed fingers. "A friend, not a customer. You see, like maybe I told you last time, me and Fred and Sal and Joe all had us a fuss, so Sal and Joe up and moved out, so we didn't do a thing but rent out their room. So we rented it to Mrs. Pike. And Mr. Pike." She flicked an ash into the basket of dirty towels. "Mrs. Pike is a very decided blonde. *She* bought me the peanuts."

"She must be cute," said Mrs. Fletcher.

"Honey, 'cute' ain't the word for what she is. I'm tellin' you, Mrs. Pike is attractive. She has her a good time. She's got a sharp eye out, Mrs. Pike has."

She dashed the comb through the air, and paused dramatically as a cloud of Mrs. Fletcher's hennaed hair floated out of the lavender teeth like a small storm-cloud.

"Hair fallin'."

"Aw, Leota."

"Uh-huh, commencin' to fall out," said Leota, combing again, and letting fall another cloud.

"Is it any dandruff in it?" Mrs. Fletcher was frowning, her hair-line eyebrows diving down toward her nose, and her wrinkled, beady-lashed eyelids batting with concentration.

"Nope." She combed again. "Just fallin' out."

"Bet it was that last perm'nent you gave me that did it," Mrs. Fletcher said cruelly. "Remember you cooked me fourteen minutes."

"You had fourteen minutes comin' to you," said Leota with finality.

"Bound to be somethin'," persisted Mrs. Fletcher.

42

"Dandruff, dandruff. I couldn't of caught a thing like that from Mr. Fletcher, could I?"

"Well," Leota answered at last, "you know what I heard in here yestiddy, one of Thelma's ladies was settin' over yonder in Thelma's booth gittin' a machineless, and I don't mean to insist or insinuate or anything, Mrs. Fletcher, but Thelma's lady just happ'med to throw out— I forgotten what she was talkin' about at the time—that you was p-r-e-g., and lots of times that'll make your hair do awful funny, fall out and God knows what all. It just ain't our fault, is the way I look at it."

There was a pause. The women stared at each other in the mirror.

"Who was it?" demanded Mrs. Fletcher.

"Honey, I really couldn't say," said Leota. "Not that you look it."

"Where's Thelma? I'll get it out of her," said Mrs. Fletcher.

"Now, honey, I wouldn't go and git mad over a little thing like that," Leota said, combing hastily, as though to hold Mrs. Fletcher down by the hair. "I'm sure it was somebody didn't mean no harm in the world. How far gone are you?"

"Just wait," said Mrs. Fletcher, and shrieked for Thelma, who came in and took a drag from Leota's cigarette.

"Thelma, honey, throw your mind back to yestiddy if you kin," said Leota, drenching Mrs. Fletcher's hair with a thick fluid and catching the overflow in a cold wet towel at her neck.

"Well, I got my lady half wound for a spiral," said Thelma doubtfully.

"This won't take but a minute," said Leota. "Who is it you got in there, old Horse Face? Just cast your mind back and try to remember who your lady was yestiddy who happ'm to mention that my customer was pregnant, that's all. She's dead to know."

Thelma drooped her blood-red lips and looked over Mrs. Fletcher's head into the mirror. "Why, honey, I ain't got the faintest," she breathed. "I really don't recollect the faintest. But I'm sure she meant no harm. I declare, I forgot my hair finally got combed and thought it was a stranger behind me."

"Was it that Mrs. Hutchinson?" Mrs. Fletcher was tensely polite.

"Mrs. Hutchinson? Oh, Mrs. Hutchinson." Thelma batted her eyes. "Naw, precious, she come on Thursday and didn't ev'm mention your name. I doubt if she ev'm knows you're on the way."

"Thelma!" cried Leota staunchly.

"All I know is, whoever it is 'll be sorry some day. Why, I just barely knew it myself!" cried Mrs. Fletcher. "Just let her wait!"

"Why? What're you gonna do to her?"

It was a child's voice, and the women looked down. A little boy was making tents with aluminum wave pinchers on the floor under the sink.

"Billy Boy, hon, mustn't bother nice ladies," Leota smiled. She slapped him brightly and behind her back waved Thelma out of the booth. "Ain't Billy Boy a sight?

44

Only three years old and already just nuts about the beauty-parlor business."

"I never saw him here before," said Mrs. Fletcher, still unmollified.

"He ain't been here before, that's how come," said Leota. "He belongs to Mrs. Pike. She got her a job but it was Fay's Millinery. He oughtn't to try on those ladies' hats, they come down over his eyes like I don't know what. They just git to look ridiculous, that's what, an' of course he's gonna put 'em on: hats. They tole Mrs. Pike they didn't appreciate him hangin' around there. Here, he couldn't hurt a thing."

"Well! I don't like children that much," said Mrs. Fletcher.

"Well!" said Leota moodily.

"Well! I'm almost tempted not to have this one," said Mrs. Fletcher. "That Mrs. Hutchinson! Just looks straight through you when she sees you on the street and then spits at you behind your back."

"Mr. Fletcher would beat you on the head if you didn't have it now," said Leota reasonably. "After going this far."

Mrs. Fletcher sat up straight. "Mr. Fletcher can't do a thing with me."

"He can't!" Leota winked at herself in the mirror.

"No, siree, he can't. If he so much as raises his voice against me, he knows good and well I'll have one of my sick headaches, and then I'm just not fit to live with. And if I really look that pregnant already—"

"Well, now, honey, I just want you to know—I

habm't told any of my ladies and I ain't goin' to tell 'em—
even that you're losin' your hair. You just get you one of
those Stork-a-Lure dresses and stop worryin'. What people don't know don't hurt nobody, as Mrs. Pike says."

"Did you tell Mrs. Pike?" asked Mrs. Fletcher sulkily.

"Well, Mrs. Fletcher, look, you ain't ever goin' to lay
eyes on Mrs. Pike or her lay eyes on you, so what dif-
funce does it make in the long run?"

"I knew it!" Mrs. Fletcher deliberately nodded her
head so as to destroy a ringlet Leota was working on
behind her ear. "Mrs. Pike!"

Leota sighed. "I reckon I might as well tell you. It
wasn't any more Thelma's lady tole me you was pregnant
than a bat."

"Not Mrs. Hutchinson?"

"Naw, Lord! It was Mrs. Pike."

"Mrs. Pike!" Mrs. Fletcher could only sputter and let
curling fluid roll into her ear. "How could Mrs. Pike possibly know I was pregnant or otherwise, when she doesn't
even know me? The nerve of some people!"

"Well, here's how it was. Remember Sunday?"

"Yes," said Mrs. Fletcher.

"Sunday, Mrs. Pike an' me was all by ourself. Mr.
Pike and Fred had gone over to Eagle Lake, sayin' they
was goin' to catch 'em some fish, but they didn't a course.
So we was settin' in Mrs. Pike's car, it's a 1939 Dodge—"

"1939, eh," said Mrs. Fletcher.

"—An' we was gettin' us a Jax beer apiece— that's
the beer that Mrs. Pike says is made right in N.O., so she
won't drink no other kind. So I seen you drive up to the
drugstore an' run in for just a secont, leavin' I reckon Mr.

46

Fletcher in the car, an' come runnin' out with looked like a perscription. So I says to Mrs. Pike, just to be makin' talk, 'Right yonder's Mrs. Fletcher, and I reckon that's Mr. Fletcher—she's one of my regular customers,' I says."

"I had on a figured print," said Mrs. Fletcher tentatively.

"You sure did," agreed Leota. "So Mrs. Pike, she give you a good look—she's very observant, a good judge of character, cute as a minute, you know—and she says, 'I bet you another Jax that lady's three months on the way.' "

"What gall!" said Mrs. Fletcher. "Mrs. Pike!"

"Mrs. Pike ain't goin' to bite you," said Leota. "Mrs. Pike is a lovely girl, you'd be crazy about her, Mrs. Fletcher. But she can't sit still a minute. We went to the travellin' freak show yestiddy after work. I got through early—nine o'clock. In the vacant store next door. What, you ain't been?"

"No, I despise freaks," declared Mrs. Fletcher.

"Aw. Well, honey, talkin' about bein' pregnant an' all, you ought to see those twins in a bottle, you really owe it to yourself."

"What twins?" asked Mrs. Fletcher out of the side of her mouth.

"Well, honey, they got these two twins in a bottle, see? Born joined plumb together—dead a course." Leota dropped her voice into a soft lyrical hum. "They was about this long—pardon—must of been full time, all right, wouldn't you say?—an' they had these two heads an' two faces an' four arms an' four legs, all kind of joined *here*. See, this face looked this-a-way, and the other face looked that-a-way, over their shoulder, see. Kinda pathetic."

"Glah!" said Mrs. Fletcher disapprovingly.

"Well, ugly? Honey, I mean to tell you—their parents was first cousins and all like that. Billy Boy, git me a fresh towel from off Teeny's stack—this 'n's wringin' wet—an' quit ticklin' my ankles with that curler. I declare! He don't miss nothin'."

"Me and Mr. Fletcher aren't one speck of kin, or he could never of had me," said Mrs. Fletcher placidly.

"Of course not!" protested Leota. "Neither is me an' Fred, not that we know of. Well, honey, what Mrs. Pike liked was the pygmies. They've got these pygmies down there, too, an' Mrs. Pike was just wild about 'em. You know, the teeniniest men in the universe? Well, honey, they can just rest back on their little bohunkus an' roll around an' you can't hardly tell if they're sittin' or standin'. That'll give you some idea. They're about forty-two years old. Just suppose it was your husband!"

"Well, Mr. Fletcher is five foot nine and one half," said Mrs. Fletcher quickly.

"Fred's five foot ten," said Leota, "but I tell him he's still a shrimp, account of I'm so tall." She made a deep wave over Mrs. Fletcher's other temple with the comb. "Well, these pygmies are a kind of a dark brown, Mrs. Fletcher. Not bad-lookin' for what they are, you know."

"I wouldn't care for them," said Mrs. Fletcher. "What does that Mrs. Pike see in them?"

"Aw, I don't know," said Leota. "She's just cute, that's all. But they got this man, this petrified man, that ever'thing ever since he was nine years old, when it goes through his digestion, see, somehow Mrs. Pike says it goes to his joints and has been turning to stone."

48

"How awful!" said Mrs. Fletcher.

"He's forty-two too. That looks like a bad age."

"Who said so, that Mrs. Pike? I bet she's forty-two," said Mrs. Fletcher.

"Naw," said Leota, "Mrs. Pike's thirty-three, born in January, an Aquarian. He could move his head—like this. A course his head and mind ain't a joint, so to speak, and I guess his stomach ain't, either—not yet, anyways. But see—his food, he eats it, and it goes down, see, and then he digests it"—Leota rose on her toes for an instant — "and it goes out to his joints and before you can say 'Jack Robinson,' it's stone—pure stone. He's turning to stone. How'd you like to be married to a guy like that? All he can do, he can move his head just a quarter of an inch. A course he *looks* just *terrible.*"

"I should think he would," said Mrs. Fletcher frostily. "Mr. Fletcher takes bending exercises every night of the world. I make him."

"All Fred does is lay around the house like a rug. I wouldn't be surprised if he woke up some day and couldn't move. The petrified man just sat there moving his quarter of an inch though," said Leota reminiscently.

"Did Mrs. Pike like the petrified man?" asked Mrs. Fletcher.

"Not as much as she did the others," said Leota deprecatingly. "And then she likes a man to be a good dresser, and all that."

"Is Mr. Pike a good dresser?" asked Mrs. Fletcher sceptically.

"Oh, well, yeah," said Leota, "but he's twelve or fourteen years older'n her. She ast Lady Evangeline about him."

"Who's Lady Evangeline?" asked Mrs. Fletcher.

"Well, it's this mind reader they got in the freak show," said Leota. "Was real good. Lady Evangeline is her name, and if I had another dollar I wouldn't do a thing but have my other palm read. She had what Mrs. Pike said was the 'sixth mind' but she had the worst manicure I ever saw on a living person."

"What did she tell Mrs. Pike?" asked Mrs. Fletcher.

"She told her Mr. Pike was as true to her as he could be and besides, would come into some money."

"Humph!" said Mrs. Fletcher. "What does he do?"

"I can't tell," said Leota, "because he don't work. Lady Evangeline didn't tell me enough about my nature or anything. And I would like to go back and find out some more about this boy. Used to go with this boy until he got married to this girl. Oh, shoot, that was about three and a half years ago, when you was still goin' to the Robert E. Lee Beauty Shop in Jackson. He married her for her money. Another fortune-teller tole me that at the time. So I'm not in love with him any more, anyway, besides being married to Fred, but Mrs. Pike thought, just for the hell of it, see, to ask Lady Evangeline was he happy."

"Does Mrs. Pike know everything about you already?" asked Mrs. Fletcher unbelievingly. "Mercy!"

"Oh, yeah, I tole her ever'thing about ever'thing, from now on back to I don't know when—to when I first started goin' out," said Leota. "So I ast Lady Evangeline for one of my questions, was he happily married, and she says, just like she was glad I ask her, 'Honey,' she says, 'naw, he idn't. You write down this day, March 8, 1941,' she says, 'and mock it down: three years from today him and her

50

won't be occupyin' the same bed.' There it is, up on the wall with them other dates—see, Mrs. Fletcher? And she says, 'Child, you ought to be glad you didn't git him, because he's so mercenary.' So I'm glad I married Fred. He sure ain't mercenary, money don't mean a thing to him. But I sure would like to go back and have my other palm read."

"Did Mrs. Pike believe in what the fortune-teller said?" asked Mrs. Fletcher in a superior tone of voice.

"Lord, yes, she's from New Orleans. Ever'body in New Orleans believes ever'thing spooky. One of 'em in New Orleans before it was raided says to Mrs. Pike one summer she was goin' to go from State to State and meet some grey-headed men, and, sure enough, she says she went on a beautician convention up to Chicago. . . ."

"Oh!" said Mrs. Fletcher. "Oh, is Mrs. Pike a beautician too?"

"Sure she is," protested Leota. "She's a beautician. I'm goin' to git her in here if I can. Before she married. But it don't leave you. She says sure enough, there was three men who was a very large part of making her trip what it was, and they all three had grey in their hair and they went in six States. Got Christmas cards from 'em. Billy Boy, go see if Thelma's got any dry cotton. Look how Mrs. Fletcher's a-drippin'."

"Where did Mrs. Pike meet Mr. Pike?" asked Mrs. Fletcher primly.

"On another train," said Leota.

"I met Mr. Fletcher, or rather he met me, in a rental library," said Mrs. Fletcher with dignity, as she watched the net come down over her head.

"Honey, me an' Fred, we met in a rumble seat eight months ago and we was practically on what you might call the way to the altar inside of half an hour," said Leota in a guttural voice, and bit a bobby pin open. "Course it don't last. Mrs. Pike says nothin' like that ever lasts."

"Mr. Fletcher and myself are as much in love as the day we married," said Mrs. Fletcher belligerently as Leota stuffed cotton into her ears.

"Mrs. Pike says it don't last," repeated Leota in a louder voice. "Now go git under the dryer. You can turn yourself on, can't you? I'll be back to comb you out. Durin' lunch I promised to give Mrs. Pike a facial. You know—free. Her bein' in the business, so to speak."

"I bet she needs one," said Mrs. Fletcher, letting the swing-door fly back against Leota. "Oh, pardon me."

A week later, on time for her appointment, Mrs. Fletcher sank heavily into Leota's chair after first removing a drug-store rental book, called *Life Is Like That*, from the seat. She stared in a discouraged way into the mirror.

"You can tell it when I'm sitting down, all right," she said.

Leota seemed preoccupied and stood shaking out a lavender cloth. She began to pin it around Mrs. Fletcher's neck in silence.

"I said you sure can tell it when I'm sitting straight on and coming at you this way," Mrs. Fletcher said.

"Why, honey, naw you can't," said Leota gloomily. "Why, I'd never know. If somebody was to come up to me on the street and say, 'Mrs. Fletcher is pregnant!' I'd say, 'Heck, she don't look it to me.' "

"If a certain party hadn't found it out and spread it around, it wouldn't be too late even now," said Mrs. Fletcher frostily, but Leota was almost choking her with the cloth, pinning it so tight, and she couldn't speak clearly. She paddled her hands in the air until Leota wearily loosened her.

"Listen, honey, you're just a virgin compared to Mrs. Montjoy," Leota was going on still absent-minded. She bent Mrs. Fletcher back in the chair and, sighing, tossed liquid from a teacup on to her head and dug both hands into her scalp. "You know Mrs. Montjoy—her husband's that premature-grey-headed fella?"

"She's in the Trojan Garden Club, is all I know," said Mrs. Fletcher.

"Well, honey," said Leota, but in a weary voice, "she come in here not the week before and not the day before she had her baby—she come in here the very selfsame day, I mean to tell you. Child, we was all plumb scared to death. There she was! Come for her shampoo an' set. Why, Mrs. Fletcher, in an hour an' twenty minutes she was layin' up there in the Babtist Hospital with a seb'm-pound son. It was that close a shave. I declare, if I hadn't been so tired I would of drank up a bottle of gin that night."

"What gall," said Mrs. Fletcher. "I never knew her at all well."

"See, her husband was waitin' outside in the car, and her bags was all packed an' in the back seat, an' she was all ready, 'cept she wanted her shampoo an' set. An' havin' one pain right after another. Her husband kep' comin' in here, scared like, but couldn't do nothin' with her a course. She yelled bloody murder, too, but she always yelled her head off when I give her a perm'nent."

"She must of been crazy," said Mrs. Fletcher. "How did she look?"

"Shoot!" said Leota.

"Well, I can guess," said Mrs. Fletcher. "Awful."

"Just wanted to look pretty while she was havin' her baby, is all," said Leota airily. "Course, we was glad to give the lady what she was after—that's our motto—but I bet a hour later she wasn't payin' no mind to them little end curls. I bet she wasn't thinkin' about she ought to have on a net. It wouldn't of done her no good if she had."

"No, I don't suppose it would," said Mrs. Fletcher.

"Yeah man! She was a-yellin'. Just like when I give her perm'nent."

"Her husband ought to make her behave. Don't it seem that way to you?" asked Mrs. Fletcher. "He ought to put his foot down."

"Ha," said Leota. "A lot he could do. Maybe some women is soft."

"Oh, you mistake me, I don't mean for her to get soft—far from it! Women have to stand up for themselves, or there's just no telling. But now you take me—I ask Mr. Fletcher's advice now and then, and he appreciates it, especially on something important, like is it time for a permanent—not that I've told him about the baby. He says, 'Why, dear, go ahead!' Just ask their *advice*."

"Huh! If I ever ast Fred's advice we'd be floatin' down the Yazoo River on a houseboat or somethin' by

54

this time," said Leota. "I'm sick of Fred. I told him to go over to Vicksburg."

"Is he going?" demanded Mrs. Fletcher.

"Sure. See, the fortune-teller—I went back and had my other palm read, since we've got to rent the room agin—said my lover was goin' to work in Vicksburg, so I don't know who she could mean, unless she meant Fred. And Fred ain't workin' here—that much is so."

"Is he going to work in Vicksburg?" asked Mrs. Fletcher. "And—"

"Sure. Lady Evangeline said so. Said the future is going to be brighter than the present. He don't want to go, but I ain't gonna put up with nothin' like that. Lays around the house an' bulls—did bull—with that good-for-nothin' Mr. Pike. He says if he goes who'll cook, but I says I never get to eat anyway—not meals. Billy Boy, take Mrs. Grover that *Screen Secrets* and leg it."

Mrs. Fletcher heard stamping feet go out the door.

"Is that that Mrs. Pike's little boy here again?" she asked, sitting up gingerly.

"Yeah, that's still him." Leota stuck out her tongue.

Mrs. Fletcher could hardly believe her eyes. "Well! How's Mrs. Pike, your attractive new friend with the sharp eyes who spreads it around town that perfect strangers are pregnant?" she asked in a sweetened tone.

"Oh, Mizziz Pike." Leota combed Mrs. Fletcher's hair with heavy strokes.

"You act like you're tired," said Mrs. Fletcher.

"Tired? Feel like it's four o'clock in the afternoon already," said Leota. "I ain't told you the awful luck we

55

had, me and Fred? It's the worst thing you ever heard of. Maybe *you* think Mrs. Pike's got sharp eyes. Shoot, there's a limit! Well, you know, we rented out our room to this Mr. and Mrs. Pike from New Orleans when Sal an' Joe Fentress got mad at us 'cause they drank up some home-brew we had in the closet—Sal an' Joe did. So, a week ago Sat'day Mr. and Mrs. Pike moved in. Well, I kinda fixed up the room, you know—put a sofa pillow on the couch and picked some ragged robbins and put in a vase, but they never did say they appreciated it. Anyway, then I put some old magazines on the table."

"I think that was lovely," said Mrs. Fletcher.

"Wait. So, come night 'fore last, Fred and this Mr. Pike, who Fred just took up with, was back from they said they was fishin', bein' as neither one of 'em has got a job to his name, and we was all settin' around in their room. So Mrs. Pike was settin' there, readin' a old *Startling G-Man Tales* that was mine, mind you, I'd bought it myself, and all of a sudden she jumps!—into the air—you'd 'a' thought she'd set on a spider—an' says, 'Canfield'—ain't that silly, that's Mr. Pike—'Canfield, my God A'mighty,' she says 'honey,' she says, 'we're rich, and you won't have to work.' Not that he turned one hand anyway. Well, me and Fred rushes over to her, and Mr. Pike, too, and there she sets, pointin' her finger at a photo in my copy of *Startling G-Man*. 'See that man?' yells Mrs. Pike. 'Remember him, Canfield?' 'Never forget a face,' says Mr. Pike. 'It's Mr. Petrie, that we stayed with him in the apartment next to ours in Toulouse Street in N.O. for six weeks. Mr. Petrie.' 'Well,' says Mrs. Pike, like she can't hold out one secont longer, 'Mr. Petrie is wanted for five hundred dollars cash, for rapin' four women in California, and I know where he is.' "

"Mercy!" said Mrs. Fletcher. "Where was he?"

At some time Leota had washed her hair and now she yanked her up by the back locks and sat her up.

"Know where he was?"

"I certainly don't," Mrs. Fletcher said. Her scalp hurt all over.

Leota flung a towel around the top of her customer's head. "Nowhere else but in that freak show! I saw him just as plain as Mrs. Pike. *He* was the petrified man!"

"Who would ever have thought that!" cried Mrs. Fletcher sympathetically.

"So Mr. Pike says, 'Well whatta you know about that,' an' he looks real hard at the photo and whistles. And she starts dancin' and singin' about their good luck. She meant our bad luck! I made a point of tellin' that fortune-teller the next time I saw her. I said, 'Listen, that magazine was layin' around the house for a month, and there was the freak show runnin' night an' day, not two steps away from my own beauty parlor, with Mr. Petrie just settin' there waitin'. An' it had to be Mr. and Mrs. Pike, almost perfect strangers.' "

"What gall," said Mrs. Fletcher. She was only sitting there, wrapped in a turban, but she did not mind.

"Fortune-tellers don't care. And Mrs. Pike, she goes around actin' like she thinks she was Mrs. God," said Leota. "So they're goin' to leave tomorrow, Mr. and Mrs. Pike. And in the meantime I got to keep that mean, bad little ole kid here, gettin' under my feet ever' minute of the day an' talkin' back too."

"Have they gotten the five hundred dollars' reward already?" asked Mrs. Fletcher.

"Well," said Leota, "at first Mr. Pike didn't want to do anything about it. Can you feature that? Said he kinda liked that ole bird and said he was real nice to 'em, lent 'em money or somethin'. But Mrs. Pike simply tole him he could just go to hell, and I can see her point. She says, 'You ain't worked a lick in six months, and here I make five hundred dollars in two seconts, and what thanks do I get for it? You go to hell, Canfield,' she says. So," Leota went on in a despondent voice, "they called up the cops and they caught the ole bird, all right, right there in the freak show where I saw him with my own eyes, thinkin' he was petrified. He's the one. Did it under his real name— Mr. Petrie. Four women in California, all in the month of August. So Mrs. Pike gits five hundred dollars. And my magazine, and right next door to my beauty parlor. I cried all night, but Fred said it wasn't a bit of use and to go to sleep, because the whole thing was just a sort of coincidence—you know: can't do nothin' about it. He says it put him clean out of the notion of goin' to Vicksburg for a few days till we rent out the room agin—no tellin' who we'll git this time."

"But can you imagine anybody knowing this old man, that's raped four women?" persisted Mrs. Fletcher, and she shuddered audibly. "Did Mrs. Pike *speak* to him when she met him in the freak show?"

Leota had begun to comb Mrs. Fletcher's hair. "I says to her, I says, 'I didn't notice you fallin' on his neck when he was the petrified man—don't tell me you didn't recognize your fine friend?' And she says, 'I didn't recognize him with that white powder all over his face. He just looked familiar.' Mrs. Pike says, 'and lots of people look familiar.' But she says that ole petrified man did put her in mind of somebody. She wondered who it was! Kep' her awake, which man she'd ever knew it reminded her of. So when she seen the photo, it all come to her. Like a flash. Mr. Petrie. The way he'd turn his head and look at her when she took him in his breakfast."

"Took him in his breakfast!" shrieked Mrs. Fletcher. "Listen—don't tell me. I'd 'a' felt something."

"Four women. I guess those women didn't have the faintest notion at the time they'd be worth a hunderd an' twenty-five bucks a piece some day to Mrs. Pike. We ast her how old the fella was then, an' she says he musta had one foot in the grave, at least. Can you beat it?"

"Not really petrified at all, of course," said Mrs. Fletcher meditatively. She drew herself up. "I'd 'a' felt something," she said proudly.

"Shoot! I did feel somethin'," said Leota. "I tole Fred when I got home I felt so funny. I said, 'Fred, that ole petrified man sure did leave me with a funny feelin'.' He says, 'Funny-haha or funny-peculiar?' and I says, 'Funny-peculiar.' " She pointed her comb into the air emphatically.

"I'll bet you did," said Mrs. Fletcher.

They both heard a crackling noise.

Leota screamed, "Billy Boy! What you doin' in my purse?"

"Aw, I'm just eatin' these ole stale peanuts up," said Billy Boy.

"You come here to me!" screamed Leota, recklessly

flinging down the comb, which scattered a whole ashtray full of bobby pins and knocked down a row of Coca-Cola bottles. "This is the last straw!"

"I caught him! I caught him!" giggled Mrs. Fletcher. "I'll hold him on my lap. You bad, bad boy, you! I guess I better learn how to spank little old bad boys," she said.

Leota's eleven o'clock customer pushed open the swing-door upon Leota paddling him heartily with the brush, while he gave angry but belittling screams which penetrated beyond the booth and filled the whole curious beauty parlor. From everywhere ladies began to gather round to watch the paddling. Billy Boy kicked both Leota and Mrs. Fletcher as hard as he could, Mrs. Fletcher with her new fixed smile.

Billy Boy stomped through the group of wild-haired ladies and went out the door, but flung back the words, "If you're so smart, why ain't you rich?"

THE KEY

IT WAS QUIET in the waiting room of the remote little station, except for the night sounds of insects. You could hear their embroidering movements in the weeds outside, which somehow gave the effect of some tenuous voice in the night, telling a story. Or you could listen to the fat thudding of the light bugs and the hoarse rushing of their big wings against the wooden ceiling. Some of the bugs were clinging heavily to the yellow globe, like idiot bees to a senseless smell.

Under this prickly light two rows of people sat in silence, their faces stung, their bodies twisted and quietly uncomfortable, expectantly so, in ones and twos, not quite asleep. No one seemed impatient, although the train was late. A little girl lay flung back in her mother's lap as though sleep had struck her with a blow.

Ellie and Albert Morgan were sitting on a bench like the others waiting for the train and had nothing to say to each other. Their names were ever so neatly and rather largely printed on a big reddish-tan suitcase strapped crookedly shut, because of a missing buckle, so that it hung apart finally like a stupid pair of lips. "Albert Morgan, Ellie Morgan, Yellow Leaf, Mississippi." They must have been driven into town in a wagon, for they and the

61

suitcase were all touched here and there with a fine yellow dust, like finger marks.

Ellie Morgan was a large woman with a face as pink and crowded as an old-fashioned rose. She must have been about forty years old. One of those black satchel purses hung over her straight, strong wrist. It must have been her savings which were making possible this trip. And to what place? you wondered, for she sat there as tense and solid as a cube, as if to endure some nameless apprehension rising and overflowing within her at the thought of travel. Her face worked and broke into strained, hardening lines, as if there had been a death—that too-explicit evidence of agony in the desire to communicate.

Albert made a slower and softer impression. He sat motionless beside Ellie, holding his hat in his lap with both hands—a hat you were sure he had never worn. He looked home-made, as though his wife had self-consciously knitted or somehow contrived a husband when she sat alone at night. He had a shock of very fine sunburned yellow hair. He was too shy for this world, you could see. His hands were like cardboard, he held his hat so still; and yet how softly his eyes fell upon its crown, moving dreamily and yet with dread over its brown surface! He was smaller than his wife. His suit was brown, too, and he wore it neatly and carefully, as though he were murmuring, "Don't look—no need to look—I am effaced." But you have seen that expression too in silent children, who will tell you what they dreamed the night before in sudden, almost hilarious, bursts of confidence.

Every now and then, as though he perceived some minute thing, a sudden alert, tantalized look would creep over the little man's face, and he would gaze slowly around him, quite slyly. Then he would bow his head again; the expression would vanish; some inner refreshment had been denied him. Behind his head was a wall poster, dirty with time, showing an old-fashioned locomotive about to crash into an open touring car filled with women in veils. No one in the station was frightened by the familiar poster, any more than they were aroused by the little man whose rising and drooping head it framed. Yet for a moment he might seem to you to be sitting there quite filled with hope.

Among the others in the station was a strong-looking young man, alone, hatless, red haired, who was standing by the wall while the rest sat on benches. He had a small key in his hand and was turning it over and over in his fingers, nervously passing it from one hand to the other, tossing it gently into the air and catching it again.

He stood and stared in distraction at the other people; so intent and so wide was his gaze that anyone who glanced after him seemed rocked like a small boat in the wake of a large one. There was an excess of energy about him that separated him from everyone else, but in the motion of his hands there was, instead of the craving for communication, something of reticence, even of secrecy, as the key rose and fell. You guessed that he was a stranger in town; he might have been a criminal or a gambler, but his eyes were widened with gentleness. His look, which traveled without stopping for long anywhere, was a hurried focusing of a very tender and explicit regard.

The color of his hair seemed to jump and move, like the flicker of a match struck in a wind. The ceiling lights were not steady but seemed to pulsate like a living and transient force, and made the young man in his preoccupation appear to tremble in the midst of his size and strength, and to fail to impress his exact outline upon the yellow walls. He was like a salamander in the fire. "Take care," you wanted to say to him, and yet also, "Come here." Nervously, and quite apart in his distraction, he continued to stand tossing the key back and forth from one hand to the other. Suddenly it became a gesture of abandonment: one hand stayed passive in the air, then seized too late: the key fell to the floor.

Everyone, except Albert and Ellie Morgan, looked up for a moment. On the floor the key had made a fierce metallic sound like a challenge, a sound of seriousness. It almost made people jump. It was regarded as an insult, a very personal question, in the quiet peaceful room where the insects were tapping at the ceiling and each person was allowed to sit among his possessions and wait for an unquestioned departure. Little walls of reproach went up about them all.

A flicker of amusement touched the young man's face as he observed the startled but controlled and obstinately blank faces which turned toward him for a moment and then away. He walked over to pick up his key.

But it had glanced and slid across the floor, and now it lay in the dust at Albert Morgan's feet.

Albert Morgan was indeed picking up the key. Across from him, the young man saw him examine it, quite slowly, with wonder written all over his face and hands, as if it had fallen from the sky. Had he failed to hear the clatter? There was something wrong with Albert. . . .

As if by decision, the young man did not terminate this wonder by claiming his key. He stood back, a peculiar flash of interest or of something more inscrutable, like resignation, in his lowered eyes.

The little man had probably been staring at the floor, thinking. And suddenly in the dark surface the small sliding key had appeared. You could see memory seize his face, twist it and hold it. What innocent, strange thing might it have brought back to life—a fish he had once spied just below the top of the water in a sunny lake in the country when he was a child? This was just as unexpected, shocking, and somehow meaningful to him. Albert sat there holding the key in his wide-open hand. How intensified, magnified, really vain all attempt at expression becomes in the afflicted! It was with an almost incandescent delight that he felt the unguessed temperature and weight of the key. Then he turned to his wife. His lips were actually trembling.

And still the young man waited, as if the strange joy of the little man took precedence with him over whatever need he had for the key. With sudden electrification he saw Ellie slip the handle of her satchel purse from her wrist and with her fingers begin to talk to her husband.

The others in the station had seen Ellie too; shallow pity washed over the waiting room like a dirty wave foaming and creeping over a public beach. In quick mumblings from bench to bench people said to each other, "Deaf and dumb!" How ignorant they were of all that the young man was seeing! Although he had no way of knowing the words Ellie said, he seemed troubled enough at the mistake the little man must have made, at his misplaced wonder and joy.

Albert was replying to his wife. On his hands he said to her, "I found it. Now it belongs to me. It is something important! Important! It means something. From now on we will get along better, have more understanding. . . . Maybe when we reach Niagara Falls we will even fall in love, the way other people have done. Maybe our marriage was really for love, after all, not for the other reason—both of us being afflicted in the same way, unable to speak, lonely because of that. Now you can stop being ashamed of me, for being so cautious and slow all my life, for taking my own time. . . . You can take hope. Because it was I who found the key. Remember that—I found it." He laughed all at once, quite silently.

Everyone stared at his impassioned little speech as it came from his fingers. They were embarrassed, vaguely aware of some crisis and vaguely affronted, but unable to interfere; it was as though they were the deaf-mutes and he the speaker. When he laughed, a few people laughed unconsciously with him, in relief, and turned away. But the young man remained still and intent, waiting at his little distance.

"This key came here very mysteriously—it is bound to mean something," the husband went on to say. He held the key up just before her eyes. "You are always praying; you believe in miracles; well, now, here is the answer. It came to me."

His wife looked self-consciously around the room and replied on her fingers, "You are always talking nonsense. Be quiet."

But she was secretly pleased, and when she saw him slowly look down in his old manner, she reached over, as if to retract what she had said, and laid her hand on his, touching the key for herself, softness making her worn hand limp. From then on they never looked around them, never saw anything except each other. They were so intent, so very solemn, wanting to have their symbols perfectly understood!

"You must see it is a symbol," he began again, his fingers clumsy and blurring in his excitement. "It is a symbol of something—something that we deserve, and that is happiness. We will find happiness in Niagara Falls."

And then, as if he were all at once shy even of her, he turned slightly away from her and slid the key into his pocket. They sat staring down at the suitcase, their hands fallen in their laps.

The young man slowly turned away from them and wandered back to the wall, where he took out a cigarette and lighted it.

Outside, the night pressed around the station like a pure stone, in which the little room might be transfixed and, for the preservation of this moment of hope, its future killed, an insect in amber. The short little train drew in, stopped, and rolled away, almost noiselessly.

Then inside, people were gone or turned in sleep or walking about, all changed from the way they had been. But the deaf-mutes and the loitering young man were still in their places.

The man was still smoking. He was dressed like a young doctor or some such person in the town, and yet he did not seem of the town. He looked very strong and active; but there was a startling quality, a willingness to be forever distracted, even disturbed, in the very reassurance of his body, some alertness which made his strength fluid and dissipated instead of withheld and greedily beautiful. His youth by now did not seem an important thing about him; it was a medium for his activity, no doubt, but as he stood there frowning and smoking you felt some apprehension that he would never express whatever might be the desire of his life in being young and strong, in standing apart in compassion, in making any intuitive present or sacrifice, or in any way of action at all—not because there was too much in the world demanding his strength, but because he was too deeply aware.

You felt a shock in glancing up at him, and when you looked away from the whole yellow room and closed your eyes, his intensity, as well as that of the room, seemed to have impressed the imagination with a shadow of itself, a blackness together with the light, the negative beside the positive. You felt as though some exact, skillful contact had been made between the surfaces of your hearts to make you aware, in some pattern, of his joy and his despair. You could feel the fullness and the emptiness of this stranger's life.

The railroad man came in swinging a lantern which he stopped suddenly in its arc. Looking uncomfortable, and then rather angry, he approached the deaf-mutes and shot his arm out in a series of violent gestures and shrugs.

Albert and Ellie Morgan were dreadfully shocked. The woman looked resigned for a moment to hopelessness. But the little man—you were startled by a look of bravado on his face.

In the station the red-haired man was speaking aloud—but to himself. "They missed their train!"

As if in quick apology, the trainman set his lantern down beside Albert's foot, and hurried away.

And as if completing a circle, the red-haired man walked over too and stood silently near the deaf-mutes. With a reproachful look at him the woman reached up and took off her hat.

They began again, talking rapidly back and forth, almost as one person. The old routine of their feeling was upon them once more. Perhaps, you thought, staring at their similarity—her hair was yellow, too—they were children together— cousins even, afflicted in the same way, sent off from home to the state institute. . . .

It was the feeling of conspiracy. They were in counter-plot against the plot of those things that pressed down upon them from outside their knowledge and their ways of making themselves understood. It was obvious that it gave the wife her greatest pleasure. But you wondered, seeing Albert, whom talking seemed rather to dishevel, whether it had not continued to be a rough and violent game which Ellie, as the older and stronger, had taught him to play with her.

"What do you think he wants?" she asked Albert, nodding at the red-haired man, who smiled faintly. And how her eyes shone! Who would ever know how deep her suspicion of the whole outside world lay in her heart, how far it had pushed her!

"What does he want?" Albert was replying quickly. "The key!"

Of course! And how fine it had been to sit there with the key hidden from the strangers and also from his wife, who had not seen where he had put it. He stole up with his hand and secretly felt the key, which must have lain in some pocket nearly against his heart. He nodded gently. The key had come there, under his eyes on the floor in the station, all of a sudden, but yet not quite unexpected. That is the way things happen to you always. But Ellie did not comprehend this.

Now she sat there as quiet as could be. It was not only hopelessness about the trip. She, too, undoubtedly felt something privately about that key, apart from what she had said or what he had told her. He had almost shared it with her—you realized that. He frowned and smiled almost at the same time. There was something— something he could almost remember but not quite—which would let him keep the key always to himself. He knew that, and he would remember it later, when he was alone.

"Never fear, Ellie," he said, a still little smile lifting his lip. "I've got it safe in a pocket. No one can find it, and there's no hole for it to fall through."

She nodded, but she was always doubting, always anxious. You could look at her troubled hands. How terrible it was, how strange, that Albert loved the key more than he loved Ellie! He did not mind missing the train. It showed in every line, every motion of his body. The key was closer—closer. The whole story began to illuminate them now, as if the lantern flame had been turned up. Ellie's anxious, hovering body could wrap him softly as a cradle, but the secret meaning, that powerful sign, that reassurance he so hopefully sought, so assuredly deserved—that had never come. There was something lacking in Ellie.

Had Ellie, with her suspicions of everything, come to know even things like this, in her way? How empty and nervous her red scrubbed hands were, how desperate to speak! Yes, she must regard it as unhappiness lying between them, as more than emptiness. She must worry about it, talk about it. You could imagine her stopping her churning to come out to his chair on the porch, to tell him that she did love him and would take care of him always, talking with the spotted sour milk dripping from her fingers. Just try to tell her that talking is useless, that care is not needed . . . And sooner or later he would always reply, say something, agree, and she would go away again. . . .

And Albert, with his face so capable of amazement, made you suspect the funny thing about talking to Ellie. Until you do, declared his round brown eyes, you can be peaceful and content that everything takes care of itself. As long as you let it alone everything goes peacefully, like an uneventful day on the farm—chores attended to, woman working in the house, you in the field, crop growing as well as can be expected, the cow giving, and the sky like a coverlet over it all—so that you're as full of yourself as a colt, in need of nothing, and nothing needing you. But when you pick up your hands and start to talk, if you don't watch carefully, this security will run away and leave you. You say something, make an observation, just to answer your wife's worryings, and everything is jolted, disturbed, laid open like the ground behind a plow, with you running along after it.

But happiness, Albert knew, is something that appears to you suddenly, that is meant for you, a thing which you reach for and pick up and hide at your breast, a shiny thing that reminds you of something alive and leaping.

Ellie sat there quiet as a mouse. She had unclasped her purse and taken out a little card with a picture of Niagara Falls on it.

"Hide it from the man," she said. She did suspect him! The red-haired man had drawn closer. He bent and saw that it was a picture of Niagara Falls.

"Do you see the little rail?" Albert began in tenderness. And Ellie loved to watch him tell her about it; she clasped her hands and began to smile and show her crooked tooth; she looked young: it was the way she had looked as a child.

"That is what the teacher pointed to with her wand on the magic-lantern slide—the little rail. You stand right here. You lean up hard against the rail. Then you can hear Niagara Falls."

"How do you hear it?" begged Ellie, nodding.

"You hear it with your whole self. You listen with your arms and your legs and your whole body. You'll never forget what hearing is, after that."

He must have told her hundreds of times in his obedience, yet she smiled with gratitude, and stared deep, deep into the tinted picture of the waterfall.

Presently she said, "By now, we'd have been there, if we hadn't missed the train."

She did not even have any idea that it was miles and days away.

She looked at the red-haired man then, her eyes all puckered up, and he looked away at last. He had seen the dust on her throat and a needle stuck in her collar where

72

she'd forgotten it, with a thread running through the eye—
the final details. Her hands were tight and wrinkled with
pressure. She swung her foot a little below her skirt, in
the new Mary Jane slipper with the hard toe.

Albert turned away too. It was then, you thought,
that he became quite frightened to think that if they
hadn't missed the train they would be hearing, at that
very moment, Niagara Falls. Perhaps they would be
standing there together, pressed against the little rail,
pressed against each other, with their lives being poured
through them, changing. . . . And how did he know what
that would be like? He bent his head and tried not to look
at his wife. He could say nothing. He glanced up once at
the stranger, with almost a pleading look, as if to say,
"Won't you come with us?"

"To work so many years, and then to miss the train,"
Ellie said.

You saw by her face that she was undauntedly wondering, unsatisfied, waiting for the future.

And you knew how she would sit and brood over this
as over their conversations together, about every misun-
derstanding, every discussion, sometimes even about some
agreement between them that had been all settled—even
about the secret and proper separation that lies between a
man and a woman, the thing that makes them what they
are in themselves, their secret life, their memory of the
past, their childhood, their dreams. This to Ellie was
unhappiness.

They had told her when she was a little girl how people who have just been married have the custom of going
to Niagara Falls on a wedding trip, to start their happi-

ness; and that came to be where she put her hope, all of it. So she saved money. She worked harder than he did, you could observe, comparing their hands, good and bad years, more than was good for a woman. Year after year she had put her hope ahead of her.

And he—somehow he had never thought that this time would come, that they might really go on the journey. He was never looking so far and so deep as Ellie—into the future, into the changing and mixing of their lives together when they should arrive at last at Niagara Falls. To him it was always something postponed, like the paying off of the mortgage.

But sitting here in the station, with the suitcase all packed and at his feet, he had begun to realize that this journey might, for a fact, take place. The key had materialized to show him the enormity of this venture. And after his first shock and pride he had simply reserved the key; he had hidden it in his pocket.

She looked unblinking into the light of the lantern on the floor. Her face looked strong and terrifying, all lighted and very near to his. But there was no joy there. You knew that she was very brave.

Albert seemed to shrink, to retreat. . . . His trembling hand went once more beneath his coat and touched the pocket where the key was lying, waiting. Would he ever remember that elusive thing about it or be sure what it might really be a symbol of? . . . His eyes, in their quick manner of filming over, grew dreamy. Perhaps he had even decided that it was a symbol not of happiness with Ellie, but of something else—something which he could have alone, for only himself, in peace, something strange and unlooked for which would come to him. . . .

The red-haired man took a second key from his pocket, and in one direct motion placed it in Ellie's red palm. It was a key with a large triangular pasteboard tag on which was clearly printed, "Star Hotel, Room 2."

He did not wait to see any more, but went out abruptly into the night. He stood still for a moment and reached for a cigarette. As he held the match close he gazed straight ahead, and in his eyes, all at once wild and searching, there was certainly, besides the simple compassion in his regard, a look both restless and weary, very much used to the comic. You could see that he despised and saw the uselessness of the thing he had done.

KEELA,
THE OUTCAST
INDIAN MAIDEN

———◆———

ONE MORNING in summertime, when all his sons and daughters were off picking plums and Little Lee Roy was all alone, sitting on the porch and only listening to the screech owls away down in the woods, he had a surprise.

First he heard white men talking. He heard two white men coming up the path from the highway. Little Lee Roy ducked his head and held his breath; then he patted all around back of him for his crutches. The chickens all came out from under the house and waited attentively on the steps.

The men came closer. It was the young man who was doing all of the talking. But when they got through the fence, Max, the older man, interrupted him. He tapped him on the arm and pointed his thumb toward Little Lee Roy.

He said, "Bud? Yonder he is."

But the younger man kept straight on talking, in an explanatory voice.

"Bud?" said Max again. "Look, Bud, yonder's the only little clubfooted nigger man was ever around Cane Springs. Is he the party?"

They came nearer and nearer to Little Lee Roy and then stopped and stood there in the middle of the yard. But the young man was so excited he did not seem to realize that they had arrived anywhere. He was only about twenty years old, very sunburned. He talked constantly, making only one gesture—raising his hand stiffly and then moving it a little to one side.

"They dressed it in a red dress, and it ate chickens alive," he said. "I sold tickets and I thought it was worth a dime, honest. They gimme a piece of paper with the thing wrote off I had to say. That was easy. 'Keela, the Outcast Indian Maiden!' I call it out through a pasteboard megaphone. Then ever' time it was fixin' to eat a live chicken, I blowed the sireen out front."

"Just tell me, Bud," said Max, resting back on the heels of his perforated tan-and-white sport shoes. "Is this nigger the one? Is that him sittin' there?"

Little Lee Roy sat huddled and blinking, a smile on his face. . . . But the young man did not look his way.

"Just took the job that time. I didn't mean to—I mean, I meant to go to Port Arthur because my brother was on a boat," he said. "My name is Steve, mister. But I worked with this show selling tickets for three months, and I never would of knowed it was like that if it hadn't been for that man." He arrested his gesture.

"Yeah, what man?" said Max in a hopeless voice.

Little Lee Roy was looking from one white man to the other, excited almost beyond respectful silence. He trembled all over, and a look of amazement and sudden life came into his eyes.

"Two years ago," Steve was saying impatiently. "And we was travelin' through Texas in those ole trucks.—See, the reason nobody ever come clost to it before was they give it a iron bar this long. And tole it if anybody come near, to shake the bar good at 'em, like this. But it couldn't say nothin'. Turned out they'd tole it it couldn't say nothin' to anybody ever, so it just kind of mumbled and growled, like a animal."

"Hee! hee!" This from Little Lee Roy, softly.

"Tell me again," said Max, and just from his look you could tell that everybody knew old Max. "Somehow I can't get it straight in my mind. Is this the boy? Is this little nigger boy the same as this Keela, the Outcast Indian Maiden?"

Up on the porch, above them, Little Lee Roy gave Max a glance full of hilarity, and then bent the other way to catch Steve's next words.

"Why, if anybody was to even come near it or even bresh their shoulder against the rope it'd growl and take on and shake its iron rod. When it would eat the live chickens it'd growl somethin' awful—you ought to heard it."

"Hee! hee!" It was a soft, almost incredulous laugh that began to escape from Little Lee Roy's tight lips, a little mew of delight.

"They'd throw it this chicken, and it would reach out

an' grab it. Would sort of rub over the chicken's neck with its thumb an' press on it good, an' then it would bite its head off."

"O.K.," said Max.

"It skint back the feathers and stuff from the neck and sucked the blood. But ever'body said it was still alive." Steve drew closer to Max and fastened his light-colored, troubled eyes on his face.

"O.K."

"Then it would pull the feathers out easy and neat-like, awful fast, an' growl the whole time, kind of moan, an' then it would commence to eat all the white meat. I'd go in an' look at it. I reckon I seen it a thousand times."

"That was you, boy?" Max demanded of Little Lee Roy unexpectedly.

But Little Lee Roy could only say, "Hee! hee!" The little man at the head of the steps where the chickens sat, one on each step, and the two men facing each other below made a pyramid.

Steve stuck his hand out for silence. "They said—I mean, I said it, out front through the megaphone, I said it myself, that it wouldn't eat nothin' but only live meat. It was supposed to be a Indian woman, see, in this red dress an' stockin's. It didn't have on no shoes, so when it drug its foot ever'body could see. . . . When it come to the chicken's heart, it would eat that too, real fast, and the heart would still be jumpin'."

"Wait a second, Bud," said Max briefly. "Say, boy, is this white man here crazy?"

Little Lee Roy burst into hysterical, deprecatory giggles. He said, "Naw suh, don't think so." He tried to catch

Steve's eye, seeking appreciation, crying, "Naw suh, don't think he crazy, mista."

Steve gripped Max's arm. "Wait! Wait!" he cried anxiously. "You ain't listenin'. I want to tell you about it. You didn't catch my name— Steve. You never did hear about that little nigger —all that happened to him? Lived in Cane Springs, Miss'ippi?"

"Bud," said Max, disengaging himself, "I don't hear anything. I got a juke box, see, so I don't have to listen."

"Look—I was really the one," said Steve more patiently, but nervously, as if he had been slowly breaking bad news. He walked up and down the bare-swept ground in front of Little Lee Roy's porch, along the row of princess feathers and snow-on-the-mountain. Little Lee Roy's turning head followed him. "I was the one—that's what I'm tellin' you."

"Suppose I was to listen to what every dope comes in Max's Place got to say, *I'd* be nuts," said Max.

"It's all me, see," said Steve. "I know that. I was the one was the cause for it goin' on an' on an' not bein' found out—such an awful thing. It was me, what I said out front through the megaphone."

He stopped still and stared at Max in despair.

"Look," said Max. He sat on the steps, and the chickens hopped off. "I know I ain't nobody but Max. I got Max's Place. I only run a place, understand, fifty yards down the highway. Liquor buried twenty feet from the premises, and no trouble yet. I ain't ever been up here before. I don't claim to been anywhere. People come to my place. Now. You're the hitch-hiker. You're tellin' me, see. You claim a lot of information. If I don't get it I don't

80

get it and I ain't complainin' about it, see. But I think you're nuts, and did from the first. I only come up here with you because I figured you's crazy."

"Maybe you don't believe I remember every word of it even now," Steve was saying gently. "I think about it at night—that an' drums on the midway. You ever hear drums on the midway?" He paused and stared politely at Max and Little Lee Roy.

"Yeh," said Max.

"Don't it make you feel sad. I remember how the drums was goin' and I was yellin', 'Ladies and gents! Do not try to touch Keela, the Outcast Indian Maiden—she will only beat your brains out with her iron rod, and eat them alive!' " Steve waved his arm gently in the air, and Little Lee Roy drew back and squealed. " 'Do not go near her, ladies and gents! I'm warnin' you!' So nobody ever did. Nobody ever come near her. Until that man."

"Sure," said Max. "That fella." He shut his eyes.

"Afterwards when he come up so bold, I remembered seein' him walk up an' buy the ticket an' go in the tent. I'll never forget that man as long as I live. To me he's a sort of—well—"

"Hero," said Max.

"I wish I could remember what he looked like. Seem like he was a tallish man with a sort of white face. Seem like he had bad teeth, but I may be wrong. I remember he frowned a lot. Kept frownin'. Whenever he'd buy a ticket, why, he'd frown."

"Ever seen him since?" asked Max cautiously, still with his eyes closed. "Ever hunt him up?"

"No, never did," said Steve. Then he went on. "He'd

frown an' buy a ticket ever' day we was in these two little
smelly towns in Texas, sometimes three-four times a day,
whether it was fixin' to eat a chicken or not."

"O.K., so he gets in the tent," said Max.

"Well, what the man finally done was, he walked right
up to the little stand where it was tied up and laid his
hand out open on the planks in the platform. He just laid
his hand out open there and said, 'Come here,' real low
and quick, that-a-way."

Steve laid his open hand on Little Lee Roy's porch
and held it there, frowning in concentration.

"I get it," said Max. "He'd caught on it was a fake."

Steve straightened up. "So ever'body yelled to git
away, git away," he continued, his voice rising, "because it
was growlin' an' carryin' on an' shakin' its iron bar like
they tole it. When I heard all that commotion—boy! I
was scared."

"You didn't know it was a fake."

Steve was silent for a moment, and Little Lee Roy
held his breath, for fear everything was all over.

"Look," said Steve finally, his voice trembling. "I
guess I was supposed to feel bad like this, and you wasn't.
I wasn't supposed to ship out on that boat from Port
Arthur and all like that. This other had to happen to me—
not you all. Feelin' responsible. You'll be O.K., mister,
but I won't. I feel awful about it. That poor little old
thing."

"Look, you got him right here," said Max quickly.
"See him? Use your eyes. He's O.K., ain't he? Looks O.K.
to me. It's just you. You're nuts, is all."

"You know—when that man laid out his open hand

on the boards, why, it just let go the iron bar," continued Steve, "let it fall down like that—bang—and act like it didn't know what to do. Then it drug itself over to where the fella was standin' an' leaned down an' grabbed holt onto that white man's hand as tight as it could an' cried like a baby. It didn't want to hit him!"

"Hee! hee! hee!"

"No sir, it didn't want to hit him. You know what it wanted?"

Max shook his head.

"It wanted him to help it. So the man said, 'Do you wanta get out of this place, whoever you are?' An' it never answered—none of us knowed it could talk—but it just wouldn't let that man's hand a-loose. It hung on, cryin' like a baby. So the man says, 'Well, wait here till I come back.' "

"Uh-huh?" said Max.

"Went off an' come back with the sheriff. Took us all to jail. But just the man owned the show and his son got took to the pen. They said I could go free. I kep' tellin' 'em I didn't know it wouldn't hit me with the iron bar an' kep' tellin' 'em I didn't know it could tell what you was sayin' to it."

"Yeh, guess you told 'em," said Max.

"By that time I felt bad. Been feelin' bad ever since. Can't hold onto a job or stay in one place for nothin' in the world. They made it stay in jail to see if it could talk or not, and the first night it wouldn't say nothin'. Some time it cried. And they undressed it an' found out it wasn't no outcast Indian woman a-tall. It was a little club-footed nigger man."

"Hee! hee!"

"You mean it was this boy here—yeh. It was him."

"Washed its face, and it was paint all over it made it look red. It all come off. And it could talk—as good as me or you. But they'd tole it not to, so it never did. They'd tole it if anybody was to come near it they was comin' to git it—and for it to hit 'em quick with that iron bar an' growl. So nobody ever come near it—until that man. I was yellin' outside, tellin' 'em to keep away, keep away. You could see where they'd whup it. They had to whup it some to make it eat all the chickens. It was awful dirty. They let it go back home free, to where they got it in the first place. They made them pay its ticket from Little Oil, Texas, to Cane Springs, Miss'ippi."

"You got a good memory," said Max.

"The way it *started* was," said Steve, in a wondering voice, "the show was just travelin' along in ole trucks through the country, and just seen this little deformed nigger man, sittin' on a fence, and just took it. It couldn't help it."

Little Lee Roy tossed his head back in a frenzy of amusement.

"I found it all out later. I was up on the Ferris wheel with one of the boys—got to talkin' up yonder in the peace an' quiet—an' said they just kind of happened up on it. Like a cyclone happens: it wasn't nothin' it could do. It was just took up." Steve suddenly paled through his sunburn. "An' they found out that back in Miss'ippi it had it a little bitty pair of crutches an' could just go runnin' on 'em!"

"And there they are," said Max.

Little Lee Roy held up a crutch and turned it about, and then snatched it back like a monkey.

"But if it hadn't been for that man, I wouldn't of knowed it till yet. If it wasn't for him bein' so bold. If he hadn't knowed what he was doin'.''

"You remember that man this fella's talkin' about, boy?" asked Max, eying Little Lee Roy.

Little Lee Roy, in reluctance and shyness, shook his head gently.

"Naw suh, I can't say as I remembas that ve'y man, suh," he said softly, looking down where just then a sparrow alighted on his child's shoe. He added happily, as if on inspiration, "Now I remembas *this* man."

Steve did not look up, but when Max shook with silent laughter, alarm seemed to seize him like a spasm in his side. He walked painfully over and stood in the shade for a few minutes, leaning his head on a sycamore tree.

"Seemed like that man just studied it out an' knowed it was somethin' wrong," he said presently, his voice coming more remotely than ever. "But I didn't know. I can't look at nothin' an' be sure what it is. Then afterwards I know. Then I see how it was."

"Yeh, but you're nuts," said Max affably.

"You wouldn't of knowed it either!" cried Steve in sudden boyish, defensive anger. Then he came out from under the tree and stood again almost pleadingly in the sun, facing Max where he was sitting below Little Lee Roy on the steps. "You'd of let it go on an' on when they made it do those things—just like I did."

"Bet I could tell a man from a woman and an Indian from a nigger though," said Max.

Steve scuffed the dust into little puffs with his worn shoe. The chickens scattered, alarmed at last.

Little Lee Roy looked from one man to the other radiantly, his hands pressed over his grinning gums.

Then Steve sighed, and as if he did not know what else he could do, he reached out and without any warning hit Max in the jaw with his fist. Max fell off the steps.

Little Lee Roy suddenly sat as still and dark as a statue, looking on.

"Say! Say!" cried Steve. He pulled shyly at Max where he lay on the ground, with his lips pursed up like a whistler, and then stepped back. He looked horrified. "How you feel?"

"Lousy," said Max thoughtfully. "Let me alone." He raised up on one elbow and lay there looking all around, at the cabin, at Little Lee Roy sitting cross-legged on the porch, and at Steve with his hand out. Finally he got up.

"I can't figure out how I could of ever knocked down an athaletic guy like you. I had to do it," said Steve. "But I guess you don't understand. I had to hit you. First you didn't believe me, and then it didn't bother you."

"That's all O.K., only hush," said Max, and added, "Some dope is always giving me the lowdown on something, but this is the first time one of 'em ever got away with a thing like this. I got to watch out."

"I hope it don't stay black long," said Steve.

"I got to be going," said Max. But he waited. "What you want to transact with Keela? You come a long way to see him." He stared at Steve with his eyes wide open now, and interested.

"Well, I was goin' to give him some money or somethin', I guess, if I ever found him, only now I ain't got any," said Steve defiantly.

"O.K.," said Max. "Here's some change for you, boy. Just take it. Go on back in the house. Go on."

Little Lee Roy took the money speechlessly, and then fell upon his yellow crutches and hopped with miraculous rapidity away through the door. Max stared after him for a moment.

"As for you"—he brushed himself off, turned to Steve and then said, "When did you eat last?"

"Well, I'll tell you," said Steve.

"Not here," said Max. "I didn't go to ask you a question. Just follow me. We serve eats at Max's Place, and I want to play the juke box. You eat, and I'll listen to the juke box."

"Well . . ." said Steve. "But when it cools off I got to catch a ride some place."

"Today while all you all was gone, and not a soul in de house," said Little Lee Roy at the supper table that night, "two white mens come heah to de house. Wouldn't come in. But talks to me about de ole times when I use to be wid de circus—"

"Hush up, Pappy," said the children.

WHY
I LIVE
AT THE P.O.

I WAS GETTING ALONG FINE with Mama, Papa-Daddy and Uncle Rondo until my sister Stella-Rondo just separated from her husband and came back home again. Mr. Whitaker! Of course I went with Mr. Whitaker first, when he first appeared here in China Grove, taking "Pose Yourself" photos, and Stella-Rondo broke us up. Told him I was one-sided. Bigger on one side than the other, which is a deliberate, calculated falsehood: I'm the same. Stella-Rondo is exactly twelve months to the day younger than I am and for that reason she's spoiled.

She's always had anything in the world she wanted and then she'd throw it away. Papa-Daddy gave her this gorgeous Add-a-Pearl necklace when she was eight years old and she threw it away playing baseball when she was nine, with only two pearls.

So as soon as she got married and moved away from home the first thing she did was separate! From Mr.

Whitaker! This photographer with the popeyes she said she trusted. Came home from one of those towns up in Illinois and to our complete surprise brought this child of two.

Mama said she like to made her drop dead for a second. "Here you had this marvelous blonde child and never so much as wrote your mother a word about it," says Mama. "I'm thoroughly ashamed of you." But of course she wasn't.

Stella-Rondo just calmly takes off this *hat,* I wish you could see it. She says, "Why, Mama, Shirley-T.'s adopted, I can prove it."

"How?" says Mama, but all I says was, "H'm!" There I was over the hot stove, trying to stretch two chickens over five people and a completely unexpected child into the bargain, without one moment's notice.

"What do you mean—'H'm!'?" says Stella-Rondo, and Mama says, "I heard that, Sister."

I said that oh, I didn't mean a thing, only that whoever Shirley-T. was, she was the spit-image of Papa-Daddy if he'd cut off his beard, which of course he'd never do in the world. Papa-Daddy's Mama's papa and sulks.

Stella-Rondo got furious! She said, "Sister, I don't need to tell you you got a lot of nerve and always did have and I'll thank you to make no future reference to my adopted child whatsoever."

"Very well," I said. "Very well, very well. Of course I noticed at once she looks like Mr. Whitaker's side too. That frown. She looks like a cross between Mr. Whitaker and Papa-Daddy."

"Well, all I can say is she isn't."

"She looks exactly like Shirley Temple to me," says Mama, but Shirley-T. just ran away from her.

So the first thing Stella-Rondo did at the table was turn Papa-Daddy against me.

"Papa-Daddy," she says. He was trying to cut up his meat. "Papa-Daddy!" I was taken completely by surprise. Papa-Daddy is about a million years old and's got this long-long beard. "Papa-Daddy, Sister says she fails to understand why you don't cut off your beard."

So Papa-Daddy l-a-y-s down his knife and fork! He's real rich. Mama says he is, he says he isn't. So he says, "Have I heard correctly? You don't understand why I don't cut off my beard?"

"Why," I says, "Papa-Daddy, of course I understand, I did not say any such of a thing, the idea!"

He says, "Hussy!"

I says, "Papa-Daddy, you know I wouldn't any more want you to cut off your beard than the man in the moon. It was the farthest thing from my mind! Stella-Rondo sat there and made that up while she was eating breast of chicken."

But he says, "So the postmistress fails to understand why I don't cut off my beard. Which job I got you through my influence with the government. 'Bird's nest'— is that what you call it?"

Not that it isn't the next to smallest P.O. in the entire state of Mississippi.

I says, "Oh, Papa-Daddy," I says, "I didn't say any such of a thing, I never dreamed it was a bird's nest, I

have always been grateful though this is the next to smallest P.O. in the state of Mississippi, and I do not enjoy
being referred to as a hussy by my own grandfather."

But Stella-Rondo says, "Yes, you did say it too. Anybody in the world could of heard you, that had ears."

"Stop right there," says Mama, looking at *me*.

So I pulled my napkin straight back through the napkin ring and left the table.

As soon as I was out of the room Mama says, "Call
her back, or she'll starve to death," but Papa-Daddy says,
"This is the beard I started growing on the Coast when I
was fifteen years old." He would of gone on till nightfall
if Shirley-T. hadn't lost the Milky Way she ate in Cairo.

So Papa-Daddy says, "I am going out and lie in the
hammock, and you can all sit here and remember my
words: I'll never cut off my beard as long as I live, even
one inch, and I don't appreciate it in you at all." Passed
right by me in the hall and went straight out and got in
the hammock.

It would be a holiday. It wasn't five minutes before
Uncle Rondo suddenly appeared in the hall in one of
Stella-Rondo's flesh-colored kimonos, all cut on the bias,
like something Mr. Whitaker probably thought was gorgeous.

"Uncle Rondo!" I says. "I didn't know who that was!
Where are you going?"

"Sister," he says, "get out of my way, I'm poisoned."

"If you're poisoned stay away from Papa-Daddy," I
says. "Keep out of the hammock. Papa-Daddy will certainly beat you on the head if you come within forty miles

of him. He thinks I deliberately said he ought to cut off his beard after he got me the P.O., and I've told him and told him and told him, and he acts like he just don't hear me. Papa-Daddy must of gone stone deaf."

"He picked a fine day to do it then," says Uncle Rondo, and before you could say "Jack Robinson" flew out in the yard.

What he'd really done, he'd drunk another bottle of that prescription. He does it every single Fourth of July as sure as shooting, and it's horribly expensive. Then he falls over in the hammock and snores. So he insisted on zigzagging right on out to the hammock, looking like a half-wit.

Papa-Daddy woke up with this horrible yell and right there without moving an inch he tried to turn Uncle Rondo against me. I heard every word he said. Oh, he told Uncle Rondo I didn't learn to read till I was eight years old and he didn't see how in the world I ever got the mail put up at the P.O., much less read it all, and he said if Uncle Rondo could only fathom the lengths he had gone to to get me that job! And he said on the other hand he thought Stella-Rondo had a brilliant mind and deserved credit for getting out of town. All the time he was just lying there swinging as pretty as you please and looping out his beard, and poor Uncle Rondo was *pleading* with him to slow down the hammock, it was making him as dizzy as a witch to watch it. But that's what Papa-Daddy likes about a hammock. So Uncle Rondo was too dizzy to get turned against me for the time being. He's Mama's only brother and is a good case of a one-track mind. Ask anybody. A certified pharmacist.

Just then I heard Stella-Rondo raising the upstairs window. While she was married she got this peculiar idea that it's cooler with the windows shut and locked. So she has to raise the window before she can make a soul hear her outdoors.

So she raises the window and says, *"Oh!"* You would have thought she was mortally wounded. Uncle Rondo and Papa-Daddy didn't even look up, but kept right on with what they were doing. I had to laugh.

I flew up the stairs and threw the door open! I says, "What in the wide world's the matter, Stella-Rondo? You mortally wounded?"

"No," she says, "I am not mortally wounded but I wish you would do me the favor of looking out that window there and telling me what you see."

So I shade my eyes and look out the window.

"I see the front yard," I says.

"Don't you see any human beings?" she says.

"I see Uncle Rondo trying to run Papa-Daddy out of the hammock," I says. "Nothing more. Naturally, it's so suffocating-hot in the house, with all the windows shut and locked, everybody who cares to stay in their right mind will have to go out and get in the hammock before the Fourth of July is over."

"Don't you notice anything different about Uncle Rondo?" asks Stella-Rondo.

"Why, no, except he's got on some terrible-looking flesh-colored contraption I wouldn't be found dead in, is all I can see," I says.

"Never mind, you won't be found dead in it, because it happens to be part of my trousseau, and Mr. Whitaker took several dozen photographs of me in it," says Stella-Rondo. "What on earth could Uncle Rondo *mean* by wearing part of my trousseau out in the broad open daylight without saying so much as 'Kiss my foot,' *knowing* I only got home this morning after my separation and hung my negligee up on the bathroom door, just as nervous as I could be?"

"I'm sure I don't know, and what do you expect me to do about it?" I says. "Jump out the window?"

"No, I expect nothing of the kind. I simply declare that Uncle Rondo looks like a fool in it, that's all," she says. "It makes me sick to my stomach."

"Well, he looks as good as he can," I says. "As good as anybody in reason could." I stood up for Uncle Rondo, please remember. And I said to Stella-Rondo, "I think I would do well not to criticize so freely if I were you and came home with a two-year-old child I had never said a word about, and no explanation whatever about my separation."

"I asked you the instant I entered this house not to refer one more time to my adopted child, and you gave me your word of honor you would not," was all Stella-Rondo would say, and started pulling out every one of her eyebrows with some cheap Kress tweezers.

So I merely slammed the door behind me and went down and made some green-tomato pickle. Somebody had to do it. Of course Mama had turned both the niggers loose; she always said no earthly power could hold one anyway on the Fourth of July, so she wouldn't even try. It turned out that Jaypan fell in the lake and came within a very narrow limit of drowning.

So Mama trots in. Lifts up the lid and says, "H'm! Not very good for your Uncle Rondo in his precarious condition, I must say. Or poor little adopted Shirley-T. Shame on you!"

That made me tired. I says, "Well, Stella-Rondo had better thank her lucky stars it was her instead of me came trotting in with that very peculiar-looking child. Now if it had been me that trotted in from Illinois and brought a peculiar-looking child of two, I shudder to think of the reception I'd of got, much less controlled the diet of an entire family."

"But you must remember, Sister, that you were never married to Mr. Whitaker in the first place and didn't go up to Illinois to live," says Mama, shaking a spoon in my face. "If you had I would of been just as overjoyed to see you and your little adopted girl as I was to see Stella-Rondo, when you wound up with your separation and came on back home."

"You would not," I says.

"Don't contradict me, I would," says Mama

But I said she couldn't convince me though she talked till she was blue in the face. Then I said, "Besides, you know as well as I do that that child is not adopted."

"She most certainly is adopted," says Mama, stiff as a poker.

I says, "Why, Mama, Stella-Rondo had her just as sure as anything in this world, and just too stuck up to admit it."

"Why, Sister," said Mama. "Here I thought we were going to have a pleasant Fourth of July, and you start right out not believing a word your own baby sister tells you!"

"Just like Cousin Annie Flo. Went to her grave denying the facts of life," I remind Mama.

"I told you if you ever mentioned Annie Flo's name I'd slap your face," says Mama, and slaps my face.

"All right, you wait and see," I says.

"I," says Mama, "I prefer to take my children's word for anything when it's humanly possible." You ought to see Mama, she weighs two hundred pounds and has real tiny feet.

Just then something perfectly horrible occurred to me.

"Mama," I says, "can that child talk?" I simply had to whisper! "Mama" I wonder if that child can be—you know—in any way? Do you realize," I says, "that she hasn't spoken one single, solitary word to a human being up to this minute? This is the way she looks," I says, and I looked like this.

Well, Mama and I just stood there and stared at each other. It was horrible!

"I remember well that Joe Whitaker frequently drank like a fish," says Mama. "I believed to my soul he drank *chemicals*." And without another word she marches to the foot of the stairs and calls Stella-Rondo.

"Stella-Rondo? O-o-o-o-o! Stella-Rondo!"

"What?" says Stella-Rondo from upstairs. Not even the grace to get up off the bed.

"Can that child of yours talk?" asks Mama.

Stella-Rondo says, "Can she what?"

"Talk! Talk!" says Mama. "Burdyburdyburdyburdy!"

So Stella-Rondo yells back, "Who says she can't talk?"

"Sister says so," says Mama.

"You didn't have to tell me, I know whose word of

honor don't mean a thing in this house," says Stella-Rondo.

And in a minute the loudest Yankee voice I ever heard in my life yells out, "OE'm Pop-OE the Sailor-r-r-r Ma-a-an!" and then somebody jumps up and down in the upstairs hall. In another second the house would of fallen down.

"Not only talks, she can tap-dance!" calls Stella-Rondo. "Which is more than some people I won't name can do."

"Why, the little precious darling thing!" Mama says, so surprised. "Just as smart as she can be!" Starts talking baby talk right there. Then she turns on me. "Sister, you ought to be thoroughly ashamed! Run upstairs this instant and apologize to Stella-Rondo and Shirley-T."

"Apologize for what?" I says. "I merely wondered if the child was normal, that's all. Now that she's proved she is, why, I have nothing further to say."

But Mama just turned on her heel and flew out, furious. She ran right upstairs and hugged the baby. She believed it was adopted. Stella-Rondo hadn't done a thing but turn her against me from upstairs while I stood there helpless over the hot stove. So that made Mama, Papa-Daddy and the baby all on Stella-Rondo's side.

Next, Uncle Rondo.

I must say that Uncle Rondo has been marvelous to me at various times in the past and I was completely unprepared to be made to jump out of my skin, the way it turned out. Once Stella-Rondo did something perfectly horrible to him—broke a chain letter from Flanders Field—and he took the radio back he had given her and gave it to me. Stella-Rondo was furious! For six months we all had to call her Stella instead of Stella-Rondo, or she wouldn't answer. I always thought Uncle Rondo had all the brains of the entire family. Another time he sent me to Mammoth Cave, with all expenses paid.

But this would be the day he was drinking that prescription, the Fourth of July.

So at supper Stella-Rondo speaks up and says she thinks Uncle Rondo ought to try to eat a little something. So finally Uncle Rondo said he would try a little cold biscuits and ketchup, but that was all. So *she* brought it to him.

"Do you think it wise to disport with ketchup in Stella-Rondo's flesh-colored kimono?" I says. Trying to be considerate! If Stella-Rondo couldn't watch out for her trousseau, somebody had to.

"Any objections?" asks Uncle Rondo, just about to pour out all the ketchup.

"Don't mind what she says, Uncle Rondo," says Stella-Rondo. "Sister has been devoting this solid afternoon to sneering out my bedroom window at the way you look."

"What's that?" says Uncle Rondo. Uncle Rondo has got the most terrible temper in the world. Anything is liable to make him tear the house down if it comes at the wrong time.

So Stella-Rondo says, "Sister says, 'Uncle Rondo certainly does look like a fool in that pink kimono!' "

Do you remember who it was really said that?

Uncle Rondo spills out all the ketchup and jumps out of his chair and tears off the kimono and throws it down on the dirty floor and puts his foot on it. It had to be sent all the way to Jackson to the cleaners and re-pleated.

"So that's your opinion of your Uncle Rondo, is it?" he says. "I look like a fool, do I? Well, that's the last straw. A whole day in this house with nothing to do, and then to hear you come out with a remark like that behind my back!"

"I didn't say any such of a thing, Uncle Rondo," I says, "and I'm not saying, who did, either. Why, I think you look all right. Just try to take care of yourself and not talk and eat at the same time," I says. "I think you better go lie down."

"Lie down my foot," says Uncle Rondo. I ought to of known by that he was fixing to do something perfectly horrible.

So he didn't do anything that night in the precarious state he was in—just played Casino with Mama and Stella-Rondo and Shirley-T. and gave Shirley-T. a nickel with a head on both sides. It tickled her nearly to death, and she called him "Papa." But at 6:30 A.M. the next morning, he threw a whole five-cent package of some unsold one-inch firecrackers from the store as hard as he could into my bedroom and they every one went off. Not one bad one in the string. Anybody else, there'd be one that wouldn't go off.

Well, I'm just terribly susceptible to noise of any kind, the doctor has always told me I was the most sensitive person he had ever seen in his whole life, and I was simply prostrated. I couldn't eat! People tell me they heard it as far as the cemetery, and old Aunt Jep Patterson, that had been holding her own so good, thought it was Judgment Day and she was going to meet her whole family. It's usually so quiet here.

And I'll tell you it didn't take me any longer than a minute to make up my mind what to do. There I was with the whole entire house on Stella-Rondo's side and turned against me. If I have anything at all I have pride.

So I just decided I'd go straight down to the P.O. There's plenty of room there in the back, I says to myself.

Well! I made no bones about letting the family catch on to what I was up to. I didn't try to conceal it.

The first thing they knew, I marched in where they were all playing Old Maid and pulled the electric oscillating fan out by the plug, and everything got real hot. Next I snatched the pillow I'd done the needlepoint on right off the davenport from behind Papa-Daddy. He went "Ugh!" I beat Stella-Rondo up the stairs and finally found my charm bracelet in her bureau drawer under a picture of Nelson Eddy.

"So that's the way the land lies," says Uncle Rondo. There he was, piecing on the ham. "Well, Sister, I'll be glad to donate my army cot if you got any place to set it up, providing you'll leave right this minute and let me get some peace." Uncle Rondo was in France.

"Thank you kindly for the cot and 'peace' is hardly the word I would select if I had to resort to firecrackers at 6:30 A.M. in a young girl's bedroom," I says back to him. "And as to where I intend to go, you seem to forget my position as postmistress of China Grove, Mississippi," I says. "I've always got the P.O."

Well, that made them all sit up and take notice.

I went out front and started digging up some four-o'clocks to plant around the P.O.

"Ah-ah-ah!" says Mama, raising the window. "Those

happen to be my four-o'clocks. Everything planted in that star is mine. I've never known you to make anything grow in your life."

"Very well," I says. "But I take the fern. Even you, Mama, can't stand there and deny that I'm the one watered that fern. And I happen to know where I can send in a box top and get a packet of one thousand mixed seeds, no two the same kind, free."

"Oh, where?" Mama wants to know.

But I says, "Too late. You 'tend to your house, and I'll 'tend to mine. You hear things like that all the time if you know how to listen to the radio Perfectly marvelous offers. Get anything you want free."

So I hope to tell you I marched in and got that radio, and they could of all bit a nail in two, especially Stella-Rondo, that it used to belong to, and she well knew she couldn't get it back, I'd sue for it like a shot. And I very politely took the sewing-machine motor I helped pay the most on to give Mama for Christmas back in 1929, and a good big calendar, with the first-aid remedies on it. The thermometer and the Hawaiian ukulele certainly were rightfully mine, and I stood on the step-ladder and got all my watermelon-rind preserves and every fruit and vegetable I'd put up, every jar. Then I began to pull the tacks out of the bluebird wall vases on the archway to the dining room.

"Who told you you could have those, Miss Priss?" says Mama, fanning as hard as she could.

"I bought 'em and I'll keep track of 'em," I says. "I'll tack 'em up one on each side the post-office window, and you can see 'em when you come to ask me for your mail, if you're so dead to see 'em."

"Not I! I'll never darken the door to that post office again if I live to be a hundred," Mama says. "Ungrateful child! After all the money we spent on you at the Normal."

"Me either," says Stella-Rondo. "You can just let my mail lie there and *rot*, for all I care. I'll never come and relieve you of a single, solitary piece."

"I should worry," I says. "And who you think's going to sit down and write you all those big fat letters and post-cards, by the way? Mr. Whitaker? Just because he was the only man ever dropped down in China Grove and you got him—unfairly —is he going to sit down and write you a lengthy correspondence after you come home giving no rhyme nor reason whatsoever for your separation and no explanation for the presence of that child? I may not have your brilliant mind, but I fail to see it."

So Mama says, "Sister, I've told you a thousand times that Stella-Rondo simply got homesick, and this child is far too big to be hers," and she says, "Now, why don't you all just sit down and play Casino?"

Then Shirley-T. sticks out her tongue at me in this perfectly horrible way. She has no more manners than the man in the moon. I told her she was going to cross her eyes like that some day and they'd stick.

"It's too late to stop me now," I says. "You should have tried that yesterday. I'm going to the P.O. and the only way you can possibly see me is to visit me there."

So Papa-Daddy says, "You'll never catch me setting foot in that post office, even if I should take a notion into my head to write a letter some place." He says, "I won't have you reachin' out of that little old window with a pair of shears and cuttin' off any beard of mine. I'm too smart for you!"

"We all are," says Stella-Rondo.

But I said, "If you're so smart, where's Mr. Whitaker?"

So then Uncle Rondo says, "I'll thank you from now on to stop reading all the orders I get on postcards and telling everybody in China Grove what you think is the matter with them," but I says, "I draw my own conclusions and will continue in the future to draw them." I says, "If people want to write their inmost secrets on penny postcards, there's nothing in the wide world you can do about it, Uncle Rondo."

"And if you think we'll ever *write* another postcard you're sadly mistaken," says Mama.

"Cutting off your nose to spite your face then," I says. "But if you're all determined to have no more to do with the U. S. mail, think of this: What will Stella-Rondo do now, if she wants to tell Mr. Whitaker to come after her?"

"Wah!" says Stella-Rondo. I knew she'd cry. She had a conniption fit right there in the kitchen.

"It will be interesting to see how long she holds out," I says. "And now—I am leaving."

"Good-bye," says Uncle Rondo.

"Oh, I declare," says Mama, "to think that a family of mine should quarrel on the Fourth of July, or the day after, over Stella-Rondo leaving old Mr. Whitaker and having the sweetest little adopted child! It looks like we'd all be glad!"

"Wah!" says Stella-Rondo, and has a fresh conniption fit.

"He left *her*—you mark my words," I says. "That's Mr. Whitaker. I know Mr. Whitaker. After all, I knew him first. I said from the beginning he'd up and leave her. I foretold every single thing that's happened."

"Where did he go?" asks Mama.

"Probably to the North Pole, if he knows what's good for him," I says.

But Stella-Rondo just bawled and wouldn't say another word. She flew to her room and slammed the door.

"Now look what you've gone and done, Sister," says Mama. "You go apologize."

"I haven't got time, I'm leaving," I says.

"Well, what are you waiting around for?" asks Uncle Rondo.

So I just picked up the kitchen clock and marched off, without saying "Kiss my foot" or anything, and never did tell Stella-Rondo good-bye.

There was a nigger girl going along on a little wagon right in front.

"Nigger girl," I says, "come help me haul these things down the hill, I'm going to live in the post office."

Took her nine trips in her express wagon. Uncle Rondo came out on the porch and threw her a nickel.

And that's the last I've laid eyes on any of my family or my family laid eyes on me for five solid days and nights. Stella-Rondo may be telling the most horrible tales in the world about Mr. Whitaker, but I haven't heard them. As I tell everybody, I draw my own conclusions.

But oh, I like it here. It's ideal, as I've been saying. You see, I've got everything cater-cornered, the way I like it. Hear the radio? All the war news. Radio, sewing machine, book ends, ironing board and that great big piano lamp—peace, that's what I like. Butter-bean vines planted all along the front where the strings are.

Of course, there's not much mail. My family are naturally the main people in China Grove, and if they prefer to vanish from the face of the earth, for all the mail they get or the mail they write, why, I'm not going to open my mouth. Some of the folks here in town are taking up for me and some turned against me. I know which is which. There are always people who will quit buying stamps just to get on the right side of Papa-Daddy.

But here I am, and here I'll stay. I want the world to know I'm happy.

And if Stella-Rondo should come to me this minute, on bended knees, and *attempt* to explain the incidents of her life with Mr. Whitaker, I'd simply put my fingers in both my ears and refuse to listen.

THE
WHISTLE

———————◆———————

NIGHT FELL. The darkness was thin, like some sleazy dress that has been worn and worn for many winters and always lets the cold through to the bones. Then the moon rose. A farm lay quite visible, like a white stone in water, among the stretches of deep woods in their colorless dead leaf. By a closer and more searching eye than the moon's, everything belonging to the Mortons might have been seen—even to the tiny tomato plants in their neat rows closest to the house, gray and featherlike, appalling in their exposed fragility. The moonlight covered everything, and lay upon the darkest shape of all, the farmhouse where the lamp had just been blown out.

Inside, Jason and Sara Morton were lying between the quilts of a pallet which had been made up close to the fireplace. A fire still fluttered in the grate, making a drowsy sound now and then, and its exhausted light beat up and down the wall, across the rafters, and over the dark pallet where the old people lay, like a bird trying to find its way out of the room.

The long-spaced, tired breathing of Jason was the only

noise besides the flutter of the fire. He lay under the quilt in a long shape like a bean, turned on his side to face the door. His lips opened in the dark, and in and out he breathed, in and out, slowly and with a rise and fall, over and over, like a conversation or a tale—a question and a sigh.

Sara lay on her back with her mouth agape, silent, but not asleep. She was staring at the dark and indistinguishable places among the rafters. Her eyes seemed opened too wide, the lids strained and limp, like openings which have been stretched shapeless and made of no more use. Once a hissing yellow flame stood erect in the old log, and her small face and pale hair, and one hand holding to the edge of the cover, were illuminated for a moment, with shadows bright blue. Then she pulled the quilt clear over her head.

Every night they lay trembling with cold, but no more communicative in their misery than a pair of window shutters beaten by a storm. Sometimes many days, weeks went by without words. They were not really old—they were only fifty; still, their lives were filled with tiredness, with a great lack of necessity to speak, with poverty which may have bound them like a disaster too great for any discussion but left them still separate and undesirous of sympathy. Perhaps, years ago, the long habit of silence may have been started in anger or passion. Who could tell now?

As the fire grew lower and lower, Jason's breathing grew heavy and solemn, and he was even beyond dreams. Completely hidden, Sara's body was as weightless as a strip of cane, there was hardly a shape to the quilt under which she was lying. Sometimes it seemed to Sara herself that it was her lack of weight which kept her from ever getting warm.

She was so tired of the cold! That was all it could do any more—make her tired. Year after year, she felt sure that she would die before the cold was over. Now, according to the Almanac, it was spring. . . . But year after year it was always the same. The plants would be set out in their frames, transplanted always too soon, and there was a freeze. . . . When was the last time they had grown tall and full, that the cold had held off and there was a crop?

Like a vain dream, Sara began to have thoughts of the spring and summer. At first she thought only simply, of the colors of green and red, the smell of the sun on the ground, the touch of leaves and of warm ripening tomatoes. Then, all hidden as she was under the quilt, she began to imagine and remember the town of Dexter in the shipping season. There in her mind, dusty little Dexter became a theater for almost legendary festivity, a place of pleasure. On every road leading in, smiling farmers were bringing in wagonloads of the most beautiful tomatoes. The packing sheds at Dexter Station were all decorated—no, it was simply that the May sun was shining. Mr. Perkins, the tall, gesturing figure, stood in the very center of everything, buying, directing, waving yellow papers that must be telegrams, shouting with grand impatience. And it was he, after all, that owned their farm now. Train after train of empty freight cars stretched away, waiting and then being filled. Was it possible to have saved out of the threat of the cold so many tomatoes in the world? Of course, for here marched in a perfect parade of

Florida packers, all the way from Florida, tanned, stock-ingless, some of them tattooed. The music box was playing in the café across the way, and the crippled man that walked like a duck was back taking poses for a dime of the young people with their heads together. With shouts of triumph the men were getting drunk, and now and then a pistol went off somewhere. In the shade the children celebrated in tomato fights. A strong, heady, sweet smell hung over everything. Such excitement! Let the packers rest, if only for a moment, thought Sara. Stretch them out, stained with sweat, under the shade tree, and one can play the guitar. The girl wrappers listen while they work. What small brown hands, red with juice! Their faces are forever sleepy and flushed; when the men speak to them they laugh. . . . And Jason and Sara themselves are standing there, standing under the burning sun near the first shed, giving over their own load, watching their own tomatoes shoved into the process, swallowed away—sorted, wrapped, loaded, dispatched in a freight car—all so fast. . . . Mr. Perkins holds out his hard, quick hand. Shake it fast! How quickly it is all over!

Sara, weightless under the quilt, could think of the celebrations of Dexter and see the vision of ripe tomatoes only in brief snatches, like the flare-up of the little fire. The rest of the time she thought only of cold, of cold going on before and after. She could not help but feel the chill of the here and now, which was not to think at all, but was for her only a trembling in the dark.

She coughed patiently and turned her head to one side. She peered over the quilt just a little and saw that the fire had at last gone out. There was left only a hulk of red log, a still, red, bent shape, like one of Jason's socks thrown down to be darned somehow. With only this to comfort her, Sara closed her eyes and fell asleep.

The husband and wife now lay perfectly still in the dark room, with Jason's hoarse, slow breathing, like the commotion of some clumsy nodding old bear trying to climb a tree, heard by nobody at all.

Every hour it was getting colder and colder. The moon, intense and white as the snow that does not fall here, drew higher in the sky, in the long night, and more distant from the earth. The farm looked as tiny and still as a seashell, with the little knob of a house surrounded by its curved furrows of tomato plants. Cold like a white pressing hand reached down and lay over the shell.

In Dexter there is a great whistle which is blown when a freeze threatens. It is known everywhere as Mr. Perkins' whistle. Now it sounded out in the clear night, blast after blast. Over the countryside lights appeared in the windows of the farms. Men and women ran out into the fields and covered up their plants with whatever they had, while Mr. Perkins' whistle blew and blew.

Jason Morton was not waked up by the great whistle. On he slept, his cavernous breathing like roars coming from a hollow tree. His right hand had been thrown out, from some deepness he must have dreamed, and lay stretched on the cold floor in the very center of a patch of moonlight which had moved across the room.

Sara felt herself waking. She knew that Mr. Perkins' whistle was blowing, what it meant—and that it now remained for her to get Jason and go out to the field. A soft. laxity, an illusion of warmth, flowed stubbornly down her body, and for a few moments she continued to lie still.

Then she was sitting up and seizing her husband by the shoulders, without saying a word, rocking him back and forth. It took all her strength to wake him. He coughed, his roaring was over, and he sat up. He said nothing either, and they both sat with bent heads and listened for the whistle. After a silence it blew again, a long, rising blast.

Promptly Sara and Jason got out of bed. They were both fully dressed, because of the cold, and only needed to put on their shoes. Jason lighted the lantern, and Sara gathered the bedclothes over her arm and followed him out.

Everything was white, and everything looked vast and extensive to them as they walked over the frozen field. White in a shadowed pit, abandoned from summer to summer, the old sorghum mill stood like the machine of a dream, with its long prostrate pole, its blunted axis.

Stooping over the little plants, Jason and Sara touched them and touched the earth. For their own knowledge, by their hands, they found everything to be true—the cold, the rightness of the warning, the need to act. Over the sticks set in among the plants they laid the quilts one by one, spreading them with a slow ingenuity. Jason took off his coat and laid it over the small tender plants by the side of the house. Then he glanced at Sara, and she reached down and pulled her dress off over her head. Her hair fell down out of its pins, and she began at once to tremble violently. The skirt was luckily long and full, and all the rest of the plants were covered by it.

Then Sara and Jason stood for a moment and stared almost idly at the field and up at the sky.

There was no wind. There was only the intense whiteness of moonlight. Why did this calm cold sink into them like the teeth of a trap? They bent their shoulders and walked silently back into the house.

The room was not much warmer. They had forgotten to shut the door behind them when the whistle was blowing so hard. They sat down to wait for morning.

Then Jason did a rare, strange thing. There long before morning he poured kerosene over some kindling and struck a light to it. Squatting, they got near it, quite gradually they drew together, and sat motionless until it all burned down. Still Sara did not move. Then Jason, in his underwear and long blue trousers, went out and brought in another load, and the big cherry log which of course was meant to be saved for the very last of winter.

The extravagant warmth of the room had sent some kind of agitation over Sara, like her memories of Dexter in the shipping season. She sat huddled in a long brown cotton petticoat, holding onto the string which went around the waist. Her mouse-colored hair, paler at the temples, was hanging loose down to her shoulders, like a child's unbound for a party. She held her knees against her numb, pendulant breasts and stared into the fire, her eyes widening.

On his side of the hearth Jason watched the fire burn too. His breath came gently, quickly, noiselessly, as though for a little time he would conceal or defend his tiredness. He lifted his arms and held out his misshapen hands to the fire.

112

At last every bit of the wood was gone. Now the cherry log was burned to ashes.

And all of a sudden Jason was on his feet again. Of all things, he was bringing the split-bottomed chair over to the hearth. He knocked it to pieces. It burned well and brightly. Sara never said word. She did not move. . . .

Then the kitchen table. To think that a solid, steady four-legged table like that, that had stood thirty years in one place, should be consumed in such a little while! Sara stared almost greedily at the waving flames.

Then when that was over, Jason and Sara sat in darkness where their bed had been, and it was colder than ever. The fire the kitchen table had made seemed wonderful to them—as if what they had never said, and what could not be, had its life, too, after all.

But Sara trembled, again pressing her hard knees against her breast. In the return of winter, of the night's cold, something strange, like fright, or dependency, a sensation of complete helplessness, took possession of her. All at once, without turning her head, she spoke.

"Jason . . ."

A silence. But only for a moment.

"Listen," said her husband's uncertain voice.

They held very still, as before, with bent heads.

Outside, as though it would exact something further from their lives, the whistle continued to blow.

THE
HITCH-HIKERS

———————◆———————

TOM HARRIS, a thirty-year-old salesman traveling in office supplies, got out of Victory a little after noon and saw people in Midnight and Louise, but went on toward Memphis. It was a base, and he was thinking he would like to do something that night.

Toward evening, somewhere in the middle of the Delta, he slowed down to pick up two hitch-hikers. One of them stood still by the side of the pavement, with his foot stuck out like an old root, but the other was playing a yellow guitar which caught the late sun as it came in a long straight bar across the fields.

Harris would get sleepy driving. On the road he did some things rather out of a dream. And the recurring sight of hitch-hikers waiting against the sky gave him the flash of a sensation he had known as a child: standing still, with nothing to touch him, feeling tall and having the world come all at once into its round shape underfoot and rush and turn through space and make his stand very precarious and lonely. He opened the car door.

"How you do?"

114

"How you do?"

Harris spoke to hitch-hikers almost formally. Now resuming his speed, he moved over a little in the seat. There was no room in the back for anybody. The man with the guitar was riding with it between his legs. Harris reached over and flicked on the radio.

"Well, music!" said the man with the guitar. Presently he began to smile. "Well, we been there a whole day in that one spot," he said softly. "Seen the sun go clear over. Course, part of the time we laid down under that one tree and taken our ease."

They rode without talking while the sun went down in red clouds and the radio program changed a few times. Harris switched on his lights. Once the man with the guitar started to sing "The One Rose That's Left in My Heart," which came over the air, played by the Aloha Boys. Then in shyness he stopped, but made a streak on the radio dial with his blackly calloused finger tip.

"I 'preciate them big 'lectric gittars some have," he said.

"Where are you going?"

"Looks like north."

"It's north," said Harris. "Smoke?"

The other man held out his hand.

"Well . . . rarely," said the man with the guitar.

At the use of the unexpected word, Harris's cheek twitched, and he handed over his pack of cigarettes. All three lighted up. The silent man held his cigarette in front of him like a piece of money, between his thumb and forefinger. Harris realized that he wasn't smoking it, but was watching it burn.

115

"My! gittin' night agin," said the man with the guitar in a voice that could assume any social surprise.

"Anything to eat?" asked Harris.

The man gave a pluck to a low string and glanced at him.

"Dewberries," said the other man. It was his only remark, and it was delivered in a slow and pondering voice.

"Some nice little rabbit come skinnin' by," said the man with the guitar, nudging Harris with a slight punch in his side, "but it run off the way it come."

The other man was so bogged in inarticulate anger that Harris could imagine him running down a cotton row after the rabbit. He smiled but did not look around.

"Now to look out for a place to sleep—is that it?" he remarked doggedly.

A pluck of the strings again, and the man yawned.

There was a little town coming up; the lights showed for twenty miles in the flat land.

"Is that Dulcie?" Harris yawned too.

"I bet you ain't got no idea where all I've slep'," the man said, turning around in his seat and speaking directly to Harris, with laughter in his face that in the light of a road sign appeared strangely teasing.

"I could eat a hamburger," said Harris, swinging out of the road under the sign in some automatic gesture of evasion. He looked out of the window, and a girl in red pants leaped onto the running board.

"Three and three beers?" she asked, smiling, with her head poked in. "Hi," she said to Harris.

"How are you?" said Harris. "That's right."

"My," said the man with the guitar. "Red sailor-boy

britches." Harris listened for the guitar note, but it did not come. "But not purty," he said.

The screen door of the joint whined, and a man's voice called, "Come on in, boys, we got girls."

Harris cut off the radio, and they listened to the nick-elodeon which was playing inside the joint and turning the window blue, red and green in turn.

"Hi," said the car-hop again as she came out with the tray. "Looks like rain."

They ate the hamburgers rapidly, without talking. A girl came and looked out of the window of the joint, lean-ing on her hand. The same couple kept dancing by behind her. There was something brassy playing, a swing record of "Love, Oh Love, Oh Careless Love."

"Same songs ever'where," said the man with the gui-tar softly. "I come down from the hills. . . . We had us owls for chickens and fox for yard dogs but we sung true."

Nearly every time the man spoke Harris's cheek twitched. He was easily amused. Also, he recognized at once any sort of attempt to confide, and then its certain and hasty retreat. And the more anyone said, the further he was drawn into a willingness to listen. I'll hear him play his guitar yet, he thought. It had got to be a pattern in his days and nights, it was almost automatic, his listen-ing, like the way his hand went to his pocket for money.

"That'n's most the same as a ballat," said the man, licking mustard off his finger. "My ma, she was the one for ballats. Little in the waist as a dirt-dauber, but her voice carried. Had her a whole lot of tunes. Long ago dead an' gone. Pa 'd come home from the courthouse drunk as a wheelbarrow, and she'd just pick up an' go sit on the front step facin' the hill an' sing. Ever'thing she knowed, she'd sing. Dead an' gone, an' the house burned down." He gulped at his beer. His foot was patting.

"This," said Harris, touching one of the keys on the guitar. "Couldn't you stop somewhere along here and make money playing this?"

Of course it was by the guitar that he had known at once that they were not mere hitch-hikers. They were tramps. They were full blown, abandoned to this. Both of them were. But when he touched it he knew obscurely that it was the yellow guitar, that bold and gay burden in the tramp's arms, that had caused him to stop and pick them up.

The man hit it flat with the palm of his hand.

"This box? Just play it for myself."

Harris laughed delightedly, but somehow he had a desire to tease him, to make him swear to his freedom.

"You wouldn't stop and play somewhere like this? For them to dance? When you know all the songs?"

Now the fellow laughed out loud. He turned and spoke completely as if the other man could not hear him. "Well, but right now I got *him.*"

"Him?" Harris stared ahead.

"He'd gripe. He don't like foolin' around. He wants to git on. You always git a partner got notions."

The other tramp belched. Harris laid his hand on the horn.

"Hurry back," said the car-hop, opening a heart-shaped pocket over her heart and dropping the tip courteously within.

"Aw river!" sang out the man with the guitar.

As they pulled out into the road again, the other man began to lift a beer bottle, and stared beseechingly, with his mouth full, at the man with the guitar.

"Drive back, mister. Sobby forgot to give her back her bottle. Drive back."

"Too late," said Harris rather firmly, speeding on into Dulcie, thinking, I was about to take directions from him.

Harris stopped the car in front of the Dulcie Hotel on the square.

" 'Preciated it," said the man, taking up his guitar.

"Wait here."

They stood on the walk, one lighted by the street light, the other in the shadow of the statue of the Confederate soldier, both caved in and giving out an odor of dust, both sighing with obedience.

Harris went across the yard and up the one step into the hotel.

Mr. Gene, the proprietor, a white-haired man with little dark freckles all over his face and hands, looked up and shoved out his arm at the same time.

"If he ain't back." He grinned. "Been about a month to the day—I was just remarking."

"Mr. Gene, I ought to go on, but I got two fellows out front. O.K., but they've just got nowhere to sleep tonight, and you know that little back porch."

"Why, it's a beautiful night out!" bellowed Mr. Gene, and he laughed silently.

"They'd get fleas in your bed," said Harris, showing the back of his hand. "But you know that old porch. It's not so bad. I slept out there once, I forget how."

119

The proprietor let his laugh out like a flood. Then he sobered abruptly.

"Sure. O.K.," he said. "Wait a minute—Mike's sick. Come here, Mike, it's just old Harris passin' through."

Mike was an ancient collie dog. He rose from a quilt near the door and moved over the square brown rug, stiffly, like a table walking, and shoved himself between the men, swinging his long head from Mr. Gene's hand to Harris's and bearing down motionless with his jaw in Harris's palm

"You sick, Mike?" asked Harris.

"Dyin' of old age, that's what he's doin'!" blurted the proprietor as if in anger.

Harris began to stroke the dog, but the familiarity in his hands changed to slowness and hesitancy. Mike looked up out of his eyes.

"His spirit's gone. You see?" said Mr. Gene pleadingly.

"Say, look," said a voice at the front door.

"Come in, Cato, and see poor old Mike," said Mr. Gene.

"I knew that was your car, Mr. Harris," said the boy. He was nervously trying to tuck a Bing Crosby cretonne shirt into his pants like a real shirt. Then he looked up and said, "They was tryin' to take your car, and down the street one of 'em like to bust the other one's head wide op'm with a bottle. Looks like you would 'a' heard the commotion. Everybody's out there. I said, 'That's Mr. Tom Harris's car, look at the out-of-town license and look at all the stuff he all time carries around with him, all bloody.' "

"He's not dead though," said Harris, kneeling on the seat of his car.

It was the man with the guitar. The little ceiling light had been turned on. With blood streaming from his broken head, he was slumped down upon the guitar, his legs bowed around it, his arms at either side, his whole body limp in the posture of a bareback rider. Harris was aware of the other face not a yard away: the man the guitar player had called Sobby was standing on the curb, with two men unnecessarily holding him. He looked more like a bystander than any of the rest, except that he still held the beer bottle in his right hand.

"Looks like if he was fixin' to hit him, *he* would of hit *him* with that gittar," said a voice. "That 'd be a real good thing to hit somebody with. Whang!"

"The way I figure this thing out is," said a penetrating voice, as if a woman were explaining it all to her husband, "the men was left to 'emselves. So—that 'n' yonder wanted to make off with the car—he's the bad one. So the good one says, 'Naw, that ain't right.' "

Or was it the other way around? thought Harris dreamily.

"So the other one says bam! bam! He whacked him over the head. And so dumb—right where the movie was letting out."

"Who's got my car keys!" Harris kept shouting. He had, without realizing it, kicked away the prop, the guitar; and he had stopped the blood with something.

Nobody had to tell him where the ramshackle little hospital was—he had been there once before, on a Delta trip. With the constable scuttling along after and then riding on the running board, glasses held tenderly in one fist, the handcuffed Sobby dragged alongside by the other, with a long line of little boys in flowered shirts accompanying him on bicycles, riding in and out of the headlight beam, with the rain falling in front of him and with Mr. Gene shouting in a sort of plea from the hotel behind and Mike beginning to echo the barking of the rest of the dogs, Harris drove in all carefulness down the long tree-dark street, with his wet hand pressed on the horn.

The old doctor came down the walk and, joining them in the car, slowly took the guitar player by the shoulders.

"I 'spec' he gonna die though," said a colored child's voice mournfully. "Wonder who goin' to git his box?"

In a room on the second floor of the two-story hotel Harris put on clean clothes, while Mr. Gene lay on the bed with Mike across his stomach.

"Ruined that Christmas tie you came in." The proprietor was talking in short breaths. "It took it out of Mike, I'm tellin' you." He sighed. "First time he's barked since Bud Milton shot up that Chinese." He lifted his head and took a long swallow of the hotel whisky, and tears appeared in his warm brown eyes. "Suppose they'd done it on the porch."

The phone rang.

"See, everybody knows you're here," said Mr. Gene.

"Ruth?" he said, lifting the receiver, his voice almost contrite.

But it was for the proprietor.

When he had hung up he said, "That little peanut— he ain't ever goin' to learn which end is up. The constable.

Got a nigger already in the jail, so he's runnin' round to find a place to put this fella of yours with the bottle, and damned if all he can think of ain't the hotel!"

"Hell, is he going to spend the night with me?"

"Well, the same thing. Across the hall. The other fella may die. Only place in town with a key but the bank, he says."

"What time is it?" asked Harris all at once.

"Oh, it ain't *late*," said Mr. Gene.

He opened the door for Mike, and the two men followed the dog slowly down the stairs. The light was out on the landing. Harris looked out of the old half-open stained-glass window.

"Is that rain?"

"It's been rainin' since dark, but you don't ever know a thing like that—it's proverbial." At the desk he held up a brown package. "Here. I sent Cato after some Memphis whisky for you. He had to do something."

"Thanks."

"I'll see you. I don't guess you're goin' to get away very shortly in the mornin'. I'm real sorry they did it in your car if they were goin' to do it."

"That's all right," said Harris. "You'd better have a little of this."

"That? It 'd kill me," said Mr. Gene.

In a drugstore Harris phoned Ruth, a woman he knew in town, and found her at home having a party.

"Tom Harris! Sent by heaven!" she cried. "I was wondering what I'd do about Carol—this *baby!*"

"What's the matter with her?"

123

"No date."

Some other people wanted to say hello from the party. He listened awhile and said he'd be out.

This had postponed the call to the hospital. He put in another nickel. . . . There was nothing new about the guitar player.

"Like I told you," the doctor said, "we don't have the facilities for giving transfusions, and he's been moved plenty without you taking him to Memphis."

Walking over to the party, so as not to use his car, making the only sounds in the dark wet street, and only partly aware of the indeterminate shapes of houses with their soft-shining fanlights marking them off, there with the rain falling mist-like through the trees, he almost forgot what town he was in and which house he was bound for.

Ruth, in a long dark dress, leaned against an open door, laughing. From inside came the sounds of at least two people playing a duet on the piano.

"He would come like this and get all wet!" she cried over her shoulder into the room. She was leaning back on her hands. "What's the matter with your little blue car? I hope you brought us a present."

He went in with her and began shaking hands, and set the bottle wrapped in the paper sack on a table.

"He never forgets!" cried Ruth.

"Drinkin' whisky!" Everybody was noisy again.

"So this is the famous 'he' that everybody talks about all the time," pouted a girl in a white dress. "Is he one of your cousins, Ruth?"

"No kin of mine, he's nothing but a vagabond," said Ruth, and led Harris off to the kitchen by the hand.

I wish they'd call me "you" when I've got here, he thought tiredly.

"More has gone on than a little bit," she said, and told him the news while he poured fresh drinks into the glasses. When she accused him of nothing, of no careless-ness or disregard of her feelings, he was fairly sure she had not heard about the assault in his car.

She was looking at him closely. "Where did you get that sunburn?"

"Well, I had to go to the Coast last week," he said.

"What did you do?"

"Same old thing." He laughed; he had started to tell her about something funny in Bay St. Louis, where an eloping couple had flagged him down in the residential section and threatened to break up if he would not carry them to the next town. Then he remembered how Ruth looked when he mentioned other places where he stopped on trips.

Somewhere in the house the phone rang and rang, and he caught himself jumping. Nobody was answering it.

"I thought you'd quit drinking," she said, picking up the bottle.

"I start and quit," he said, taking it from her and pouring his drink. "Where's my date?"

"Oh, she's in Leland," said Ruth.

They all drove over in two cars to get her.

She was a slight little thing, with her nightgown in some sort of little bag. She came out when they blew the horn, before he could go in after her. . . .

"Let's go holler off the bridge," said somebody in the car ahead.

They drove over a little gravel road, miles through the misty fields, and came to the bridge out in the middle of nowhere.

"Let's dance," said one of the boys. He grabbed Carol around the waist, and they began to tango over the boards.

"Did you miss me?" asked Ruth. She stayed by him, standing in the road.

"Woo-hoo!" they cried.

"I wish I knew what makes it holler back," said one girl. "There's nothing anywhere. Some of my kinfolks can't even hear it."

"Yes, it's funny," said Harris, with a cigarette in his mouth.

"Some people say it's an old steamboat got lost once."

"Might be."

They drove around and waited to see if it would stop raining.

Back in the lighted rooms at Ruth's he saw Carol, his date, give him a strange little glance. At the moment he was serving her with a drink from the tray.

"Are you the one everybody's 'miratin' and gyratin' over?" she said, before she would put her hand out.

"Yes," he said, "I come from afar." He placed the strongest drink from the tray in her hand, with a little flourish.

"Hurry back!" called Ruth.

In the pantry Ruth came over and stood by him while he set more glasses on the tray and then followed him out to the kitchen. Was she at all curious about him? he wondered. For a moment, when they were simply close together, her lips parted, and she stared off at nothing;

her jealousy seemed to let her go free. The rainy wind from the back porch stirred her hair.

As if under some illusion, he set the tray down and told her about the two hitch-hikers.

Her eyes flashed.

"What a—stupid thing!" Furiously she seized the tray when he reached for it.

The phone was ringing again. Ruth glared at him.

It was as though he had made a previous engagement with the hitch-hikers.

Everybody was meeting them at the kitchen door.

"Aha!" cried one of the men, Jackson. "He tries to put one over on you, girls. Somebody just called up, Ruth, about the murder in Tom's car."

"Did he die?" asked Harris, without moving.

"I knew all about it!" cried Ruth, her cheeks flaming. "He told me all about it. It practically ruined his car. Didn't it!"

"Wouldn't he get into something crazy like that?"

"It's because he's an angel," said the girl named Carol, his date, speaking in a hollow voice from her high-ball glass.

"Who phoned?" asked Harris.

"Old Mrs. Daggett, that old lady about a million years old that's always calling up. She was right there."

Harris phoned the doctor's home and woke the doctor's wife. The guitar player was still the same.

"This is so exciting, tell us all," said a fat boy. Harris knew he lived fifty miles up the river and had driven down under the impression that there would be a bridge game.

"It was just a fight."

"Oh, he wouldn't tell you, he never talks. I'll tell you," said Ruth. "Get your drinks, for goodness' sake."

So the incident became a story. Harris grew very tired of it.

"It's marvelous the way he always gets in with some-body and then something happens," said Ruth, her eyes completely black.

"Oh, he's my hero," said Carol, and she went out and stood on the back porch.

"Maybe you'll still be here tomorrow," Ruth said to Harris, taking his arm. "Will you be detained, maybe?"

"If he dies," said Harris.

He told them all good-bye.

"Let's all go to Greenville and get a Coke," said Ruth.

"No," he said. "Good night."

" 'Aw river,' " said the girl in the white dress. "Isn't that what the little man said?"

"Yes," said Harris, the rain falling on him, and he refused to spend the night or to be taken in a car back to the hotel.

In the antlered lobby, Mr. Gene bent over asleep under a lamp by the desk phone. His freckles seemed to come out darker when he was asleep.

Harris woke him. "Go to bed," he said. "What was the idea? Anything happened?"

"I just wanted to tell you that little buzzard's up in 202. Locked and double-locked, handcuffed to the bed, but I wanted to tell you."

"Oh. Much obliged."

"All a gentleman could do," said Mr. Gene. He was drunk. "Warn you what's sleepin' under your roof."

"Thanks," said Harris. "It's almost morning. Look."

"Poor Mike can't sleep," said Mr. Gene. "He scrapes somethin' when he breathes. Did the other fella poop out?"

"Still unconscious. No change," said Harris. He took the bunch of keys which the proprietor was handing him.

"You keep 'em," said Mr. Gene.

In the next moment Harris saw his hand tremble and he took hold of it.

"A murderer!" whispered Mr. Gene. All his freckles stood out. "Here he came . . . with not a word to say . . ."

"Not a murderer yet," said Harris, starting to grin.

When he passed 202 and heard no sound, he remembered what old Sobby had said, standing handcuffed in front of the hospital, with nobody listening to him. "I was jist tired of him always uppin' an' makin' a noise about ever'thing."

In his room, Harris lay down on the bed without undressing or turning out the light. He was too tired to sleep. Half blinded by the unshaded bulb he stared at the bare plaster walls and the equally white surface of the mirror above the empty dresser. Presently he got up and turned on the ceiling fan, to create some motion and sound in the room. It was a defective fan which clicked with each revolution, on and on. He lay perfectly still beneath it, with his clothes on, unconsciously breathing in a rhythm related to the beat of the fan.

He shut his eyes suddenly. When they were closed,

in the red darkness he felt all patience leave him. It was like the beginning of desire. He remembered the girl dropping money into her heart-shaped pocket, and remembered a disturbing possessiveness, which meant nothing, Ruth leaning on her hands. He knew he would not be held by any of it. It was for relief, almost, that his thoughts turned to pity, to wonder about the two tramps, their conflict, the sudden brutality when his back was turned. How would it turn out? It was in this suspense that it was more acceptable to him to feel the helplessness of his life.

He could forgive nothing in this evening. But it was too like other evenings, this town was too like other towns, for him to move out of this lying still clothed on the bed, even into comfort or despair. Even the rain—there was often rain, there was often a party, and there had been other violence not of his doing—other fights, not quite so pointless, but fights in his car; fights, unheralded confessions, sudden love-making—none of any of this his, not his to keep, but belonging to the people of these towns he passed through, coming out of their rooted pasts and their mock rambles, coming out of their time. He himself had no time. He was free; helpless. He wished he knew how the guitar player was, if he was still unconscious, if he felt pain.

He sat up on the bed and then got up and walked to the window.

"Tom!" said a voice outside in the dark.

Automatically he answered and listened. It was a girl. He could not see her, but she must have been standing on the little plot of grass that ran around the side of the hotel. Wet feet, pneumonia, he thought. And he was so tired he thought of a girl from the wrong town.

He went down and unlocked the door. She ran in as far as the middle of the lobby as though from impetus. It was Carol, from the party.

"You're wet," he said. He touched her.

"Always raining." She looked up at him, stepping back. "How are you?"

"O.K., fine," he said.

"I was wondering," she said nervously. "I knew the light would be you. I hope I didn't wake up anybody." Was old Sobby asleep? he wondered.

"Would you like a drink? Or do you want to go to the All-Nite and get a Coca-Cola?" he said.

"It's open," she said, making a gesture with her hand. "The All-Nite's open—I just passed it."

They went out into the mist, and she put his coat on with silent protest, in the dark street not drunken but womanly.

"You didn't remember me at the party," she said, and did not look up when he made his exclamation. "They say you never forget anybody, so I found out they were wrong about that anyway."

"They're often wrong," he said, and then hurriedly, "Who are you?"

"We used to stay at the Manning Hotel on the Coast every summer—I wasn't grown. Carol Thames. Just dances and all, but you had just started to travel then, it was on your trips, and you—you talked at intermission."

He laughed shortly, but she added:

"You talked about yourself."

They walked past the tall wet church, and their steps echoed.

"Oh, it wasn't so long ago—five years," she said. Under a magnolia tree she put her hand out and stopped him, looking up at him with her child's face. "But when I saw you again tonight I wanted to know how you were getting along."

He said nothing, and she went on.

"You used to play the piano."

They passed under a street light, and she glanced up as if to look for the little tic in his cheek.

"Out on the big porch where they danced," she said, walking on. "Paper lanterns . . ."

"I'd forgotten that, is one thing sure," he said. "Maybe you've got the wrong man. I've got cousins galore who all play the piano."

"You'd put your hands down on the keyboard like you'd say, 'Now this is how it really is!' " she cried, and turned her head away. "I guess I was crazy about you, though."

"Crazy about me then?" He struck a match and held a cigarette between his teeth.

"No—yes, and now too!" she cried sharply, as if driven to deny him.

They came to the little depot where a restless switch engine was hissing, and crossed the black street. The past and present joined like this, he thought, it never happened often to me, and it probably won't happen again. He took her arm and led her through the dirty screen door of the All-Nite.

He waited at the counter while she sat down by the

wall table and wiped her face all over with her handkerchief. He carried the black coffees over to the table
himself, smiling at her from a little distance. They sat
under a calendar with some picture of giant trees being cut
down.

They said little. A fly bothered her. When the coffee
was all gone he put her into the old Cadillac taxi that
always stood in front of the depot.

Before he shut the taxi door he said, frowning, "I
appreciate it. . . . You're sweet."

Now she had torn her handkerchief. She held it up
and began to cry. "What's sweet about me?" It was the
look of bewilderment in her face that he would remember.

"To come out, like this—in the rain—to be here. . . ."
He shut the door, partly from weariness.

She was holding her breath. "I hope your friend
doesn't die," she said. "All I hope is your friend gets
well."

But when he woke up the next morning and phoned
the hospital, the guitar player was dead. He had been
dying while Harris was sitting in the All-Nite.

"It *was* a murderer," said Mr. Gene, pulling Mike's
ears. "That was just plain murder. No way anybody could
call that an affair of honor."

The man called Sobby did not oppose an invitation to
confess. He stood erect and turning his head about a little, and almost smiled at all the men who had come to
see him. After one look at him Mr. Gene, who had come
with Harris, went out and slammed the door behind him.

All the same, Sobby had found little in the night, asleep or awake, to say about it. "I done it, sure," he said. "Didn't ever'body see me, or was they blind?"

They asked him about the man he had killed.

"Name Sanford," he said, standing still, with his foot out, as if he were trying to recall something particular and minute. "But he didn't have nothing and he didn't have no folks. No more'n me. Him and me, we took up together two weeks back." He looked up at their faces as if for support. "He was uppity, though. He bragged. He carried a gittar around." He whimpered. "It was his notion to run off with the car."

Harris, fresh from the barbershop, was standing in the filling station where his car was being polished.

A ring of little boys in bright shirt-tails surrounded him and the car, with some colored boys waiting behind them.

"Could they git all the blood off the seat and the steerin' wheel, Mr. Harris?"

He nodded. They ran away.

"Mr. Harris," said a little colored boy who stayed. "Does you want the box?"

"The what?"

He pointed, to where it lay in the back seat with the sample cases. "The po' kilt man's gittar. Even the police-mans didn't want it."

"No," said Harris, and handed it over.

A MEMORY

ONE SUMMER MORNING when I was a child I lay on the sand after swimming in the small lake in the park. The sun beat down—it was almost noon. The water shone like steel, motionless except for the feathery curl behind a distant swimmer. From my position I was looking at a rectangle brightly lit, actually glaring at me, with sun, sand, water, a little pavilion, a few solitary people in fixed attitudes, and around it all a border of dark rounded oak trees, like the engraved thunderclouds surrounding illustrations in the Bible. Ever since I had begun taking painting lessons, I had made small frames with my fingers, to look out at everything.

Since this was a weekday morning, the only persons who were at liberty to be in the park were either children, who had nothing to occupy them, or those older people whose lives are obscure, irregular, and consciously of no worth to anything: this I put down as my observation at that time. I was at an age when I formed a judgment upon every person and every event which came under my eye, although I was easily frightened. When a person, or a happening, seemed to me not in keeping with my opinion, or even my hope or expectation, I was terrified by a vision of abandonment and wildness which tore my heart with a kind of sorrow. My father and mother, who believed that I saw nothing in the world which was not strictly coaxed into place like a vine on our garden trellis to be presented to my eyes, would have been badly concerned if they had guessed how frequently the weak and inferior and strangely turned examples of what was to come showed themselves to me.

I do not know even now what it was that I was waiting to see; but in those days I was convinced that I almost saw it at every turn. To watch everything about me I regarded grimly and possessively as a *need*. All through this summer I had lain on the sand beside the small lake, with my hands squared over my eyes, finger tips touching, looking out by this device to see everything: which appeared as a kind of projection. It did not matter to me what I looked at; from any observation I would conclude that a secret of life had been nearly revealed to me—for I was obsessed with notions about concealment, and from the smallest gesture of a stranger I would wrest what was to me a communication or a presentiment.

This state of exaltation was heightened, or even brought about, by the fact that I was in love then for the first time: I had identified love at once. The truth is that never since has any passion I have felt remained so hopelessly unexpressed within me or appeared so grotesquely altered in the outward world. It is strange that sometimes, even now, I remember unadulteratedly a certain morning when I touched my friend's wrist (as if by accident, and he pretended not to notice) as we passed on the stairs in school. I must add, and this is not so strange, that the child was not actually my friend. We had never exchanged a word or even a nod of recognition; but it was possible during that entire year for me to think endlessly on this minute and brief encounter which we endured on the stairs, until it would swell with a sudden and overwhelming beauty, like a rose forced into premature bloom for a great occasion.

My love had somehow made me doubly austere in my observations of what went on about me. Through some intensity I had come almost into a dual life, as observer and dreamer. I felt a necessity for absolute conformity to my ideas in any happening I witnessed. As a result, all day long in school I sat perpetually alert, fearing for the untoward to happen. The dreariness and regularity of the school day were a protection for me, but I remember with exact clarity the day in Latin class when the boy I loved (whom I watched constantly) bent suddenly over and brought his handkerchief to his face. I saw red—vermilion—blood flow over the handkerchief and his square-shaped hand; his nose had begun to bleed. I remember the very moment: several of the older girls laughed at the confusion and distraction; the boy rushed from the room; the teacher spoke sharply in warning. But this small happening which had closed in upon my friend was a tremendous shock to me; it was unforeseen, but at the same time dreaded; I recognized it, and suddenly I leaned heavily on my arm and fainted. Does this explain why, ever since that day, I have been unable to bear the sight of blood?

I never knew where this boy lived, or who his parents were. This occasioned during the year of my love a constant uneasiness in me. It was unbearable to think that his house might be slovenly and unpainted, hidden by tall trees, that his mother and father might be shabby—dishonest—crippled—dead. I speculated endlessly on the dangers of his home. Sometimes I imagined that his house might catch on fire in the night and that he might die. When he would walk into the schoolroom the next morning, a look of unconcern and even stupidity on his face would dissipate my dream; but my fears were increased through his unconsciousness of them, for I felt a mystery deeper than danger which hung about him. I watched everything he did, trying to learn and translate and verify. I could reproduce for you now the clumsy weave, the exact shade of faded blue in his sweater. I remember how he used to swing his foot as he sat at his desk—softly, barely not touching the floor. Even now it does not seem trivial.

As I lay on the beach that sunny morning, I was thinking of my friend and remembering in a retarded, dilated, timeless fashion the incident of my hand brushing his wrist. It made a very long story. But like a needle going in and out among my thoughts were the children running on the sand, the upthrust oak trees growing over the clean pointed roof of the white pavilion, and the slowly changing attitudes of the grown-up people who had avoided the city and were lying prone and laughing on the water's edge. I still would not care to say which was more real—the dream I could make blossom at will, or the sight of the bathers. I am presenting them, you see, only as simultaneous.

I did not notice how the bathers got there, so close to me. Perhaps I actually fell asleep, and they came out then.

Sprawled close to where I was lying, at any rate, appeared a group of loud, squirming, ill-assorted people who seemed thrown together only by the most confused accident, and who seemed driven by foolish intent to insult each other, all of which they enjoyed with a hilarity which astonished my heart. There were a man, two women, two young boys. They were brown and roughened, but not foreigners; when I was a child such people were called "common." They wore old and faded bathing suits which did not hide either the energy or the fatigue of their bodies, but showed it exactly.

The boys must have been brothers, because they both had very white straight hair, which shone like thistles in the red sunlight. The older boy was greatly overgrown—he protruded from his costume at every turn. His cheeks were ballooned outward and hid his eyes, but it was easy for me to follow his darting, sly glances as he ran clumsily around the others, inflicting pinches, kicks, and idiotic sounds upon them. The smaller boy was thin and defiant; his white bangs were plastered down where he had thrown himself time after time headfirst into the lake when the older child chased him to persecute him.

Lying in leglike confusion together were the rest of the group, the man and the two women. The man seemed completely given over to the heat and glare of the sun; his relaxed eyes sometimes squinted with faint amusement over the brilliant water and the hot sand. His arms were flabby and at rest. He lay turned on his side, now and then scooping sand in a loose pile about the legs of the older woman.

She herself stared fixedly at his slow, undeliberate

movements, and held her body perfectly still. She was unnaturally white and fatly aware, in a bathing suit which had no relation to the shape of her body. Fat hung upon her upper arms like an arrested earthslide on a hill. With the first motion she might make, I was afraid that she would slide down upon herself into a terrifying heap. Her breasts hung heavy and widening like pears into her bathing suit. Her legs lay prone one on the other like shadowed bulwarks, uneven and deserted, upon which, from the man's hand, the sand piled higher like the teasing threat of oblivion. A slow, repetitious sound I had been hearing for a long time unconsciously, I identified as a continuous laugh which came through the motionless open pouched mouth of the woman.

The younger girl, who was lying at the man's feet, was curled tensely upon herself. She wore a bright green bathing suit like a bottle from which she might, I felt, burst in a rage of churning smoke. I could feel the genie-like rage in her narrowed figure as she seemed both to crawl and to lie still, watching the man heap the sand in his careless way about the larger legs of the older woman. The two little boys were running in wobbly ellipses about the others, pinching them indiscriminately and pitching sand into the man's roughened hair as though they were not afraid of him. The woman continued to laugh, almost as she would hum an annoying song. I saw that they were all resigned to each other's daring and ugliness.

There had been no words spoken among these people, but I began to comprehend a progression, a circle of answers, which they were flinging toward one another in their own way, in the confusion of vulgarity and hatred which twined among them all like a wreath of steam rising from the wet sand. I saw the man lift his hand filled with crumbling sand, shaking it as the woman laughed, and pour it down inside her bathing suit between her bulbous descending breasts. There it hung, brown and shapeless, making them all laugh. Even the angry girl laughed, with an insistent hilarity which flung her to her feet and tossed her about the beach, her stiff, cramped legs jumping and tottering. The little boys pointed and howled. The man smiled, the way panting dogs seem to be smiling, and gazed about carelessly at them all and out over the water. He even looked at me, and included me. Looking back, stunned, I wished that they all were dead.

But at that moment the girl in the green bathing suit suddenly whirled all the way around. She reached rigid arms toward the screaming children and joined them in a senseless chase. The small boy dashed headfirst into the water, and the larger boy churned his overgrown body through the blue air onto a little bench, which I had not even known was there! Jeeringly he called to the others, who laughed as he jumped, heavy and ridiculous, over the back of the bench and tumbled exaggeratedly in the sand below. The fat woman leaned over the man to smirk, and the child pointed at her, screaming. The girl in green then came running toward the bench as though she would destroy it, and with a fierceness which took my breath away, she dragged herself through the air and jumped over the bench. But no one seemed to notice, except the smaller boy, who flew out of the water to dig his fingers into her side, in mixed congratulation and derision; she pushed him angrily down into the sand.

I closed my eyes upon them and their struggles but I could see them still, large and almost metallic, with painted smiles, in the sun. I lay there with my eyes pressed shut, listening to their moans and their frantic squeals. It seemed to me that I could hear also the thud and the fat impact of all their ugly bodies upon one another. I tried to withdraw to my most inner dream, that of touching the wrist of the boy I loved on the stair; I felt the shudder of my wish shaking the darkness like leaves where I had closed my eyes; I felt the heavy weight of sweetness which always accompanied this memory; but the memory itself did not come to me.

I lay there, opening and closing my eyes. The brilliance and then the blackness were like some alternate experiences of night and day. The sweetness of my love seemed to bring the dark and to swing me gently in its suspended wind; I sank into familiarity; but the story of my love, the long narrative of the incident on the stairs, had vanished. I did not know, any longer, the meaning of my happiness; it held me unexplained.

Once when I looked up, the fat woman was standing opposite the smiling man. She bent over and in a condescending way pulled down the front of her bathing suit, turning it outward, so that the lumps of mashed and folded sand came emptying out. I felt a peak of horror, as though her breasts themselves had turned to sand, as though they were of no importance at all and she did not care.

When finally I emerged again from the protection of my dream, the undefined austerity of my love, I opened my eyes onto the blur of an empty beach. The group of

142

strangers had gone. Still I lay there, feeling victimized by the sight of the unfinished bulwark where they had piled and shaped the wet sand around their bodies, which changed the appearance of the beach like the ravages of a storm. I looked away, and for the object which met my eye, the small worn white pavilion, I felt pity suddenly overtake me, and I burst into tears.

That was my last morning on the beach. I remember continuing to lie there, squaring my vision with my hands, trying to think ahead to the time of my return to school in winter. I could imagine the boy I loved walking into a classroom, where I would watch him with this hour on the beach accompanying my recovered dream and added to my love. I could even foresee the way he would stare back, speechless and innocent, a medium-sized boy with blond hair, his unconscious eyes looking beyond me and out the window, solitary and unprotected.

CLYTIE

IT WAS LATE AFTERNOON, with heavy silver clouds which looked bigger and wider than cotton fields, and presently it began to rain. Big round drops fell, still in the sunlight, on the hot tin sheds, and stained the white false fronts of the row of stores in the little town of Farr's Gin. A hen and her string of yellow chickens ran in great alarm across the road, the dust turned river-brown, and the birds flew down into it immediately, sitting out little pockets in which to take baths. The bird dogs got up from the doorways of the stores, shook themselves down to the tail, and went to lie inside. The few people standing with long shadows on the level road moved over into the post office. A little boy kicked his bare heels into the sides of his mule, which proceeded slowly through the town toward the country.

After everyone else had gone under cover, Miss Clytie Farr stood still in the road, peering ahead in her near-sighted way, and as wet as the little birds.

She usually came out of the old big house about this time in the afternoon, and hurried through the town. It used to be that she ran about on some pretext or other, and for a while she made soft-voiced explanations that nobody could hear, and after that she began to charge up

144

bills, which the postmistress declared would never be paid any more than anyone else's, even if the Farrs were too good to associate with other people. But now Clytie came for nothing. She came every day, and no one spoke to her any more: she would be in such a hurry, and couldn't see who it was. And every Saturday they expected her to be run over, the way she darted out into the road with all the horses and trucks.

It might be simply that Miss Clytie's wits were all leaving her, said the ladies standing in the door to feel the cool, the way her sister's had left her; and she would just wait there to be told to go home. She would have to wring out everything she had on—the waist and the jumper skirt, and the long black stockings. On her head was one of the straw hats from the furnishing store, with an old black satin ribbon pinned to it to make it a better hat, and tied under the chin. Now, under the force of the rain, while the ladies watched, the hat slowly began to sag down on each side until it looked even more absurd and done for, like an old bonnet on a horse. And indeed it was with the patience almost of a beast that Miss Clytie stood there in the rain and stuck her long empty arms out a little from her sides, as if she were waiting for something to come along the road and drive her to shelter.

In a little while there was a clap of thunder.

"Miss Clytie! Go in out of the rain, Miss Clytie!" someone called.

The old maid did not look around, but clenched her hands and drew them up under her armpits, and sticking out her elbows like hen wings, she ran out of the street, her poor hat creaking and beating about her ears.

"Well, there goes Miss Clytie," the ladies said, and one of them had a premonition about her.

Through the rushing water in the sunken path under the four wet black cedars, which smelled bitter as smoke, she ran to the house.

"Where the devil have you been?" called the older sister, Octavia, from an upper window.

Clytie looked up in time to see the curtain fall back.

She went inside, into the hall, and waited, shivering. It was very dark and bare. The only light was falling on the white sheet which covered the solitary piece of furniture, an organ. The red curtains over the parlor door, held back by ivory hands, were still as tree trunks in the airless house. Every window was closed, and every shade was down, though behind them the rain could still be heard.

Clytie took a match and advanced to the stair post, where the bronze cast of Hermes was holding up a gas fixture; and at once above this, lighted up, but quite still, like one of the unmovable relics of the house, Octavia stood waiting on the stairs.

She stood solidly before the violet-and-lemon-colored glass of the window on the landing, and her wrinkled, unresting fingers took hold of the diamond cornucopia she always wore in the bosom of her long black dress. It was an unwithered grand gesture of hers, fondling the cornucopia.

"It is not enough that we are waiting here— hungry," Octavia was saying, while Clytie waited below. "But you must sneak away and not answer when I call you. Go off and wander about the streets. Common—common—!"

"Never mind, Sister," Clytie managed to say.

"But you always return."

"Of course. . . ."

"Gerald is awake now, and so is Papa," said Octavia, in the same vindicative voice—a loud voice, for she was usually calling.

Clytie went to the kitchen and lighted the kindling in the wood stove. As if she were freezing cold in June, she stood before its open door, and soon a look of interest and pleasure lighted her face, which had in the last years grown weather-beaten in spite of the straw hat. Now some dream was resumed. In the street she had been thinking about the face of a child she had just seen. The child, playing with another of the same age, chasing it with a toy pistol, had looked at her with such an open, serene, trusting expression as she passed by! With this small, peaceful face still in her mind, rosy like these flames, like an inspiration which drives all other thoughts away, Clytie had forgotten herself and had been obliged to stand where she was in the middle of the road. But the rain had come down, and someone had shouted at her, and she had not been able to reach the end of her meditations.

It had been a long time now, since Clytie had first begun to watch faces, and to think about them.

Anyone could have told you that there were not more than 150 people in Farr's Gin, counting Negroes. Yet the number of faces seemed to Clytie almost infinite. She knew now to look slowly and carefully at a face; she was convinced that it was impossible to see it all at once. The first thing she discovered about a face was always that she had never seen it before. When she began to look at people's actual countenances there was no more familiarity in the world for her. The most profound, the most moving sight in the whole world must be a face. Was it possible to comprehend the eyes and the mouths of other people, which concealed she knew not what, and secretly asked for still another unknown thing? The mysterious smile of the old man who sold peanuts by the church gate returned to her; his face seemed for a moment to rest upon the iron door of the stove, set into the lion's mane. Other people said Mr. Tom Bate's Boy, as he called himself, stared away with a face as clean-blank as a watermelon seed, but to Clytie, who observed grains of sand in his eyes and in his old yellow lashes, he might have come out of a desert, like an Egyptian.

But while she was thinking of Mr. Tom Bate's Boy, there was a terrible gust of wind which struck her back, and she turned around. The long green window shade billowed and plunged. The kitchen window was wide open—she had done it herself. She closed it gently. Octavia, who never came all the way downstairs for any reason, would never have forgiven her for an open window, if she knew. Rain and sun signified ruin, in Octavia's mind. Going over the whole house, Clytie made sure that everything was safe. It was not that ruin in itself could distress Octavia. Ruin or encroachment, even upon priceless treasures and even in poverty, held no terror for her; it was simply some form of prying from without, and this she would not forgive. All of that was to be seen in her face.

Clytie cooked the three meals on the stove, for they all ate different things, and set the three trays. She had to carry them in proper order up the stairs. She frowned in concentration, for it was hard to keep all the dishes straight, to make them come out right in the end, as Old Lethy could have done. They had had to give up the cook long ago when their father suffered the first stroke. Their father had been fond of Old Lethy, she had been his nurse in childhood, and she had come back out of the country to see him when she heard he was dying. Old Lethy had come and knocked at the back door. And as usual, at the first disturbance, front or back, Octavia had peered down from behind the curtain and cried, "Go away! Go away! What the devil have you come *here* for?" And although Old Lethy and their father had both pleaded that they might be allowed to see each other, Octavia had shouted as she always did, and sent the intruder away. Clytie had stood as usual, speechless in the kitchen, until finally she had repeated after her sister, "Lethy, go away." But their father had not died. He was, instead, paralyzed, blind, and able only to call out in unintelligible sounds and to swallow liquids. Lethy still would come to the back door now and then, but they never let her in, and the old man no longer heard or knew enough to beg to see her. There was only one caller admitted to his room. Once a week the barber came by appointment to shave him. On this occasion not a word was spoken by anyone.

Clytie went up to her father's room first and set the tray down on a little marble table they kept by his bed.

"I want to feed Papa," said Octavia, taking the bowl from her hands.

"You fed him last time," said Clytie.

Relinquishing the bowl, she looked down at the pointed face on the pillow. Tomorrow was the barber's

day, and the sharp black points, at their longest, stuck
out like needles all over the wasted cheeks. The old man's
eyes were half closed. It was impossible to know what he
felt. He looked as though he were really far away,
neglected, free. . . . Octavia began to feed him.

Without taking her eyes from her father's face, Clytie
suddenly began to speak in rapid, bitter words to her sister, the wildest words that came to her head. But soon
she began to cry and gasp, like a small child who has been
pushed by the big boys into the water.

"That is enough," said Octavia.

But Clytie could not take her eyes from her father's
unshaven face and his still-open mouth.

"And I'll feed him tomorrow if I want to," said
Octavia. She stood up. The thick hair, growing back after
an illness and dyed almost purple, fell over her forehead.
Beginning at her throat, the long accordion pleats which
fell the length of her gown opened and closed over her
breasts as she breathed. "Have you forgotten Gerald?"
she said. "And I am hungry too."

Clytie went back to the kitchen and brought her sister's supper.

Then she brought her brother's.

Gerald's room was dark, and she had to push through the
usual barricade. The smell of whisky was everywhere; it
even flew up in the striking of the match when she lighted
the jet.

"It's night," said Clytie presently.

Gerald lay on his bed looking at her. In the bad light
he resembled his father.

"There's some more coffee down in the kitchen," said Clytie.

"Would you bring it to me?" Gerald asked. He stared at her in an exhausted, serious way.

She stooped and held him up. He drank the coffee while she bent over him with her eyes closed, resting.

Presently he pushed her away and fell back on the bed, and began to describe how nice it was when he had a little house of his own down the street, all new, with all conveniences, gas stove, electric lights, when he was married to Rosemary. Rosemary—she had given up a job in the next town, just to marry him. How had it happened that she had left him so soon? It meant nothing that he had threatened time and again to shoot her, it was nothing at all that he had pointed the gun against her breast. She had not understood. It was only that he had relished his contentment. He had only wanted to play with her. In a way he had wanted to show her that he loved her above life and death.

"Above life and death," he repeated closing his eyes.

Clytie did not make an answer, as Octavia always did during these scenes, which were bound to end in Gerald's tears.

Outside the closed window a mockingbird began to sing. Clytie held back the curtain and pressed her ear against the glass. The rain had stopped. The bird's song sounded in liquid drops down through the pitch-black trees and the night.

"Go to hell," Gerald said. His head was under the pillow.

She took up the tray, and left Gerald with his face

hidden. It was not necessary for her to look at any of their faces. It was their faces which came between.

Hurrying, she went down to the kitchen and began to eat her own supper.

Their faces came between her face and another. It was their faces which had come pushing in between, long ago, to hide some face that had looked back at her. And now it was hard to remember the way it looked, or the time when she had seen it first. It must have been when she was young. Yes, in a sort of arbor, hadn't she laughed, leaned forward . . . and that vision of a face—which was a little like all the other faces, the trusting child's, the innocent old traveler's, even the greedy barber's and Lethy's and the wandering peddlers' who one by one knocked and went unanswered at the door—and yet different, yet far more—this face had been very close to hers, almost familiar, almost accessible. And then the face of Octavia was thrust between, and at other times the apoplectic face of her father, the face of her brother Gerald and the face of her brother Henry with the bullet hole through the forehead. . . . It was purely for a resemblance to a vision that she examined the secret, mysterious, unrepeated faces she met in the street of Farr's Gin.

But there was always an interruption. If anyone spoke to her, she fled. If she saw she was going to meet someone on the street, she had been known to dart behind a bush and hold a small branch in front of her face until the person had gone by. When anyone called her by name, she turned first red, then white, and looked somehow, as one of the ladies in the store remarked, *disappointed*.

She was becoming more frightened all the time, too.

People could tell because she never dressed up any more. For years, every once in a while, she would come out in what was called an "outfit," all in hunter's green, a hat that came down around her face like a bucket, a green silk dress, even green shoes with pointed toes. She would wear the outfit all one day, if it was a pretty day, and then next morning she would be back in the faded jumper with her old hat tied under the chin, as if the outfit had been a dream. It had been a long time now since Clytie had dressed up so that you could see her coming.

Once in a while when a neighbor, trying to be kind or only being curious, would ask her opinion about anything—such as a pattern of crochet—she would not run away; but, giving a thin trapped smile, she would say in a childish voice, "It's nice." But, the ladies always added, nothing that came anywhere close to the Farrs' house was nice for long.

"It's nice," said Clytie when the old lady next door showed her the new rosebush she had planted, all in bloom.

But before an hour was gone, she came running out of her house screaming, "My sister Octavia says you take that rosebush up! My sister Octavia says you take that rosebush up and move it away from our fence! If you don't I'll kill you! You take it away."

And on the other side of the Farrs lived a family with a little boy who was always playing in his yard. Octavia's cat would go under the fence, and he would take it and hold it in his arms. He had a song he sang to the Farrs' cat. Clytie would come running straight out of the house, flaming with her message from Octavia. "Don't you do that! Don't you do that!" she would cry in anguish. "If you do that again, I'll have to kill you!"

And she would run back to the vegetable patch and begin to curse.

The cursing was new, and she cursed softly, like a singer going over a song for the first time. But it was something she could not stop. Words which at first horrified Clytie poured in a full, light stream from her throat, which soon, nevertheless, felt strangely relaxed and rested. She cursed all alone in the peace of the vegetable garden. Everybody said, in something like deprecation, that she was only imitating her older sister, who used to go out to that same garden and curse in that same way, years ago, but in a remarkably loud, commanding voice that could be heard in the post office.

Sometimes in the middle of her words Clytie glanced up to where Octavia, at her window, looked down at her. When she let the curtain drop at last, Clytie would be left there speechless.

Finally, in a gentleness compounded of fright and exhaustion and love, an overwhelming love, she would wander through the gate and out through the town, gradually beginning to move faster, until her long legs gathered a ridiculous, rushing speed. No one in town could have kept up with Miss Clytie, they said, giving them an even start.

She always ate rapidly, too, all alone in the kitchen, as she was eating now. She bit the meat savagely from the heavy silver fork and gnawed the little chicken bone until it was naked and clean.

Halfway upstairs, she remembered Gerald's second

pot of coffee, and went back for it. After she had carried the other trays down again and washed the dishes, she did not forget to try all the doors and windows to make sure that everything was locked up absolutely tight.

The next morning, Clytie bit into smiling lips as she cooked breakfast. Far out past the secretly opened window a freight train was crossing the bridge in the sunlight. Some Negroes filed down the road going fishing, and Mr. Tom Bate's Boy, who was going along, turned and looked at her through the window.

Gerald had appeared dressed and wearing his spectacles, and announced that he was going to the store today. The old Farr furnishing store did little business now, and people hardly missed Gerald when he did not come; in fact, they could hardly tell when he did because of the big boots strung on a wire, which almost hid the cagelike office. A little high-school girl could wait on anybody who came in.

Now Gerald entered the dining room.

"How are you this morning, Clytie?" he asked.

"Just fine, Gerald, how are you?"

"I'm going to the store," he said.

He sat down stiffly, and she laid a place on the table before him.

From above, Octavia screamed, "Where in the devil is my thimble, you stole my thimble, Clytie Farr, you carried it away, my little silver thimble!"

"It's started," said Gerald intensely. Clytie saw his fine, thin, almost black lips spread in a crooked line. "How can a man live in the house with women? How can he?"

155

He jumped up, and tore his napkin exactly in two. He walked out of the dining room without eating the first bite of his breakfast. She heard him going back upstairs into his room.

"My thimble!" screamed Octavia.

She waited one moment. Crouching eagerly, rather like a little squirrel, Clytie ate part of her breakfast over the stove before going up the stairs.

At nine Mr. Bobo, the barber, knocked at the front door.

Without waiting, for they never answered the knock, he let himself in and advanced like a small general down the hall. There was the old organ that was never uncovered or played except for funerals, and then nobody was invited. He went ahead, under the arm of the tiptoed male statue and up the dark stairway. There they were, lined up at the head of the stairs, and they all looked at him with repulsion. Mr. Bobo was convinced that they were every one mad. Gerald, even, had already been drinking, at nine o'clock in the morning.

Mr. Bobo was short and had never been anything but proud of it, until he had started coming to this house once a week. But he did not enjoy looking up from below at the soft, long throats, the cold, repelled, high-reliefed faces of those Farrs. He could only imagine what one of those sisters would do to him if he made one move. (As if he would!) As soon as he arrived upstairs, they all went off and left him. He pushed out his chin and stood with his round legs wide apart, just looking around. The upstairs hall was absolutely bare. There was not even a chair to sit down in.

"Either they sell away their furniture in the dead of night," said Mr. Bobo to the people of Farr's Gin, "or else they're just too plumb mean to use it."

Mr. Bobo stood and waited to be summoned, and wished he had never started coming to this house to shave old Mr. Farr. But he had been so surprised to get a letter in the mail. The letter was on such old, yellowed paper that at first he thought it must have been written a thousand years ago and never delivered. It was signed "Octavia Farr," and began without even calling him "Dear Mr. Bobo." What it said was: "Come to this residence at nine o'clock each Friday morning until further notice, where you will shave Mr. James Farr."

He thought he would go one time. And each time after that, he thought he would never go back—especially when he never knew when they would pay him anything. Of course, it was something to be the only person in Farr's Gin allowed inside the house (except for the undertaker, who had gone there when young Henry shot himself, but had never to that day spoken of it). It was not easy to shave a man as bad off as Mr. Farr, either—not anything like as easy as to shave a corpse or even a fighting-drunk field hand. Suppose you were like this, Mr. Bobo would say: you couldn't move your face; you couldn't hold up your chin, or tighten your jaw, or even bat your eyes when the razor came close. The trouble with Mr. Farr was his face made no resistance to the razor. His face didn't hold.

"I'll never go back," Mr. Bobo always ended to his customers. "Not even if they paid me. I've seen enough."

Yet here he was again, waiting before the sickroom door.

"This is the last time," he said. "By God!"

And he wondered why the old man did not die.

Just then Miss Clytie came out of the room. There she came in her funny, sideways walk, and the closer she got to him the more slowly she moved.

"Now?" asked Mr. Bobo nervously.

Clytie looked at his small, doubtful face. What fear raced through his little green eyes! His pitiful, greedy, small face—how very mournful it was, like a stray kitten's. What was it that this greedy little thing was so desperately needing?

Clytie came up to the barber and stopped. Instead of telling him that he might go in and shave her father, she put out her hand and with breathtaking gentleness touched the side of his face.

For an instant afterward, she stood looking at him inquiringly, and he stood like a statue, like the statue of Hermes.

Then both of them uttered a despairing cry. Mr. Bobo turned and fled, waving his razor around in a circle, down the stairs and out the front door; and Clytie, pale as a ghost, stumbled against the railing. The terrible scent of bay rum, of hair tonic, the horrible moist scratch of an invisible beard, the dense, popping green eyes—what had she got hold of with her hand! She could hardly bear it— the thought of that face.

From the closed door to the sickroom came Octavia's shouting voice.

"Clytie! Clytie! You haven't brought Papa the rain water! Where in the devil is the rain water to shave Papa?"

Clytie moved obediently down the stairs.

Her brother Gerald threw open the door of his room and called after her, "What now? This is a madhouse! Somebody was running past my room, I heard it. Where do you keep your men? Do you have to bring them home?" He slammed the door again, and she heard the barricade going up.

Clytie went through the lower hall and out the back door. She stood beside the old rain barrel and suddenly felt that this object, now, was her friend, just in time, and her arms almost circled it with impatient gratitude. The rain barrel was full. It bore a dark, heavy, penetrating fragrance, like ice and flowers and the dew of night.

Clytie swayed a little and looked into the slightly moving water. She thought she saw a face there.

Of course. It was the face she had been looking for, and from which she had been separated. As if to give a sign, the index finger of a hand lifted to touch the dark cheek.

Clytie leaned closer, as she had leaned down to touch the face of the barber.

It was a wavering, inscrutable face. The brows were drawn together as if in pain. The eyes were large, intent, almost avid, the nose ugly and discolored as if from weeping, the mouth old and closed from any speech. On either side of the head dark hair hung down in a disreputable and wild fashion. Everything about the face frightened and shocked her with its signs of waiting, of suffering.

For the second time that morning, Clytie recoiled, and as she did so, the other recoiled in the same way.

Too late, she recognized the face. She stood there completely sick at heart, as though the poor, half-remembered vision had finally betrayed her.

"Clytie! Clytie! The water! The water!" came Octavia's monumental voice.

Clytie did the only thing she could think of to do. She bent her angular body further, and thrust her head into the barrel, under the water, through its glittering surface into the kind, featureless depth, and held it there.

When Old Lethy found her, she had fallen forward into the barrel, with her poor ladylike black-stockinged legs up-ended and hung apart like a pair of tongs.

think, is a large, elongated old woman with electric-looking hair and curly lips. She has spent her life trying to escape from the parlor-like jaws of self-consciousness. Her late marriage has set in upon her nerves like a retriever nosing and puffing through old dead leaves out in the woods. When she walks around the room she looks remote and nebulous, out on the fringe of habitation, and rather as if she must have been cruelly trained—otherwise she couldn't do actual, immediate things, like answering the telephone or putting on a hat. But she has gone further than you'd think: into club work. Surrounded by other more suitably exclaiming women, she belongs to the Daughters of the American Revolution and the United Daughters of the Confederacy, attending teas. Her long, disquieted figure towering in the candlelight of other women's houses looks like something accidental. Any occasion, and she dresses her hair like a unicorn horn. She even sings, and is requested to sing. She even writes some of the songs she sings ("O Trees in the Evening"). She has a voice that dizzies other ladies like an organ note, and amuses men like a halloo down the well. It's full of a hollow wind and echo, winding out through the wavery hope of her mouth. Do people know of her perpetual amazement? Back in safety she wonders, her untidy head trembles in the domestic dark. She remembers how everyone in Natchez will suddenly grow quiet around her. Old Mrs. Marblehall, Mr. Marblehall's wife: she even goes out in the rain, which Southern women despise above everything, in big neat biscuit-colored galoshes, for which she "ordered off." She is only looking around—servile, undelighted, sleepy, expensive, tortured Mrs. Marblehall, pinning her mind with a pin to her husband's diet. She wants to tempt him, she tells him. What would he like best, that he can have?

There is Mr. Marblehall's ancestral home. It's not so wonderfully large—it has only four columns—but you always look toward it, the way you always glance into tunnels and see nothing. The river is after it now, and the little back garden has assuredly crumbled away, but the box maze is there on the edge like a trap, to confound the Mississippi River. Deep in the red wall waits the front door—it weighs such a lot, it is perfectly solid, all one piece, black mahogany. . . . And you see—one of *them* is always going in it. There is a knocker shaped like a gasping fish on the door. You have every reason in the world to imagine the inside is dark, with old things about. There's many a big, deathly-looking tapestry, wrinkling and thin, many a sofa shaped like an S. Brocades as tall as the wicked queens in Italian tales stand gathered before the windows. Everything is draped and hooded and shaded, of course, unaffectionate but close. Such rosy lamps! The only sound would be a breath against the prisms, a stirring of the chandelier. It's like old eyelids, the house with one of its shutters, in careful working order, slowly opening outward. Then the little son softly comes and stares out like a kitten, with button nose and pointed ears and little fuzz of silky hair running along the top of his head.

The son is the worst of all. Mr. and Mrs. Marblehall had a child! When both of them were terribly old, they had this little, amazing, fascinating son. You can see how people are taken aback, how they jerk and throw up their hands every time they so much as think about it. At least, Mr. Marblehall sees them. He thinks Natchez people do nothing themselves, and really, most of them have done or could do the same thing. This son is six years old now. Close up, he has a monkey look, a very penetrating look. He has very sparse Japanese hair, tiny little pearly teeth, long little wilted fingers. Every day he is slowly and expensively dressed and taken to the Catholic school. He looks quietly and maliciously absurd, out walking with old Mr. Marblehall or old Mrs. Marblehall, placing his small booted foot on a little green worm, while they stop and wait on him. Everybody passing by thinks that he looks quite as if he thinks his parents had him just to show they could. You see, it becomes complicated, full of vindictiveness.

But now, as Mr. Marblehall walks as briskly as possible toward the river where there is sun, you have to merge him back into his proper blur, into the little party-giving town he lives in. Why look twice at him? There has been an old Mr. Marblehall in Natchez ever since the first one arrived back in 1818—with a theatrical presentation of Otway's *Venice*, ending with *A Laughable Combat between Two Blind Fiddlers*—an actor! Mr. Marblehall isn't so important. His name is on the list, he is forgiven, but nobody gives a hoot about any old Mr. Marblehall. He could die, for all they care; some people even say, "Oh, is he still alive?" Mr. Marblehall walks and walks, and now and then he is driven in his ancient fringed carriage with the candle burners like empty eyes in front. And yes, he is supposed to travel for his health. But why consider his absence? There isn't any other place besides Natchez, and

even if there were, it would hardly be likely to change
Mr. Marblehall if it were brought up against him. Big
fingers could pick him up off the Esplanade and take him
through the air, his old legs still measuredly walking in a
dangle, and set him down where he could continue that
same old Natchez stroll of his in the East or the West or
Kingdom Come. What difference could anything make
now about old Mr. Marblehall—so late? A week or two
would go by in Natchez and then there would be Mr.
Marblehall, walking down Catherine Street again, still
exactly in the same degree alive and old.

People naturally get bored. They say, "Well, he
waited till he was sixty years old to marry, and what did
he want to marry for?" as though what he did were the
excuse for their boredom and their lack of concern. Even
the thought of his having a stroke right in front of one of
the Pilgrimage houses during Pilgrimage Week makes
them only sigh, as if to say it's nobody's fault but his own
if he wants to be so insultingly and precariously well-pre-
served. He ought to have a little black boy to follow
around after him. Oh, his precious old health, which never
had reason to be so inspiring! Mr. Marblehall has a for-
mal, reproachful look as he stands on the corners arranging
himself to go out into the traffic to cross the streets. It's
as if he's thinking of shaking his stick and saying, "Well,
look! I've done it, don't you see?" But really, nobody pays
much attention to his look. He is just like other people to
them. He could have easily danced with a troupe of angels
in Paradise every night, and they wouldn't have guessed.
Nobody is likely to find out that he is leading a double
life.

The funny thing is he just recently began to lead this double life. He waited until he was sixty years old. Isn't he crazy? Before that, he'd never done anything. He didn't know what to do. Everything was for all the world like his first party. He stood about, and looked in his father's books, and long ago he went to France, but he didn't like it.

Drive out any of these streets in and under the hills and you find yourself lost. You see those scores of little galleried houses nearly alike. See the yellowing China trees at the eaves, the round flower beds in the front yards, like bites in the grass, listen to the screen doors whining, the ice wagons dragging by, the twittering noises of children. Nobody ever looks to see who is living in a house like that. These people come out themselves and sprinkle the hose over the street at this time of day to settle the dust, and after they sit on the porch, they go back into the house, and you hear the radio for the next two hours. It seems to mourn and cry for them. They go to bed early.

Well, old Mr. Marblehall can easily be seen standing beside a row of zinnias growing down the walk in front of that little house, bending over, easy, easy, so as not to strain anything, to stare at the flowers. Of course he planted them! They are covered with brown—each petal is a little heart-shaped pocket of dust. They don't have any smell, you know. It's twilight, all amplified with locusts screaming; nobody could see anything. Just what Mr. Marblehall is bending over the zinnias for is a mystery, any way you look at it. But there he is, quite visible, alive and old, leading his double life.

There's his other wife, standing on the night-stained

porch by a potted fern, screaming things to a neighbor. This wife is really worse than the other one. She is more solid, fatter, shorter, and while not so ugly, funnier looking. She looks like funny furniture—an unornamented stair post in one of these little houses, with her small monotonous round stupid head—or sometimes like a woodcut of a Bavarian witch, forefinger pointing, with scratches in the air all around her. But she's so static she scarcely moves, from her thick shoulders down past her cylindered brown dress to her short, stubby house slippers. She stands still and screams to the neighbors.

This wife thinks Mr. Marblehall's name is Mr. Bird. She says, "I declare I told Mr. Bird to go to bed, and look at him! I don't understand him!" All her devotion is combustible and goes up in despair. This wife tells everything she knows. Later, after she tells the neighbors, she will tell Mr. Marblehall. Cymbal-breasted, she fills the house with wifely complaints. She calls, "After I get Mr. Bird to bed, what does he do then? He lies there stretched out with his clothes on and don't have one word to say. Know what he does?"

And she goes on, while her husband bends over the zinnias, to tell what Mr. Marblehall (or Mr. Bird) does in bed. She does tell the truth. He reads *Terror Tales* and *Astonishing Stories*. She can't see anything to them: they scare her to death. These stories are about horrible and fantastic things happening to nude women and scientists. In one of them, when the characters open bureau drawers, they find a woman's leg with a stocking and garter on. Mrs. Bird had to shut the magazine. "The glutinous shadows," these stories say, "the red-eyed, muttering old crone," "the moonlight on her thigh," "an ancient cult of sun worshipers," "an altar suspiciously stained . . ." Mr. Marblehall doesn't feel as terrified as all that, but he reads on and on. He is killing time. It is richness without taste, like some holiday food. The clock gets a fruity bursting tick, to get through midnight—then leisurely, leisurely on. When time is passing it's like a bug in his ear. And then Mr. Bird—he doesn't even want a shade on the light, this wife moans respectably. He reads under a bulb. She can tell you how he goes straight through a stack of magazines. "He might just as well not have a family," she always ends, unjustly, and rolls back into the house as if she had been on a little wheel all this time.

But the worst of them all is the other little boy. Another little boy just like the first one. He wanders around the bungalow full of tiny little schemes and jokes. He has lost his front tooth, and in this way he looks slightly different from Mr. Marblehall's other little boy— more shocking. Otherwise, you couldn't tell them apart if you wanted to. They both have that look of cunning little jugglers, violently small under some spotlight beam, preoccupied and silent, amusing themselves. Both of the children will go into sudden fits and tantrums that frighten their mothers and Mr. Marblehall to death. Then they can get anything they want. But this little boy, the one who's lost the tooth, is the smarter. For a long time he supposed that his mother was totally solid, down to her thick separated ankles. But when she stands there on the porch screaming to the neighbors, she reminds him of those flares that charm him so, that they leave burning in the street at night—the dark solid ball, then, tongue-like, the wicked, yellow, continuous, enslaving blaze on the stem. He knows what his father thinks.

Perhaps one day, while Mr. Marblehall is standing there gently bent over the zinnias, this little boy is going to write on a fence, "Papa leads a double life." He finds out things you wouldn't find out. He is a monkey.

You see, one night he is going to follow Mr. Marblehall (or Mr. Bird) out of the house. Mr. Marblehall has said as usual that he is leaving for one of his health trips. He is one of those correct old gentlemen who are still going to the wells and drinking the waters—exactly like his father, the late old Mr. Marblehall. But why does he leave on foot? This will occur to the little boy.

So he will follow his father. He will follow him all the way across town. He will see the shining river come winding around. He will see the house where Mr. Marblehall turns in at the wrought-iron gate. He will see a big speechless woman come out and lead him in by the heavy door. He will not miss those rosy lamps beyond the many-folded draperies at the windows. He will run around the fountains and around the Japonica trees, past the stone figure of the pigtailed courtier mounted on the goat, down to the back of the house. From there he can look far up at the strange upstairs rooms. In one window the other wife will be standing like a giant, in a long-sleeved gathered nightgown, combing her electric hair and breaking it off each time in the comb. From the next window the other little boy will look out secretly into the night, and see him—or not see him. That would be an interesting

169

thing, a moment of strange telepathies. (Mr. Marblehall can imagine it.) Then in the corner room there will suddenly be turned on the bright, naked light. Aha! Father!

Mr. Marblehall's little boy will easily climb a tree there and peep through the window. There, under a stark shadeless bulb, on a great four-poster with carved griffins, will be Mr. Marblehall, reading *Terror Tales,* stretched out and motionless.

Then everything will come out.

At first, nobody will believe it.

Or maybe the policeman will say, "Stop! How dare you!"

Maybe, better than that, Mr. Marblehall himself will confess his duplicity—how he has led two totally different lives, with completely different families, two sons instead of one. What an astonishing, unbelievable, electrifying confession that would be, and how his two wives would topple over, how his sons would cringe! To say nothing of most men aged sixty-six. So thinks self-consoling Mr. Marblehall.

You will think, what if nothing ever happens? What if there is no climax, even to this amazing life? Suppose old Mr. Marblehall simply remains alive, getting older by the minute, shuttling, still secretly, back and forth?

Nobody cares. Not an inhabitant of Natchez, Mississippi, cares if he is deceived by old Mr. Marblehall. Neither does anyone care that Mr. Marblehall has finally caught on, he thinks, to what people are supposed to do. This is it: they endure something inwardly—for a time secretly; they establish a past, a memory; thus they store up life. He has done this; most remarkably, he has even multiplied his life by deception; and plunging deeper and deeper he speculates upon some glorious finish, a great explosion of revelations . . . the future.

But he still has to kill time, and get through the clocking nights. Otherwise he dreams that he is a great blazing butterfly stitching up a net; which doesn't make sense.

Old Mr. Marblehall! He may have years ahead yet in which to wake up bolt upright in the bed under the naked bulb, his heart thumping, his old eyes watering and wild, imagining that if people knew about his double life, they'd die.

FLOWERS
FOR
MARJORIE

———◆———

HE WAS ONE OF THE MODEST, the shy, the sandy haired—
one of those who would always have preferred waiting to
one side. . . . A row of feet rested beside his own where
he looked down. Beyond was the inscribed base of the
drinking fountain which stemmed with a troubled sound
up into the glare of the day. The feet were in Vs, all still.
Then down at the end of the bench, one softly began to
pat. It made an innuendo at a dainty pink chewing-gum
wrapper blowing by.

He would not look up. When the chewing-gum wrapper blew over and tilted at his foot, he spat at some
sensing of invitation and kicked it away. He held a toothpick in his mouth.

Someone spoke. "You goin' to join the demonstration
at two o'clock?"

Howard lifted his gaze no further than the baggy cor-
duroy knees in front of his own.

"Demonstration . . . ?" The tasteless toothpick stuck to his lips; what he said was indistinct.

But he snapped the toothpick finally with his teeth and puffed it out of his mouth. It landed in the grass like a little tent. He was surprised at the sight of it, and at his neatness and proficiency in blowing it out. And that little thing started up all the pigeons, His eyes ached when they whirled all at once, as though a big spoon stirred them in the sunshine. He closed his eyes upon their flying opal-changing wings.

And then, with his eyes shut, he had to think about Marjorie. Always now like something he had put off, the thought of her was like a wave that hit him when he was tired, rising impossibly out of stagnancy and deprecation while he sat in the park, towering over his head, pounding, falling, going back and leaving nothing behind it.

He stood up, looked at the position of the sun, and slowly started back to her.

He was panting from the climb of four flights, and his hand groped for the knob in the hall shadows. As soon as he opened the door he shrugged and threw his hat on the bed, so Marjorie would not ask him how he came out looking about the job at Columbus Circle; for today, he had not gone back to inquire.

Nothing was said, and he sat for a while on the couch, his hands spread on his knees. Then, before he would meet her eye, he looked at the chair in the room, which neither one would use, and there lay Marjorie's coat with a flower stuck in the buttonhole. He gave a silent despairing laugh that turned into a cough.

173

Marjorie said, "I walked around the block—and look what I found." She too was looking only at the pansy, full of pride.

It was bright yellow. She only found it, Howard thought, but he winced inwardly, as though she had displayed some power of the spirit. He simply had to sit and stare at her, his hands drawn back into his pockets, feeling a match.

Marjorie sat on the little trunk by the window, her round arm on the sill, her soft cut hair now and then blowing and streaming like ribbon-ends over her curling hand where she held her head up. It was hard to remember, in this city of dark, nervous, loud-spoken women, that in Victory, Mississippi, all girls were like Marjorie—and that Marjorie was in turn like his home. . . . Or was she? There were times when Howard would feel lost in the one little room. Marjorie often seemed remote now, or it might have been the excess of life in her rounding body that made her never notice any more the single and lonely life around her, the very pressing life around her. He could only look at her. . . . Her breath whistled a little between her parted lips as she stirred in some momentary discomfort.

Howard lowered his eyes and once again he saw the pansy. There it shone, a wide-open yellow flower with dark red veins and edges. Against the sky-blue of Marjorie's old coat it began in Howard's anxious sight to lose its identity of flower-size and assume the gradual and large curves of a mountain on the horizon of a desert, the veins becoming crevasses, the delicate edges the giant worn lips of a sleeping crater. His heart jumped to his mouth. . . .

He snatched the pansy from Marjorie's coat and tore its petals off and scattered them on the floor and jumped on them!

Marjorie watched him in silence, and slowly he realized that he had not acted at all, that he had only had a terrible vision. The pansy still blazed on the coat, just as the pigeons had still flown in the park when he was hungry. He sank back onto the couch, trembling with the desire and the pity that had overwhelmed him, and said harshly, "How long before your time comes?"

"Oh, Howard."

"Oh, Howard,"—that was Marjorie. The softness, the reproach—how was he to stop it, ever?

"What did you say?" he asked her.

"Oh, Howard, can't you keep track of the time? Always asking me . . ." She took a breath and said, "In three more months—the end of August."

"This is May," he told her. . . . He almost warned her. "This is May."

"May, June, July, August." She rattled the time off.

"You know for sure—you're certain, it will happen when you say?" He gazed at her.

"Why, of course, Howard, those things always happen when they're supposed to. Nothing can stop me from having the baby, that's sure." Tears came slowly into her eyes.

"Don't cry, Marjorie!" he shouted at her. "Don't cry, don't cry!"

"Even if you don't want it," she said.

He beat his fist down on the old dark red cloth that covered the couch. He felt emotion climbing hand over

175

hand up his body, with its strange and perfect agility. Helplessly he shut his eyes.

"I expect you can find work before then, Howard," she said.

He stood up in wonder: let it be the way she says. He looked searchingly around the room, pressed by tenderness, and softly pulled the pansy from the coat.

Holding it out he crossed to her and dropped soberly onto the floor beside her. His eyes were large. He gave her the flower.

She whispered to him. "We haven't been together in so long." She laid her calm warm hand on his head, covering over the part in his hair, holding him to her side, while he drew deep breaths of the cloverlike smell of her tightening skin and her swollen thighs.

Why, this is not possible! he was thinking. The ticks of the cheap alarm clock grew louder and louder as he buried his face against her, feeling new desperation every moment in the time-marked softness and the pulse of her sheltering body.

But she was talking.

"If they would only give you some paving work for the three months, we could scrape something out of that to pay a nurse, maybe, for a little while afterwards, after the baby comes—"

He jumped to his feet, his muscles as shocked by her words as if they had hurled a pick at the pavement in Columbus Circle at that moment. His sharp words overlaid her murmuring voice.

"Work?" he said sternly, backing away from her, speaking loudly from the middle of the room, almost as if he copied his pose and his voice somehow from the agita-tors in the park. "When did I ever work? A year ago . . . six months . . . back in Mississippi . . . I've forgotten! Time isn't as easy to count up as you think! I wouldn't know what to do now if they did give me work. I've for-gotten! It's all past now. . . . And I don't believe it any more—they won't give me work now—they never will—"

He stopped, and for a moment a look shone in his face, as if he had caught sight of a mirage. Perhaps he could imagine ahead of him some regular and steady divi-sion of the day and night, with breakfast appearing in the morning. Then he laughed gently, and moved even further back until he stood against the wall, as far as possible away from Marjorie, as though she were faithless and strange, allied to the other forces.

"Why, Howard, you don't even hope you'll find work any more," she whispered.

"Just because you're going to have a baby, just because that's a thing that's bound to happen, just because you can't go around forever with a baby inside your belly, and it will really happen that the baby is born—that doesn't mean everything else is going to happen and change!" He shouted across at her desperately, leaning against the wall. "That doesn't mean that I will find work! It doesn't mean we aren't starving to death." In some ges-ture of his despair he had brought his little leather purse from his pocket, and was swinging it violently back and forth. "You may not know it, but you're the only thing left in the world that hasn't stopped!"

The purse, like a little pendulum, slowed down in his hand. He stared at her intently, and then his working mouth drooped, and he stood there holding the purse as still as possible in his palms.

But Marjorie sat as undismayed as anyone could ever be, there on the trunk, looking with her head to one side. Her fullness seemed never to have touched his body. Away at his distance, backed against the wall, he regarded her world of sureness and fruitfulness and comfort, grown forever apart, safe and hopeful in pregnancy, as if he thought it strange that this world, too, should not suffer.

"Have you had anything to eat?" she was asking him.

He was astonished at her; he hated her, then. Inquiring out of her safety into his hunger and weakness! He flung the purse violently to the floor, where it struck softly like the body of a shot bird. It was empty.

Howard walked unsteadily about and came to the stove. He picked up a small clean bent saucepan, and put it down again. They had taken it with them wherever they had moved, from room to room. His hand went to the objects on the shelf as if he were blind. He got hold of the butcher knife. Holding it gently, he turned toward Marjorie.

"Howard, what are you going to do?" she murmured in a patient, lullaby-like voice, as she had asked him so many times.

They were now both far away, remote from each other, detached. Like a flash of lightning he changed his hold on the knife and thrust it under her breast.

The blood ran down the edge of the handle and dripped regularly into her open hand which she held in her lap. How strange! he thought wonderingly. She still leaned back on her other arm, but she must have borne down too heavily upon it, for before long her head bowed slowly over, and her forehead touched the window sill. Her hair began to blow from the back of her head and after a few minutes it was all turned the other way. Her arm that had rested on the window sill in a raised position was just as it was before. Her fingers were relaxed, as if she had just let something fall. There were little white cloudy markings on her nails. It was perfect balance, Howard thought, staring at her arm. That was why Marjorie's arm did not fall. When he finally looked down there was blood everywhere; her lap was like a bowl.

Yes, of course, he thought; for it had all been impossible. He went to wash his hands. The clock ticked dreadfully, so he threw it out the window. Only after a long time did he hear it hit the courtyard below.

His head throbbing in sudden pain, he stooped and picked up his purse. He went out, after closing the door behind him gently.

There in the city the sun slanted onto the streets. It lay upon a thin gray cat watching in front of a barber's pole; as Howard passed, she licked herself overneatly, staring after him. He set his hat on straight and walked through a crowd of children who surged about a jumping rope, chanting and jumping around him with their lips hanging apart. He crossed a street and a messenger boy banged into him with the wheel of his bicycle, but it never hurt at all.

He walked up Sixth Avenue under the shade of the L, and kept setting his hat on straight. The little spurts of wind tried to take it off and blow it away. How far he would have had to chase it! . . . He reached a crowd of people who were watching a machine behind a window; it made doughnuts very slowly. He went to the next door, where he saw another window full of colored prints of the Virgin Mary and nearly all kinds of birds and animals, and down below these a shelf of little gray pasteboard boxes in which were miniature toilets and night jars to be used in playing jokes, and in the middle box a bulb attached to a long tube, with a penciled sign, "Palpitator—the Imitation Heart. Show her you Love her." An organ grinder immediately removed his hat and played "Valencia."

He went on and in a doorway watched how the auctioneer leaned out so intimately and waved a pair of gold candlesticks at some men who puffed smoke straight up against the brims of their hats. He passed another place, with the same pictures of the Virgin Mary pinned with straight pins to the door facing, in case they had not been seen the first time. On a dusty table near his hand was a glass-ball paperweight. He reached out with shy joy and touched it, it was so small and round. There was a little scene inside made of bits of colored stuff. That was a bright land under the glass; he would like to be there. It made him smile: it was like everything made small and illuminated and flowering, not too big now. He turned the ball upside down with a sort of instinct, and in shocked submission and pity saw the landscape deluged in a small fury of snow. He stood for a moment fascinated, and then, suddenly aware of his great size, he put the paperweight back where he had found it, and stood shaking in the door. A man passing by dropped a dime into his open hand.

Then he found himself in the tunnel of a subway. All

along the tile wall was written, "God sees me, God sees me, God sees me, God sees me"—four times where he walked by. He read the signs, "Entrance" and "Exit Only," and where someone had printed "Nuts!" under both words. He looked at himself in a chewing-gum-machine mirror and straightened his hat before entering the train.

In the car he looked above the heads of the people at the pictures on the advertisements, and saw many couples embracing and smiling. A beggar came through with a cane and sang "Let Me Call You Sweetheart" like a blind man, and he too was given a dime. As Howard left the car a guard told him to watch his step. He clutched his hat. The wind blew underground, too, whistling down the tracks after the trains. He went up the stairs between two old warm Jewish women.

Up above, he went into a bar and had a drink of whisky, and though he could not pay for that, he had a nickel left over from the subway ride. In the back he heard a slot machine being played. He moved over and stood for a while between two friendly men and then put in the nickel. The many nickels that poured spurting and clanging out of the hole sickened him; they fell all over his legs, and he backed up against the dusty red curtain. His hat slid off onto the floor. They all rushed to pick it up, and some of them gave him handfuls of nickels to hold and bought him drinks with the rest. One of them said, "Fella, you ought not to let all hell loose that way." It was a Southern man. Howard agreed that they should all have drinks around and that his fortune belonged to them all.

But after he had walked around outside awhile he still

had nowhere in his mind to go. He decided to try the W.P.A. office and Miss Ferguson. Miss Ferguson knew him. There was an old habit he used to have of going up to see her.

He went into the front office. He could see Miss Ferguson through the door, typing the same as ever.

"Oh, Miss Ferguson!" he called softly, leaning forward in all his confidence. He reached up, ready to remove his hat, but she went on typing.

"Oh, Miss Ferguson!"

A woman who did not know him at all came into the room.

"Did you receive a card to call?" she asked.

"Miss Ferguson," he repeated, peering around her red arm to keep his eye on the typewriter.

"Miss Ferguson is busy," said the red-armed woman.

If he could only tell Miss Ferguson everything, everything in his life! Howard was thinking. Then it would come clear, and Miss Ferguson would write a note on a little card and hand it to him, tell him exactly where he could go and what he could do.

When the red-armed woman walked out of the office, Howard tried to win Miss Ferguson over. She could be very sympathetic.

"Somebody told me you could type!" he called softly, in complimentary tones.

Miss Ferguson looked up. "Yes, that's right. I can type," she said, and went on typing.

"I got something to tell you," Howard said. He smiled at her.

"Some other time," replied Miss Ferguson over the

sound of the keys. "I'm busy now. You'd better go home and sleep it off, h'm?"

Howard dropped his arm. He waited, and tried desperately to think of an answer to that. He was gazing into the water cooler, in which minute air bubbles swam. But he could think of nothing.

He lifted his hat with a strange jauntiness which may have stood for pride.

"Good-bye, Miss Ferguson!"

And he was back on the street.

He walked further and further. It was late when he turned into a large arcade, and when he followed someone through a free turnstile, a woman marched up to him and said, "You are the ten millionth person to enter Radio City, and you will broadcast over a nationwide red-and-blue network tonight at six o'clock, Eastern standard time. What is your name, address, and phone number? Are you married? Accept these roses and the key to the city."

She gave him a great heavy key and an armful of bright red roses. He tried to give them back to her at first, but she had not waited a moment. A ring of men with hawklike faces aimed cameras at him and all took his picture, to the flashing of lights.

"What is your occupation?"

"Are you married?"

Almost in his face a large woman with feathery furs and a small brown wire over one tooth was listening, and others were waiting behind her.

He watched for an opening, and when they were not looking he broke through and ran.

He ran down Sixth Avenue as fast as he could, ablaze

with horror, the roses nodding like heads in his arm, the key prodding his side. With his free hand he held determinedly to his hat. Doorways and intersections blurred past. All shining within was a restaurant beside him, but now it was too late to be hungry. He wanted only to get home. He could not see easily, but traffic seemed to stop softly when he ran thundering by; horses under the L drew up, and trucks kindly contracted, as if on a bellows, in front of him. People seemed to melt out of his way. He thought that maybe he was dead, and now in the end everything and everybody was afraid of him.

When he reached his street his breath was gone. There were the children playing. They were afraid of him and let him by. He ran into the courtyard, and stopped still.

There on the walk was the clock.

It lay on its face, and scattered about it in every direction were wheels and springs and bits of glass. He bent over and looked at the tiny little pieces.

At last he climbed the stairs. Somehow he tried to unlock the door with the key to the city. But the door was not locked at all, and when he got inside, he looked over to the window and there was Marjorie on the little trunk. Then the roses gave out deep waves of fragrance. He stroked their soft leaves. Marjorie's arm had fallen down; the balance was gone, and now her hand hung out the window as if to catch the wind.

Then Howard knew for a fact that everything had stopped. It was just as he had feared, just as he had dreamed. He had had a dream to come true.

He backed away slowly, until he was out of the room. Then he ran down the stairs.

On the street corner the first person he saw was a policeman watching pigeons flying.

Howard went up and stood for a little while beside him.

"Do you know what's up there in that room?" he asked finally. He was embarrassed to be asking anything of a policeman and to be holding such beautiful flowers.

"What is that?" asked the policeman.

Howard bent his head and buried his eyes, nose, and mouth in the roses. "A dead woman. Marjorie is dead."

Although the street-intersection sign was directly over their heads, and in the air where the pigeons flew the chimes of a clock were striking six, even the policeman did not seem for a moment to be sure of the time and place they were in, but had to consult his own watch and pocket effects.

"Oh!" and "So!" the policeman kept saying, while Howard in perplexity turned his head from side to side. He looked at him steadily, memorizing for all time the nondescript, dusty figure with the wide gray eyes and the sandy hair. "And I don't suppose the red drops on your pants are rose petals, are they?"

He grasped the staring man finally by the arm.

"Don't be afraid, big boy. *I'll* go up with you," he said.

They turned and walked back side by side. When the roses slid from Howard's fingers and fell on their heads all along the sidewalk, the little girls ran stealthily up and put them in their hair.

A CURTAIN
OF GREEN

EVERY DAY one summer in Larkin's Hill, it rained a little. The rain was a regular thing, and would come about two o'clock in the afternoon.

One day, almost as late as five o'clock, the sun was still shining. It seemed almost to spin in a tiny groove in the polished sky, and down below, in the trees along the street and in the rows of flower gardens in the town, every leaf reflected the sun from a hardness like a mirror surface. Nearly all the women sat in the windows of their houses, fanning and sighing, waiting for the rain.

Mrs. Larkin's garden was a large, densely grown plot running downhill behind the small white house where she lived alone now, since the death of her husband. The sun and the rain that beat down so heavily that summer had not kept her from working there daily. Now the intense light like a tweezers picked out her clumsy, small figure in its old pair of men's overalls rolled up at the sleeves and trousers, separated it from the thick leaves, and made it look strange and yellow as she worked with a hoe—overvigorous, disreputable, and heedless.

Within its border of hedge, high like a wall, and visible only from the upstairs windows of the neighbors, this slanting, tangled garden, more and more over-abundant and confusing, must have become so familiar to Mrs. Larkin that quite possibly by now she was unable to conceive of any other place. Since the accident in which her husband was killed, she had never once been seen anywhere else. Every morning she might be observed walking slowly, almost timidly, out of the white house, wearing a pair of the untidy overalls, often with her hair streaming and tangled where she had neglected to comb it. She would wander about for a little while at first, uncertainly, deep among the plants and wet with their dew, and yet not quite putting out her hand to touch anything. And then a sort of sturdiness would possess her—stabilize her; she would stand still for a moment, as if a blindfold were being removed; and then she would kneel in the flowers and begin to work.

She worked without stopping, almost invisibly, submerged all day among the thick, irregular, sloping beds of plants. The servant would call her at dinnertime, and she would obey; but it was not until it was completely dark that she would truthfully give up her labor and with a drooping, submissive walk appear at the house, slowly opening the small low door at the back. Even the rain would bring only a pause to her. She would move to the shelter of the pear tree, which in mid-April hung heavily almost to the ground in brilliant full leaf, in the center of the garden.

It might seem that the extreme fertility of her garden formed at once a preoccupation and a challenge to Mrs.

Larkin. Only by ceaseless activity could she cope with the rich blackness of this soil. Only by cutting, separating, thinning and tying back in the clumps of flowers and bushes and vines could she have kept them from over-reaching their boundaries and multiplying out of all reason. The daily summer rains could only increase her vigilance and her already excessive energy. And yet, Mrs. Larkin rarely cut, separated, tied back. . . . To a certain extent, she seemed not to seek for order, but to allow an overflowering, as if she consciously ventured forever a little farther, a little deeper, into her life in the garden.

She planted every kind of flower that she could find or order from a catalogue—planted thickly and hastily, without stopping to think, without any regard for the ideas that her neighbors might elect in their club as to what consti-tuted an appropriate vista, or an effect of restfulness, or even harmony of color. Just to what end Mrs. Larkin worked so strenuously in her garden, her neighbors could not see. She certainly never sent a single one of her fine flowers to any of them. They might get sick and die, and she would never send a flower. And if she thought of *beauty* at all (they regarded her stained overalls, now almost of a color with the leaves), she certainly did not strive for it in her garden. It was impossible to enjoy look-ing at such a place. To the neighbors gazing down from their upstairs windows it had the appearance of a sort of jungle, in which the slight, heedless form of its owner daily lost itself.

At first, after the death of Mr. Larkin—for whose father, after all, the town had been named—they had called upon the widow with decent frequency. But she had not appreciated it, they said to one another. Now, occasionally, they looked down from their bedroom windows as they brushed studiously at their hair in the morning; they found her place in the garden, as they might have run their fingers toward a city on a map of a foreign country, located her from their distance almost in curiosity, and then forgot her.

Early that morning they had heard whistling in the Larkin garden. They had recognized Jamey's tune, and had seen him kneeling in the flowers at Mrs. Larkin's side. He was only the colored boy who worked in the neighborhood by the day. Even Jamey, it was said, Mrs. Larkin would tolerate only now and then. . . .

Throughout the afternoon she had raised her head at intervals to see how fast he was getting along in his transplanting. She had to make him finish before it began to rain. She was busy with the hoe, clearing one of the last patches of uncultivated ground for some new shrubs. She bent under the sunlight, chopping in blunt, rapid, tireless strokes. Once she raised her head far back to stare at the flashing sky. Her eyes were dull and puckered, as if from long impatience or bewilderment. Her mouth was a sharp line. People said she never spoke.

But memory tightened about her easily, without any prelude of warning or even despair. She would see promptly, as if a curtain had been jerked quite unceremoniously away from a little scene, the front porch of the white house, the shady street in front, and the blue automobile in which her husband approached, driving home from work. It was a summer day, a day from the summer before. In the freedom of gaily turning her head, a motion she was now forced by memory to repeat as she hoed the ground, she could see again the tree that was going to fall. There had been no warning. But there was the enormous tree, the fragrant chinaberry tree, suddenly tilting, dark and slow like a cloud, leaning down to her husband. From her place on the front porch she had spoken in a soft voice to him, never so intimate as at that moment, "You can't be hurt." But the tree had fallen, had struck the car exactly so as to crush him to death. She had waited there on the porch for a time afterward, not moving at all—in a sort of recollection—as if to reach under and bring out from obliteration her protective words and to try them once again . . . so as to change the whole happening. It was accident that was incredible, when her love for her husband was keeping him safe.

She continued to hoe the breaking ground, to beat down the juicy weeds. Presently she became aware that hers was the only motion to continue in the whole slackened place. There was no wind at all now. The cries of the birds had hushed. The sun seemed clamped to the side of the sky. Everything had stopped once again, the stillness had mesmerized the stems of the plants, and all the leaves went suddenly into thickness. The shadow of the pear tree in the center of the garden lay callous on the ground. Across the yard, Jamey knelt, motionless.

"Jamey!" she called angrily.

But her voice hardly carried in the dense garden. She felt all at once terrified, as though her loneliness had been pointed out by some outside force whose finger parted the hedge. She drew her hand for an instant to her breast.

An obscure fluttering there frightened her, as though the force babbled to her, The bird that flies within your heart could not divide this cloudy air . . . She stared without expression at the garden. She was clinging to the hoe, and she stared across the green leaves toward Jamey.

A look of docility in the Negro's back as he knelt in the plants began to infuriate her. She started to walk toward him, dragging the hoe vaguely through the flowers behind her. She forced herself to look at him, and noticed him closely for the first time—the way he looked like a child. As he turned his head a little to one side and negligently stirred the dirt with his yellow finger, she saw, with a sort of helpless suspicion and hunger, a soft, rather deprecating smile on his face; he was lost in some impossible dream of his own while he was transplanting the little shoots. He was not even whistling; even that sound was gone.

She walked nearer to him—he must have been deaf!— almost stealthily bearing down upon his laxity and his absorption, as if that glimpse of the side of his face, that turned-away smile, were a teasing, innocent, flickering and beautiful vision—some mirage to her strained and wandering eyes.

Yet a feeling of stricture, of a responding hopelessness almost approaching ferocity, grew with alarming quickness about her. When she was directly behind him she stood quite still for a moment, in the queer sheathed manner she had before beginning her gardening in the morning. Then she raised the hoe above her head; the clumsy sleeves both fell back, exposing the thin, unsunburned whiteness of her arms, the shocking fact of their youth.

She gripped the handle tightly, tightly, as though convinced that the wood of the handle could feel, and that all her strength could indent its surface with pain. The head of Jamey, bent there below her, seemed witless, terrifying, wonderful, almost inaccessible to her, and yet in its explicit nearness meant surely for destruction, with its clustered hot woolly hair, its intricate, glistening ears, its small brown branching streams of sweat, the bowed head holding so obviously and so deadly its ridiculous dream.

Such a head she could strike off, intentionally, so deeply did she know, from the effect of a man's danger and death, its cause in oblivion; and so helpless was she, too helpless to defy the workings of accident, of life and death, of unaccountability. . . . Life and death, she thought, gripping the heavy hoe, life and death, which now meant nothing to her but which she was compelled continually to wield with both her hands, ceaselessly asking, Was it not possible to compensate? to punish? to protest? Pale darkness turned for a moment through the sunlight, like a narrow leaf blown through the garden in a wind.

In that moment, the rain came. The first drop touched her upraised arm. Small, close sounds and coolness touched her.

Sighing, Mrs. Larkin lowered the hoe to the ground and laid it carefully among the growing plants. She stood still where she was, close to Jamey, and listened to the rain falling. It was so gentle. It was so full—the sound of the end of waiting.

In the light from the rain, different from sunlight, everything appeared to gleam unreflecting from within itself in its quiet arcade of identity. The green of the small zinnia shoots was very pure, almost burning. One by one, as the rain reached them, all the individual little plants shone out, and then the branching vines. The pear tree gave a soft rushing noise, like the wings of a bird alighting. She could sense behind her, as if a lamp were lighted in the night, the signal-like whiteness of the house. Then Jamey, as if in the shock of realizing the rain had come, turned his full face toward her, questions and delight intensifying his smile, gathering up his aroused, stretching body. He stammered some disconnected words, shyly.

She did not answer Jamey or move at all. She would not feel anything now except the rain falling. She listened for its scattered soft drops between Jamey's words, its quiet touching of the spears of the iris leaves, and a clear sound like a bell as it began to fall into a pitcher the cook had set on the doorstep.

Finally, Jamey stood there quietly, as if waiting for his money, with his hand trying to brush his confusion away from before his face. The rain fell steadily. A wind of deep wet fragrance beat against her.

Then as if it had swelled and broken over a daily levee, tenderness tore and spun through her sagging body.

It has come, she thought senselessly, her head lifting and her eyes looking without understanding at the sky which had begun to move, to fold nearer in softening, dissolving clouds. It was almost dark. Soon the loud and gentle night of rain would come. It would pound upon the steep roof of the white house. Within, she would lie in her bed and hear the rain. On and on it would fall, beat and fall. The day's work would be over in the garden.

193

She would lie in bed, her arms tired at her sides and in motionless peace: against that which was inexhaustible, there was no defense.

Then Mrs. Larkin sank in one motion down into the flowers and lay there, fainting and streaked with rain. Her face was fully upturned, down among the plants, with the hair beaten away from her forehead and her open eyes closing at once when the rain touched them. Slowly her lips began to part. She seemed to move slightly, in the sad adjustment of a sleeper.

Jamey ran jumping and crouching about her, drawing in his breath alternately at the flowers breaking under his feet and at the shapeless, passive figure on the ground. Then he became quiet, and stood back at a little distance and looked in awe at the unknowing face, white and rested under its bombardment. He remembered how something had filled him with stillness when he felt her standing there behind him looking down at him, and he would not have turned around at that moment for anything in the world. He remembered all the while the oblivious crash of the windows next door being shut when the rain started. . . . But now, in this unseen place, it was he who stood looking at poor Mrs. Larkin.

He bent down and in a horrified, piteous, beseeching voice he began to call her name until she stirred.

"Miss Lark'! Miss Lark'!"

Then he jumped nimbly to his feet and ran out of the garden.

A VISIT
OF CHARITY

———————◆———————

IT WAS MID-MORNING—a very cold, bright day. Holding a potted plant before her, a girl of fourteen jumped off the bus in front of the Old Ladies' Home, on the outskirts of town. She wore a red coat, and her straight yellow hair was hanging down loose from the pointed white cap all the little girls were wearing that year. She stopped for a moment beside one of the prickly dark shrubs with which the city had beautified the Home, and then proceeded slowly toward the building, which was of whitewashed brick and reflected the winter sunlight like a block of ice. As she walked vaguely up the steps she shifted the small pot from hand to hand; then she had to set it down and remove her mittens before she could open the heavy door.

"I'm a Campfire Girl. . . . I have to pay a visit to some old lady," she told the nurse at the desk. This was a woman in a white uniform who looked as if she were cold; she had close-cut hair which stood up on the very top of her head exactly like a sea wave. Marian, the little girl, did not tell her that this visit would give her a minimum of only three points in her score.

195

"Acquainted with any of our residents?" asked the nurse. She lifted one eyebrow and spoke like a man.

"With any old ladies? No—but—that is, any of them will do," Marian stammered. With her free hand she pushed her hair behind her ears, as she did when it was time to study Science.

The nurse shrugged and rose. "You have a nice *multiflora cineraria* there," she remarked as she walked ahead down the hall of closed doors to pick out an old lady.

There was loose, bulging linoleum on the floor. Marian felt as if she were walking on the waves, but the nurse paid no attention to it. There was a smell in the hall like the interior of a clock. Everything was silent until, behind one of the doors, an old lady of some kind cleared her throat like a sheep bleating. This decided the nurse. Stopping in her tracks, she first extended her arm, bent her elbow, and leaned forward from the hips—all to examine the watch strapped to her wrist; then she gave a loud double-rap on the door.

"There are two in each room," the nurse remarked over her shoulder.

"Two what?" asked Marian without thinking. The sound like a sheep's bleating almost made her turn around and run back.

One old woman was pulling the door open in short, gradual jerks, and when she saw the nurse a strange smile forced her old face dangerously awry. Marian, suddenly propelled by the strong, impatient arm of the nurse, saw next the side-face of another old woman, even older, who was lying flat in bed with a cap on and a counterpane drawn up to her chin.

"Visitor," said the nurse, and after one more shove she was off up the hall.

Marian stood tongue-tied; both hands held the potted plant. The old woman, still with that terrible, square smile (which was a smile of welcome) stamped on her bony face, was waiting. . . . Perhaps she said something. The old woman in bed said nothing at all, and she did not look around.

Suddenly Marian saw a hand, quick as a bird claw, reach up in the air and pluck the white cap off her head. At the same time, another claw to match drew her all the way into the room, and the next moment the door closed behind her.

"My, my, my," said the old lady at her side.

Marian stood enclosed by a bed, a washstand and a chair; the tiny room had altogether too much furniture. Everything smelled wet—even the bare floor. She held onto the back of the chair, which was wicker and felt soft and damp. Her heart beat more and more slowly, her hands got colder and colder, and she could not hear whether the old women were saying anything or not. She could not see them very clearly. How dark it was! The window shade was down, and the only door was shut. Marian looked at the ceiling. . . . It was like being caught in a robbers' cave, just before one was murdered.

"Did you come to be our little girl for a while?" the first robber asked.

Then something was snatched from Marian's hand— the little potted plant.

"Flowers!" screamed the old woman. She stood holding the pot in an undecided way. "Pretty flowers," she added.

197

Then the old woman in bed cleared her throat and spoke. "They are not pretty," she said, still without looking around, but very distinctly.

Marian suddenly pitched against the chair and sat down in it.

"Pretty flowers," the first old woman insisted. "Pretty—pretty . . ."

Marian wished she had the little pot back for just a moment—she had forgotten to look at the plant herself before giving it away. What did it look like?

"Stinkweeds," said the other old woman sharply. She had a bunchy white forehead and red eyes like a sheep. Now she turned them toward Marian. The fogginess seemed to rise in her throat again, and she bleated, "Who—are—you?"

To her surprise, Marian could not remember her name. "I'm a Campfire Girl," she said finally.

"Watch out for the germs," said the old woman like a sheep, not addressing anyone.

"One came out last month to see us," said the first old woman.

A sheep or a germ? wondered Marian dreamily, holding onto the chair.

"Did not!" cried the other old woman.

"Did so! Read to us out of the Bible, and we enjoyed it!" screamed the first.

"Who enjoyed it!" said the woman in bed. Her mouth was unexpectedly small and sorrowful, like a pet's.

"We enjoyed it," insisted the other. "You enjoyed it—I enjoyed it."

"We all enjoyed it," said Marian, without realizing that she had said a word.

The first old woman had just finished putting the potted plant high, high on the top of the wardrobe, where it could hardly be seen from below. Marian wondered how she had ever succeeded in placing it there, how she could ever have reached so high.

"You mustn't pay any attention to old Addie," she now said to the little girl. "She's ailing today."

"Will you shut your mouth?" said the woman in bed. "I am not."

"You're a story."

"I can't stay but a minute—really, I can't," said Marian suddenly. She looked down at the wet floor and thought that if she were sick in here they would have to let her go.

With much to-do the first old woman sat down in a rocking chair—still another piece of furniture!—and began to rock. With the fingers of one hand she touched a very dirty cameo pin on her chest. "What do you do at school?" she asked.

"I don't know . . ." said Marian. She tried to think but she could not.

"Oh, but the flowers are beautiful," the old woman whispered. She seemed to rock faster and faster; Marian did not see how anyone could rock so fast.

"Ugly," said the woman in bed.

"If we bring flowers—" Marian began, and then fell silent. She had almost said that if Campfire Girls brought flowers to the Old Ladies' Home, the visit would count one extra point, and if they took a Bible with them on the bus and read it to the old ladies, it counted double. But the old woman had not listened, anyway; she was rocking and watching the other one, who watched back from the bed.

"Poor Addie is ailing. She has to take medicine—see?" she said, pointing a horny finger at a row of bottles on the table, and rocking so high that her black comfort shoes lifted off the floor like a little child's.

"I am no more sick than you are," said the woman in bed.

"Oh, yes you are!"

"I just got more sense than you have, that's all," said the other old woman, nodding her head.

"That's only the contrary way she talks when *you all* come," said the first old lady with sudden intimacy. She stopped the rocker with a neat pat of her feet and leaned toward Marian. Her hand reached over—it felt like a petunia leaf, clinging and just a little sticky.

"Will you hush! Will you hush!" cried the other one.

Marian leaned back rigidly in her chair.

"When I was a little girl like you, I went to school and all," said the old woman in the same intimate, menacing voice. "Not here—another town. . . ."

"Hush!" said the sick woman. "You never went to school. You never came and you never went. You never were anything—only here. You never were born! You don't know anything. Your head is empty, your heart and hands and your old black purse are all empty, even that little old box that you brought with you you brought empty—you showed it to me. And yet you talk, talk, talk,

talk, talk all the time until I think I'm losing my mind! Who are you? You're a stranger—a perfect stranger! Don't you know you're a stranger? Is it possible that they have actually done a thing like this to anyone—sent them in a stranger to talk, and rock, and tell away her whole long rigmarole? Do they seriously suppose that I'll be able to keep it up, day in, day out, night in, night out, living in the same room with a terrible old woman—forever?"

Marian saw the old woman's eyes grow bright and turn toward her. This old woman was looking at her with despair and calculation in her face. Her small lips suddenly dropped apart, and exposed a half circle of false teeth with tan gums.

"Come here, I want to tell you something," she whispered. "Come here!"

Marian was trembling, and her heart nearly stopped beating altogether for a moment.

"Now, now, Addie," said the first old woman. "That's not polite. Do you know what's really the matter with old Addie today?" She, too, looked at Marian; one of her eyelids drooped low.

"The matter?" the child repeated stupidly. "What's the matter with her?"

"Why, she's mad because it's her birthday!" said the first old woman, beginning to rock again and giving a little crow as though she had answered her own riddle.

"It is not, it is not!" screamed the old woman in bed. "It is not my birthday, no one knows when that is but myself, and will you please be quiet and say nothing more, or I'll go straight out of my mind!" She turned her eyes toward Marian again, and presently she said in the soft, foggy voice, "When the worst comes to the worst, I ring this bell, and the nurse comes." One of her hands was drawn out from under the patched counterpane—a thin little hand with enormous black freckles. With a finger which would not hold still she pointed to a little bell on the table among the bottles.

"How old are you?" Marian breathed. Now she could see the old woman in bed very closely and plainly, and very abruptly, from all sides, as in dreams. She wondered about her—she wondered for a moment as though there was nothing else in the world to wonder about. It was the first time such a thing had happened to Marian.

"I won't tell!"

The old face on the pillow, where Marian was bending over it, slowly gathered and collapsed. Soft whimpers came out of the small open mouth. It was a sheep that she sounded like—a little lamb. Marian's face drew very close, the yellow hair hung forward.

"She's crying!" She turned a bright, burning face up to the first old woman.

"That's Addie for you," the old woman said spitefully.

Marian jumped up and moved toward the door. For the second time, the claw almost touched her hair, but it was not quick enough. The little girl put her cap on.

"Well, it was a real visit," said the old woman, following Marian through the doorway and all the way out into the hall. Then from behind she suddenly clutched the child with her sharp little fingers. In an affected, high-pitched whine she cried, "Oh, little girl, have you a penny to spare for a poor old woman that's not got anything of her own? We don't have a thing in the world— not a penny for candy—not a thing! Little girl, just a nickel—a penny—"

Marian pulled violently against the old hands for a moment before she was free. Then she ran down the hall, without looking behind her and without looking at the nurse, who was reading *Field & Stream* at her desk. The nurse, after another triple motion to consult her wrist watch, asked automatically the question put to visitors in all institutions: "Won't you stay and have dinner with *us*?"

Marian never replied. She pushed the heavy door open into the cold air and ran down the steps.

Under the prickly shrub she stooped and quickly, without being seen, retrieved a red apple she had hidden there.

Her yellow hair under the white cap, her scarlet coat, her bare knees all flashed in the sunlight as she ran to meet the big bus rocketing through the street.

"Wait for me!" she shouted. As though at an imperial command, the bus ground to a stop.

She jumped on and took a big bite out of the apple.

DEATH OF
A TRAVELING
SALESMAN

———◆———

R. J. BOWMAN, who for fourteen years had traveled for a
shoe company through Mississippi, drove his Ford along a
rutted dirt path. It was a long day! The time did not seem
to clear the noon hurdle and settle into soft afternoon.
The sun, keeping its strength here even in winter, stayed
at the top of the sky, and every time Bowman stuck his
head out of the dusty car to stare up the road, it seemed to
reach a long arm down and push against the top of his
head, right through his hat—like the practical joke of an
old drummer, long on the road. It made him feel all the
more angry and helpless. He was feverish, and he was not
quite sure of the way.

This was his first day back on the road after a long
siege of influenza. He had had very high fever, and
dreams, and had become weakened and pale, enough to
tell the difference in the mirror, and he could not think
clearly. . . . All afternoon, in the midst of his anger, and

for no reason, he had thought of his dead grandmother. She had been a comfortable soul. Once more Bowman wished he could fall into the big feather bed that had been in her room. . . . Then he forgot her again.

This desolate hill country! And he seemed to be going the wrong way—it was as if he were going back, far back. There was not a house in sight. . . . There was no use wishing he were back in bed, though. By paying the hotel doctor his bill he had proved his recovery. He had not even been sorry when the pretty trained nurse said good-bye. He did not like illness, he distrusted it, as he distrusted the road without signposts. It angered him. He had given the nurse a really expensive bracelet, just because she was packing up her bag and leaving.

But now—what if in fourteen years on the road he had never been ill before and never had an accident? His record was broken, and he had even begun almost to question it. . . . He had gradually put up at better hotels, in the bigger towns, but weren't they all, eternally, stuffy in summer and drafty in winter? Women? He could only remember little rooms within little rooms, like a nest of Chinese paper boxes, and if he thought of one woman he saw the worn loneliness that the furniture of that room seemed built of. And he himself—he was a man who always wore rather wide-brimmed black hats, and in the wavy hotel mirrors had looked something like a bull-fighter, as he paused for that inevitable instant on the landing, walking downstairs to supper. . . . He leaned out of the car again, and once more the sun pushed at his head.

Bowman had wanted to reach Beulah by dark, to go to

bed and sleep off his fatigue. As he remembered, Beulah was fifty miles away from the last town, on a graveled road. This was only a cow trail. How had he ever come to such a place? One hand wiped the sweat from his face, and he drove on.

He had made the Beulah trip before. But he had never seen this hill or this petering-out path before—or that cloud, he thought shyly, looking up and then down quickly—any more than he had seen this day before. Why did he not admit he was simply lost and had been for miles? . . . He was not in the habit of asking the way of strangers, and these people never knew where the very roads they lived on went to; but then he had not even been close enough to anyone to call out. People standing in the fields now and then, or on top of the haystacks, had been too far away, looking like leaning sticks or weeds, turning a little at the solitary rattle of his car across their countryside, watching the pale sobered winter dust where it chunked out behind like big squashes down the road. The stares of these distant people had followed him solidly like a wall, impenetrable, behind which they turned back after he had passed.

The cloud floated there to one side like the bolster on his grandmother's bed. It went over a cabin on the edge of a hill, where two bare chinaberry trees clutched at the sky. He drove through a heap of dead oak leaves, his wheels stirring their weightless sides to make a silvery melancholy whistle as the car passed through their bed. No car had been along this way ahead of him. Then he saw that he was on the edge of a ravine that fell away, a red erosion, and that this was indeed the road's end.

He pulled the brake. But it did not hold, though he put all his strength into it. The car, tipped toward the edge, rolled a little. Without doubt, it was going over the bank.

He got out quietly, as though some mischief had been done him and he had his dignity to remember. He lifted his bag and sample case out, set them down, and stood back and watched the car roll over the edge. He heard something—not the crash he was listening for, but a slow, unuproarious crackle. Rather distastefully he went to look over, and he saw that his car had fallen into a tangle of immense grapevines as thick as his arm, which caught it and held it, rocked it like a grotesque child in a dark cradle, and then, as he watched, concerned somehow that he was not still inside it, released it gently to the ground.

He sighed.

Where am I? he wondered with a shock. Why didn't I do something? All his anger seemed to have drifted away from him. There was the house, back on the hill. He took a bag in each hand and with almost childlike willingness went toward it. But his breathing came with difficulty, and he had to stop to rest.

It was a shotgun house, two rooms and an open passage between, perched on the hill. The whole cabin slanted a little under the heavy heaped-up vine that covered the roof, light and green, as though forgotten from summer. A woman stood in the passage.

He stopped still. Then all of a sudden his heart began to behave strangely. Like a rocket set off, it began to leap and expand into uneven patterns of beats which showered into his brain, and he could not think. But in scattering and falling it made no noise. It shot up with great power, almost elation, and fell gently, like acrobats into nets. It began to pound profoundly, then waited irresponsibly, hitting in some sort of inward mockery first at his ribs, then against his eyes, then under his shoulder blades, and against the roof of his mouth when he tried to say, "Good afternoon, madam." But he could not hear his heart—it was as quiet as ashes falling. This was rather comforting; still, it was shocking to Bowman to feel his heart beating at all.

Stock-still in his confusion, he dropped his bags, which seemed to drift in slow bulks gracefully through the air and to cushion themselves on the gray prostrate grass near the doorstep.

As for the woman standing there, he saw at once that she was old. Since she could not possibly hear his heart, he ignored the pounding and now looked at her carefully, and yet in his distraction dreamily, with his mouth open.

She had been cleaning the lamp, and held it, half blackened, half clear, in front of her. He saw her with the dark passage behind her. She was a big woman with a weather-beaten but unwrinkled face; her lips were held tightly together, and her eyes looked with a curious dulled brightness into his. He looked at her shoes, which were like bundles. If it were summer she would be bare-foot. . . . Bowman, who automatically judged a woman's age on sight, set her age at fifty. She wore a formless garment of some gray coarse material, rough-dried from a washing, from which her arms appeared pink and unexpectedly round. When she never said a word, and sustained her quiet pose of holding the lamp, he was convinced of the strength in her body.

"Good afternoon, madam," he said.

She stared on, whether at him or at the air around him he could not tell, but after a moment she lowered her eyes to show that she would listen to whatever he had to say.

"I wonder if you would be interested—" He tried once more. "An accident—my car . . ."

Her voice emerged low and remote, like a sound across a lake. "Sonny he ain't here."

"Sonny?"

"Sonny ain't here now."

Her son—a fellow able to bring my car up, he decided in blurred relief. He pointed down the hill. "My car's in the bottom of the ditch. I'll need help."

"Sonny ain't here, but he'll be here."

She was becoming clearer to him and her voice stronger, and Bowman saw that she was stupid.

He was hardly surprised at the deepening postponement and tedium of his journey. He took a breath, and heard his voice speaking over the silent blows of his heart. "I was sick. I am not strong yet. . . . May I come in?"

He stooped and laid his big black hat over the handle on his bag. It was a humble motion, almost a bow, that instantly struck him as absurd and betraying of all his weakness. He looked up at the woman, the wind blowing his hair. He might have continued for a long time in this unfamiliar attitude; he had never been a patient man, but when he was sick he had learned to sink submissively into the pillows, to wait for his medicine. He waited on the woman.

Then she, looking at him with blue eyes, turned and held open the door, and after a moment Bowman, as if convinced in his action, stood erect and followed her in.

Inside, the darkness of the house touched him like a professional hand, the doctor's. The woman set the half-cleaned lamp on a table in the center of the room and pointed, also like a professional person, a guide, to a chair with a yellow cowhide seat. She herself crouched on the hearth, drawing her knees up under the shapeless dress.

At first he felt hopefully secure. His heart was quieter. The room was enclosed in the gloom of yellow pine boards. He could see the other room, with the foot of an iron bed showing, across the passage. The bed had been made up with a red-and-yellow pieced quilt that looked like a map or a picture, a little like his grandmother's girlhood painting of Rome burning.

He had ached for coolness, but in this room it was cold. He stared at the hearth with dead coals lying on it and iron pots in the corners. The hearth and smoked chimney were of the stone he had seen ribbing the hills, mostly slate. Why is there no fire? he wondered.

And it was so still. The silence of the fields seemed to enter and move familiarly through the house. The wind used the open hall. He felt that he was in a mysterious, quiet, cool danger. It was necessary to do what? . . . To talk.

"I have a nice line of women's low-priced shoes . . ." he said.

But the woman answered, "Sonny 'll be here. He's strong. Sonny 'll move your car."

"Where is he now?"

"Farms for Mr. Redmond."

Mr. Redmond. Mr. Redmond. That was someone he would never have to encounter, and he was glad. Somehow the name did not appeal to him. . . . In a flare of touchiness and anxiety, Bowman wished to avoid even mention of unknown men and their unknown farms.

"Do you two live here alone?" He was surprised to hear his old voice, chatty, confidential, inflected for selling shoes, asking a question like that—a thing he did not even want to know.

"Yes. We are alone."

He was surprised at the way she answered. She had taken a long time to say that. She had nodded her head in a deep way too. Had she wished to affect him with some sort of premonition? he wondered unhappily. Or was it only that she would not help him, after all, by talking with him? For he was not strong enough to receive the impact of unfamiliar things without a little talk to break their fall. He had lived a month in which nothing had happened except in his head and his body—an almost inaudible life of heartbeats and dreams that came back, a life of fever and privacy, a delicate life which had left him weak to the point of—what? Of begging. The pulse in his palm leapt like a trout in a brook.

He wondered over and over why the woman did not go ahead with cleaning the lamp. What prompted her to stay there across the room, silently bestowing her presence upon him? He saw that with her it was not a time for doing little tasks. Her face was grave; she was feeling how right she was. Perhaps it was only politeness. In

211

docility he held his eyes stiffly wide; they fixed themselves on the woman's clasped hands as though she held the cord they were strung on.

Then, "Sonny's coming," she said.

He himself had not heard anything, but there came a man passing the window and then plunging in at the door, with two hounds beside him. Sonny was a big enough man, with his belt slung low about his hips. He looked at least thirty. He had a hot, red face that was yet full of silence. He wore muddy blue pants and an old military coat stained and patched. World War? Bowman wondered. Great God, it was a Confederate coat. On the back of his light hair he had a wide filthy black hat which seemed to insult Bowman's own. He pushed down the dogs from his chest. He was strong, with dignity and heaviness in his way of moving. . . . There was the resemblance to his mother.

They stood side by side. . . . He must account again for his presence here.

"Sonny, this man, he had his car to run off over the prec'pice an' wants to know if you will git it out for him," the woman said after a few minutes.

Bowman could not even state his case.

Sonny's eyes lay upon him.

He knew he should offer explanations and show money—at least appear either penitent or authoritative. But all he could do was to shrug slightly.

Sonny brushed by him going to the window, followed by the eager dogs, and looked out. There was effort even in the way he was looking, as if he could throw his sight out like a rope. Without turning Bowman felt that his own eyes could have seen nothing: it was too far.

"Got me a mule out there an' got me a block an' tackle," said Sonny meaningfully. "I *could* catch me my mule an' git me my ropes, an' before long I'd git your car out the ravine."

He looked completely around the room, as if in meditation, his eyes roving in their own distance. Then he pressed his lips firmly and yet shyly together, and with the dogs ahead of him this time, he lowered his head and strode out. The hard earth sounded, cupping to his powerful way of walking—almost a stagger.

Mischievously, at the suggestion of those sounds, Bowman's heart leapt again. It seemed to walk about inside him.

"Sonny's goin' to do it," the woman said. She said it again, singing it almost, like a song. She was sitting in her place by the hearth.

Without looking out, he heard some shouts and the dogs barking and the pounding of hoofs in short runs on the hill. In a few minutes Sonny passed under the window with a rope, and there was a brown mule with quivering, shining, purple-looking ears. The mule actually looked in the window. Under its eyelashes it turned target-like eyes into his. Bowman averted his head and saw the woman looking serenely back at the mule, with only satisfaction in her face.

She sang a little more, under her breath. It occurred to him, and it seemed quite marvelous, that she was not really talking to him, but rather following the thing that came about with words that were unconscious and part of her looking.

So he said nothing, and this time when he did not reply he felt a curious and strong emotion, not fear, rise up in him.

This time, when his heart leapt, something—his soul—seemed to leap too, like a little colt invited out of a pen. He stared at the woman while the frantic nimbleness of his feeling made his head sway. He could not move; there was nothing he could do, unless perhaps he might embrace this woman who sat there growing old and shapeless before him.

But he wanted to leap up, to say to her, I have been sick and I found out then, only then, how lonely I am. Is it too late? My heart puts up a struggle inside me, and you may have heard it, protesting against emptiness. . . . It should be full, he would rush on to tell her, thinking of his heart now as a deep lake, it should be holding love like other hearts. It should be flooded with love. There would be a warm spring day . . . Come and stand in my heart, whoever you are, and a whole river would cover your feet and rise higher and take your knees in whirlpools, and draw you down to itself, your whole body, your heart too.

But he moved a trembling hand across his eyes, and looked at the placid crouching woman across the room. She was still as a statue. He felt ashamed and exhausted by the thought that he might, in one more moment, have tried by simple words and embraces to communicate some strange thing—something which seemed always to have just escaped him . . .

Sunlight touched the furthest pot on the hearth. It was late afternoon. This time tomorrow he would be somewhere on a good graveled road, driving his car past things that happened to people, quicker than their happening. Seeing ahead to the next day, he was glad, and knew that this was no time to embrace an old woman. He could feel in his pounding temples the readying of his blood for motion and for hurrying away.

"Sonny's hitched up your car by now," said the woman. "He'll git it out the ravine right shortly."

"Fine!" he cried with his customary enthusiasm.

Yet it seemed a long time that they waited. It began to get dark. Bowman was cramped in his chair. Any man should know enough to get up and walk around while he waited. There was something like guilt in such stillness and silence.

But instead of getting up, he listened. . . . His breathing restrained, his eyes powerless in the growing dark, he listened uneasily for a warning sound, forgetting in wariness what it would be. Before long he heard something—soft, continuous, insinuating.

"What's that noise?" he asked, his voice jumping into the dark. Then wildly he was afraid it would be his heart beating so plainly in the quiet room, and she would tell him so.

"You might hear the stream," she said grudgingly.

Her voice was closer. She was standing by the table. He wondered why she did not light the lamp. She stood there in the dark and did not light it.

Bowman would never speak to her now, for the time was past. I'll sleep in the dark, he thought, in his bewilderment pitying himself.

Heavily she moved on to the window. Her arm, vaguely white, rose straight from her full side and she pointed out into the darkness.

"That white speck's Sonny," she said, talking to herself.

He turned unwillingly and peered over her shoulder; he hesitated to rise and stand beside her. His eyes searched the dusky air. The white speck floated smoothly toward her finger, like a leaf on a river, growing whiter in the dark. It was as if she had shown him something secret, part of her life, but had offered no explanation. He looked away. He was moved almost to tears, feeling for no reason that she had made a silent declaration equivalent to his own. His hand waited upon his chest.

Then a step shook the house, and Sonny was in the room. Bowman felt how the woman left him there and went to the other man's side.

"I done got your car out, mister," said Sonny's voice in the dark. "She's settin' a-waitin' in the road, turned to go back where she come from."

"Fine!" said Bowman, projecting his own voice to loudness. "I'm surely much obliged—I could never have done it myself—I was sick. . . ."

"I could do it easy," said Sonny.

Bowman could feel them both waiting in the dark, and he could hear the dogs panting out in the yard, waiting to bark when he should go. He felt strangely helpless and resentful. Now that he could go, he longed to stay. From what was he being deprived? His chest was rudely shaken by the violence of his heart. These people cherished something here that he could not see, they withheld some ancient promise of food and warmth and light. Between them they had a conspiracy. He thought of the way she had moved away from him and gone to Sonny, she had flowed toward him. He was shaking with cold, he was tired, and it was not fair. Humbly and yet angrily he stuck his hand into his pocket.

"Of course I'm going to pay you for everything—"

"We don't take money for such," said Sonny's voice belligerently.

"I want to pay. But do something more . . . Let me stay—tonight. . . ." He took another step toward them. If only they could see him, they would know his sincerity, his real need! His voice went on, "I'm not very strong yet, I'm not able to walk far, even back to my car, maybe, I don't know—I don't know exactly where I am—"

He stopped. He felt as if he might burst into tears. What would they think of him!

Sonny came over and put his hands on him. Bowman felt them pass (they were professional too) across his chest, over his hips. He could feel Sonny's eyes upon him in the dark.

"You ain't no revenuer come sneakin' here, mister, ain't got no gun?"

To this end of nowhere! And yet *he* had come. He made a grave answer. "No."

"You can stay."

"Sonny," said the woman, "you'll have to borry some fire."

"I'll go git it from Redmond's," said Sonny.

"What?" Bowman strained to hear their words to each other.

"Our fire, it's out, and Sonny's got to borry some, because its dark an' cold," she said.

"But matches—I have matches—"

"We don't have no need for 'em," she said proudly. "Sonny's goin' after his own fire."

"I'm goin' to Redmond's," said Sonny with an air of importance, and he went out.

After they had waited a while, Bowman looked out the window and saw a light moving over the hill. It spread itself out like a little fan. It zigzagged along the field, darting and swift, not like Sonny at all. . . . Soon enough, Sonny staggered in, holding a burning stick behind him in tongs, fire flowing in his wake, blazing light into the corners of the room.

"We'll make a fire now," the woman said, taking the brand.

When that was done she lit the lamp. It showed its dark and light. The whole room turned golden-yellow like some sort of flower, and the walls smelled of it and seemed to tremble with the quiet rushing of the fire and the waving of the burning lampwick in its funnel of light.

The woman moved among the iron pots. With the tongs she dropped hot coals on top of the iron lids. They made a set of soft vibrations, like the sound of a bell far away.

She looked up and over at Bowman, but he could not answer. He was trembling. . . .

"Have a drink, mister?" Sonny asked. He had brought in a chair from the other room and sat astride it with his folded arms across the back. Now we are all visible to one another, Bowman thought, and cried, "Yes sir, you bet, thanks!"

"Come after me and do just what I do," said Sonny.

It was another excursion into the dark. They went through the hall, out to the back of the house, past a shed and a hooded well. They came to a wilderness of thicket.

"Down on your knees," said Sonny.

"What?" Sweat broke out on his forehead.

He understood when Sonny began to crawl through a sort of tunnel that the bushes made over the ground. He followed, startled in spite of himself when a twig or a thorn touched him gently without making a sound, clinging to him and finally letting him go.

Sonny stopped crawling and, crouched on his knees, began to dig with both his hands into the dirt. Bowman shyly struck matches and made a light. In a few minutes Sonny pulled up a jug. He poured out some of the whisky into a bottle from his coat pocket, and buried the jug again. "You never know who's liable to knock at your door," he said, and laughed. "Start back," he said, almost formally. "Ain't no need for us to drink outdoors, like hogs."

At the table by the fire, sitting opposite each other in their chairs, Sonny and Bowman took drinks out of the bottle, passing it across. The dogs slept; one of them was having a dream.

"This is good," said Bowman. "This is what I needed." It was just as though he were drinking the fire off the hearth.

"He makes it," said the woman with quiet pride.

She was pushing the coals off the pots, and the smells of corn bread and coffee circled the room. She set everything on the table before the men, with a bone-handled knife stuck into one of the potatoes, splitting out its golden fiber. Then she stood for a minute looking at them, tall and full above them where they sat. She leaned a little toward them.

"You all can eat now," she said, and suddenly smiled.

Bowman had just happened to be looking at her. He set his cup back on the table in unbelieving protest. A pain pressed at his eyes. He saw that she was not an old woman. She was young, still young. He could think of no number of years for her. She was the same age as Sonny, and she belonged to him. She stood with the deep dark corner of the room behind her, the shifting yellow light scattering over her head and her gray formless dress, trembling over her tall body when it bent over them in its sudden communication. She was young. Her teeth were shining and her eyes glowed. She turned and walked slowly and heavily out of the room, and he heard her sit down on the cot and then lie down. The pattern on the quilt moved.

"She's goin' to have a baby," said Sonny, popping a bite into his mouth.

Bowman could not speak. He was shocked with knowing what was really in this house. A marriage, a fruitful marriage. That simple thing. Anyone could have had that.

Somehow he felt unable to be indignant or protest, although some sort of joke had certainly been played upon him. There was nothing remote or mysterious here—only something private. The only secret was the ancient communication between two people. But the memory of the woman's waiting silently by the cold hearth, of the man's stubborn journey a mile away to get fire, and how they finally brought out their food and drink and filled the room proudly with all they had to show, was suddenly too clear and too enormous within him for response. . . .

"You ain't as hungry as you look," said Sonny.

The woman came out of the bedroom as soon as the men had finished, and ate her supper while her husband stared peacefully into the fire.

Then they put the dogs out, with the food that was left.

"I think I'd better sleep here by the fire, on the floor," said Bowman.

He felt that he had been cheated, and that he could afford now to be generous. Ill though he was, he was not going to ask them for their bed. He was through with asking favors in this house, now that he understood what was there.

"Sure, mister."

But he had not known yet how slowly he understood. They had not meant to give him their bed. After a little interval they both rose and looking at him gravely went into the other room.

He lay stretched by the fire until it grew low and dying. He watched every tongue of blaze lick out and vanish. "There will be special reduced prices on all footwear during the month of January," he found himself repeating quietly, and then he lay with his lips tight shut.

How many noises the night had! He heard the stream running, the fire dying, and he was sure now that he heard his heart beating, too, the sound it made under his ribs. He heard breathing, round and deep, of the man and his wife in the room across the passage. And that was all. But emotion swelled patiently within him, and he wished that the child were his.

He must get back to where he had been before. He stood weakly before the red coals and put on his overcoat. It felt too heavy on his shoulders. As he started out he looked and saw that the woman had never got through with cleaning the lamp. On some impulse he put all the money from his billfold under its fluted glass base, almost ostentatiously.

Ashamed, shrugging a little, and then shivering, he took his bags and went out. The cold of the air seemed to lift him bodily. The moon was in the sky.

On the slope he began to run, he could not help it. Just as he reached the road, where his car seemed to sit in the moonlight like a boat, his heart began to give off tremendous explosions like a rifle, bang bang bang.

He sank in fright onto the road, his bags falling about him. He felt as if all this had happened before. He covered his heart with both hands to keep anyone from hearing the noise it made.

But nobody heard it.

POWERHOUSE

———————◆———————

POWERHOUSE is playing!

He's here on tour from the city—"Powerhouse and His Keyboard"—"Powerhouse and His Tasmanians"—think of the things he calls himself! There's no one in the world like him. You can't tell what he is. "Nigger man"?—he looks more Asiatic, monkey, Jewish, Babylonian, Peruvian, fanatic, devil. He has pale gray eyes, heavy lids, maybe horny like a lizard's, but big glowing eyes when they're open. He has African feet of the greatest size, stomping, both together, on each side of the pedals. He's not coal black—beverage colored—looks like a preacher when his mouth is shut, but then it opens—vast and obscene. And his mouth is going every minute: like a monkey's when it looks for something. Improvising, coming on a light and childish melody—*smooch*—he loves it with his mouth.

Is it possible that he could be this! When you have him there performing for you, that's what you feel. You know people on a stage—and people of a darker race—so likely to be marvelous, frightening.

This is a white dance. Powerhouse is not a show-off like the Harlem boys, not drunk, not crazy—he's in a trance; he's a person of joy, a fanatic. He listens as much as he performs, a look of hideous, powerful rapture on his face. Big arched eyebrows that never stop traveling, like a Jew's—wandering-Jew eyebrows. When he plays he beats down piano and seat and wears them away. He is in motion every moment—what could be more obscene? There he is with his great head, fat stomach, and little round piston legs, and long yellow-sectioned strong big fingers, at rest about the size of bananas. Of course you know how he sounds—you've heard him on records—but still you need to see him. He's going all the time, like skating around the skating rink or rowing a boat. It makes everybody crowd around, here in this shadowless steel-trussed hall with the rose-like posters of Nelson Eddy and the testimonial for the mind-reading horse in handwriting magnified five hundred times. Then all quietly he lays his finger on a key with the promise and serenity of a sibyl touching the book.

Powerhouse is so monstrous he sends everybody into oblivion. When any group, any performers, come to town, don't people always come out and hover near, leaning inward about them, to learn what it is? What is it? Listen. Remember how it was with the acrobats. Watch them carefully, hear the least word, especially what they say to one another, in another language—don't let them escape you; it's the only time for hallucination, the last time. They can't stay. They'll be somewhere else this time tomorrow.

Powerhouse has as much as possible done by signals. Everybody, laughing as if to hide a weakness, will sooner or later hand him up a written request. Powerhouse reads each one, studying with a secret face: that is the face which looks like a mask—anybody's; there is a moment when he makes a decision. Then a light slides under his eyelids, and he says, "92!" or some combination of figures—never a name. Before a number the band is all frantic, misbehaving, pushing, like children in a schoolroom, and he is the teacher getting silence. His hands over the keys, he says sternly, "You-all ready? You-all ready to do some serious walking?"—waits—then, STAMP. Quiet. STAMP, for the second time. This is absolute. Then a set of rhythmic kicks against the floor to communicate the tempo. Then, O Lord! say the distended eyes from beyond the boundary of the trumpets, Hello and good-bye, and they are all down the first note like a waterfall.

This note marks the end of any known discipline. Powerhouse seems to abandon them all—he himself seems lost—down in the song, yelling up like somebody in a whirlpool—not guiding them—hailing them only. But he knows, really. He cries out, but he must know exactly. "Mercy! . . . What I say! . . . Yeah!" And then drifting, listening—"Where that skin beater?"—wanting drums, and starting up and pouring it out in the greatest delight and brutality. On the sweet pieces such a leer for everybody! He looks down so benevolently upon all our faces and whispers the lyrics to us. And if you could hear him at this moment on "Marie, the Dawn is Breaking"! He's going up the keyboard with a few fingers in some very derogatory triplet-routine, he gets higher and higher, and then he looks over the end of the piano, as if over a cliff. But not in a show-off way—the song makes him do it.

He loves the way they all play, too—all those next to him. The far section of the band is all studious, wearing glasses, every one—they don't count. Only those playing around Powerhouse are the real ones. He has a bass fiddler from Vicksburg, black as pitch, named Valentine, who plays with his eyes shut and talking to himself, very young: Powerhouse has to keep encouraging him. "Go on, go on, give it up, bring it on out there!" When you heard him like that on records, did you know he was really pleading?

He calls Valentine out to take a solo.

"What you going to play?" Powerhouse looks out kindly from behind the piano; he opens his mouth and shows his tongue, listening.

Valentine looks down, drawing against his instrument, and says without a lip movement, " 'Honeysuckle Rose.' "

He has a clarinet player named Little Brother, and loves to listen to anything he does. He'll smile and say, "Beautiful!" Little Brother takes a step forward when he plays and stands at the very front, with the whites of his eyes like fishes swimming. Once when he played a low note, Powerhouse muttered in dirty praise, "He went clear downstairs to get that one!"

After a long time, he holds up the number of fingers to tell the band how many choruses still to go—usually five. He keeps his directions down to signals.

It's a bad night outside. It's a white dance, and nobody dances, except a few straggling jitterbugs and two elderly couples. Everybody just stands around the band and watches Powerhouse. Sometimes they steal glances at one another, as if to say, Of course, you know how it is with *them*—Negroes—band leaders—they would play the same way, giving all they've got, for an audience of one. . . . When somebody, no matter who, gives everything, it makes people feel ashamed for him.

Late at night they play the one waltz they will ever consent to play—by request, "Pagan Love Song." Powerhouse's head rolls and sinks like a weight between his waving shoulders. He groans, and his fingers drag into the keys heavily, holding on to the notes, retrieving. It is a sad song.

"You know what happened to me?" says Powerhouse.

Valentine hums a response, dreaming at the bass.

"I got a telegram my wife is dead," says Powerhouse, with wandering fingers.

"Uh-huh?"

His mouth gathers and forms a barbarous O while his fingers walk up straight, unwillingly, three octaves.

"Gypsy? Why how come her to die, didn't you just phone her up in the night last night long distance?"

"Telegram say—here the words: Your wife is dead." He puts 4/4 over the 3/4.

"Not but four words?" This is the drummer, an unpopular boy named Scoot, a disbelieving maniac.

Powerhouse is shaking his vast cheeks. "What the hell was she trying to do? What was she up to?"

"What name has it got signed, if you got a telegram?" Scoot is spitting away with those wire brushes.

Little Brother, the clarinet player, who cannot now speak, glares and tilts back.

"Uranus Knockwood is the name signed." Power-

227

house lifts his eyes open. "Ever heard of him?" A bubble shoots out on his lip like a plate on a counter.

Valentine is beating slowly on with his palm and scratching the strings with his long blue nails. He is fond of a waltz, Powerhouse interrupts him.

"I don't know him. Don't know who he is." Valentine shakes his head with the closed eyes.

"Say it agin."

"Uranus Knockwood."

"That ain't Lenox Avenue."

"It ain't Broadway."

"Ain't ever seen it wrote out in any print, even for horse racing."

"Hell, that's on a star, boy, ain't it?" Crash of the cymbals.

"What the hell was she up to?" Powerhouse shudders. "Tell me, tell me, tell me." He makes triplets, and begins a new chorus. He holds three fingers up.

"You say you got a telegram." This is Valentine, patient and sleepy, beginning again.

Powerhouse is elaborate. "Yas, the time I go out, go way downstairs along a long cor-ri-dor to where they puts us: coming back along the cor-rid-or: steps out and hands me a telegram: Your wife is dead."

"Gypsy?" The drummer like a spider over his drums.

"Aaaaaaaaa!" shouts Powerhouse, flinging out both powerful arms for three whole beats to flex his muscles, then kneading a dough of bass notes. His eyes glitter. He plays the piano like a drum sometimes—why not?

"Gypsy? Such a dancer?"

"Why you don't hear it straight from your agent?

228

Why it ain't come from headquarters? What you been doing, getting telegrams in the *corridor*, signed nobody?"

They all laugh. End of that chorus.

"What time is it?" Powerhouse calls. "What the hell place is this? Where is my watch and, chain?"

"I hang it on you," whimpers Valentine. "It still there."

There it rides on Powerhouse's great stomach, down where he can never see it.

"Sure did hear some clock striking twelve while ago. Must be *midnight*."

"It going to be intermission," Powerhouse declares, lifting up his finger with the signet ring.

He draws the chorus to an end. He pulls a big Northern hotel towel out of the deep pocket in his vast, special-cut tux pants and pushes his forehead into it.

"If she went and killed herself!" he says with a hidden face. "If she up and jumped out that window!" He gets to his feet, turning vaguely, wearing the towel on his head.

"Ha, ha!"

"Sheik, sheik!"

"She wouldn't do that." Little Brother sets down his clarinet like a precious vase, and speaks. He still looks like an East Indian queen, implacable, divine, and full of snakes. "You ain't going to expect people doing what they says over long distance."

"Come on!" roars Powerhouse. He is already at the back door, he has pulled it wide open, and with a wild, gathered-up face is smelling the terrible night.

Powerhouse, Valentine, Scoot and Little Brother step outside into the drenching rain.

"Well, they emptying buckets," says Powerhouse in a mollified voice. On the street he holds his hands out and turns up the blanched palms like sieves.

A hundred dark, ragged, silent, delighted Negroes have come around from under the eaves of the hall, and follow wherever they go.

"Watch out Little Brother don't shrink," says Powerhouse. "You just the right size now, clarinet don't suck you in. You got a dry throat, Little Brother, you in the desert?" He reaches into the pocket and pulls out a paper of mints. "Now hold 'em in your mouth—don't chew 'em. I don't carry around nothing without limit."

"Go in that joint and have beer," says Scoot, who walks ahead.

"Beer? Beer? You know what beer is? What do they say is beer? What's beer? Where I been?"

"Down yonder where it say World Cafe—that do?" They are in Negrotown now.

Valentine patters over and holds open a screen door warped like a sea shell, bitter in the wet, and they walk in, stained darker with the rain and leaving footprints. Inside, sheltered dry smells stand like screens around a table covered with a red-checkered cloth, in the center of which flies hang onto an obelisk-shaped ketchup bottle. The midnight walls are checkered again with admonishing "Not Responsible" signs and black-figured, smoky calendars. It is a waiting, silent, limp room. There is a burned-out-looking nickelodeon and right beside it a long-necked wall instrument labeled "Business Phone, Don't Keep Talking." Circled phone numbers are written up everywhere. There is a worn-out peacock feather hanging by a thread to an old, thin, pink, exposed light bulb, where it slowly turns around and around, whoever breathes.

A waitress watches.

"Come here, living statue, and get all this big order of beer we fixing to give."

"Never seen you before anywhere." The waitress moves and comes forward and slowly shows little gold leaves and tendrils over her teeth. She shoves up her shoulders and breasts. "How I going to know who you might be? Robbers? Coming in out of the black of night right at midnight, setting down so big at my table?"

"Boogers," says Powerhouse, his eyes opening lazily as in a cave.

The girl screams delicately with pleasure. O Lord, she likes talk and scares.

"Where you going to find enough beer to put out on this here table?"

She runs to the kitchen with bent elbows and sliding steps.

"Here's a million nickels," says Powerhouse, pulling his hand out of his pocket and sprinkling coins out, all but the last one, which he makes vanish like a magician.

Valentine and Scoot take the money over to the nickelodeon, which looks as battered as a slot machine, and read all the names of the records out loud.

"Whose 'Tuxedo Junction'?" asks Powerhouse.

"You know whose."

"Nickelodeon, I request you please to play 'Empty Red Blues' and let Bessie Smith sing."

Silence: they hold it like a measure.

"Bring me all those nickels on back here," says Powerhouse. "Look at that! What you tell me the name of this place?"

"White dance, week night, raining, Alligator, Mississippi, long ways from home."

"Uh-huh."

"Sent for You Yesterday and Here You Come Today" plays.

The waitress, setting the tray of beer down on a back table, comes up taut and apprehensive as a hen. "Says in the kitchen, back there putting their eyes to little hole peeping out, that you is Mr. Powerhouse. . . . They knows from a picture they seen."

"They seeing right tonight, that is him," says Little Brother.

"You him?"

"That is him in the flesh," says Scoot.

"Does you wish to touch him?" asks Valentine. "Because he don't bite."

"You passing through?"

"Now you got everything right."

She waits like a drop, hands languishing together in front.

"Little-Bit, ain't you going to bring the beer?"

She brings it, and goes behind the cash register and smiles, turning different ways. The little fillet of gold in her mouth is gleaming.

"The Mississippi River's here," she says once.

Now all the watching Negroes press in gently and bright-eyed through the door, as many as can get in. One is a little boy in a straw sombrero which has been coated with aluminum paint all over.

Powerhouse, Valentine, Scoot and Little Brother drink beer, and their eyelids come together like curtains. The wall and the rain and the humble beautiful waitress waiting on them and the other Negroes watching enclose them.

"Listen!" whispers Powerhouse, looking into the ketchup bottle and slowly spreading his performer's hands over the damp, wrinkling cloth with the red squares. "Listen how it is. My wife gets missing me. Gypsy. She goes to the window. She looks out and sees you know what. Street. Sign saying Hotel. People walking. Somebody looks up. Old man. She looks down, out the window. Well? . . . *Ssssst! Plooey!* What she do? Jump out and bust her brains all over the world."

He opens his eyes.

"That's it," agrees Valentine. "You gets a telegram."

"Sure she misses you," Little Brother adds.

"No, it's night time." How softly he tells them! "Sure. It's the night time. She say, What do I hear? Footsteps walking up the hall? That him? Footsteps go on off. It's not me. I'm in Alligator, Mississippi, she's crazy. Shaking all over. Listens till her ears and all grow out like old music-box horns but still she can't hear a thing. She says, All right! I'll jump out the window then. Got on her nightgown. I know that nightgown, and her thinking there. Says, Ho hum, all right, and jumps out the window. Is she mad at me! Is she crazy! She don't leave *nothing* behind her!"

"Ya! Ha!"

"Brains and insides everywhere, Lord, Lord." All the watching Negroes stir in their delight, and to their higher delight he says affectionately, "Listen! Rats in here."

"That must be the way, boss."

"Only, naw, Powerhouse, that ain't true. That sound too *bad*."

"Does? I even know who finds her," cries Powerhouse. "That no-good pussyfooted crooning creeper, that creeper that follow around after me, coming up like weeds behind me, following around after me everything I do and messing around on the trail I leave. Bets my numbers, sings my songs, gets close to my agent like a Betsy-bug; when I going out he just coming in. I got him now! I got my eye on him."

"Know who he is?"

"Why, it's that old Uranus Knockwood!"

"Ya! Ha!"

"Yeah, and he coming now, he going to find Gypsy. There he is, coming around that corner, and Gypsy kadoodling down, oh-oh, watch out! *Ssssst! Plooey!* See, there she is in her little old nightgown, and her insides and brains all scattered round."

A sigh fills the room.

"Hush about her brains. Hush about her insides."

"Ya! Ha! You talking about her brains and insides— old Uranus Knockwood," says Powerhouse, "look down and say Jesus! He say, Look here what I'm walking round in!"

They all burst into halloos of laughter. Powerhouse's face looks like a big hot iron stove.

"Why, he picks her up and carries her off!" he says.

"Ya! Ha!"

"Carries her *back* around the corner. . . ."

"Oh, Powerhouse!"

234

"You know him."

"Uranus Knockwood!"

"Yeahhh!"

"He take our wives when we gone!"

"He come in when we goes out!"

"Uh-huh!"

"He go out when we comes in!"

"Yeahhh!"

"He standing behind the door!"

"Old Uranus Knockwood."

"You know him."

"Middle-size man."

"Wears a hat."

"That's him."

Everybody in the room moans with pleasure. The little boy in the fine silver hat opens a paper and divides out a jelly roll among his followers.

And out of the breathless ring somebody moves forward like a slave, leading a great logy Negro with bursting eyes, and says, "This here is Sugar-Stick Thompson, that dove down to the bottom of July Creek and pulled up all those drownded white people fall out of a boat. Last summer, pulled up fourteen."

"Hello," says Powerhouse, turning and looking around at them all with his great daring face until they nearly suffocate.

Sugar-Stick, their instrument, cannot speak; he can only look back at the others.

"Can't even swim. Done it by holding his breath," says the fellow with the hero.

Powerhouse looks at him seekingly.

"I his half brother," the fellow puts in.

They step back.

"Gypsy say," Powerhouse rumbles gently again, looking at *them*, " 'What is the use? I'm gonna jump out so far—so far. . . .' *Ssssst*—!"

"Don't, boss, don't do it agin," says Little Brother.

"It's awful," says the waitress. "I hates that Mr. Knockwoods. All that the truth?"

"Want to see the telegram I got from him?" Powerhouse's hand goes to the vast pocket.

"Now wait, now wait, boss." They all watch him.

"It must be the real truth," says the waitress, sucking in her lower lip, her luminous eyes turning sadly, seeking the windows.

"No, babe, it ain't the truth." His eyebrows fly up, and he begins to whisper to her out of his vast oven mouth. His hand stays in his pocket. "Truth is something worse, I ain't said what, yet. It's something hasn't come to me, but I ain't saying it won't. And when it does, then want me to tell you?" He sniffs all at once, his eyes come open and turn up, almost too far. He is dreamily smiling.

"Don't, boss, don't, Powerhouse!"

"Oh!" the waitress screams.

"Go on git out of here!" bellows Powerhouse, taking his hand out of his pocket and clapping after her red dress.

The ring of watchers breaks and falls away.

"*Look* at that! Intermission is up," says Powerhouse.

He folds money under a glass, and after they go out, Valentine leans back in and drops a nickel in the nickelodeon behind them, and it lights up and begins to play "The Goona Goo." The feather dangles still.

*   *   *

"Take a telegram!" Powerhouse shouts suddenly up into the rain over the street. "Take a answer. Now what was that name?"

They get a little tired.

"Uranus Knockwood."

"You ought to know."

"Yas? Spell it to me."

They spell it all the ways it could be spelled. It puts them in a wonderful humor.

"Here's the answer. I got it right here. 'What in the hell you talking about? Don't make any difference: I gotcha.' Name signed: Powerhouse."

"That going to reach him, Powerhouse?" Valentine speaks in a maternal voice.

"Yas, yas."

All hushing, following him up the dark street at a distance, like old rained-on black ghosts, the Negroes are afraid they will die laughing.

Powerhouse throws back his vast head into the steaming rain, and a look of hopeful desire seems to blow somehow like a vapor from his own dilated nostrils over his face and bring a mist to his eyes.

"Reach him and come out the other side."

"That's it, Powerhouse, that's it. You got him now."

Powerhouse lets out a long sigh.

"But ain't you going back there to call up Gypsy long distance, the way you did last night in that other place? I seen a telephone. . . . Just to see if she there at home?"

There is a measure of silence. That is one crazy drummer that's going to get his neck broken some day.

"No," growls Powerhouse. "No! How many thousand times tonight I got to say No?"

He holds up his arm in the rain.

"You sure-enough unroll your voice some night, it about reach up yonder to her," says Little Brother, dismayed.

They go on up the street, shaking the rain off and on them like birds.

Back in the dance hall, they play "San" (99). The jitterbugs start up like windmills stationed over the floor, and in their orbits—one circle, another, a long stretch and a zigzag—dance the elderly couples with old smoothness, undisturbed and stately.

When Powerhouse first came back from intermission, no doubt full of beer, they said, he got the band tuned up again in his own way. He didn't strike the piano keys for pitch—he simply opened his mouth and gave falsetto howls—in A, D and so on—they tuned by him. Then he took hold of the piano, as if he saw it for the first time in his life, and tested it for strength, hit it down in the bass, played an octave with his elbow, lifted the top, looked inside, and leaned against it with all his might. He sat down and played it for a few minutes with outrageous force and got it under his power—a bass deep and coarse as a sea net—then produced something glimmering and fragile, and smiled. And who could ever remember any of the things he says? They are just inspired remarks that roll out of his mouth like smoke.

They've requested "Somebody Loves Me," and he's already done twelve or fourteen choruses, piling them up nobody knows how, and it will be a wonder if he ever gets through. Now and then he calls and shouts, " 'Somebody loves me! Somebody loves me, I wonder who!' " His mouth gets to be nothing but a volcano. "I wonder who!"

"Maybe . . ." He uses all his right hand on a trill.

"Maybe . . ." He pulls back his spread fingers, and looks out upon the place where he is. A vast, impersonal and yet furious grimace transfigures his wet face.

". . . Maybe it's you!"

A WORN
PATH

———————◆———————

It was December—a bright frozen day in the early
morning. Far out in the country there was an old Negro
woman with her head tied in a red rag, coming along a
path through the pinewoods. Her name was Phoenix
Jackson. She was very old and small and she walked slowly
in the dark pine shadows, moving a little from side to side
in her steps, with the balanced heaviness and lightness of
a pendulum in a grandfather clock. She carried a thin,
small cane made from an umbrella, and with this she kept
tapping the frozen earth in front of her. This made a grave
and persistent noise in the still air, that seemed medita-
tive like the chirping of a solitary little bird.

She wore a dark striped dress reaching down to her
shoe tops, and an equally long apron of bleached sugar
sacks, with a full pocket: all neat and tidy, but every time
she took a step she might have fallen over her shoelaces,
which dragged from her unlaced shoes. She looked straight
ahead. Her eyes were blue with age. Her skin had a pattern all its own of numberless branching wrinkles and as
though a whole little tree stood in the middle of her fore-

head, but a golden color ran underneath, and the two knobs of her cheeks were illumined by a yellow burning under the dark. Under the red rag her hair came down on her neck in the frailest of ringlets, still black, and with an odor like copper.

Now and then there was a quivering in the thicket. Old Phoenix said, "Out of my way, all you foxes, owls, beetles, jack rabbits, coons and wild animals! . . . Keep out from under these feet, little bob-whites. . . . Keep the big wild hogs out of my path. Don't let none of those come running my direction. I got a long way." Under her small black-freckled hand her cane, limber as a buggy whip, would switch at the brush as if to rouse up any hiding things.

On she went. The woods were deep and still. The sun made the pine needles almost too bright to look at, up where the wind rocked. The cones dropped as light as feathers. Down in the hollow was the mourning dove—it was not too late for him.

The path ran up a hill. "Seem like there is chains about my feet, time I get this far," she said, in the voice of argument old people keep to use with themselves. "Something always take a hold of me on this hill—pleads I should stay."

After she got to the top she turned and gave a full, severe look behind her where she had come. "Up through pines," she said at length. "Now down through oaks."

Her eyes opened their widest, and she started down gently. But before she got to the bottom of the hill a bush caught her dress.

Her fingers were busy and intent, but her skirts were

full and long, so that before she could pull them free in one place they were caught in another. It was not possible to allow the dress to tear. "I in the thorny bush," she said. "Thorns, you doing your appointed work. Never want to let folks pass, no sir. Old eyes thought you was a pretty little *green* bush."

Finally, trembling all over, she stood free, and after a moment dared to stoop for her cane.

"Sun so high!" she cried, leaning back and looking, while the thick tears went over her eyes. "The time getting all gone here."

At the foot of this hill was a place where a log was laid across the creek.

"Now comes the trial," said Phoenix.

Putting her right foot out, she mounted the log and shut her eyes. Lifting her skirt, leveling her cane fiercely before her, like a festival figure in some parade, she began to march across. Then she opened her eyes and she was safe on the other side.

"I wasn't as old as I thought," she said.

But she sat down to rest. She spread her skirts on the bank around her and folded her hands over her knees. Up above her was a tree in a pearly cloud of mistletoe. She did not dare to close her eyes, and when a little boy brought her a plate with a slice of marble-cake on it she spoke to him. "That would be acceptable," she said. But when she went to take it there was just her own hand in the air.

So she left that tree, and had to go through a barbed-wire fence. There she had to creep and crawl, spreading her knees and stretching her fingers like a baby trying to climb the steps. But she talked loudly to herself: she could not let her dress be torn now, so late in the day, and she could not pay for having her arm or her leg sawed off if she got caught fast where she was.

At last she was safe through the fence and risen up out in the clearing. Big dead trees, like black men with one arm, were standing in the purple stalks of the withered cotton field. There sat a buzzard.

"Who you watching?"

In the furrow she made her way along.

"Glad this not the season for bulls," she said, looking sideways, "and the good Lord made his snakes to curl up and sleep in the winter. A pleasure I don't see no two-headed snake coming around that tree, where it come once. It took a while to get by him, back in the summer."

She passed through the old cotton and went into a field of dead corn. It whispered and shook and was taller than her head. "Through the maze now," she said, for there was no path.

Then there was something tall, black, and skinny there, moving before her.

At first she took it for a man. It could have been a man dancing in the field. But she stood still and listened, and it did not make a sound. It was as silent as a ghost.

"Ghost," she said sharply, "who be you the ghost of? For I have heard of nary death close by."

But there was no answer—only the ragged dancing in the wind.

She shut her eyes, reached out her hand, and touched a sleeve. She found a coat and inside that an emptiness, cold as ice.

"You scarecrow," she said. Her face lighted. "I ought

to be shut up for good," she said with laughter. "My senses is gone. I too old. I the oldest people I ever know. Dance, old scarecrow," she said, "while I dancing with you."

She kicked her foot over the furrow, and with mouth drawn down, shook her head once or twice in a little strutting way. Some husks blew down and whirled in streamers about her skirts.

Then she went on, parting her way from side to side with the cane, through the whispering field. At last she came to the end, to a wagon track where the silver grass blew between the red ruts. The quail were walking around like pullets, seeming all dainty and unseen.

"Walk pretty," she said. "This the easy place. This the easy going."

She followed the track, swaying through the quiet bare fields, through the little strings of trees silver in their dead leaves, past cabins silver from weather, with the doors and windows boarded shut, all like old women under a spell sitting there. "I walking in their sleep," she said, nodding her head vigorously.

In a ravine she went where a spring was silently flowing through a hollow log. Old Phoenix bent and drank. "Sweet-gum makes the water sweet," she said, and drank more. "Nobody know who made this well, for it was here when I was born."

The track crossed a swampy part where the moss hung as white as lace from every limb. "Sleep on, alligators, and blow your bubbles." Then the track went into the road.

Deep, deep the road went down between the high

green-colored banks. Overhead the live-oaks met, and it was as dark as a cave.

A black dog with a lolling tongue came up out of the weeds by the ditch. She was meditating, and not ready, and when he came at her she only hit him a little with her cane. Over she went in the ditch, like a little puff of milkweed.

Down there, her senses drifted away. A dream visited her, and she reached her hand up, but nothing reached down and gave her a pull. So she lay there and presently went to talking. "Old woman," she said to herself, "that black dog come up out of the weeds to stall you off, and now there he sitting on his fine tail, smiling at you."

A white man finally came along and found her—a hunter, a young man, with his dog on a chain.

"Well, Granny!" he laughed. "What are you doing there?"

"Lying on my back like a June-bug waiting to be turned over, mister," she said, reaching up her hand.

He lifted her up, gave her a swing in the air, and set her down. "Anything broken, Granny?"

"No sir, them old dead weeds is springy enough," said Phoenix, when she had got her breath. "I thank you for your trouble."

"Where do you live, Granny?" he asked, while the two dogs were growling at each other.

"Away back yonder, sir, behind the ridge. You can't even see it from here."

"On your way home?"

"No sir, I going to town."

"Why, that's too far! That's as far as I walk when I come out myself, and I get something for my trouble." He patted the stuffed bag he carried, and there hung down a little closed claw. It was one of the bob-whites, with its beak hooked bitterly to show it was dead. "Now you go on home, Granny!"

"I bound to go to town, mister," said Phoenix. "The time come around."

He gave another laugh, filling the whole landscape. "I know you old colored people! Wouldn't miss going to town to see Santa Claus!"

But something held old Phoenix very still. The deep lines in her face went into a fierce and different radiation. Without warning, she had seen with her own eyes a flashing nickel fall out of the man's pocket onto the ground.

"How old are you, Granny?" he was saying.

"There is no telling, mister," she said, "no telling."

Then she gave a little cry and clapped her hands and said, "Git on away from here, dog! Look! Look at that dog!" She laughed as if in admiration. "He ain't scared of nobody. He a big black dog." She whispered, "Sic him!"

"Watch me get rid of that cur," said the man. "Sic him, Pete! Sic him!"

Phoenix heard the dogs fighting, and heard the man running and throwing sticks. She even heard a gunshot. But she was slowly bending forward by that time, further and further forward, the lids stretched down over her eyes, as if she were doing this in her sleep. Her chin was lowered almost to her knees. The yellow palm of her hand came out from the fold of her apron. Her fingers slid down and along the ground under the piece of money with the grace and care they would have in lifting an egg from under a setting hen. Then she slowly straightened up, she stood erect, and the nickel was in her apron pocket. A bird flew by. Her lips moved. "God watching me the whole time. I come to stealing."

The man came back, and his own dog panted about them. "Well, I scared him off that time," he said, and then he laughed and lifted his gun and pointed it at Phoenix.

She stood straight and faced him.

"Doesn't the gun scare you?" he said, still pointing it.

"No, sir, I seen plenty go off closer by, in my day, and for less than what I done," she said, holding utterly still.

He smiled, and shouldered the gun. "Well, Granny," he said, "you must be a hundred years old, and scared of nothing. I'd give you a dime if I had any money with me. But you take my advice and stay home, and nothing will happen to you."

"I bound to go on my way, mister," said Phoenix. She inclined her head in the red rag. Then they went in different directions, but she could hear the gun shooting again and again over the hill.

She walked on. The shadows hung from the oak trees to the road like curtains. Then she smelled wood-smoke, and smelled the river, and she saw a steeple and the cabins on their steep steps. Dozens of little black children whirled around her. There ahead was Natchez shining. Bells were ringing. She walked on.

In the paved city it was Christmas time. There were red and green electric lights strung and crisscrossed everywhere, and all turned on in the daytime. Old Phoenix would have been lost if she had not distrusted her eyesight and depended on her feet to know where to take her.

She paused quietly on the sidewalk where people were passing by. A lady came along in the crowd, carrying an armful of red-, green- and silver-wrapped presents; she gave off perfume like the red roses in hot summer, and Phoenix stopped her.

"Please, missy, will you lace up my shoe?" She held up her foot.

"What do you want, Grandma?"

"See my shoe," said Phoenix. "Do all right for out in the country, but wouldn't look right to go in a big building."

"Stand still then, Grandma," said the lady. She put her packages down on the sidewalk beside her and laced and tied both shoes tightly.

"Can't lace 'em with a cane," said Phoenix. "Thank you, missy. I doesn't mind asking a nice lady to tie up my shoe, when I gets out on the street."

Moving slowly and from side to side, she went into the big building, and into a tower of steps, where she walked up and around and around until her feet knew to stop.

She entered a door, and there she saw nailed up on the wall the document that had been stamped with the gold seal and framed in the gold frame, which matched the dream that was hung up in her head.

"Here I be," she said. There was a fixed and ceremonial stiffness over her body.

"A charity case, I suppose," said an attendant who sat at the desk before her.

But Phoenix only looked above her head. There was

sweat on her face, the wrinkles in her skin shone like a bright net.

"Speak up, Grandma," the woman said. "What's your name? We must have your history, you know. Have you been here before? What seems to be the trouble with you?"

Old Phoenix only gave a twitch to her face as if a fly were bothering her.

"Are you deaf?" cried the attendant.

But then the nurse came in.

"Oh, that's just old Aunt Phoenix," she said. "She doesn't come for herself—she has a little grandson. She makes these trips just as regular as clockwork. She lives away back off the Old Natchez Trace." She bent down. "Well, Aunt Phoenix, why don't you just take a seat? We won't keep you standing after your long trip." She pointed.

The old woman sat down, bolt upright in the chair.

"Now, how is the boy?" asked the nurse.

Old Phoenix did not speak.

"I said, how is the boy?"

But Phoenix only waited and stared straight ahead, her face very solemn and withdrawn into rigidity.

"Is his throat any better?" asked the nurse. "Aunt Phoenix, don't you hear me? Is your grandson's throat any better since the last time you came for the medicine?"

With her hands on her knees, the old woman waited, silent, erect and motionless, just as if she were in armor.

"You mustn't take up our time this way, Aunt Phoenix," the nurse said. "Tell us quickly about your grandson, and get it over. He isn't dead, is he?"

At last there came a flicker and then a flame of comprehension across her face, and she spoke.

"My grandson. It was my memory had left me. There I sat and forgot why I made my long trip."

"Forgot?" The nurse frowned. "After you came so far?"

Then Phoenix was like an old woman begging a dignified forgiveness for waking up frightened in the night. "I never did go to school, I was too old at the Surrender," she said in a soft voice. "I'm an old woman without an education. It was my memory fail me. My little grandson, he is just the same, and I forgot it in the coming."

"Throat never heals, does it?" said the nurse, speaking in a loud, sure voice to old Phoenix. By now she had a card with something written on it, a little list. "Yes. Swallowed lye. When was it?—January—two-three years ago—"

Phoenix spoke unasked now. "No, missy, he not dead, he just the same. Every little while his throat begin to close up again, and he not able to swallow. He not get his breath. He not able to help himself. So the time come around, and I go on another trip for the soothing medicine."

"All right. The doctor said as long as you came to get it, you could have it," said the nurse. "But it's an obstinate case."

"My little grandson, he sit up there in the house all wrapped up, waiting by himself," Phoenix went on. "We is the only two left in the world. He suffer and it don't seem to put him back at all. He got a sweet look. He going to last. He wear a little patch quilt and peep out holding his mouth open like a little bird. I remembers so plain now. I not going to forget him again, no, the whole enduring time. I could tell him from all the others in creation."

"All right." The nurse was trying to hush her now. She brought her a bottle of medicine. "Charity," she said, making a check mark in a book.

Old Phoenix held the bottle close to her eyes, and then carefully put it into her pocket.

"I thank you," she said.

"It's Christmas time, Grandma," said the attendant. "Could I give you a few pennies out of my purse?"

"Five pennies is a nickel," said Phoenix stiffly.

"Here's a nickel," said the attendant.

Phoenix rose carefully and held out her hand. She received the nickel and then fished the other nickel out of her pocket and laid it beside the new one. She stared at her palm closely, with her head on one side.

Then she gave a tap with her cane on the floor.

"This is what come to me to do," she said. "I going to the store and buy my child a little windmill they sells, made out of paper. He going to find it hard to believe there such a thing in the world. I'll march myself back where he waiting, holding it straight up in this hand."

She lifted her free hand, gave a little nod, turned around, and walked out of the doctor's office. Then her slow step began on the stairs, going down.

THE
WIDE NET
AND OTHER
STORIES

To My Mother
Chestina Andrews Welty

FIRST LOVE

———◆———

Whatever happened, it happened in extraordinary times, in a season of dreams, and in Natchez it was the bitterest winter of them all. The north wind struck one January night in 1807 with an insistent penetration, as if it followed the settlers down by their own course, screaming down the river bends to drive them further still. Afterwards there was the strange drugged fall of snow. When the sun rose the air broke into a thousand prisms as close as the flash-and-turn of gulls' wings. For a long time afterwards it was so clear that in the evening the little companion-star to Sirius could be seen plainly in the heavens by travelers who took their way by night, and Venus shone in the daytime in all its course through the new transparency of the sky.

The Mississippi shuddered and lifted from its bed, reaching like a somnambulist driven to go in new places; the ice stretched far out over the waves. Flatboats and rafts continued to float downstream, but with unsignalling passengers submissive and huddled, mere bundles of sticks; bets were laid on shore as to whether they were alive or dead, but it was impossible to prove it either way.

The coated moss hung in blue and shining garlands over the trees along the changed streets in the morning.

The town of little galleries was all laden roofs and silence. In the fastness of Natchez it began to seem then that the whole world, like itself, must be in a transfiguration. The only clamor came from the animals that suffered in their stalls, or from the wildcats that howled in closer rings each night from the frozen cane. The Indians could be heard from greater distances and in greater numbers than had been guessed, sending up placating but proud messages to the sun in continual ceremonies of dancing. The red percussion of their fires could be seen night and day by those waiting in the dark trance of the frozen town. Men were caught by the cold, they dropped in its snare-like silence. Bands of travelers moved closer together, with intenser caution, through the glassy tunnels of the Trace, for all proportion went away, and they followed one another like insects going at dawn through the heavy grass. Natchez people turned silently to look when a solitary man that no one had ever seen before was found and carried in through the streets, frozen the way he had crouched in a hollow tree, gray and huddled like a squirrel, with a little bundle of goods clasped to him.

Joel Mayes, a deaf boy twelve years old, saw the man brought in and knew it was a dead man, but his eyes were for something else, something wonderful. He saw the breaths coming out of people's mouths, and his dark face, losing just now a little of its softness, showed its secret desire. It was marvelous to him when the infinite designs of speech became visible in formations on the air, and he watched with awe that changed to tenderness whenever people met and passed in the road with an exchange of words. He walked alone, slowly through the silence, with the sturdy and yet dreamlike walk of the orphan, and let his own breath out through his lips, pushed it into the air, and whatever word it was it took the shape of a tower. He was as pleased as if he had had a little conversation with someone. At the end of the street, where he turned into the Inn, he always bent his head and walked faster, as if all frivolity were done, for he was boot-boy there.

He had come to Natchez some time in the summer. That was through great worlds of leaves, and the whole journey from Virginia had been to him a kind of childhood wandering in oblivion. He had remained to himself: always to himself at first, and afterwards too—with the company of Old Man McCaleb who took him along when his parents vanished in the forest, were cut off from him, and in spite of his last backward look, dropped behind. Arms bent on destination dragged him forward through the sharp bushes, and leaves came toward his face which he finally put his hands out to stop. Now that he was a boot-boy, he had thought little, frugally, almost stonily, of that long time . . . until lately Old Man McCaleb had reappeared at the Inn, bound for no telling where, his tangled beard like the beards of old men in dreams; and in the act of cleaning his boots, which were uncommonly heavy and burdensome with mud, Joel came upon a little part of the old adventure, for there it was, dark and crusted. . . came back to it, and went over it again. . . .

He rubbed, and remembered the day after his parents had left him, the day when it was necessary to hide from the Indians. Old Man McCaleb, his stern face lighting in the most unexpected way, had herded them, the whole party alike, into the dense cane brake, deep down off the Trace—the densest part, where it grew as thick and locked as some kind of wild teeth. There they crouched, and each one of them, man, woman, and child, had looked at all the others from a hiding place that seemed the least safe of all, watching in an eager wild instinct for any movement or betrayal. Crouched by his bush, Joel had cried; all his understanding would desert him suddenly and because he could not hear he could not see or touch or find a familiar thing in the world. He wept, and Old Man McCaleb first felled the excited dog with the blunt end of his axe, and then he turned a fierce face toward him and lifted the blade in the air, in a kind of ecstasy of protecting the silence they were keeping. Joel had made a sound. . . . He gasped and put his mouth quicker than thought against the earth. He took the leaves in his mouth. . . . In that long time of lying motionless with the men and women in the cane brake he had learned what silence meant to other people. Through the danger he had felt acutely, even with horror, the nearness of his compan-ions, a speechless embrace of which he had had no warning, a powerful, crushing unity. The Indians had then gone by, followed by an old woman—in solemn, single file, careless of the inflaming arrows they carried in their quivers, dangling in their hands a few strings of catfish. They passed in the length of the old woman's yawn. Then one by one McCaleb's charges had to rise up and come out of the hiding place. There was little talking together, but a kind of shame and shuffling. As soon as the party reached Natchez, their little cluster dissolved completely. The old man had given each of them one long, rather for-

lorn look for a farewell, and had gone away, no less preoccupied than he had ever been. To the man who had
saved his life Joel lifted the gentle, almost indifferent face
of the child who has asked for nothing. Now he remembered the white gulls flying across the sky behind the old
man's head.

Joel had been deposited at the Inn, and there was
nowhere else for him to go, for it stood there and marked
the foot of the long Trace, with the river back of it. So he
remained. It was a noncommittal arrangement: he never
paid them anything for his keep, and they never paid him
anything for his work. Yet time passed, and he became a
little part of the place where it passed over him. A small
private room became his own; it was on the ground floor
behind the saloon, a dark little room paved with stones
with its ceiling rafters curved not higher than a man's
head. There was a fireplace and one window, which
opened on the courtyard filled always with the tremor of
horses. He curled up every night on a highbacked bench,
when the weather turned cold he was given a collection
of old coats to sleep under, and the room was almost
excessively his own, as it would have been a stray kitten's
that came to the same spot every night. He began to keep
his candlestick carefully polished, he set it in the center
of the puncheon table, and at night when it was lighted
all the messages of love carved into it with a knife in Spanish words, with a deep Spanish gouging, came out in black
relief, for anyone to read who came knowing the language.

Late at night, nearer morning, after the travelers had
all certainly pulled off their boots to fall into bed, he
waked by habit and passed with the candle shielded up the

259

stairs and through the halls and rooms, and gathered up the boots. When he had brought them all down to his table he would sit and take his own time cleaning them, while the firelight would come gently across the paving stones. It seemed then that his whole life was safely alighted, in the sleep of everyone else, like a bird on a bough, and he was alone in the way he liked to be. He did not despise boots at all—he had learned boots; under his hand they stood up and took a good shape. This was not a slave's work, or a child's either. It had dignity: it was dangerous to walk about among sleeping men. More than once he had been seized and the life half shaken out of him by a man waking up in a sweat of suspicion or nightmare, but he dealt nimbly as an animal with the violence and quick frenzy of dreamers. It might seem to him that the whole world was sleeping in the lightest of trances, which the least movement would surely wake; but he only walked softly, stepping around and over, and got back to his room. Once a rattlesnake had shoved its head from a boot as he stretched out his hand; but that was not likely to happen again in a thousand years.

It was in his own room, on the night of the first snowfall, that a new adventure began for him. Very late in the night, toward morning, Joel sat bolt upright in bed and opened his eyes to see the whole room shining brightly, like a brimming lake in the sun. Boots went completely out of his head, and he was left motionless. The candle was lighted in its stick, the fire was high in the grate, and from the window a wild tossing illumination came, which he did not even identify at first as the falling of snow. Joel was left in the shadow of the room, and there before him, in the center of the strange multiplied light, were two men in black capes sitting at his table. They sat in profile to him, tall under the little arch of the rafters, facing each other across the good table he used for everything, and talking together. They were not of Natchez, and their names were not in the book. Each of them had a white glitter upon his boots—it was the snow; their capes were drawn together in front, and in the blackness of the folds, snowflakes were just beginning to melt.

Joel had never been able to hear the knocking at a door, and still he knew what that would be; and he surmised that these men had never knocked even lightly to enter his room. When he found that at some moment outside his knowledge or consent two men had seemingly fallen from the clouds onto the two stools at his table and had taken everything over for themselves, he did not keep the calm heart with which he had stood and regarded all men up to Old Man McCaleb, who snored upstairs.

He did not at once betray the violation that he felt. Instead, he simply sat, still bolt upright, and looked with the feasting the eyes do in secret—at their faces, the one eye of each that he could see, the cheeks, the half-hidden mouths—the faces each firelit, and strange with a common reminiscence or speculation. . . . Perhaps he was saved from giving a cry by knowing it could be heard. Then the gesture one of the men made in the air transfixed him where he waited.

One of the two men lifted his right arm—a tense, yet gentle and easy motion—and made the dark wet cloak fall back. To Joel it was like the first movement he had ever

seen, as if the world had been up to that night inanimate.
It was like the signal to open some heavy gate or pad-
dock, and it did open to his complete astonishment upon a
panorama in his own head, about which he knew first of
all that he would never be able to speak—it was nothing
but brightness, as full as the brightness on which he had
opened his eyes. Inside his room was still another interior, this meeting upon which all the light was turned,
and within that was one more mystery, all that was being
said. The men's heads were inclined together against the
blaze, their hair seemed light and floating. Their elbows
rested on the boards, stirring the crumbs where Joel had
eaten his biscuit. He had no idea of how long they had
stayed when they got up and stretched their arms and
walked out through the door, after blowing the candle
out.

When Joel woke up again at daylight, his first thought
was of Indians, his next of ghosts, and then the vision of
what had happened came back into his head. He took a
light beating for forgetting to clean the boots, but then he
forgot the beating. He wondered for how long a time the
men had been meeting in his room while he was asleep,
and whether they had ever seen him, and what they might
be going to do to him, whether they would take him each
by the arm and drag him on further, through the leaves.
He tried to remember everything of the night before, and
he could, and then of the day before, and he rubbed belat-
edly at a boot in a long and deepening dream. His memory
could work like the slinging of a noose to catch a wild
pony. It reached back and hung trembling over the very
moment of terror in which he had become separated from

his parents, and then it turned and started in the opposite direction, and it would have discerned some shape, but he would not let it, of the future. In the meanwhile, all day long, everything in the passing moment and each little deed assumed the gravest importance. He divined every change in the house, in the angle of the doors, in the height of the fires, and whether the logs had been stirred by a boot or had only fallen in an empty room. He was seized and possessed by mystery. He waited for night. In his own room the candlestick now stood on the table covered with the wonder of having been touched by unknown hands in his absence and seen in his sleep.

It was while he was cleaning boots again that the identity of the men came to him all at once. Like part of his meditations, the names came into his mind. He ran out into the street with this knowledge rocking in his head, remembering then the tremor of a great arrival which had shaken Natchez, caught fast in the grip of the cold, and shaken it through the lethargy of the snow, and it was clear now why the floors swayed with running feet and unsteady hands shoved him aside at the bar. There was no one to inform him that the men were Aaron Burr and Harman Blennerhassett, but he knew. No one had pointed out to him any way that he might know which was which, but he knew that: it was Burr who had made the gesture.

They came to his room every night, and indeed Joel had not expected that the one visit would be the end. It never occurred to him that the first meeting did not mark a beginning. It took a little time always for the snow to melt from their capes—for it continued all this time to snow. Joel sat up with his eyes wide open in the shadows and looked out like the lone watcher of a conflagration. The room grew warm, burning with the heat from the little grate, but there was something of fire in all that happened. It was from Aaron Burr that the flame was springing, and it seemed to pass across the table with certain words and through the sudden nobleness of the gesture, and touch Blennerhassett. Yet the breath of their speech was no simple thing like the candle's gleam between them. Joel saw them still only in profile, but he could see that the secret was endlessly complex, for in two nights it was apparent that it could never be all told. All that they said never finished their conversation. They would always have to meet again. The ring Burr wore caught the firelight repeatedly and started it up again in the intricate whirlpool of a signet. Quicker and fuller still was his eye, darting its look about, but never at Joel. Their eyes had never really seen his room . . . the fine polish he had given the candlestick, the clean boards from which he had scraped the crumbs, the wooden bench where he was himself, from which he put outward—just a little, carelessly—his hand. . . . Everything in the room was conquest, all was a dream of delights and powers beyond its walls. . . . The light-filled hair fell over Burr's sharp forehead, his cheek grew taut, his smile was sudden, his lips drove the breath through. The other man's face, with its quiet mouth, for he was the listener, changed from ardor to gloom and back to ardor. . . . Joel sat still and looked from one man to the other.

At first he believed that he had not been discovered. Then he knew that they had learned somehow of his presence, and that it had not stopped them. Somehow that appalled him. . . . They were aware that if it were only before him, they could talk forever in his room. Then he put it that they accepted him. One night, in his first realization of this, his defect seemed to him a kind of hospitality. A joy came over him, he was moved to gaiety, he felt wit stirring in his mind, and he came out of his hiding place and took a few steps toward them. Finally, it was too much: he broke in upon the circle of their talk, and set food and drink from the kitchen on the table between them. His hands were shaking, and they looked at him as if from great distances, but they were not surprised, and he could smell the familiar black wetness of travelers' clothes steaming up from them in the firelight. Afterwards he sat on the floor perfectly still, with Burr's cloak hanging just beside his own shoulder. At such moments he felt a dizziness as if the cape swung him about in a great arc of wonder, but Aaron Burr turned his full face and looked down at him only with gravity, the high margin of his brows lifted above tireless eyes.

There was a kind of dominion promised in his gentlest glance. When he first would come and throw himself down to talk and the fire would flame up and the reflections of the snowy world grew bright, even the clumsy table seemed to change its substance and to become a part of a ceremony. He might have talked in another language, in which there was nothing but evocation. When he was seen so plainly, all his movements and his looks seemed part of a devotion that was curiously patient and had the illusion of wisdom all about it. Lights shone in his eyes like travelers' fires seen far out on the river. Always he talked, his talking was his appearance, as if there were no eyes, nose, or mouth to remember; in his face there was every subtlety and eloquence, and no features, no kindness, for there was no awareness whatever of the present. Looking up from the floor at his speaking face, Joel knew all at once some secret of temptation and an anguish that would reach out after it like a closing hand. He would allow Burr to take him with him wherever it was that he meant to go.

Sometimes in the nights Joel would feel himself surely under their eyes, and think they must have come; but that would be a dream, and when he sat up on his bench he often saw nothing more than the dormant firelight stretched on the empty floor, and he would have a strange feeling of having been deserted and lost, not quite like anything he had ever felt in his life. It was likely to be early dawn before they came.

When they were there, he sat restored, though they paid no more attention to him than they paid the presence of the firelight. He brought all the food he could manage to give them; he saved a little out of his own suppers, and one night he stole a turkey pie. He might have been their safety, for the way he sat up so still and looked at them at moments like a father at his playing children. He never for an instant wished for them to leave, though he would so long for sleep that he would stare at them finally in bewilderment and without a single flicker of the eyelid. Often they would talk all night. Blennerhassett's wide vague face would grow out of devotion into exhaustion. But Burr's hand would always reach across and take him by the shoulder as if to rouse him from a dull sleep, and the radiance of his own face would heighten always with the passing of time. Joel sat quietly, waiting for the full revelation of the meetings. All his love went out to the talkers. He would not have known how to hold it back.

In the idle mornings, in some morning need to go looking at the world, he wandered down to the Esplanade and stood under the trees which bent heavily over his head. He frowned out across the ice-covered racetrack and out upon the river. There was one hour when the river was the color of smoke, as if it were more a thing of the woods than an element and a power in itself. It seemed to belong to the woods, to be gentle and watched over, a tethered and grazing pet of the forest, and then when the light spread higher and color stained the world, the river would leap suddenly out of the shining ice around, into its full-grown torrent of life, and its strength and its churning passage held Joel watching over it like the spell unfolding by night in his room. If he could not speak to the river, and he could not, still he would try to read in the river's blue and violet skeins a working of the momentous event. It was hard to understand. Was any scheme a man had, however secret and intact, always broken upon by the very current of its working? One day, in anguish, he saw a raft torn apart in midstream and the men scattered from it. Then all that he felt move in his heart at the sight of the inscrutable river went out in hope for the two men and their genius that he sheltered.

It was when he returned to the Inn that he was given a notice to paste on the saloon mirror saying that the trial of Aaron Burr for treason would be held at the end of the month at Washington, capitol of Mississippi Territory, on the campus of Jefferson College, where the crowds might be amply accommodated. In the meanwhile, the arrival of the full, armed flotilla was being awaited, and the price of whisky would not be advanced in this tavern, but there would be a slight increase in the tariff on a bed upstairs, depending on how many slept in it.

The month wore on, and now it was full moonlight. Late at night the whole sky was lunar, like the surface of the moon brought as close as a cheek. The luminous ranges of all the clouds stretched one beyond the other in heavenly order. They seemed to be the streets where Joel was walking through the town. People now lighted their houses in entertainments as if they copied after the sky, with Burr in the center of them always, dancing with the women, talking with the men. They followed and formed cotillion figures about the one who threatened or lured them, and their minuets skimmed across the nights like a pebble expertly skipped across water. Joel would watch them take sides and watch the arguments, all the frilled motions and the toasts, and he thought they were to decide whether Burr was good or evil. But all the time, Joel believed, when he saw Burr go dancing by, that did not touch him at all. Joel knew his eyes saw nothing there and went always beyond the room, although usually the most beautiful woman there was somehow in his arms when the set was over. Sometimes they drove him in their carriages down to the Esplanade and pointed out the moon to him, to end the evening. There they sat showing everything to Aaron Burr, nodding with a magnificence that approached fatigue toward the reaches of the ice that stretched over the river like an impossible bridge, some extension to the West of the Natchez Trace; and a radiance as soft and near as rain fell on their hands and faces, and on the plumes of the breaths from the horses' nostrils, and they were as gracious and as grand as Burr.

Each day that drew the trial closer, men talked more hotly on the corners and the saloon at the Inn shook with debate; every night Burr was invited to a finer and later ball; and Joel waited. He knew that Burr was being allotted, by an almost specific consent, this free and unmolested time till dawn, to meet in conspiracy, for the sake of continuing and perfecting the secret. This knowledge Joel gathered to himself by being, himself, everywhere; it decreed his own suffering and made it secret and filled with private omens.

One day he was driven to know everything. It was the morning he was given a little fur cap, and he set it on his head and started out. He walked through the dark trodden snow all the way up the Trace to the Bayou Pierre. The great trees began to break that day. The pounding of their explosions filled the subdued air; to Joel it was as if a great foot had stamped on the ground. And at first he thought he saw the fulfillment of all the rumor and promise—the flotilla coming around the bend, and he did not know whether he felt terror or pride. But then he saw that what covered the river over was a chain of great perfect trees floating down, lying on their sides in postures like slain giants and heroes of battle, black cedars and stone-white sycamores, magnolias with their heavy leaves shining as if they were in bloom, a long procession. Then it was terror that he felt.

He went on. He was not the only one who had made

the pilgrimage to see what the original flotilla was like, that had been taken from Burr. There were many others: there was Old Man McCaleb, at a little distance. . . . In care not to show any excitement of expectation, Joel made his way through successive little groups that seemed to meditate there above the encampment of militia on the snowy bluff, and looked down at the water.

There was no galley there. There were nine small flat-boats tied to the shore. They seemed so small and delicate that he was shocked and distressed, and looked around at the faces of the others, who looked coolly back at him. There was no sign of a weapon about the boats or anywhere, except in the hands of the men on guard. There were barrels of molasses and whisky, rolling and knocking each other like drowned men, and stowed to one side of one of the boats, in a dark place, a strange little collection of blankets, a silver bridle with bells, a book swollen with water, and a little flute with a narrow ridge of snow along it. Where Joel stood looking down upon them, the boats floated in clusters of three, as small as water-lilies on a still bayou. A canoe filled with crazily wrapped-up Indians passed at a little distance, and with severe open mouths the Indians all laughed.

But the soldiers were sullen with cold, and very grave or angry, and Old Man McCaleb was there with his beard flying and his finger pointing prophetically in the direction of upstream. Some of the soldiers and all the women nodded their heads, as though they were the easiest believers, and one woman drew her child tightly to her. Joel shivered. Two of the young men hanging over the edge of the bluff flung their arms in sudden exhilaration about each other's shoulders, and a look of wildness came over their faces.

Back in the streets of Natchez, Joel met part of the militia marching and stood with his heart racing, back out of the way of the line coming with bright guns tilted up in the sharp air. Behind them, two of the soldiers dragged along a young dandy whose eyes glared at everything. There where they held him he was trying over and over again to make Aaron Burr's gesture, and he never convinced anybody.

Joel went in all three times to the militia's encampment on the Bayou Pierre, the last time on the day before the trial was to begin. Then out beyond a willow point a rowboat with one soldier in it kept laconic watch upon the north.

Joel returned on the frozen path to the Inn, and stumbled into his room, and waited for Burr and Blennerhassett to come and talk together. His head ached. . . . All his walking about was no use. Where did people learn things? Where did they go to find them? How far?

Burr and Blennerhassett talked across the table, and it was growing late on the last night. Then there in the doorway with a fiddle in her hand stood Blennerhassett's wife, wearing breeches, come to fetch him home. The fiddle she had simply picked up in the Inn parlor as she came through, and Joel did not think she bothered now to speak at all. But she waited there before the fire, still a child and so clearly related to her husband that their sudden movements at the encounter were alike and made at the same time, They stood looking at each other there in the firelight like creatures balancing together on a raft, and then she lifted the bow and began to play.

Joel gazed at the girl, not much older than himself. She leaned her cheek against the fiddle. He had never examined a fiddle at all, and when she began to play it she frightened and dismayed him by her almost insect-like motions, the pensive antennae of her arms, her mask of a countenance. When she played she never blinked her eye. Her legs, fantastic in breeches, were separated slightly, and from her bent knees she swayed back and forth as if she were weaving the tunes with her body. The sharp odor of whisky moved with her. The slits of her eyes were milky. The songs she played seemed to him to have no beginnings and no endings, but to be about many hills and valleys, and chains of lakes. She, like the men, knew of a place. . . . All of them spoke of a country.

And quite clearly, and altogether to his surprise, Joel saw a sight that he had nearly forgotten. Instead of the fire on the hearth, there was a mimosa tree in flower. It was in the little back field at his home in Virginia and his mother was leading him by the hand. Fragile, delicate, cloud-like it rose on its pale trunk and spread its long level arms. His mother pointed to it. Among the trembling leaves the feathery puffs of sweet bloom filled the tree like thousands of paradisical birds all alighted at an instant. He had known then the story of the Princess Labam, for his mother had told it to him, how she was so radiant that she sat on the roof-top at night and lighted the city. It seemed to be the mimosa tree that lighted the garden, for its brightness and fragrance overlaid all the rest. Out of its graciousness this tree suffered their presence and shed its splendor upon him and his mother. His mother pointed again, and its scent swayed like the Asiatic princess moving up and down the pink steps of its branches. Then the vision was gone. Aaron Burr sat in front of the fire, Blennerhassett faced him, and Blennerhassett's wife played on the violin.

There was no compassion in what this woman was doing, he knew that—there was only a frightening thing, a stern allurement. Try as he might, he could not comprehend it, though it was so calculated. He had instead a sensation of pain, the ends of his fingers were stinging. At first he did not realize that he had heard the sounds of her song, the only thing he had ever heard. Then all at once as she held the lifted bow still for a moment he gasped for breath at the interruption, and he did not care to learn her purpose or to wonder any longer, but bent his head and listened for the note that she would fling down upon them. And it was so gentle then, it touched him with surprise; it made him think of animals sleeping on their cushioned paws.

For a moment his love went like sound into a myriad life and was divided among all the people in his room. While they listened, Burr's radiance was somehow quenched, or theirs was raised to equal it, and they were all alike. There was one thing that shone in all their faces, and that was how far they were from home, how far from everywhere that they knew. Joel put his hand to his own face, and hid his pity from them while they listened to the endless tunes.

But she ended them. Sleep all at once seemed to overcome her whole body. She put down the fiddle and took

Blennerhassett by both hands. He seemed tired too, more tired than talking could ever make him. He went out when she led him. They went wrapped under one cloak, his arm about her.

Burr did not go away immediately. First he walked up and down before the fire. He turned each time with diminishing violence, and light and shadow seemed to stream more softly with his turning cloak. Then he stood still. The firelight threw its changes over his face. He had no one to talk to. His boots smelled of the fire's closeness. Of course he had forgotten Joel, he seemed quite alone. At last with a strange naturalness, almost with a limp, he went to the table and stretched himself full length upon it.

He lay on his back. Joel was astonished. That was the way they laid out the men killed in duels in the Inn yard; and that was the table they laid them on.

Burr fell asleep instantly, so quickly that Joel felt he should never be left alone. He looked at the sleeping face of Burr, and the time and the place left him, and all that Burr had said that he had tried to guess left him too—he knew nothing in the world except the sleeping face. It was quiet. The eyes were almost closed, only dark slits lay beneath the lids. There was a small scar on the cheek. The lips were parted. Joel thought, I could speak if I would, or I could hear. Once I did each thing. . . . Still he listened . . . and it seemed that all that would speak, in this world, was listening. Burr was silent; he demanded nothing, nothing. . . . A boy or a man could be so alone in his heart that he could not even ask a question. In such silence as falls over a lonely man there is childlike supplication, and all arms might wish to open to him, but there is no speech. This was Burr's last night: Joel knew that. This was the moment before he would ride away. Why would the heart break so at absence? Joel knew that it was because nothing had been told. The heart is secret even when the moment it dreamed of has come, a moment when there might have been a revelation. . . . Joel stood motionless; he lifted his gaze from Burr's face and stared at nothing. . . . If love does a secret thing always, it is to reach backward, to a time that could not be known—for it makes a history of the sorrow and the dream it has contemplated in some instant of recognition. What Joel saw before him he had a terrible wish to speak out loud, but he would have had to find names for the places of the heart and the times for its shadowy and tragic events, and they seemed of great magnitude, heroic and terrible and splendid, like the legends of the mind. But for lack of a way to tell how much was known, the boundaries would lie between him and the others, all the others, until he died.

Presently Burr began to toss his head and to cry out. He talked, his face drew into a dreadful set of grimaces, which it followed over and over. He could never stop talking. Joel was afraid of these words, and afraid that eavesdroppers might listen to them. Whatever words they were, they were being taken by some force out of his dream. In horror, Joel put out his hand. He could never in his life have laid it across the mouth of Aaron Burr, but he thrust it into Burr's spread-out fingers. The fingers closed and did not yield; the clasp grew so fierce that it hurt his hand, but he saw that the words had stopped.

As if a silent love had shown him whatever new thing

275

he would ever be able to learn, Joel had some wisdom in his fingers now which only this long month could have brought. He knew with what gentleness to hold the burning hand. With the gravity of his very soul he received the furious pressure of this man's dream. At last Burr drew his arm back beside his quiet head, and his hand hung like a child's in sleep, released in oblivion.

The next morning, Joel was given a notice to paste on the saloon mirror that conveyances might be rented at the Inn daily for the excursion to Washington for the trial of Mr. Burr, payment to be made in advance. Joel went out and stood on a corner, and joined with a group of young boys walking behind the militia.

It was warm—a "false spring" day. The little procession from Natchez, decorated and smiling in all they owned or whatever they borrowed or chartered or rented, moved grandly through the streets and on up the Trace. To Joel, somewhere in the line, the blue air that seemed to lie between the high banks held it all in a mist, softly colored, the fringe waving from a carriage top, a few flags waving, a sword shining when some gentleman made a flourish. High up on their horses a number of the men were wearing their Revolutionary War uniforms, as if to reiterate that Aaron Burr fought once at their sides as a hero.

Under the spreading live-oaks at Washington, the trial opened like a festival. There was a theatre of benches, and a promenade; stalls were set out under the trees and glasses of whisky, and colored ribbons, were sold. Joel sat somewhere among the crowds. Breezes touched the yellow and violet of dresses and stirred them, horses pawed the ground, and the people pressed upon him and seemed more real than those in dreams, and yet their pantomime was like those choruses and companies whose movements are like the waves running together. A hammer was then pounded, there was sudden attention from all the spectators, and Joel felt the great solidifying of their silence.

He had dreaded the sight of Burr. He had thought there might be some mark or disfigurement that would come from his panic. But all his grace was back upon him, and he was smiling to greet the studious faces which regarded him. Before their bright façade others rose first, declaiming men in turn, and then Burr.

In a moment he was walking up and down with his shadow on the grass and the patches of snow. He was talking again, talking now in great courtesy to everybody. There was a flickering light of sun and shadow on his face.

Then Joel understood. Burr was explaining away, smoothing over all that he had held great enough to have dreaded once. He walked back and forth elegantly in the sun, turning his wrist ever so airily in its frill, making light of his dream that had terrified him. And it was the deed they had all come to see. All around Joel they gasped, smiled, pressed one another's arms, nodded their heads; there were tender smiles on the women's faces. They were at Aaron Burr's feet at last, learning their superiority. They loved him now, in their condescension. They leaned forward in delight at the parading spectacle he was making. And when it was over for the day, they shook each other's hands, and Old Man McCaleb could be seen spitting on the ground, in the anticipation of another day as good as this one.

Blennerhassett did not come that night.

Burr came very late. He walked in the door, looked down at Joel where he sat among his boots, and suddenly stooped and took the dirty cloth out of his hand. He put his face quickly into it and pressed and rubbed it against his skin. Joel saw that all his clothes were dirty and ragged. The last thing he did was to set a little cap of turkey feathers on his head. Then he went out.

Joel followed him along behind the dark houses and through a ravine. Burr turned toward the Halfway Hill. Joel turned too, and he saw Burr walk slowly up and open the great heavy gate.

He saw him stop beside a tall camellia bush as solid as a tower and pick up one of the frozen buds which were shed all around it on the ground. For a moment he held it in the palm of his hand, and then he went on. Joel, following behind, did the same. He held the bud, and studied the burned edges of its folds by the pale half-light of the East. The bud came apart in his hand, its layers like small velvet shells, still iridescent, the shriveled flower inside. He held it tenderly and yet timidly, in a kind of shame, as though all disaster lay pitifully disclosed now to the eyes.

He knew the girl Burr had often danced with under the rings of tapers when she came out in a cloak across the shadowy hill. Burr stood, quiet and graceful as he had always been as her partner at the balls. Joel felt a pain like a sting while she first merged with the dark figure and then drew back. The moon, late-risen and waning, came out of the clouds. Aaron Burr made the gesture there in the distance, toward the West, where the clouds hung still and red, and when Joel looked at him in the light he saw as she must have seen the absurdity he was dressed in, the feathers on his head. With a curious feeling of revenge upon her, he watched her turn, draw smaller within her own cape, and go away.

Burr came walking down the hill, and passed close to the camellia bush where Joel was standing. He walked stiffly in his mock Indian dress with the boot polish on his face. The youngest child in Natchez would have known that this was a remarkable and wonderful figure that had humiliated itself by disguise.

Pausing in an open space, Burr lifted his hand once more and a slave led out from the shadows a majestic horse with silver trappings shining in the light of the moon. Burr mounted from the slave's hand in all the clarity of his true elegance, and sat for a moment motionless in the saddle. Then he cut his whip through the air, and rode away.

Joel followed him on foot toward the Liberty Road. As he walked through the streets of Natchez he felt a strange mourning to know that Burr would never come again by that way. If he had left in disguise, the thirst that was in his face was the same as it had ever been. He had eluded judgment, that was all he had done, and Joel was glad while he still trembled. Joel would never know now the true course, or the true outcome of any dream: this was all he felt. But he walked on, in the frozen path into the wilderness, on and on. He did not see how he could ever go back and still be the boot-boy at the Inn.

THE WIDE NET

———◆———

This story is for
JOHN FRAISER ROBINSON

WILLIAM WALLACE JAMIESON'S wife Hazel was going to have a baby. But this was October, and it was six months away, and she acted exactly as though it would be tomorrow. When he came in the room she would not speak to him, but would look as straight at nothing as she could, with her eyes glowing. If he only touched her she stuck out her tongue or ran around the table. So one night he went out with two of the boys down the road and stayed out all night. But that was the worst thing yet, because when he came home in the early morning Hazel had vanished. He went through the house not believing his eyes, balancing with both hands out, his yellow cowlick rising on end, and then he turned the kitchen inside out looking for her, but it did no good. Then when he got back to the front room he saw she had left him a little letter, in an envelope. That was doing something behind someone's back. He took out the letter, pushed it open, held it out at a distance from his eyes. . . . After one look he was scared to read the exact words, and he crushed the whole thing in his hand instantly, but what it had said was that

281

she would not put up with him after that and was going to the river to drown herself.

"Drown herself. . . . But she's in mortal fear of the water!"

He ran out front, his face red like the red of the picked cotton field he ran over, and down in the road he gave a loud shout for Virgil Thomas, who was just going in his own house, to come out again. He could just see the edge of Virgil, he had almost got in, he had one foot inside the door.

They met half-way between the farms, under the shade-tree.

"Haven't you had enough of the night?" asked Virgil. There they were, their pants all covered with dust and dew, and they had had to carry the third man home flat between them.

"I've lost Hazel, she's vanished, she went to drown herself."

"Why, that ain't like Hazel," said Virgil.

William Wallace reached out and shook him. "You heard me. Don't you know we have to drag the river?"

"Right this minute?"

"You ain't got nothing to do till spring."

"Let me go set foot inside the house and speak to my mother and tell her a story, and I'll come back."

"This will take the wide net," said William Wallace. His eyebrows gathered, and he was talking to himself.

"How come Hazel to go and do that way?" asked Virgil as they started out.

William Wallace said, "I reckon she got lonesome."

"That don't argue—drown herself for getting lonesome. My mother gets lonesome."

"Well," said William Wallace. "It argues for Hazel."

"How long is it now since you and her was married?"

"Why, it's been a year."

"It don't seem that long to me. A year!"

"It was this time last year. It seems longer," said William Wallace, breaking a stick off a tree in surprise. They walked along, kicking at the flowers on the road's edge. "I remember the day I seen her first, and that seems a long time ago. She was coming along the road holding a little frying-size chicken from her grandma, under her arm, and she had it real quiet. I spoke to her with nice manners. We knowed each other's names, being bound to, just didn't know each other to speak to. I says, 'Where are you taking the fryer?' and she says, 'Mind your manners,' and I kept on till after while she says, 'If you want to walk me home, take littler steps.' So I didn't lose time. It was just four miles across the field and full of blackberries, and from the top of the hill there was Dover below, looking sizeable-like and clean, spread out between the two churches like that. When we got down, I says to her, 'What kind of water's in this well?' and she says, 'The best water in the world.' So I drew a bucket and took out a dipper and she drank and I drank. I didn't think it was that remarkable, but I didn't tell her."

"What happened that night?" asked Virgil.

"We ate the chicken," said William Wallace, "and it was tender. Of course that wasn't all they had. The night

I was trying their table out, it sure had good things to eat from one end to the other. Her mama and papa sat at the head and foot and we was face to face with each other across it, with I remember a pat of butter between. They had real sweet butter, with a tree drawed down it, elegant-like. Her mama eats like a man. I had brought her a whole hat-ful of berries and she didn't even pass them to her husband. Hazel, she would leap up and take a pitcher of new milk and fill up the glasses. I had heard how they couldn't have a singing at the church without a fight over her."

"Oh, she's a pretty girl, all right," said Virgil. "It's a pity for the ones like her to grow old, and get like their mothers."

"Another thing will be that her mother will get wind of this and come after me," said William Wallace.

"Her mother will eat you alive," said Virgil.

"She's just been watching her chance," said William Wallace. "Why did I think I could stay out all night."

"Just something come over you."

"First it was just a carnival at Carthage, and I had to let them guess my weight . . . and after that . . ."

"It was nice to be sitting on your neck in a ditch singing," prompted Virgil, "in the moonlight. And playing on the harmonica like you can play."

"Even if Hazel did sit home knowing I was drunk, that wouldn't kill her," said William Wallace. "What she knows ain't ever killed her yet. . . . She's smart, too, for a girl," he said.

"She's a lot smarter than her cousin in Beula," said Virgil. "And especially Edna Earle, that never did get to be what you'd call a heavy thinker. Edna Earle could sit and ponder all day on how the little tail of the 'C' got through the 'L' in a Coca-Cola sign."

"Hazel *is* smart," said William Wallace. They walked on. "You ought to see her pantry shelf, it looks like a hundred jars when you open the door. I don't see how she could turn around and jump in the river."

"It's a woman's trick."

"I always behaved before. Till the one night—last night."

"Yes, but the one night," said Virgil. "And she was waiting to take advantage."

"She jumped in the river because she was scared to death of the water and that was to make it worse," he said. "She remembered how I used to have to pick her up and carry her over the oak-log bridge, how she'd shut her eyes and make a dead-weight and hold me round the neck, just for a little creek. I don't see how she brought herself to jump."

"Jumped backwards," said Virgil. "Didn't look."

When they turned off, it was still early in the pink and green fields. The fumes of morning, sweet and bitter, sprang up where they walked. The insects ticked softly, their strength in reserve; butterflies chopped the air, going to the east, and the birds flew carelessly and sang by fits and starts, not the way they did in the evening in sustained and drowsy songs.

"It's a pretty *day* for sure," said William Wallace. "It's a pretty *day* for it."

"I don't see a sign of her ever going along here," said Virgil.

"Well," said William Wallace. "She wouldn't have dropped anything. I never saw a girl to leave less signs of where she's been."

"Not even a plum seed," said Virgil, kicking the grass.

In the grove it was so quiet that once William Wallace gave a jump, as if he could almost hear a sound of himself wondering where she had gone. A descent of energy came down on him in the thick of the woods and he ran at a rabbit and caught it in his hands.

"Rabbit . . . Rabbit . . ." He acted as if he wanted to take it off to himself and hold it up and talk to it. He laid a palm against its pushing heart. "Now . . . There now . . ."

"Let her go, William Wallace, let her go." Virgil, chewing on an elderberry whistle he had just made, stood at his shoulder: "What do you want with a live rabbit?"

William Wallace squatted down and set the rabbit on the ground but held it under his hand. It was a little, old, brown rabbit. It did not try to move. "See there?"

"Let her go."

"She can go if she wants to, but she don't want to."

Gently he lifted his hand. The round eye was shining at him sideways in the green gloom.

"Anybody can freeze a *rabbit,* that wants to," said Virgil. Suddenly he gave a far-reaching blast on the whistle, and the rabbit went in a streak. "Was you out catching cotton-tails, or was you out catching your wife?" he said, taking the turn to the open fields. "I come along to keep you on the track."

* * *

"Who'll we get, now?" They stood on top of a hill and William Wallace looked critically over the countryside. "Any of the Malones?"

"I was always scared of the Malones," said Virgil. "Too many *of* them."

"This is my day with the net, and they would have to watch out," said William Wallace. "I reckon some Malones, and the Doyles, will be enough. The six Doyles and their dogs, and you and me, and two little nigger boys is enough, with just a few Malones."

"That ought to be enough," said Virgil, "no matter what."

"I'll bring the Malones, and you bring the Doyles," said William Wallace, and they separated at the spring.

When William Wallace came back, with a string of Malones just showing behind him on the hilltop, he found Virgil with the two little Rippen boys waiting behind him, solemn little towheads. As soon as he walked up, Grady, the one in front, lifted his hand to signal silence and caution to his brother Brucie who began panting merrily and untrustworthily behind him.

Brucie bent readily under William Wallace's hand-pat, and gave him a dreamy look out of the tops of his round eyes, which were pure green-and-white like clover tops. William Wallace gave him a nickel. Grady hung his head; his white hair lay in a little tail in the nape of his neck.

"Let's let them come," said Virgil.

"Well, they can come then, but if we keep letting everybody come it is going to be too many," said William Wallace.

"They'll appreciate it, those little-old boys," said Virgil. Brucie held up at arm's length a long red thread with a bent pin tied on the end; and a look of helpless and intense interest gathered Grady's face like a drawstring—his eyes, one bright with a sty, shone pleadingly under his white bangs, and he snapped his jaw and tried to speak. . . . "Their papa was drowned in the Pearl River," said Virgil.

There was a shout from the gully.

"Here come all the Malones," cried William Wallace. "I asked four of them would they come, but the rest of the family invited themselves."

"Did you ever see a time when they didn't," said Virgil. "And yonder from the other direction comes the Doyles, still with biscuit crumbs on their cheeks, I bet, now it's nothing to do but eat as their mother said."

"If two little niggers would come along now, or one big nigger," said William Wallace. And the words were hardly out of his mouth when two little Negro boys came along, going somewhere, one behind the other, stepping high and gay in their overalls, as though they waded in honeydew to the waist.

"Come here, boys. What's your names?"

"Sam and Robbie Bell."

"Come along with us, we're going to drag the river."

"You hear that, Robbie Bell?" said Sam.

They smiled.

The Doyles came noiselessly, their dogs made all the fuss. The Malones, eight giants with great long black eyelashes, were already stamping the ground and pawing each other, ready to go. Everybody went up together to see Doc.

Old Doc owned the wide net. He had a house on top of the hill and he sat and looked out from a rocker on the front porch.

"Climb the hill and come in!" he began to intone across the valley. "Harvest's over . . . slipped up on everybody . . . cotton's picked, gone to the gin . . . hay cut . . . molasses made around here. . . . Big explosion's over, supervisors elected, some pleased, some not. . . . We're hearing talk of war!"

When they got closer, he was saying, "Many's been saved at revival, twenty-two last Sunday including a Doyle, ought to counted two. Hope they'll be a blessing to Dover community besides a shining star in Heaven. Now what?" he asked, for they had arrived and stood gathered in front of the steps.

"If nobody is using your wide net, could we use it?" asked William Wallace.

"You just used it a month ago," said Doc. "It ain't your turn."

Virgil jogged William Wallace's arm and cleared his throat. "This time is kind of special," he said. "We got reason to think William Wallace's wife Hazel is in the river, drowned."

"What reason have you got to think she's in the river drowned?" asked Doc. He took out his old pipe. "I'm asking the husband."

"Because she's not in the house," said William Wallace.

"Vanished?" and he knocked out the pipe.

"Plum vanished."

"Of course a thousand things could have happened to her," said Doc, and he lighted the pipe.

"Hand him up the letter, William Wallace," said Virgil. "We can't wait around till Doomsday for the net while Doc sits back thinkin'."

"I tore it up, right at the first," said William Wallace. "But I know it by heart. It said she was going to jump straight in the Pearl River and that I'd be sorry."

"Where do you come in, Virgil?" asked Doc.

"I was in the same place William Wallace sat on his neck in, all night, and done as much as he done, and come home the same time."

"You-all were out cuttin' up, so Lady Hazel has to jump in the river, is that it? Cause and effect? Anybody want to argue with me? Where do these others come in, Doyles, Malones, and what not?"

"Doc is the smartest man around," said William Wallace, turning to the solidly waiting Doyles, "but it sure takes time."

"These are the ones that's collected to drag the river for her," said Virgil.

"Of course I am not going on record to say so soon that *I* think she's drowned," Doc said, blowing out blue smoke.

"Do you think . . ." William Wallace mounted a step, and his hands both went into fists. "Do you think she was *carried off*?"

"Now that's the way to argue, see it from all sides," said Doc promptly. "But who by?"

Some Malone whistled, but not so you could tell which one.

"There's no booger around the Dover section that goes around carrying off young girls that's married," stated Doc.

"She was always scared of the Gypsies." William Wallace turned scarlet. "She'd sure turn her ring around on her finger if she passed one, and look in the other direction so they couldn't see she was pretty and carry her off. They come in the end of summer."

"Yes, there are the Gypsies, kidnappers since the world began. But was it to be you that would pay the grand ransom?" asked Doc. He pointed his finger. They all laughed then at how clever old Doc was and clapped William Wallace on the back. But that turned into a scuffle and they fell to the ground.

"Stop it, or you can't have the net," said Doc. "You're scaring my wife's chickens."

"It's time we was gone," said William Wallace.

The big barking dogs jumped to lean their front paws on the men's chests.

"My advice remains, Let well enough alone," said Doc. "Whatever this mysterious event will turn out to be, it has kept one woman from talking a while. However, Lady Hazel is the prettiest girl in Mississippi, you've never seen a prettier one and you never will. A golden-haired girl." He got to his feet with the nimbleness that was always his surprise, and said, "I'll come along with you."

* * *

The path they always followed was the Old Natchez Trace. It took them through the deep woods and led them out down below on the Pearl River, where they could begin dragging it upstream to a point near Dover. They walked in silence around William Wallace, not letting him carry anything, but the net dragged heavily and the buckets were full of clatter in a place so dim and still.

Once they went through a forest of cucumber trees and came up on a high ridge. Grady and Brucie who were running ahead all the way stopped in their tracks; a whistle had blown and far down and far away a long freight train was passing. It seemed like a little festival procession, moving with the slowness of ignorance or a dream, from distance to distance, the tiny pink and gray cars like secret boxes. Grady was counting the cars to himself, as if he could certainly see each one clearly, and Brucie watched his lips, hushed and cautious, the way he would watch a bird drinking. Tears suddenly came to Grady's eyes, but it could only be because a tiny man walked along the top of the train, walking and moving on top of the moving train.

They went down again and soon the smell of the river spread over the woods, cool and secret. Every step they took among the great walls of vines and among the passion-flowers started up a little life, a little flight.

"We're walking along in the changing-time," said Doc. "Any day now the change will come. It's going to turn from hot to cold, and we can kill the hog that's ripe and have fresh meat to eat. Come one of these nights and we can wander down here and tree a nice possum. Old Jack Frost will be pinching things up. Old Mr. Winter will be standing in the door. Hickory tree there will be yellow. Sweet-gum red, hickory yellow, dogwood red, sycamore yellow." He went along rapping the tree trunks with his knuckle. "Magnolia and live-oak never die. Remember that. Persimmons will all get fit to eat, and the nuts will be dropping like rain all through the woods here. And run, little quail, run, for we'll be after you too."

They went on and suddenly the woods opened upon light, and they had reached the river. Everyone stopped, but Doc talked on ahead as though nothing had happened. "Only today," he said, "today, in October sun, it's all gold—sky and tree and water. Everything just before it changes looks to be made of gold."

William Wallace looked down, as though he thought of Hazel with the shining eyes, sitting at home and looking straight before her, like a piece of pure gold, too precious to touch.

Below them the river was glimmering, narrow, soft, and skin-colored, and slowed nearly to stillness. The shining willow trees hung round them. The net that was being drawn out, so old and so long-used, it too looked golden, strung and tied with golden threads.

Standing still on the bank, all of a sudden William Wallace, on whose word they were waiting, spoke up in a voice of surprise. "What is the name of this river?"

They looked at him as if he were crazy not to know the name of the river he had fished in all his life. But a deep frown was on his forehead, as if he were compelled to wonder what people had come to call this river, or to think

293

there was a mystery in the name of a river they all knew so well, the same as if it were some great far torrent of waves that dashed through the mountains somewhere, and almost as if it were a river in some dream, for they could not give him the name of that.

"Everybody knows Pearl River is named the Pearl River," said Doc.

A bird note suddenly bold was like a stone thrown into the water to sound it.

"It's deep here," said Virgil, and jogged William Wallace. "Remember?"

William Wallace stood looking down at the river as if it were still a mystery to him. There under his feet which hung over the bank it was transparent and yellow like an old bottle lying in the sun, filling with light.

Doc clattered all his paraphernalia.

Then all of a sudden all the Malones scattered jumping and tumbling down the bank. They gave their loud shout. Little Brucie started after them, and looked back.

"Do you think she jumped?" Virgil asked William Wallace.

II

Since the net was so wide, when it was all stretched it reached from bank to bank of the Pearl River, and the weights would hold it all the way to the bottom. Jug-like sounds filled the air, splashes lifted in the sun, and the party began to move upstream. The Malones with great groans swam and pulled near the shore, the Doyles swam and pushed from behind with Virgil to tell them how to do it best; Grady and Brucie with his thread and pin trotted along the sandbars hauling buckets and lines. Sam and Robbie Bell, naked and bright, guided the old oarless rowboat that always drifted at the shore, and in it, sitting up tall with his hat on, was Doc—he went along without ever touching water and without ever taking his eyes off the net. William Wallace himself did everything but most of the time he was out of sight, swimming about under water or diving, and he had nothing to say any more.

The dogs chased up and down, in and out of the water, and in and out of the woods.

"Don't let her get too heavy, boys," Doc intoned regularly, every few minutes, "and she won't let nothing through."

"She won't let nothing through, she won't let nothing through," chanted Sam and Robbie Bell, one at his front and one at his back.

The sandbars were pink or violet drifts ahead. Where the light fell on the river, in a wandering from shore to shore, it was leaf-shaped spangles that trembled softly, while the dark of the river was calm. The willow trees leaned overhead under muscadine vines, and their trailing leaves hung like waterfalls in the morning air. The thing that seemed like silence must have been the endless cry of all the crickets and locusts in the world, rising and falling.

Every time William Wallace took hold of a big eel that slipped the net, the Malones all yelled, "Rassle with him, son!"

"Don't let her get too heavy, boys," said Doc.

"This is hard on catfish," William Wallace said once.

There were big and little fishes, dark and bright, that they caught, good ones and bad ones, the same old fish.

"This is more shoes than I ever saw got together in any store," said Virgil when they emptied the net to the bottom. "Get going!" he shouted in the next breath.

The little Rippens who had stayed ahead in the woods stayed ahead on the river. Brucie, leading them all, made small jumps and hops as he went, sometimes on one foot, sometimes on the other.

The winding river looked old sometimes, when it ran wrinkled and deep under high banks where the roots of trees hung down, and sometimes it seemed to be only a young creek, shining with the colors of wildflowers. Sometimes sandbars in the shapes of fishes lay nose to nose across, without the track of even a bird.

"Here comes some alligators," said Virgil. "Let's let them by."

They drew out on the shady side of the water, and three big alligators and four middle-sized ones went by, taking their own time.

"Look at their great big old teeth!" called a shrill voice. It was Grady making his only outcry, and the alligators were not showing their teeth at all.

"The better to eat folks with," said Doc from his boat, looking at him severely.

"Doc, you are bound to declare all you know," said Virgil. "Get going!"

When they started off again the first thing they caught in the net was the baby alligator.

"That's just what we wanted!" cried the Malones.

They set the little alligator down on a sandbar and

he squatted perfectly still; they could hardly tell when it was he started to move. They watched with set faces his incredible mechanics, while the dogs after one bark stood off in inquisitive humility, until he winked.

"He's ours!" shouted all the Malones. "We're taking him home with us!"

"He ain't nothing but a little-old baby," said William Wallace.

The Malones only scoffed, as if he might be only a baby but he looked like the oldest and worst lizard.

"What are you going to do with him?" asked Virgil.

"Keep him."

"I'd be more careful what I took out of this net," said Doc.

"Tie him up and throw him in the bucket," the Malones were saying to each other, while Doc was saying, "Don't come running to me and ask me what to do when he gets big."

They kept catching more and more fish, as if there was no end in sight.

"Look, a string of lady's beads," said Virgil. "Here, Sam and Robbie Bell."

Sam wore them around his head, with a knot over his forehead and loops around his ears, and Robbie Bell walked behind and stared at them.

In a shadowy place something white flew up. It was a heron, and it went away over the dark treetops. William Wallace followed it with his eyes and Brucie clapped his hands, but Virgil gave a sigh, as if he knew that when you go looking for what is lost, everything is a sign.

An eel slid out of the net.

"Rassle with him, son!" yelled the Malones. They swam like fiends.

"The Malones are in it for the fish," said Virgil.

It was about noon that there was a little rustle on the bank.

"Who is that yonder?" asked Virgil, and he pointed to a little undersized man with short legs and a little straw hat with a band around it, who was following along on the other side of the river.

"Never saw him and don't know his brother," said Doc.

Nobody had ever seen him before.

"Who invited you?" cried Virgil hotly. "Hi . . . !" and he made signs for the little undersized man to look at him, but he would not.

"Looks like a crazy man, from here," said the Malones.

"Just don't pay any attention to him and maybe he'll go away," advised Doc.

But Virgil had already swum across and was up on the other bank. He and the stranger could be seen exchanging a word apiece and then Virgil put out his hand the way he would pat a child and patted the stranger to the ground. The little man got up again just as quickly, lifted his shoulders, turned around, and walked away with his hat tilted over his eyes.

When Virgil came back he said, "Little-old man claimed he was harmless as a baby. I told him to just try horning in on this river and anything in it."

"What did he look like up close?" asked Doc.

"I wasn't studying how he looked," said Virgil. "But

I don't like anybody to come looking at me that I am not familiar with." And he shouted, "Get going!"

"Things are moving in too great a rush," said Doc.

Brucie darted ahead and ran looking into all the bushes, lifting up their branches and looking underneath.

"Not one of the Doyles has spoke a word," said Virgil.

"That's because they're not talkers," said Doc.

All day William Wallace kept diving to the bottom. Once he dived down and down into the dark water, where it was so still that nothing stirred, not even a fish, and so dark that it was no longer the muddy world of the upper river but the dark clear world of deepness, and he must have believed this was the deepest place in the whole Pearl River, and if she was not here she would not be anywhere. He was gone such a long time that the others stared hard at the surface of the water, through which the bubbles came from below. So far down and all alone, had he found Hazel? Had he suspected down there, like some secret, the real, the true trouble that Hazel had fallen into, about which words in a letter could not speak . . . how (who knew?) she had been filled to the brim with that elation that they all remembered, like their own secret, the elation that comes of great hopes and changes, sometimes simply of the harvest time, that comes with a little course of its own like a tune to run in the head, and there was nothing she could do about it—they knew—and so it had turned into this? It could be nothing but the old trouble that William Wallace was finding out, reaching and turning in the gloom of such depths.

"Look down yonder," said Grady softly to Brucie.

He pointed to the surface, where their reflections lay colorless and still side by side. He touched his brother gently as though to impress him.

"That's you and me," he said.

Brucie swayed precariously over the edge, and Grady caught him by the seat of his overalls. Brucie looked, but showed no recognition. Instead, he backed away, and seemed all at once unconcerned and spiritless, and pressed the nickel William Wallace had given him into his palm, rubbing it into his skin. Grady's inflamed eyes rested on the brown water. Without warning he saw something . . . perhaps the image in the river seemed to be his father, the drowned man—with arms open, eyes open, mouth open. . . . Grady stared and blinked, again something wrinkled up his face.

And when William Wallace came up it was in an agony from submersion, which seemed an agony of the blood and of the very heart, so woeful he looked. He was staring and glaring around in astonishment, as if a long time had gone by, away from the pale world where the brown light of the sun and the river and the little party watching him trembled before his eyes.

"What did you bring up?" somebody called—was it Virgil?

One of his hands was holding fast to a little green ribbon of plant, root and all. He was surprised, and let it go.

It was afternoon. The trees spread softly, the clouds hung wet and tinted. A buzzard turned a few slow wheels in the sky, and drifted upwards. The dogs promenaded the banks.

"It's time we ate fish," said Virgil.

On a wide sandbar on which seashells lay they dragged up the haul and built a fire.

Then for a long time among clouds of odors and smoke, all half-naked except Doc, they cooked and ate catfish. They ate until the Malones groaned and all the Doyles stretched out on their faces, though for long after, Sam and Robbie Bell sat up to their own little table on a cypress stump and ate on and on. Then they all were silent and still, and one by one fell asleep.

"There ain't a thing better than fish," muttered William Wallace. He lay stretched on his back in the glimmer and shade of trampled sand. His sunburned forehead and cheeks seemed to glow with fire. His eyelids fell. The shadow of a willow branch dipped and moved over him. "There is nothing in the world as good as . . . fish. The fish of Pearl River." Then slowly he smiled. He was asleep.

But it seemed almost at once that he was leaping up, and one by one up sat the others in their ring and looked at him, for it was impossible to stop and sleep by the river.

"You're feeling as good as you felt last night," said Virgil, setting his head on one side.

"The excursion is the same when you go looking for your sorrow as when you go looking for your joy," said Doc.

But William Wallace answered none of them anything, for he was leaping all over the place and all, over them and the feast and the bones of the feast, trampling the sand, up and down, and doing a dance so crazy that he would die next. He took a big catfish and hooked it to his belt buckle and went up and down so that they all hollered, and the tears of laughter streaming down his cheeks made him put his hand up, and the two days' growth of beard began to jump out, bright red.

But all of a sudden there was an even louder cry, something almost like a cheer, from everybody at once, and all pointed fingers moved from William Wallace to the river. In the center of three light-gold rings across the water was lifted first an old hoary head ("It has whiskers!" a voice cried) and then in an undulation loop after loop and hump after hump of a long dark body, until there were a dozen rings of ripples, one behind the other, stretching all across the river, like a necklace.

"The King of the Snakes!" cried all the Malones at once, in high tenor voices and leaning together.

"The King of the Snakes," intoned old Doc in his profound bass.

"He looked you in the eye."

William Wallace stared back at the King of the Snakes with all his might.

It was Brucie that darted forward, dangling his little thread with the pin tied to it, going toward the water.

"That's the King of the Snakes!" cried Grady, who always looked after him.

Then the snake went down.

The little boy stopped with one leg in the air, spun around on the other, and sank to the ground.

"Git up," Grady whispered. "It was just the King of the Snakes. He went off whistling. Git up. It wasn't a thing but the King of the Snakes."

Brucie's green eyes opened, his tongue darted out, and he sprang up; his feet were heavy, his head light, and he rose like a bubble coming to the surface.

Then thunder like a stone loosened and rolled down the bank.

They all stood unwilling on the sandbar, holding to the net. In the eastern sky were the familiar castles and the round towers to which they were used, gray, pink, and blue, growing darker and filling with thunder. Lightning flickered in the sun along their thick walls. But in the west the sun shone with such a violence that in an illumination like a long-prolonged glare of lightning the heavens looked black and white; all color left the world, the goldenness of everything was like a memory, and only heat, a kind of glamor and oppression, lay on their heads. The thick heavy trees on the other side of the river were brushed with mile-long streaks of silver, and a wind touched each man on the forehead. At the same time there was a long roll of thunder that began behind them, came up and down mountains and valleys of air, passed over their heads, and left them listening still. With a small, near noise a mockingbird followed it, the little white bars of its body flashing over the willow trees.

"We are here for a storm now," Virgil said. "We will have to stay till it's over."

They retreated a little, and hard drops fell in the leathery leaves at their shoulders and about their heads.

"Magnolia's the loudest tree there is in a storm," said Doc.

Then the light changed the water, until all about them

the woods in the rising wind seemed to grow taller and blow inward together and suddenly turn dark. The rain struck heavily. A huge tail seemed to lash through the air and the river broke in a wound of silver. In silence the party crouched and stooped beside the trunk of the great tree, which in the push of the storm rose full of a fragrance and unyielding weight. Where they all stared, past their tree, was another tree, and beyond that another and another, all the way down the bank of the river, all towering and darkened in the storm.

"The outside world is full of endurance," said Doc. "Full of endurance."

Robbie Bell and Sam squatted down low and embraced each other from the start.

"Runs in our family to get struck by lightnin'," said Robbie Bell. "Lightnin' drawed a pitchfork right on our grandpappy's cheek, stayed till he died. Pappy got struck by some bolts of lightnin' and was dead three days, dead as that-there axe."

There was a succession of glares and crashes.

"This'n's goin' to be either me or you," said Sam. "Here come a little bug. If he go to the left, be me, and to the right, be you."

But at the next flare a big tree on the hill seemed to turn into fire before their eyes, every branch, twig, and leaf, and a purple cloud hung over it.

"Did you hear that crack?" asked Robbie Bell. "That were its bones."

"Why do you little niggers talk so much!" said Doc. "Nobody's profiting by this information."

"We always talks this much," said Sam, "but now everybody so quiet, they hears us."

The great tree, split and on fire, fell roaring to earth. Just at its moment of falling, a tree like it on the opposite bank split wide open and fell in two parts.

"Hope they ain't goin' to be no balls of fire come rollin' over the water and fry all the fishes with they scales on," said Robbie Bell.

The water in the river had turned purple and was filled with sudden currents and whirlpools. The little willow trees bent almost to its surface, bowing one after another down the bank and almost breaking under the storm. A great curtain of wet leaves was borne along before a blast of wind, and every human being was covered.

"Now us got scales," wailed Sam. "Us is the fishes."

"Hush up, little-old colored children," said Virgil. "This isn't the way to act when somebody takes you out to drag a river."

"Poor lady's-ghost, I bet it is scareder than us," said Sam.

"All I hoping is, us don't find her!" screamed Robbie Bell.

William Wallace bent down and knocked their heads together. After that they clung silently in each other's arms, the two black heads resting, with wind-filled cheeks and tight-closed eyes, one upon the other until the storm was over.

"Right over yonder is Dover," said Virgil. "We've come all the way. William Wallace, you have walked on a sharp rock and cut your foot open."

III

In Dover it had rained, and the town looked somehow like new. The wavy heat of late afternoon came down from the watertank and fell over everything like shiny mosquito-netting. At the wide place where the road was paved and patched with tar, it seemed newly embedded with Coca-Cola tops. The old circus posters on the store were nearly gone, only bits, the snowflakes of white horses, clinging to its side. Morning-glory vines started almost visibly to grow over the roofs and cling round the ties of the railroad track, where bluejays lighted on the rails, and umbrella chinaberry trees hung heavily over the whole town, dripping intermittently upon the tin roofs.

Each with his counted fish on a string, the members of the river-dragging party walked through the town. They went toward the town well, and there was Hazel's mother's house, but no sign of her yet coming out. They all drank a dipper of the water, and still there was not a soul on the street. Even the bench in front of the store was empty, except for a little corn-shuck doll.

But something told them somebody had come, for after one moment people began to look out of the store and out of the post office. All the bird dogs woke up to see the Doyle dogs and such a large number of men and boys materialize suddenly with such a big catch of fish, and they ran out barking. The Doyle dogs joyously barked back. The bluejays flashed up and screeched above the town, whipping through their tunnels in the chinaberry

306

trees. In the café a nickel clattered inside a music box and a love song began to play. The whole town of Dover began to throb in its wood and tin, like an old tired heart, when the men walked through once more, coming around again and going down the street carrying the fish, so drenched, exhausted, and muddy that no one could help but admire them.

William Wallace walked through the town as though he did not see anybody or hear anything. Yet he carried his great string of fish held high where it could be seen by all. Virgil came next, imitating William Wallace exactly, then the modest Doyles crowded by the Malones, who were holding up their alligator, tossing it in the air, even, like a father tossing his child. Following behind and pointing authoritatively at the ones in front strolled Doc, with Sam and Robbie Bell still chanting in his wake. In and out of the whole little line Grady and Brucie jerked about. Grady, with his head ducked, and stiff as a rod, walked with a springy limp; it made him look forever angry and unapproachable. Under his breath he was whispering, "Sty, sty, git out of my eye, and git on somebody passin' by." He traveled on with narrowed shoulders, and kept his eye unerringly upon his little brother, wary and at the same time proud, as though he held a flying June-bug on a string. Brucie, making a twanging noise with his lips, had shot forth again, and he was darting rapidly everywhere at once, delighted and tantalized, running in circles around William Wallace, pointing to his fish. A frown of pleasure like the print of a bird's foot was stamped between his faint brows, and he trotted in some unknown realm of delight.

"Did you ever see so many fish?" said the people in Dover.

"How much are your fish, mister?"

"Would you sell your fish?"

"Is that all the fish in Pearl River?"

"How much you sell them all for? Everybody's?"

"Three dollars," said William Wallace suddenly, and loud.

The Malones were upon him and shouting, but it was too late.

And just as William Wallace was taking the money in his hand, Hazel's mother walked solidly out of her front door and saw it.

"You can't head her mother off," said Virgil. "Here she comes in full bloom."

But William Wallace turned his back on her, that was all, and on everybody, for that matter, and that was the breaking-up of the party.

Just as the sun went down, Doc climbed his back steps, sat in his chair on the back porch where he sat in the evenings, and lighted his pipe. William Wallace hung out the net and came back and Virgil was waiting for him, so they could say good evening to Doc.

"All in all," said Doc, when they came up, "I've never been on a better river-dragging, or seen better behavior. If it took catching catfish to move the Rock of Gibraltar, I believe this outfit could move it."

"Well, we didn't catch Hazel," said Virgil.

"What did you say?" asked Doc.

"He don't really pay attention," said Virgil. "I said, 'We didn't catch Hazel.' "

"Who says Hazel was to be caught?" asked Doc. "She wasn't in there. Girls don't like the water—remember that. Girls don't just haul off and go jumping in the river to get back at their husbands. They got other ways."

"Didn't you ever think she was in there?" asked William Wallace. "The whole time?"

"Nary once," said Doc.

"He's just smart," said Virgil, putting his hand on William Wallace's arm. "It's only because we didn't find her that he wasn't looking for her."

"I'm beholden to you for the net, anyway," said William Wallace.

"You're welcome to borry it again," said Doc.

On the way home Virgil kept saying, "Calm down, calm down, William Wallace."

"If he wasn't such an old skinny man I'd have wrung his neck for him," said William Wallace. "He had no business coming."

"He's too big for his britches," said Virgil. "Don't nobody know everything. And just because it's his net. Why does it have to be his net?"

"If it wasn't for being polite to old men, I'd have skinned him alive," said William Wallace.

"I guess he don't really know nothing about wives at all, his wife's so deaf," said Virgil.

"He don't know Hazel," said William Wallace. "I'm

the only man alive knows Hazel: would she jump in the river or not, and I say she would. She jumped in because I was sitting on the back of my neck in a ditch singing, and that's just what she ought to done. Doc ain't got no right to say one word about it."

"Calm down, calm down, William Wallace," said Virgil.

"If it had been you that talked like that, I'd have broke every bone in your body," said William Wallace. "Just let you talk like that. You're my age and size."

"But I ain't going to talk like that," said Virgil. "What have I done the whole time but keep this river-dragging going straight and running even, without no hitches? You couldn't have drug the river a foot without me."

"What are you talking about! Without who!" cried William Wallace. "This wasn't your river-dragging! It wasn't your wife!" He jumped on Virgil and they began to fight.

"Let me up." Virgil was breathing heavily.

"Say it was my wife. Say it was my river-dragging."

"Yours!" Virgil was on the ground with William Wallace's hand putting dirt in his mouth.

"Say it was my net."

"Your net!"

"Get up then."

They walked along getting their breath, and smelling the honeysuckle in the evening. On a hill William Wallace looked down, and at the same time there went drifting by the sweet sounds of music outdoors. They were having the Sacred Harp Sing on the grounds of an old white church glimmering there at the crossroads, far below. He stared away as if he saw it minutely, as if he could see a lady in

310

white take a flowered cover off the organ, which was set on a little slant in the shade, dust the keys, and start to pump and play. . . . He smiled faintly, as he would at his mother, and at Hazel, and at the singing women in his life, now all one young girl standing up to sing under the trees the oldest and longest ballads there were.

Virgil told him good night and went into his own house and the door shut on him.

When he got to his own house, William Wallace saw to his surprise that it had not rained at all. But there, curved over the roof, was something he had never seen before as long as he could remember, a rainbow at night. In the light of the moon, which had risen again, it looked small and of gauzy material, like a lady's summer dress, a faint veil through which the stars showed.

He went up on the porch and in at the door, and all exhausted he had walked through the front room and through the kitchen when he heard his name called. After a moment, he smiled, as if no matter what he might have hoped for in his wildest heart, it was better than that to hear his name called out in the house. The voice came out of the bedroom.

"What do you want?" he yelled, standing stock-still.

Then she opened the bedroom door with the old complaining creak, and there she stood. She was not changed a bit.

"How do you feel?" he said.

"I feel pretty good. Not too good," Hazel said, looking mysterious.

"I cut my foot," said William Wallace, taking his shoe off so she could see the blood.

"How in the world did you do that?" she cried, with a step back.

"Dragging the river. But it don't hurt any longer."

"You ought to have been more careful," she said. "Supper's ready and I wondered if you would ever come home, or if it would be last night all over again. Go and make yourself fit to be seen," she said, and ran away from him.

After supper they sat on the front steps a while.

"Where were you this morning when I came in?" asked William Wallace when they were ready to go in the house.

"I was hiding," she said. "I was still writing on the letter. And then you tore it up."

"Did you watch me when I was reading it?"

"Yes, and you could have put out your hand and touched me, I was so close."

But he bit his lip, and gave her a little tap and slap, and then turned her up and spanked her.

"Do you think you will do it again?" he asked.

"I'll tell my mother on you for this!"

"Will you do it again?"

"No!" she cried.

"Then pick yourself up off my knee."

It was just as if he had chased her and captured her again. She lay smiling in the crook of his arm. It was the same as any other chase in the end.

"I will do it again if I get ready," she said. "Next time will be different, too."

Then she was ready to go in, and rose up and looked out from the top step, out across their yard where the

China tree was and beyond, into the dark fields where the lightning-bugs flickered away. He climbed to his feet too and stood beside her, with the frown on his face, trying to look where she looked. And after a few minutes she took him by the hand and led him into the house, smiling as if she were smiling down on him.

A STILL
MOMENT

———————◆———————

LORENZO DOW rode the Old Natchez Trace at top speed
upon a race horse, and the cry of the itinerant Man of
God, "I must have souls! And souls I must have!" rang
in his own windy ears. He rode as if never to stop, toward
his night's appointment.

It was the hour of sunset. All the souls that he had
saved and all those he had not took dusky shapes in the
mist that hung between the high banks, and seemed by
their great number and density to block his way, and
showed no signs of melting or changing back into mist,
so that he feared his passage was to be difficult forever.
The poor souls that were not saved were darker and more
pitiful than those that were, and still there was not any of
the radiance he would have hoped to see in such a con-
gregation.

"Light up, in God's name!" he called, in the pain of
his disappointment.

Then a whole swarm of fireflies instantly flickered all
around him, up and down, back and forth, first one golden
light and then another, flashing without any of the weari-

ness that had held back the souls. These were the signs sent from God that he had not seen the accumulated radiance of saved souls because he was not able, and that his eyes were more able to see the fire flies of the Lord than His blessed souls.

"Lord, give me the strength to see the angels when I am in Paradise," he said. "Do not let my eyes remain in this failing proportion to my loving heart always."

He gasped and held on. It was that day's complexity of horse-trading that had left him in the end with a Spanish race horse for which he was bound to send money in November from Georgia. Riding faster on the beast and still faster until he felt as if he were flying he sent thoughts of love with matching speed to his wife Peggy in Massachusetts. He found it effortless to love at a distance. He could look at the flowering trees and love Peggy in fullness, just as he could see his visions and love God. And Peggy, to whom he had not spoken until he could speak fateful words ("Would she accept of such an object as him?"), Peggy, the bride, with whom he had spent a few hours of time, showing of herself a small round handwriting, declared all in one letter, her first, that she felt the same as he, and that the fear was never of separation, but only of death.

Lorenzo well knew that it was Death that opened underfoot, that rippled by at night, that was the silence the birds did their singing in. He was close to death, closer than any animal or bird. On the back of one horse after another, winding them all, he was always riding toward it or away from it, and the Lord sent him directions with protection in His mind.

Just then he rode into a thicket of Indians taking aim with their new guns. One stepped out and took the horse by the bridle, it stopped at a touch, and the rest made a closing circle. The guns pointed.

"Incline!" The inner voice spoke sternly and with its customary lightning-quickness.

Lorenzo inclined all the way forward and put his head to the horse's silky mane, his body to its body, until a bullet meant for him would endanger the horse and make his death of no value. Prone he rode out through the circle of Indians, his obedience to the voice leaving him almost fearless, almost careless with joy.

But as he straightened and pressed ahead, care caught up with him again. Turning half-beast and half-divine, dividing himself like a heathen Centaur, he had escaped his death once more. But was it to be always by some metamorphosis of himself that he escaped, some humiliation of his faith, some admission to strength and argumentation and not frailty? Each time when he acted so it was at the command of an instinct that he took at once as the word of an angel, until too late, when he knew it was the word of the devil. He had roared like a tiger at Indians, he had submerged himself in water blowing the savage bubbles of the alligator, and they skirted him by. He had prostrated himself to appear dead, and deceived bears. But all the time God would have protected him in His own way, less hurried, more divine.

Even now he saw a serpent crossing the Trace, giving out knowing glances.

He cried, "I know you now!", and the serpent gave

him one look out of which all the fire had been taken, and went away in two darts into the tangle.

He rode on, all expectation, and the voices in the throats of the wild beasts went, almost without his noticing when, into words. "Praise God," they said. "Deliver us from one another." Birds especially sang of divine love which was the one ceaseless protection. "Peace, in peace," were their words so many times when they spoke from the briars, in a courteous sort of inflection, and he turned his countenance toward all perched creatures with a benevolence striving to match their own.

He rode on past the little intersecting trails, letting himself be guided by voices and by lights. It was battle-sounds he heard most, sending him on, but sometimes ocean sounds, that long beat of waves that would make his heart pound and retreat as heavily as they, and he despaired again in his failure in Ireland when he took a voyage and persuaded with the Catholics with his back against the door, and then ran away to their cries of "Mind the white hat!" But when he heard singing it was not the militant and sharp sound of Wesley's hymns, but a soft, tireless and tender air that had no beginning and no end, and the softness of distance, and he had pleaded with the Lord to find out if all this meant that it was wicked, but no answer had come.

Soon night would descend, and a camp-meeting ground ahead would fill with its sinners like the sky with its stars. How he hungered for them! He looked in prescience with a longing of love over the throng that waited while the flames of the torches threw change, change,

317

change over their faces. How could he bring them enough,
if it were not divine love and sufficient warning of all that
could threaten them? He rode on faster. He was a filler of
appointments, and he filled more and more, until his journeys up and down creation were nothing but a shuttle,
driving back and forth upon the rich expanse of his vision.
He was homeless by his own choice, he must be everywhere at some time, and somewhere soon. There
hastening in the wilderness on his flying horse he gave
the night's torch-lit crowd a premature benediction, he
could not wait. He spread his arms out, one at a time for
safety, and he wished, when they would all be gathered
in by his tin horn blasts and the inspired words would go
out over their heads, to brood above the entire and pas-
sionate life of the wide world, to become its rightful part.

He peered ahead. "Inhabitants of Time! The wilderness is your souls on earth!" he shouted ahead into the
treetops. "Look about you, if you would view the condi-
tions of your spirit, put here by the good Lord to show
you and afright you. These wild places and these trails of
awesome loneliness lie nowhere, nowhere, but in your
heart."

A dark man, who was James Murrell the outlaw, rode his
horse out of a cane brake and began going along beside
Lorenzo without looking at him. He had the alternately
proud and aggrieved look of a man believing himself to
be an instrument in the hands of a power, and when he
was young he said at once to strangers that he was being
used by Evil, or sometimes he stopped a traveler by shouting, "Stop! I'm the Devil!" He rode along now talking

and drawing out his talk, by some deep control of the voice gradually slowing the speed of Lorenzo's horse down until both the horses were softly trotting. He would have wondered that nothing he said was heard, not knowing that Lorenzo listened only to voices of whose heavenly origin he was more certain.

Murrell riding along with his victim-to-be, Murrell riding, was Murrell talking. He told away at his long tales, with always a distance and a long length of time flowing through them, and all centered about a silent man. In each the silent man would have done a piece of evil, a robbery or a murder, in a place of long ago, and it was all made for the revelation in the end that the silent man was Murrell himself, and the long story had happened yesterday, and the place *here*—the Natchez Trace. It would only take one dawning look for the victim to see that all of this was another story and he himself had listened his way into it, and that he too was about to recede in time (to where the dread was forgotten) for some listener and to live for a listener in the long ago. Destroy the present!—that must have been the first thing that was whispered in Murrell's heart—the living moment and the man that lives in it must die before you can go on. It was his habit to bring the journey—which might even take days—to a close with a kind of ceremony. Turning his face at last into the face of the victim, for he had never seen him before now, he would tower up with the sudden height of a man no longer the tale teller but the speechless protagonist, silent at last, one degree nearer the hero. Then he would murder the man.

But it would always start over. This man going forward was going backward with talk. He saw nothing, observed no world at all. The two ends of his journey pulled at him always and held him in a nowhere, half asleep, smiling and witty, dangling his predicament. He was a murderer whose final stroke was over-long post-poned, who had to bring himself through the greatest tedium to act, as if the whole wilderness, where he was born, were his impediment. But behind him and before him he kept in sight a victim, he saw a man fixed and stayed at the point of death—no matter how the man's eyes denied it, a victim, hands spreading to reach as if for the first time for life. Contempt! That is what Murrell gave that man.

Lorenzo might have understood, if he had not been in haste, that Murrell in laying hold of a man meant to solve his mystery of being. It was as if other men, all but himself, would lighten their hold on the secret, upon assault, and let it fly free at death. In his violence he was only treating of enigma. The violence shook his own body first, like a force gathering, and now he turned in the sad-dle.

Lorenzo's despair had to be kindled as well as his ecstasy, and could not come without that kindling. Before the awe-filled moment when the faces were turned up under the flares, as though an angel hand tipped their chins, he had no way of telling whether he would enter the sermon by sorrow or by joy. But at this moment the face of Murrell was turned toward him, turning at last, all soli-tary, in its full, and Lorenzo would have seized the man at once by his black coat and shaken him like prey for a lost soul, so instantly was he certain that the false fire was in his heart instead of the true fire. But Murrell, quick when he was quick, had put his own hand out, a restraining hand, and laid it on the wavelike flesh of the Spanish race horse, which quivered and shuddered at the touch.

They had come to a great live-oak tree at the edge of a low marsh-land. The burning sun hung low, like a head lowered on folded arms, and over the long reaches of violet trees the evening seemed still with thought. Lorenzo knew the place from having seen it among many in dreams, and he stopped readily and willingly. He drew rein, and Murrell drew rein, he dismounted and Murrell dismounted, he took a step, and Murrell was there too; and Lorenzo was not surprised at the closeness, how Murrell in his long dark coat and over it his dark face darkening still, stood beside him like a brother seeking light.

But in that moment instead of two men coming to stop by the great forked tree, there were three.

From far away, a student, Audubon, had been approaching lightly on the wilderness floor, disturbing nothing in his lightness. The long day of beauty had led him this certain distance. A flock of purple finches that he tried for the first moment to count went over his head. He made a spelling of the soft *pet* of the ivory-billed woodpecker. He told himself always: remember.

Coming upon the Trace, he looked at the high cedars, azure and still as distant smoke overhead, with their silver roots trailing down on either side like the veins of deepness in this place, and he noted some fact to his memory—this earth that wears but will not crumble or slide or turn to dust, they say it exists in one other spot in the world, Egypt—and then forgot it. He walked quietly. All life used this Trace, and he liked to see the animals move along it in direct, oblivious journeys, for they had begun it and made it, the buffalo and deer and the small running creatures before man ever knew where he wanted to go, and birds flew a great mirrored course above. Walking beneath them Audubon remembered how in the cities he had seen these very birds in his imagination, calling them up whenever he wished, even in the hard and glittering outer parlors where if an artist were humble enough to wait, some idle hand held up promised money. He walked lightly and he went as carefully as he had started at two that morning, crayon and paper, a gun, and a small bottle of spirits disposed about his body. *(Note: "The mocking birds so gentle that they would scarcely move out of the way.")* He looked with care; great abundance had ceased to startle him, and he could see things one by one. In Natchez they had told him of many strange and marvelous birds that were to be found here. Their descriptions had been exact, complete, and wildly varying, and he took them for inventions and believed that like all the worldly things that came out of Natchez, they would be disposed of and shamed by any man's excursion into the reality of Nature.

In the valley he appeared under the tree, a sure man, very sure and tender, as if the touch of all the earth rubbed upon him and the stains of the flowery swamp had made him so.

Lorenzo welcomed him and turned fond eyes upon him. To transmute a man into an angel was the hope that drove him all over the world and never let him flinch from a meeting or withhold good-byes for long. This hope insistently divided his life into only two parts, journey and rest. There could be no night and day and love and despair and longing and satisfaction to make partitions in the single ecstasy of this alternation. All things were speech.

"God created the world," said Lorenzo, "and it exists to give testimony. Life is the tongue: speak."

But instead of speech there happened a moment of deepest silence.

Audubon said nothing because he had gone without speaking a word for days. He did not regard his thoughts for the birds and animals as susceptible, in their first change, to words. His long playing on the flute was not in its origin a talking to himself. Rather than speak to order or describe, he would always draw a deer with a stroke across it to communicate his need of venison to an Indian. He had only found words when he discovered that there is much otherwise lost that can be noted down each item in its own day, and he wrote often now in a journal, not wanting anything to be lost the way it had been, all the past, and he would write about a day, "Only sorry that the Sun Sets."

Murrell, his cheated hand hiding the gun, could only continue to smile at Lorenzo, but he remembered in malice that he had disguised himself once as an Evangelist, and his final words to this victim would have been, "One of my disguises was what you are."

Then in Murrell Audubon saw what he thought of as "acquired sorrow"—that cumbrousness and darkness from which the naked Indian, coming just as he was made from God's hand, was so lightly free. He noted the eyes—the dark kind that loved to look through chinks, and saw neither closeness nor distance, light nor shade, wonder nor familiarity. They were narrowed to contract the heart, narrowed to make an averting plan. Audubon knew the finest-drawn tendons of the body and the working of their power, for he had touched them, and he supposed then that in man the enlargement of the eye to see started a motion in the hands to make or do, and that the narrowing of the eye stopped the hand and contracted the heart. Now Murrell's eyes followed an ant on a blade of grass, up the blade and down, many times in the single moment. Audubon had examined the Cave-In Rock where one robber had lived his hiding life, and the air in the cave was the cavelike air that enclosed this man, the same odor, flinty and dark. O secret life, he thought—is it true that the secret is withdrawn from the true disclosure, that man is a cave man, and that the openness I see, the ways through forests, the rivers brimming light, the wide arches where the birds fly, are dreams of freedom? If my origin is withheld from me, is my end to be unknown too? Is the radiance I see closed into an interval between two darks, or can it not illuminate them both and discover at last, though it cannot be spoken, what was thought hidden and lost?

In that quiet moment a solitary snowy heron flew down not far away and began to feed beside the marsh water.

At the single streak of flight, the ears of the race horse lifted, and the eyes of both horses filled with the soft lights of sunset, which in the next instant were reflected in the eyes of the men too as they all looked into the west toward the heron, and all eyes seemed infused with a sort of wildness.

Lorenzo gave the bird a triumphant look, such as a man may bestow upon his own vision, and thought, Nearness is near, lighted in a marsh-land, feeding at sunset. Praise God, His love has come visible.

Murrell, in suspicion pursuing all glances, blinking into a haze, saw only whiteness ensconced in darkness, as if it were a little luminous shell that drew in and held the eyesight. When he shaded his eyes, the brand "H.T." on his thumb thrust itself into his own vision, and he looked at the bird with the whole plan of the Mystic Rebellion darting from him as if in rays of the bright reflected light, and he stood looking proudly, leader as he was bound to become of the slaves, the brigands and outcasts of the entire Natchez country, with plans, dates, maps burning like a brand into his brain, and he saw himself proudly in a moment of prophecy going down rank after rank of successively bowing slaves to unroll and flaunt an awesome great picture of the Devil colored on a banner.

Audubon's eyes embraced the object in the distance and he could see it as carefully as if he held it in his hand. It was a snowy heron alone out of its flock. He watched it steadily, in his care noting the exact inevitable things. When it feeds it muddies the water with its foot. . . . It was as if each detail about the heron happened slowly in time, and only once. He felt again the old stab of wonder—what structure of life bridged the reptile's scale and the heron's feather? That knowledge too had been lost. He watched without moving. The bird was defenseless in the world except for the intensity of its life, and he wondered, how can heat of blood and speed of heart defend it? Then he thought, as always as if it were new and unbelievable, it has nothing in space or time to prevent its flight. And he waited, knowing that some birds will wait for a sense of their presence to travel to men before they will fly away from them.

Fixed in its pure white profile it stood in the precipitous moment, a plumicorn on its head, its breeding dress extended in rays, eating steadily the little water creatures. There was a little space between each man and the others, where they stood overwhelmed. No one could say the three had ever met, or that this moment of intersection had ever come in their lives, or its promise fulfilled. But before them the white heron rested in the grasses with the evening all around it, lighter and more serene than the evening, flight closed in its body, the circuit of its beauty closed, a bird seen and a bird still, its motion calm as if it were offered: Take my flight. . . .

What each of them had wanted was simply *all*. To save all souls, to destroy all men, to see and to record all life that filled this world—all, all—but now a single frail yearning seemed to go out of the three of them for a moment and to stretch toward this one snowy, shy bird in the marshes. It was as if three whirlwinds had drawn together at some center, to find there feeding in peace a snowy heron. Its own slow spiral of flight could lake it away in its own time, but for a little it held them still, it laid quiet over them, and they stood for a moment unburdened. . . .

Murrell wore no mask, for his face was that, a face
that was aware while he was somnolent, a face that
watched for him, and listened for him, alert and nearly
brutal, the guard of a planner. He was quick without that
he might be slow within, he staved off time, he wandered
and plotted, and yet his whole desire mounted in him
toward the end (was this the end—the sight of a bird feeding at dusk?), toward the instant of confession. His
incessant deeds were thick in his heart now, and flinging
himself to the ground he thought wearily, when all these
trees are cut down, and the Trace lost, then my
Conspiracy that is yet to spread itself will be disclosed,
and all the stone-loaded bodies of murdered men will be
pulled up, and all everywhere will know poor Murrell.
His look pressed upon Lorenzo, who stared upward, and
Audubon, who was taking out his gun, and his eyes
squinted up to them in pleading, as if to say, "How soon
may I speak, and how soon will you pity me?" Then he
looked back to the bird, and he thought if it would look
at him a dread penetration would fill and gratify his heart.

Audubon in each act of life was aware of the mysterious origin he half-concealed and half-sought for. People
along the way asked him in their kindness or their rudeness
if it were true, that he was born a prince, and was the Lost
Dauphin, and some said it was his secret, and some said
that that was what he wished to find out before he died.
But if it was his identity that he wished to discover, or if
it was what a man had to seize beyond that, the way for
him was by endless examination, by the care for every
bird that flew in his path and every serpent that shone
underfoot. Not one was enough; he looked deeper and

deeper, on and on, as if for a particular beast or some legendary bird. Some men's eyes persisted in looking outward when they opened to look inward, and to their delight, there outflung was the astonishing world under the sky. When a man at last brought himself to face some mirror-surface he still saw the world looking back at him, and if he continued to look, to look closer and closer, what then? The gaze that looks outward must be trained without rest, to be indomitable. It must see as slowly as Murrell's ant in the grass, as exhaustively as Lorenzo's angel of God, and then, Audubon dreamed, with his mind going to his pointed brush, it must see like this, and he tightened his hand on the trigger of the gun and pulled it, and his eyes went closed. In memory the heron was all its solitude, its total beauty. All its whiteness could be seen from all sides at once, its pure feathers were as if counted and known and their array one upon the other would never be lost. But it was not from that memory that he could paint.

His opening eyes met Lorenzo's, close and flashing, and it was on seeing horror deep in them, like fires in abysses, that he recognized it for the first time. He had never seen horror in its purity and clarity until now, in bright blue eyes. He went and picked up the bird. He had thought it to be a female, just as one sees the moon as female; and so it was. He put it in his bag, and started away. But Lorenzo had already gone on, leaning a-tilt on the horse which went slowly.

Murrell was left behind, but he was proud of the dispersal, as if he had done it, as if he had always known that three men in simply being together and doing a thing can, by their obstinacy, take the pride out of one another.

Each must go away alone, each send the others away alone. He himself had purposely kept to the wildest country in the world, and would have sought it out, the loneliest road. He looked about with satisfaction, and hid. Travelers were forever innocent, he believed: that was his faith. He lay in wait; his faith was in innocence and his knowledge was of ruin; and had these things been shaken? Now, what could possibly be outside his grasp? Churning all about him like a cloud about the sun was the great folding descent of his thought. Plans of deeds made his thoughts, and they rolled and mingled about his ears as if he heard a dark voice that rose up to overcome the wilderness voice, or was one with it. The night would soon come; and he had gone through the day.

Audubon, splattered and wet, turned back into the wilderness with the heron warm under his hand, his head still light in a kind of trance. It was undeniable, on some Sunday mornings, when he turned over and over his drawings they seemed beautiful to him, through what was dramatic in the conflict of life, or what was exact. What he would draw, and what he had seen, became for a moment one to him then. Yet soon enough, and it seemed to come in that same moment, like Lorenzo's horror and the gun's firing, he knew that even the sight of the heron which surely he alone had appreciated, had not been all his belonging, and that never could any vision, even any simple sight, belong to him or to any man. He knew that the best he could make would be, after it was apart from his hand, a dead thing and not a live thing, never the essence, only a sum of parts; and that it would always meet with a stranger's sight, and never be one with the beauty in any other man's head in the world. As he had seen the bird most purely at its moment of death, in some fatal way, in his care for looking outward, he saw his long labor most revealingly at the point where it met its limit. Still carefully, for he was trained to see well in the dark, he walked on into the deeper woods, noting all sights, all sounds, and was gentler than they as he went.

In the woods that echoed yet in his ears, Lorenzo riding slowly looked back. The hair rose on his head and his hands began to shake with cold, and suddenly it seemed to him that God Himself, just now, thought of the Idea of Separateness. For surely He had never thought of it before, when the little white heron was flying down to feed. He could understand God's giving Separateness first and then giving Love to follow and heal in its wonder; but God had reversed this, and given Love first and then Separateness, as though it did not matter to Him which came first. Perhaps it was that God never counted the moments of Time; Lorenzo did that, among his tasks of love. Time did not occur to God. Therefore—did He even know of it? How to explain Time and Separateness back to God, Who had never thought of them, Who could let the whole world come to grief in a scattering moment?

Lorenzo brought his cold hands together in a clasp and stared through the distance at the place where the bird had been as if he saw it still; as if nothing could really take away what had happened to him, the beautiful little vision of the feeding bird. Its beauty had been greater than he could account for. The sweat of rapture poured down from his forehead, and then he shouted into the marshes.

"Tempter!"

He whirled forward in the saddle and began to hurry the horse to its high speed. His camp ground was far away still, though even now they must be lighting the torches and gathering in the multitudes, so that at the appointed time he would duly appear in their midst, to deliver his address on the subject of "In that day when all hearts shall be disclosed."

Then the sun dropped below the trees, and the new moon, slender and white, hung shyly in the west.

ASPHODEL

———◆———

IT WAS A CLOUDLESS DAY—a round hill where the warm winds blew. It was noon, and without a shadow the line of columns rose in perfect erectness from the green vines. There was a quiver of birdsong. A little company of three women stood fixed on the slope before the ruin, holding wicker baskets between them. They were not young. There were identical looks of fresh mourning on their faces. A wind blew down from the columns, and the white dimity fluttered about their elbows.

"Look—"

"Asphodel."

It was a golden ruin: six Doric columns, with the entablature unbroken over the first two, full-facing the approach. The sky was pure, transparent, and round like a shell over this hill.

The three women drew nearer, in postures that were still from ministrations, and that came from a mourning procession.

"This is Asphodel," they repeated, looking modestly upward to the frieze of maidens that was saturated with sunlight and seemed to fill with color, and before which the branch of a leafy tree was trembling.

332

"If there's one place in the solid world where Miss Sabina would never look for us, it's Asphodel," they said. "She forbade it," they said virtuously. "She would never tolerate us to come, to Mr. Don McInnis's Asphodel, or even to say his name."

"Her funeral was yesterday, and we've cried our eyes dry," said one of the three. "And as for saying Mr. Don's name out loud, of course he is dead too." And they looked from one to the other—Cora, Phoebe, and Irene, all old maids, in hanging summer cottons, carrying picnic baskets. The way was so narrow they had come in a buggy, then walked.

There was not a shadow. It was high noon. A honey locust bent over their heads, sounding with the bees that kept at its bee-like flowers.

"This is the kind of day I could just *eat!*" cried Cora ardently.

They were another step forward. A little stream spread from rock to rock and over the approach. Then their shoes were off, and their narrow maiden feet hung trembling in the rippling water. The wind had shaken loose their gray and scanty hair. They smiled at one another.

"I used to be scared of little glades," said Phoebe. "I used to think something, something wild, would come and carry me off."

Then they were laughing freely all at once, drying their feet on the other side of the stream. The mockingbirds seemed to imitate flutes in the midday air. The horse they had unhitched champed on the hill, always visible—

an old horse that seemed about to run, his mane fluttering in the light and his tail flaunted like a decoration he had only just put on.

Then the baskets were opened, the cloth was spread with the aromatic ham and chicken, spices and jellies, fresh breads and a cake, peaches, bananas, figs, pomegranates, grapes, and a thin dark bottle of blackberry cordial.

"There's one basket left in the buggy," said Irene, always the last to yield. "I like to have a little something saved back."

The women reclined before the food, beside the warm and weighty pedestal. Above them the six columns seemed to be filled with the inhalations of summer and to be suspended in the resting of noon.

They pressed at the pomegranate stains on their mouths. And then they began to tell over Miss Sabina's story, their voices serene and alike: how she looked, the legend of her beauty when she was young, the house where she was born and what happened in it, and how she came out when she was old, and her triumphal way, and the pitiful end when she toppled to her death in a dusty place where she was a stranger, that she had despised and deplored.

"Miss Sabina's house stood on the high hill," Cora said, but the lips of the others moved with hers. It was like an old song they carried in their memory, the story of the two houses separated by a long, winding, difficult, untravelled road—a curve of the old Natchez Trace—but actually situated almost back to back on the ring of hills, while completely hidden from each other, like the reliefs on opposite sides of a vase.

"It commanded the town that came to be at its foot. Her house was a square of marble and stone, the front was as dark as pitch under the magnolia trees. Not one blade of grass grew in the hard green ground, but in some places a root stuck up like a serpent. Inside, the house was all wood, dark wood carved and fluted, long hallways, great staircases of walnut, ebony beds that filled a room, even mahogany roses in the ceilings, where the chandeliers hung down like red glass fruit. There was one completely dark inside room. The house was a labyrinth set with statues—Venus, Hermes, Demeter, and with singing ocean shells on draped pedestals.

"Miss Sabina's father came bringing Mr. Don McInnis home, and proposed the marriage to him. She was no longer young for suitors; she was instructed to submit. On the marriage night the house was ablaze, and lighted the town and the wedding guests climbing the hill. We were there. The presents were vases of gold, gold cups, statues of Diana. . . . And the bride . . . We had not forgotten it yesterday when we drew it from the chest—the stiff white gown she wore! It never made a rustle when she gave him her hand. It was spring, the flowers in the baskets were purple hyacinths and white lilies that wilted in the heat and showed their blue veins. Ladies fainted from the scent; the gentlemen were without exception drunk, and Mr. Don McInnis, with his head turning quickly from side to side, like an animal's, opened his mouth and laughed."

Irene said: "A great, profane man like all the McInnis men of Asphodel, Mr. Don McInnis. He was the last of his own, just as she was the last of hers. The hope was in him, and he knew it. He had a sudden way of laughter, like a rage, that pointed his eyebrows that were yellow, and changed his face. That night he stood astride . . . astride the rooms, the guests, the flowers, the tapers, the bride and her father with his purple face. 'What, Miss Sabina?' he would roar, though she had never said a word, not one word . . . waiting in the stiffened gown that took then its odor of burning wax. We remembered that, that roar, that 'What, Miss Sabina?' and we whispered it among ourselves later when we embroidered together, as though it were a riddle that young ladies could not answer. He seemed never to have said any other thing to her. He was dangerous that first night, swaying with drink, trampling the scattered flowers, led up to a ceremony there before all our eyes, Miss Sabina so rigid by his side. He was a McInnis, a man that would be like a torch carried into a house."

The three old maids, who lay like a faded garland at the foot of the columns, paused in peaceful silence. When the story was taken up again, it was in Phoebe's delicate and gentle way, for its narrative was only part of memory now, and its beginning and ending might seem mingled and freed in the blue air of the hill.

"She bore three children, two boys and a girl, and one by one they died as they reached maturity. There was Minerva and she was drowned—before her wedding day. There was Theo, coming out from the university in his gown of the law, and killed in a fall off the wild horse he was bound to ride. And there was Lucian, the youngest, shooting himself publicly on the courthouse steps, drunk in the broad daylight.

"Who can tell what will happen in this world!" said Phoebe, and she looked placidly up into the featureless sky overhead.

"It all served to make Miss Sabina prouder than ever," Irene said. "She was born grand, with a will to impose, and now she had only Mr. Don left, to impose it upon. But he was a McInnis. He had the wildness we all worshipped that first night, since he was not to be ours to love. He was unfaithful—maybe always—maybe once—"

"We told the news," said Cora. "We went in a body up the hill and into the house, weeping and wailing, hardly daring to name the name or the deed."

"It was in the big hall by the statues of the Seasons, and she stood up to listen to us all the way through," Irene murmured. "She didn't move—she didn't blink her eye. We stood there in our little half-circle not daring to come closer. Then she reached out both her arms as though she would embrace us all, and made fists with her hands, with the sharp rings cutting into her, and called down the curse of heaven on everybody's head—his, and the woman's, and the dead children's, and ours. Then she walked out, and the door of her bedroom closed."

"We ran away," said Phoebe languidly. "We ran down the steps and in and out of the boxwood garden, around the fountain, all clutching one another as though we were pursued, and away through the street, crying. She never shed a tear, whatever happened, but we shed enough for everybody."

Cora said: "By that time, her father was dead and there was no one to right the wrong. And Mr. Don—he only flourished. He wore white linen suits summer and winter. She declared the lightning would strike him for the destruction he had brought on her, but it never struck. She never closed her eyes a single night, she was so outraged and so undone. She would not eat a bite for anybody. We carried things up to her—soups, birds, wines, frozen surprises, cold shapes, one after the other. She only pushed them away. It could have been thought that life with the beast was the one thing in the living world to be pined after. But 'How can I hate him enough?' she said over and over. 'How can I show him the hate I have for him?' She implored us to tell her."

"We heard he was running away to Asphodel," said Irene, "and taking the woman. And when we went and told Miss Sabina, she would not wait any longer for an act of God to punish him, though we took her and held her till she pushed us from her side."

"She drove Mr. Don out of the house," said Cora, to whom the cordial was now passed. "Drove him out with a whip, in the broad daylight. It was a day like this, in summer—I remember the magnolias that made the air so heavy and full of sleep. It was just after dinner time and all the population came out and stood helpless to see, as if in a dream. Like a demon she sprang from the door and rushed down the long iron steps, driving him before her with the buggy whip, that had a purple tassel. He walked straight ahead as if to humor her, with his white hat lifted and held in his hand."

"We followed at a little distance behind her, in case she should faint," said Phoebe. "But we were the ones who were near to fainting, when she set her feet in the gateway after driving him through, and called at the top of her voice for the woman to come forward. She longed to whip her there and then. But no one came forward. She swore that we were hiding and protecting some wretched creature, that we were all in league. Miss Sabina put a great blame on the whole town."

"When Asphodel burned that night," said Cora, "and we all saw the fire raging on the sky, we ran and told her, and she was gratified—but from that moment remote from us and grand. And she laid down the law that the name of Don McInnis and the name of Asphodel were not to cross our lips again. . . ."

The prodigious columns shone down and appeared tremulous with the tender light of summer which enclosed them all around, in equal and shadowless flame. They seemed to flicker with the flight of birds.

"Miss Sabina," said Irene, "for the rest of her life was proceeding through the gateway and down the street, and all her will was turned upon the population."

"She was painted to be beautiful and terrible in the face, all dark around the eyes," said Phoebe, "in the way of grand ladies of the South grown old. She wore a fine jet-black wig of great size, for she had lost her hair by some illness or violence. She went draped in the heavy brocades from her family trunks, which she hung about herself in some bitter disregard. She would do no more than pin them and tie them into place. Through such a weight of material her knees pushed slowly, her progress was hampered but she came on. Her look was the challenging one when looks met, though only Miss Sabina knew why there had to be any clangor of encounter among peaceable people. *We* knew she had been beautiful. Her hands were small, and as hot to the touch as a child's under the sharp diamonds. One hand, the right one, curved round and clenched an ebony stick mounted with the gold head of a lion."

"She took her stick and went down the street proclaiming and wielding her power," said Cora. "Her power reached over the whole population—white and black, men and women, children, idiots, and animals—even strangers. Her law was laid over us, her riches were distributed upon us; we were given a museum and a statue, a waterworks. And we stood in fear of her, old and young and like ourselves. At the May Festival when she passed by, all the maypoles became hopelessly tangled, one by one. Her good wish and her censure could be as clearly told apart as a white horse from a black one. All news was borne to her first, and she interrupted every news-bearer. 'You don't have to tell me: I know. The woman is dead. The child is born. The man is proved a thief.' There would be a time when she appeared at the door of every house on the street, pounding with her cane. She dominated every ceremony, set the times for weddings and for funerals, even for births, and she named the children. She ordered lives about and moved people from one place to another in the town, brought them together or drove them apart, with the mystical and rigorous devotion of a priestess in a story; and she prophesied all the things beforehand. She foretold disaster, and was ready with hot breads and soups to send by running Negroes to every house the moment it struck. And she expected her imparted recipes to be used forever after, and no other. We are eating Miss Sabina's cake now. . . ."

"But at the end of the street there was one door where Miss Sabina had never entered," said Phoebe. "The door of the post office. She acted as if the post office had no existence in the world, or else she called it a dirty little room with the door standing wide open to the flies. All the hate she had left in her when she was old went out to a little four-posted whitewashed building, the post office. It was beyond her domain. For there we might still be apart in a dream, and she did not know what it was."

"But in the end, she came in," said Irene.

"We were there," she said. "It was mail time, and we each had a letter in our hands. We heard her come to the end of the street, the heavy staggering figure coming to the beat of the cane. We were silent all at once. When Miss Sabina is at the door, there is no other place in the world but where you stand, and no other afternoon but that one, past or future. We held onto our letters as onto all faraway or ephemeral things at that moment, to our secret hope or joy and our despair too, which she might require of us."

"When she entered," said Cora, "and took her stand in the center of the floor, a little dog saw who it was and trotted out, and alarm like the vibration from the firebell trembled in the motes of the air, and the crowded room seemed to shake, to totter. We looked at one another in greater fear of her than ever before in our lives, and we would have run away or spoken to her first, except for a premonition that this time was the last, this demand the final one."

"It was as if the place of the smallest and the longest-permitted indulgence, the little common green, were to

341

be invaded when the time came for the tyrant to die,"
said Phoebe.

The three old maids sighed gently. The grapes they
held upon their palms were transparent in the light, so that
the little black seeds showed within.

"But when Miss Sabina spoke," said Irene, "she said,
'Give me my letter.' And Miss Sabina never got a letter
in her life. She never knew a soul beyond the town. We
told her there was no letter for her, but she cried out again,
'Give me my letter!' We told her there was none, and we
went closer and tried to gather her to us. But she said,
'Give me that.' And she took our letters out of our hands.
'Your lovers!' she said, and tore them in two. We let her
do just as she would. But she was not satisfied. 'Open
up!' she said to the postmistress, and she beat upon the little communicating door. So the postmistress had to open
up, and Miss Sabina went in to the inner part. We all
drew close. We glanced at one another with our eyes
grown bright, like people under a spell, for she was bent
upon destruction."

"A fury and a pleasure seemed to rise inside her, that
went out like lightning through her hands," said Cora.
"She threw down her stick, she advanced with her bare
hands. She seized upon everything before her, and tore it
to pieces. She dragged the sacks about, and the wastebas-
kets, and the contents she scattered like snow. Even the
ink pad she flung against the wall, and it left a purple
mark like a grape stain that will never wear off.

"She was possessed then, before our eyes, as she could
never have been possessed. She raged. She rocked from
side to side, she danced. Miss Sabina's arms moved like a

harvester's in the field, to destroy all that was in the little room. In her frenzy she tore all the letters to pieces, and even put bits in her mouth and appeared to eat them.

"Then she stood still in the little room. She had finished. We had not yet moved when she lay toppled on the floor, her wig fallen from her head and her face awry like a mask.

"'A stroke.' That is what we said, because we did not know how to put a name to the end of her life. . . ."

Here in the bright sun where the three old maids sat beside their little feast, Miss Sabina's was an old story, closed and complete. In some intoxication of the time and the place, they recited it and came to the end. Now they lay stretched on their sides on the ground, their summer dresses spread out, little smiles forming on their mouths, their eyes half-closed, Phoebe with a juicy green leaf between her teeth. Above them like a dream rested the bright columns of Asphodel, a dream like the other side of their lamentations.

All at once there was a shudder in the vines growing up among the columns. Out into the radiant light with one foot forward had stepped a bearded man. He stood motionless as one of the columns, his eyes bearing without a break upon the three women. He was as rude and golden as a lion. He did nothing, and he said nothing while the birds sang on. But he was naked.

The white picnic cloth seemed to have stirred of itself and spilled out the half-eaten fruit and shattered the bottle of wine as the three old maids first knelt, then stood, and with a cry clung with their arms upon one another. As if they heard a sound in the vibrant silence, they were compelled to tarry in the very act of flight. In a soft little chorus of screams they waited, looking back over their shoulders, with their arms stretched before them. Then their shoes were left behind them, and the three made a little line across the brook, and across the field in an aisle that opened among the mounds of wild roses. With the suddenness of birds they had all dropped to earth at the same moment and as if by magic risen on the other side of the fence, beside a "No Trespassing" sign.

They stood wordless together, brushing and plucking at their clothes, while quite leisurely the old horse trotted towards them across this pasture that was still, for him, unexplored.

The bearded man had not moved once.

Cora spoke. "That was Mr. Don McInnis."

"It was not," said Irene. "It was a vine in the wind."

Phoebe was bent over to pull a thorn from her bare foot. "But we thought he was dead."

"That was just as much Mr. Don as this is I," said Cora, "and I would swear to that in a court of law."

"He was naked," said Irene.

"He was buck-naked," said Cora. "He was as naked as an old goat. He must be as old as the hills."

"I didn't look," declared Phoebe. But there at one side she stood bowed and trembling as if from a fateful encounter.

"No need to cry about it, Phoebe," said Cora. "If it's Mr. Don, it's Mr. Don."

They consoled one another, and hitched the horse, and then waited still in their little cluster, looking back.

"What Miss Sabina wouldn't have given to see him!"

cried Cora at last. "What she wouldn't have told him, what she wouldn't have done to him!"

But at that moment, as their gaze was fixed on the ruin, a number of goats appeared between the columns of Asphodel, and with a little leap started down the hill. Their nervous little hooves filled the air with a shudder and palpitation.

"Into the buggy!"

Tails up, the goats leapt the fence as if there was nothing they would rather do.

Cora, Irene, and Phoebe were inside the open buggy, the whip was raised over the old horse.

"There are more and more coming still," cried Irene.

There were billy-goats and nanny-goats, old goats and young, a whole thriving herd. Their little beards all blew playfully to the side in the wind of their advancement.

"They are bound to catch up," cried Irene.

"Throw them something," said Cora, who held the reins.

At their feet was the basket that had been saved out, with a napkin of biscuits and bacon on top.

"Here, billy-goats!" they cried.

Leaning from the sides of the buggy, their sleeves fluttering, each one of them threw back biscuits with both hands.

"Here, billy-goats!" they cried, but the little goats were prancing so close, their inquisitive noses were almost in the spokes of the wheels.

"It won't stop them," said Phoebe. "They're not satisfied in the least, it only makes them curious."

Cora was standing up in the open buggy, driving it

like a chariot. "Give them the little baked hen, then," she said, and they threw it behind.

The little goats stopped, with their heads flecked to one side, and then their horns met over the prize.

There was a turn, and Asphodel was out of sight. The road went into a ravine and wound into the shade. . . .

"We escaped," said Cora.

"I am thankful Miss Sabina did not live to see us then," said Irene. "She would have been ashamed of us— barefooted and running. She would never have given up the little basket we had saved back."

"He ought not to be left at liberty," cried Cora. She spoke soothingly to the old horse whose haunches still trembled, and then said, "I have a good mind to report him to the law!"

There was the great house where Miss Sabina had lived, high on the coming hill.

But Phoebe laughed aloud as they made the curve. Her voice was soft, and she seemed to be still in a tender dream and an unconscious celebration—as though the picnic were not already set rudely in the past, but were the enduring and intoxicating present, still the phenomenon, the golden day.

THE WINDS

———————◆———————

WHEN JOSIE FIRST WOKE UP in the night she thought the big girls of the town were having a hay-ride. Choruses and cries of what she did not question to be joy came stealing through the air. At once she could see in her mind the source of it, the Old Natchez Trace, which was at the edge of her town, an old dark place where the young people went, and it was called both things, the Old Natchez Trace and Lover's Lane. An excitement touched her and she could see in her imagination the leaning wagon coming, the long white-stockinged legs of the big girls hung down in a fringe on one side of the hay—then as the horses made a turn, the boys' black stockings stuck out the other side.

But while her heart rose longingly to the pitch of their delight, hands reached under her and she was lifted out of bed.

"Don't be frightened," said her father's voice into her ear, as if he told her a secret.

Am I old? Am I invited? she wondered, stricken.

The chorus seemed to envelop her, but it was her father's thin nightshirt she lay against in the dark.

347

"I still say it's a shame to wake them up." It was her mother's voice coming from the doorway, though strangely argumentative for so late in the night.

Then they were all moving in the stirring darkness, all in their nightgowns, she and Will being led by their mother and father, and they in turn with their hands out as if they were being led by something invisible. They moved off the sleeping porch into the rooms of the house. The calls and laughter of the older children came closer, and Josie thought that at any moment their voices would all come together, and they would sing their favorite round, "Row, row, row your boat, gently down the stream—merrily, merrily, merrily, merrily—"

"Don't turn on the lights," said her father, as if to keep the halls and turnings secret within. They passed the front bedroom; she knew it by the scent of her mother's verbena sachet and the waist-shape of the mirror which showed in the dark. But they did not go in there. Her father put little coats about them, not their right ones. In her sleep she seemed to have dreamed the sounds of all the windows closing, upstairs and down. Coming out of the guest-room was a sound like a nest of little mice in the hay; in a flash of pride and elation Josie discovered it to be the empty bed rolling around and squeaking on its wheels. Then close beside them was a small musical tinkle against the floor, and she knew the sound; it was Will's Tinker-Toy tower coming apart and the wooden spools and rods scattering down.

"Oh boy!" cried Will, spreading his arms high in his sleep and beginning to whirl about. "The house is falling down!"

"Hush," said their mother, catching him.

"Never mind," said their father, smoothing Josie's hair but speaking over her head. "Downstairs."

The hour had never seemed so late in their house as when they made this slow and unsteady descent. Josie thought again of Lover's Lane. The stairway gave like a chain, the pendulum shivered in the clock.

They moved into the living room. The summer matting was down on the floor, cracked and lying in little ridges under their sandals, smelling of its stains and dust, of thin green varnish, and of its origin in China. The sheet of music open on the piano had caved in while they slept, and gleamed faintly like a shell in the shimmer and flow of the strange light. Josie's drawing of the plaster-cast of Joan of Arc, which it had taken her all summer to do for her mother, had rolled itself tightly up on the desk like a diploma. Were they all going away and leave that? They wandered separately for a moment looking like strangers at the wicker chairs. The cretonne pillows smelled like wet stones. Outside the beseeching cries rose and fell, and drew nearer. The curtains hung almost still, like poured cream, down the windows, but on the table the petals shattered all at once from a bowl of roses. Then the chorus of wildness and delight seemed to come almost into their street, though still it held its distance, exactly like the wandering wagon filled with the big girls and boys at night.

Will in his little shirt was standing straight up with his eyes closed, erect as a spinning top.

"He'll sleep through it," said their mother. "You take him, and I'll take the girl." With a little push, she divided the children; she was unlike herself. Then their mother and father sat down opposite each other in the wicker chairs. They were waiting.

"Is it a moonlight picnic?" asked Josie.

"It's a storm," said her father. He answered her questions formally in a kind of deep courtesy always, which did not depend on the day or night. "This is the equinox."

Josie gave a leap at that and ran to the front window and looked out.

"Josie!"

She was looking for the big girl who lived in the double-house across the street. There was a strange fluid lightning which she now noticed for the first time to be filling the air, violet and rose, and soundless of thunder; and the eyes of the double-house seemed to open and shut with it.

"Josie, come back."

"I see Cornella. I see Cornella in the equinox, there in her high-heeled shoes."

"Nonsense," said her father. "Nonsense, Josie."

But she stood with her back to all of them and looked, saying, "I see Cornella."

"How many times have I told you that you need not concern yourself with—Cornella!" The way her mother said her name was not diminished now.

"I see Cornella. She's on the outside, Mama, outside in the storm, and she's in the equinox."

But her mother would not answer.

"Josie, don't you understand—I want to keep us close together," said her father. She looked back at him. "Once in an equinoctial storm," he said cautiously over the sleep-

350

ing Will, "a man's little girl was blown away from him into a haystack out in a field."

"The wind will come after Cornella," said Josie.

But he called her back.

The house shook as if a big drum were being beaten down the street.

Her mother sighed. "Summer is over."

Josie drew closer to her, with a sense of consolation. Her mother's dark plait was as warm as her arm, and she tugged at it. In the coming of these glittering flashes and the cries and the calling voices of the equinox, summer was turning into the past. The long ago . . .

"What is the equinox?" she asked.

Her father made an explanation. "A seasonal change, you see, Josie—like the storm we had in winter. You remember that."

"No, sir," she said. She clung to her mother.

"She couldn't remember it next morning," said her mother, and looked at Will, who slept up against his father with his hands in small fists.

"You mustn't be frightened, Josie," said her father again. "You have my word that this is a good strong house." He had built it before she was born. But in the equinox Josie stayed with her mother, though the lightning stamped the pattern of her father's dressing gown on the room.

With the pulse of the lightning the wide front window was oftener light than dark, and the persistence of illumination seemed slowly to be waking something that slept longer than Josie had slept, for her trembling body turned under her mother's hand.

"Be still," said her mother. "It's soon over."

They looked at one another, parents and children, as if through a turning wheel of light, while they waited in their various attitudes against the wicker arabesques and the flowered cloth. When the wind rose still higher, both mother and father went all at once silent, Will's eyes lifted open, and all their gazes confronted one another. Then in a single flickering, Will's face was lost in sleep. The house moved softly like a boat that has been stepped into.

Josie lay drifting in the chair, and where she drifted was through the summertime, the way of the past. . . .

It seemed to her that there should have been more time for the monkey-man—for the premonition, the organ coming from the distance, the crisis in the house, "Is there a penny upstairs or down?", the circle of following children, their downcast looks of ecstasy, and for the cold imploring hand of the little monkey.

She woke only to hunt for signs of the fairies, and counted nothing but a footprint smaller than a bird-claw. All of the sand pile went into a castle, and it was a rite to stretch on her stomach and put her mouth to the door. "O my Queen!" and the coolness of the whisper would stir the grains of sand within. Expectant on the floor were spread the sycamore leaves, Will's fur rugs with the paws, head, and tail. "I am thine eternally, my Queen, and will serve thee always and I will be enchanted with thy love forever." It was delicious to close both eyes and wait a length of time. Then, supposing a mocking-bird sang in the tree, "I ask for my first wish, to be made to understand the tongue of birds." They called her back because they had no memory of magic. Even a June-bug, if he were caught and released, would turn into a being, and this was forgotten in the way people summoned one another.

Polishing the dark hall clock as though it was through her tending that the time was brought, the turbaned cook would be singing, "Dere's a Hole in de Bottom of de Sea." "How old will I get to be, Johanna?" she would ask as she ran through the house. "Ninety-eight." "How old is Will going to be?" "Ninety-nine." Then she was out the door. Her bicycle was the golden Princess, the name in a scroll in front. She would take her as early as possible. So as to touch nothing, to make no print on the earliness of the day, she rode with no hands, no feet, touching nowhere but the one place, moving away into the leaves, down the swaying black boards of the dewy alley. They called her back. She hung from and circled in order the four round posts, warm and filled with weight, on the porch. Green arched ferns, like great exhalations, spread from the stands. The porch was deep and wide and painted white with a blue ceiling, and the swing, like three sides of a box, was white too under its long quiet chains. She ran and jumped, secure that the house was theirs and identical with them—the pale smooth house seeming not to yield to any happening, with the dreamlike arch of the roof over the entrance like the curve of their upper lips.

All the children came running and jumping out. She went along chewing nasturtium stems and sucking the honey from four-o'clock flowers, out for whatever figs and pomegranates came to hand. She floated a rose petal dry in her mouth, and sucked on the spirals of honeysuckle and the knobs of purple clover. She wore crowns. She added flower necklaces as the morning passed, then bracelets, and applied transfer-pictures to her forehead and arms and legs—a basket of roses, a windmill, Columbus's ships, ruins of Athens. But always oblivious, off in the shade, the big girls reclined or pressed their flowers in a book, or filled whole baking-powder cans with four-leaf-clovers they found.

And watching it all from the beginning, the morning going by, was the double-house. This worn old house was somehow in disgrace, as if it had been born into it and could not help it. Josie was sorry, and sorry that it looked like a face, with its wide-apart upper windows, the nose-like partition between the two sagging porches, the chimneys rising in listening points at either side, and the roof across which the birds sat. It watched, and by not being what it should have been, the house was inscrutable. There was always some noise of disappointment to be heard coming from within—a sigh, a thud, something dropped. There were eight children in all that came out of it—all sizes, and all tow-headed, as if they might in some way all be kin under that roof, and they had a habit of arranging themselves in the barren yard in a little order, like an octave, and staring out across the street at the rest of the neighborhood—as if to state, in their rude way, "This is us." Everyone was cruelly prevented from playing with the children of the double-house, no matter how in their humility they might change—in the course of the summer they would change to an entirely new set, with the movings in and out, though somehow there were always exactly eight. Cornella, being nearly grown and being transformed by age, was not to be counted simply as a forbidden playmate—yet sometimes, as if she wanted to be just that, she chased after them, or stood in the middle while they ran a ring around her.

In the morning was Cornella's time of preparation. She was forever making ready. Big girls are usually idle, but Cornella, as occupied as a child, vigorously sunned her hair, or else she had always just washed it and came out busily to dry it. It was bright yellow, wonderfully silky and long, and she would bend her neck and toss her hair over her head before her face like a waterfall. And her hair was as constant a force as a waterfall to Josie, under whose eyes alone it fell. Cornella, Cornella, let down thy hair, and the King's son will come climbing up.

Josie watched her, for there was no one else to see, how she shook it and played with it and presently began to brush it, over and over, out in public. But always through the hiding hair she would be looking out, steadily out, over the street. Josie, who followed her gaze, felt the emptiness of their street too, and could not understand why at such a moment no one could be as pitiful as only the old man driving slowly by in the cart, and no song could be as sad as his song,

> "Milk, milk,
> Buttermilk!
> Sweet potatoes—Irish potatoes—green peas—
> And buttermilk!"

But Cornella, instead of being moved by this sad moment, in which Josie's love began to go toward her, stamped her foot. She was angry, angry. To see her then, oppression touched Josie and held her quite still. Called in to dinner before she could understand, she felt a conviction: I will never catch up with her. No matter how old I get, I will never catch up with Cornella. She felt that daring and risking everything went for nothing; she would never take a poison wild strawberry into her mouth again in the hope of finding out the secret and the punishment of the world, for Cornella, whom she might love, had stamped her foot, and had as good as told her, "You will never catch up." All that she ran after in the whole summer world came to life in departure before Josie's eyes and covered her vision with wings. It kept her from eating her dinner to think of all that she had caught or meant to catch before the time was gone—June-bugs in the banana plants to fly before breakfast on a thread, lightning-bugs that left a bitter odor in the palms of the hands, butterflies with their fierce and haughty faces, bees in a jar. A great tempest of droning and flying seemed to have surrounded her as she ran, and she seemed not to have moved without putting her hand out after something that flew ahead. . . .

"There! I thought you were asleep," said her father.

She turned in her chair. The house had stirred.

"Show me their tracks," muttered Will. "Just show me their tracks."

As though the winds were changed back into songs, Josie seemed to hear "Beautiful Ohio" slowly picked out in the key of C down the hot afternoon. That was Cornella. Through the tied-back curtains of parlors the other big girls, with rats in their hair and lace insertions in their white dresses, practiced forever on one worn little waltz, up and down the street, for they took lessons.

"Come spend the day with me." "See who can eat a banana down without coming up to breathe." That was Josie and her best friend, smirking at each other.

They wandered at a trot, under their own parasols. In the vacant field, in the center of summer, was a chinaberry tree, as dark as a cloud in the middle of the day. Its frail flowers or its bitter yellow balls lay trodden always over the whole of the ground. There was a little path that came through the hedge and went its way to this tree, and there was an old low seat built part-way around the trunk, on which was usually lying an abandoned toy of some kind. Here beside the nurses stood the little children, whose level eyes stared at the rosettes on their garters.

"How do you do?"

"How do you do?"

"I remembers you. Where you all think you goin'?"

"We don't have to answer."

They went to the drugstore and treated each other. It was behind the latticed partition. How well she knew its cut-out pasteboard grapes whose color was put on a little to one side. Her elbows slid smoothly out on the cold camp marble that smelled like hyacinths. "You say first." "No, you. First you love me last you hate me." When they were full of sweets it was never too late to take the long way home. They ran through the park and drank from the fountain. Moving slowly as sunlight over the grass were the broad and dusty backs of pigeons. They stopped and made a clover-chain and hung it on a statue.

They groveled in the dirt under the bandstand hunting for lost money, but when they found a dead bird with its feathers cool as rain, they ran out in the sun. Old Biddy Felix came to make a speech, he stood up and shouted with no one to listen—"The time flies, the time flies!"—and his arm and hand flew like a bat in the ragged sleeve. Walking the seesaw she held her breath for him. They floated magnolia leaves in the horse trough, themselves taking the part of the wind and waves, and suddenly remembering who they were. They closed in upon the hot tamale man, fixing their frightened eyes on his lantern and on his scars.

Josie never came and she never went without touching the dragon—the Chinese figure in the garden on the corner that in biting held rain water in the cavern of its mouth. And never did it seem so still, so utterly of stone, as when all the children said goodbye as they always did on that corner, and she was left alone with it. Stone dragons opened their mouths and begged to swallow the day, they loved to eat the summer. It was painful to think of even pony-rides gobbled, the way they all went, the children, every one (except from the double-house) crammed into the basket with their heads stuck up like candy-almonds in a treat. She backed all the way home from the dragon.

But she had only to face the double-house in her meditations, and then she could invoke Cornella. Thy name is Corn, and thou art like the ripe corn, beautiful Cornella. And before long the figure of Cornella would be sure to appear. She would dart forth from one old screen door of the double-house, trailed out by the nagging odor of cabbage cooking. She would have just bathed and dressed, for it took her so long, and her bright hair would be done in puffs and curls with a bow behind.

Cornella was not even a daughter in her side of the house, she was only a niece or cousin, there only by the frailest indulgence. She would come out with this frailty about her, come without a hat, without anything. Between the double-house and the next house was the strongest fence that could be built, and no ball had ever come back that went over it. It reached all the way out to the street. So Cornella could never see if anyone might be coming, unless she came all the way out to the curb and leaned around the corner of the fence. Josie knew the way it would happen, and yet it was like new always. At the opening of the door, the little towheads would scatter, dash to the other side of the partition, disappear as if by consent. Then lightly down the steps, down the walk, Cornella would come, in some kind of secrecy swaying from side to side, her skirts swinging round, and the sidewalk echoing smally to her pumps with the Baby Louis heels. Then, all alone, Cornella would turn and gaze away down the street, as if she could see far, far away, in a little pantomime of hope and apprehension that would not permit Josie to stir.

But the moment came when without meaning to she lifted her hand softly, and made a sign to Cornella. She almost said her name.

And Cornella—what was it she had called back across the street, the flash of what word, so furious and yet so frail and thin? It was more furious than even the stamping of her foot, only a single word.

Josie took her hand down. In a seeking humility she stood there and bore her shame to attend Cornella. Cornella herself would stand still, haughtily still, waiting as if in pride, until a voice old and cracked would call her too, from the upper window, "Cornella, Cornella!" And she would have to turn around and go inside to the old woman, her hair ribbon and her sash in pale bows that sank down in the back.

Then for Josie the sun on her bangs stung, and the pity for ribbons drove her to a wild capering that would end in a tumble.

Will woke up with a yell like a wild Indian.

"Here, let me hold him," said his mother. Her voice had become soft; time had passed. She took Will on her lap.

Josie opened her eyes. The lightning was flowing like the sea, and the cries were like waves at the door. Her parents' faces were made up of hundreds of very still moments.

"Tomahawks!" screamed Will.

"Mother, don't let him—" Josie said uneasily.

"Never mind. You talk in your sleep too," said her mother.

She experienced a kind of shock, a small shock of detachment, like the time in the picture-show when a little blurred moment of the summer's May Festival had been thrown on the screen and there was herself, ribbon in hand, weaving once in and once out, a burning and abandoned look in the flicker of her face as though no one in the world would ever see her.

Her mother's hand stretched to her, but Josie broke away. She lay with her face hidden in the pillow. . . . The summer day became vast and opalescent with twilight. The calming and languid smell of manure came slowly to meet her as she passed through the back gate and went out to the pasture among the mounds of wild roses. "Daisy," she had only to say once, in her quietest voice, for she felt very near to the cow. There she walked, not even eating—Daisy, the small tender Jersey with her soft violet nose, walking and presenting her warm side. Josie bent to lean her forehead against her. Here the tears from her eyes could go rolling down Daisy's shining coarse hairs, and Daisy did not move or speak but held patient, richly compassionate and still. . . .

"You're not frightened any more, are you, Josie?" asked her father.

"No, sir," she said, with her face buried. . . . She thought of the evening, the sunset, the stately game played by the flowering hedge when the vacant field was theirs. "Here comes the duke a-riding, riding, riding . . . What are you riding here for, here for?" while the hard iron sound of the Catholic Church bell tolled at twilight for unknown people. "The fairest one that I can see . . . London Bridge is falling down . . . Lady Moon, Lady Moon, show your shoe . . . I measure my love to show you . . ." Under the fiery windows, how small the children were. "Fox in the morning!—Geese in the evening!—How many have you got?—More than you can ever catch!" The children were rose-colored too. Fading, rolling shouts cast long flying shadows behind them, and to watch them she

stood still. Above everything in the misty blue dome of
the sky was the full white moon. So it is, for a true thing,
round, she thought, and where she waited a hand seemed
to reach around and take her under the loose-hanging hair,
and words in her thoughts came shaped like grapes in her
throat. She felt lonely. She would stop a runner. "Did you
know the moon was round?" "I did. Annie told me last
summer." The game went on. But I must find out everything about the moon, Josie thought in the solemnity of
evening. The moon and tides. O moon! O tides! I ask
thee. I ask thee. Where dost thou rise and fall? As if it
were this knowledge which she would allow to enter her
heart, for which she had been keeping room, and as if it
were the moon, known to be round, that would go floating
through her dreams forever and never leave her, she
looked steadily up at the moon. The moon looked down at
her, full with all the lonely time to go.

When night was about to fall, the time came to bring
out her most precious possession, the steamboat she had
made from a shoe-box. In all boats the full-moon, half-
moon, and new moon were cut out of each side for the
windows, with tissue-paper through which shone the
unsteady candle inside. She knew this journey ahead of
time as if it were long ago, the hushing noise the boat
made being dragged up the brick walk by the string, the
leap it had to take across the three-cornered missing place
over the big root, the spreading smell of warm wax in the
evening, and the remembered color of the daylight turning. Coming to meet the boat was another boat, shining
and gliding as if by itself.

Children greeted each other dreamily at twilight.

"Choo-choo!"

"Choo-choo!"

And something made her turn after that and see how Cornella stood and looked across at them, all dressed in gauze, looking as if the street were a river flowing along between, and she did not speak at all. Josie understood: she *could* not. It seemed to her as she guided her warm boat under the brightening moon that Cornella would have turned into a tree if she could, there in the front yard of the double-house, and that the center of the tree would have to be seen into before her heart was bared, so undaunted and so filled with hope. . . .

"I'll shoot you dead!" screamed Will.

"Hush, hush," said their mother.

Her father held up his hand and said, "Listen."

Then their house was taken to the very breast of the storm.

Josie lay as still as an animal, and in panic thought of the future . . . the sharp day when she would come running out of the field holding the ragged stems of the quick-picked goldenrod and the warm flowers thrust out for a present for somebody. The future was herself bringing presents, the season of gifts. When would the day come when the wind would fall and they would sit in silence on the fountain rim, their play done, and the boys would crack the nuts under their heels? If they would bring the time around once more, she would lose nothing that was given, she would hoard the nuts like a squirrel.

For the first time in her life she thought, might the same wonders never come again? Was each wonder original and alone like the falling star, and when it fell did it bury itself beyond where you hunted it? Should she hope to see it snow twice, and the teacher running again to open the window, to hold out her black cape to catch it as it came down, and then going up and down the room quickly, quickly, to show them the snowflakes? . . .

"Mama, where is my muff that came from Marshall Field's?"

"It's put away, it was your grandmother's present." (But it came from those far fields.) "Are you dreaming?" Her mother felt of her forehead.

"I want my little muff to hold." She ached for it. "Mother, give it to me."

"Keep still," said her mother softly.

Her father came over and kissed her, and as if a new kiss could bring a memory, she remembered the night. . . . It was that very night. How could she have forgotten and nearly let go what was closest of all? . . .

The whole way, as they walked slowly after supper past the houses, and the wet of sprinkled lawns was rising like a spirit over the streets, the locusts were filling the evening with their old delirium, the swell that would rise and die away.

In the Chautauqua when they got there, there was a familiar little cluster of stars beyond the hole in the top of the tent, but the canvas sides gave off sighs and stirred, and a knotted rope knocked outside. It was war time where there were grown people, and the vases across the curtained stage held little bunches of flags on sticks which drooped and wilted like flowers before their eyes. Josie and Will sat waiting on the limber board in the front row, their feet hanging into the spice-clouds of sawdust. The curtains parted. Waiting with lifted hands was a company with a sign beside them saying "The Trio." All were ladies, one in red, one in white, and one in blue, and after one smile which touched them all at the same instant, like a match struck in their faces, they began to play a piano, a cornet, and a violin.

At first, in the hushed disappointment which filled the Chautauqua tent in beginning moments, the music had been sparse and spare, like a worn hedge through which the hiders can be seen. But then, when hope had waned, there had come a little transition to another key, and the woman with the cornet had stepped forward, raising her instrument.

If morning-glories had come out of the horn instead of those sounds, Josie would not have felt a more astonished delight. She was pierced with pleasure. The sounds that so tremulously came from the striving of the lips were welcome and sweet to her. Between herself and the lifted cornet there was no barrier, there was only the stale, expectant air of the old shelter of the tent. The cornetist was beautiful. There in the flame-like glare that was somehow shadowy, she had come from far away, and the long times of the world seemed to be about her. She was draped heavily in white, shaded with blue, like a Queen, and she stood braced and looking upward like the figure-head on a Viking ship. As the song drew out, Josie could see the slow appearance of a little vein in her cheek. Her closed eyelids seemed almost to whir and yet to rest motionless, like the wings of a humming-bird, when she reached the high note. The breaths she took were fearful, and a little medallion of some kind lifted each time on her breast. Josie listened in mounting care and suspense, as if the performance led in some direction away—as if a destination were being shown her.

And there not far away, with her face all wild, was Cornella, listening too, and still alone. In some alertness Josie turned and looked back for her parents, but they were far back in the crowd; they did not see her, they were not listening. She was let free, and turning back to the cornetist, who was transfixed beneath her instrument, she bent gently forward and closed her hands together over her knees.

"Josie!" whispered Will, prodding her.

"That's my name." But she would not talk to him.

She had come home tired, in a dream. But after the light had been turned out on the sleeping porch, and the kisses of her family were put on her cheek, she had not fallen asleep. She could see out from the high porch that the town was dark, except where beyond the farthest rim of trees the old cotton-seed mill with its fiery smokestack and its lights forever seemed an inland boat that waited for the return of the sea. It came over her how the beauty of the world had come with its sign and stridden through their town that night; and it seemed to her that a proclamation had been made in the last high note of the lady trumpeteer when her face had become set in its passion, and that after that there would be no more waiting and no more time left for the one who did not take heed and follow. . . .

* * *

There was a breaking sound, the first thunder.

"You see!" said her father. He struck his palms together, and it thundered again. "It's over."

"Back to bed, every last one of you," said her mother, as if it had all been something done to tease her, and now her defiance had won. She turned a light on and off.

"Pow!" cried Will, and then toppled into his father's arms, and was carried up the stairs.

From then on there was only the calm steady falling of rain.

Josie was placed in her winter-time bed. They would think her asleep, for they had all kissed one another in a kind of triumph to do for the rest of the night. The rain was a sleeper's sound. She listened for a time to a tapping that came at her window, like a plea from outside. . . . From whom? She could not know. Cornella, sweet summertime, the little black monkey, poor Biddy Felix, the lady with the horn whose lips were parted? Had they after all asked something of her? There, outside, was all that was wild and beloved and estranged, and all that would beckon and leave her, and all that was beautiful. She wanted to follow, and by some metamorphosis she would take them in—all—every one. . . .

The first thing next morning Josie ran outdoors to see what signs the equinox had left. The sun was shining. Will was already out, gruffly exhorting himself, digging in his old hole to China. The double-house across the street looked as if its old age had come upon it at last. Nobody was to be seen at the windows, and not a child was near.

The whole façade drooped and gave way in the soft light, like the face of an old woman fallen asleep in church. In all the trees in all the yards the leaves were slowly dropping, one by one, as if in breath after breath.

There at Josie's foot on the porch was something. It was a folded bit of paper, wet and pale and thin, trembling in the air and clinging to the pedestal of the column, as though this were the residue of some great wave that had rolled upon the rock and then receded for another time. It was a fragment of a letter. It was written not properly in ink but in indelible pencil, and so its message had not been washed away as it might have been.

Josie knelt down and took the paper in both hands, and without moving read all that was there. Then she went to her room and put it into her most secret place, the little drawstring bag that held her dancing shoes. The name Cornella was on it, and it said, "O my darling I have waited so long when are you coming for me? Never a day or a night goes by that I do not ask When? When? When?". . .

THE
PURPLE HAT

———————◆———————

IT WAS in a bar, a quiet little hole in the wall. It was four
o'clock in the afternoon. Beyond the open door the rain
fell, the heavy color of the sea, in air where the sunlight
was still suspended. Its watery reflection lighted the room,
as a room might have lighted a mouse-hole. It was in New
Orleans.

There was a bartender whose mouth and eyes curved
downward from the divide of his baby-pink nose, as if he
had combed them down, like his hair; he always just said
nothing. The seats at his bar were black oilcloth knobs,
worn and smooth and as much alike as six pebbles on the
beach, and yet the two customers had chosen very partic-
ularly the knobs they would sit on. They had come in
separately out of the wet, and had each chosen an end
stool, and now sat with the length of the little bar between
them. The bartender obviously did not know either one;
he rested his eyes by closing them. . . .

The fat customer, with a rather affable look about
him, said he would have a rye. The unshaven young man
with the shaking hands, though he had come in first, only

369

looked fearfully at a spot on the counter before him until
the bartender, as if he could hear silent prayer, covered the
spot with a drink.

The fat man swallowed, and began at once to look a
little cosy and prosperous. He seemed ready to speak, if
the moment came. . . .

There was a calm roll of thunder, no more than a
shifting of the daily rain clouds over Royal Street.

Then—"Rain or shine," the fat man spoke, "she'll be
there."

The bartender stilled his cloth on the bar, as if mop-
ping up made a loud noise, and waited.

"Why, at the Palace of Pleasure," said the fat man.
He was really more heavy and solid than he was simply
fat.

The bartender leaned forward an inch on his hand.

"The lady will be at the Palace of Pleasure," said the
fat man in his drowsy voice. "The lady with the purple
hat."

Then the fat man turned on the black knob, put his
elbow on the counter, and rested his cheek on his hand,
where he could see all the way down the bar. For a
moment his eyes seemed dancing there, above one of those
hands so short and so plump that you are always counting the fingers . . . really helpless-looking hands for so
large a man.

The young man stared back without much curiosity,
looking at the affable face much the way you stare out at
a little station where your train is passing through. His
hand alone found its place on his small glass.

"Oh, the hat she wears is a creation," said the fat man,

almost dreamily, yet not taking his eyes from the young man. It was strange that he did not once regard the bartender, who after all had done him the courtesy of asking a polite question or two, or at least the same as asked. "A great and ancient and bedraggled purple hat."

There was another rumble overhead. Here they seemed to inhabit the world that was just beneath the thunder. The fat man let it go by, lifting his little finger like a pianist. Then he went on.

"Sure, she's one of those thousands of middle-aged women who come every day to the Palace, would not be kept away by anything on earth. . . . Most of them are dull enough, drab old creatures, all of them, walking in with their big black purses held wearily by the handles like suitcases packed for a trip. No one has ever been able to find out how all these old creatures can leave their lives at home like that to gamble . . . what their husbands think . . . who keeps the house in order . . . who pays. . . . At any rate, she is one like the rest, except for the hat, and except for the young man that always meets her there, from year to year. . . . And I think she is a ghost."

"Ghost!" said the bartender—noncommittally, just as he might repeat an order.

"For this reason," said the fat man.

A reminiscent tone came into his voice which seemed to put the silent thin young man on his guard. He made the beginning of a gesture toward the bottle. The bartender was already filling his glass.

"In thirty years she has not changed," said the fat man. "Neither has she changed her hat. Dear God, how the moths must have hungered for that hat. But she has kept it in full bloom on her head, that monstrosity—purple, too, as if she were beautiful in the bargain. She has not aged, but she keeps her middle-age. The young man, on the other hand, must change—I'm sure he's not always the same young man. For thirty years," he said, "she's met a young man at the dice table every afternoon, rain or shine, at five o'clock, and gambles till midnight and tells him goodbye, and still it looks to be always the same young man—always young, but a little stale, a little tired . . . the smudge of a sideburn. . . . She finds them, she does. She picks them. Where I don't know, unless New Orleans, as I've always had a guess, is the birthplace of ready-made victims."

"Who are you?" asked the young man. It was the sort of idle voice in which the greatest wildness sometimes speaks out at last in a quiet bar.

"In the Palace of Pleasure there is a little catwalk along beneath the dome," said the fat man. His rather small, mournful lips, such as big men often have, now parted in a vague smile. "I am the man whose eyes look out over the gambling room. I am the armed man that everyone knows to be watching, at all they do. I don't believe my position is dignified by a title." Nevertheless, he looked rather pleased. "I have watched her every day for thirty years and I think she is a ghost. I have seen her murdered twice," said the fat man.

The bartender's enormous sad black eyebrows raised, like hoods on baby-carriages, and showed his round eyes.

The fat man lifted his other fat little hand and studied, or rather showed off, a ruby ring that he wore on his little finger. "That carpet, if you have ever been there, in the Palace of Pleasure, is red, but from up above, it changes and gives off light between the worn criss-crossing of the aisles like the facets of a well-cut ruby," he said, speaking in a declarative manner as if he had been waiting for a chance to deliver this enviable comparison. "The tables and chandeliers are far down below me, points in its interior. . . . Life in the ruby. And yet somehow all that people do is clear and lucid and authentic there, as if it were magnified in the red lens, not made smaller. I can see everything in the world from my catwalk. You mustn't think I brag. . . ." He looked all at once from his ring straight at the young man's face, which was as drained and white as ever, expressionless, with a thin drop of whisky running down his cheek where he had blundered with his glass.

"I have seen this old and disgusting creature in her purple hat every night, quite plainly, for thirty years, and to my belief she has been murdered twice. I suppose it will take the third time." He himself smoothly tossed down a drink.

The bartender leaned over and filled the young man's glass.

"It's within the week, within the month, that she comes back. Once she was shot point-blank— that was the first time. The young man was hot-headed then. I saw her carried out bleeding from the face. We hush those things, you know, at the Palace. There are no signs afterwards, no trouble. . . . The soft red carpet . . . Within the month she was back—with her young man meeting her at the table just after five."

The bartender put his head to one side.

"The only good of shooting her was, it made a brief period of peace there," said the fat man. "I wouldn't scoff, if I were you." He did seem the least bit fretted by that kind of interruption.

"The second time took into account the hat," he went on. "And I do think her young man was on his way toward the right idea that time, the secret. I think he had learned something. Or he wanted it all kept more quiet, or he was a new one. . . ." He looked at the young man at the other end of the bar with a patient, compassionate expression, or it may have been the inevitably tender contour of his round cheeks. "It is time that I told you about the hat. It is quite a hat. A great, wide, deep hat such as has no fashion and never knew there was fashion and change. It serves her to come out in winter and summer. Those are old plush flowers that trim it—roses? Poppies? A man wouldn't know easily. And you would never know if you only met her wearing the hat that a little glass vial with a plunger helps decorate the crown. You would have to see it from above. . . . Or you would need to be the young man sitting beside her at the gambling table when, at some point in the evening, she takes the hat off and lays it carefully in her lap, under the table. . . . Then you might notice the little vial, and be attracted to it and wish to take it out and examine it at your pleasure off in the washroom—to admire the handle, for instance, which is red glass, like the petal of an artificial flower."

The bartender suddenly lifted his hand to his mouth as if it held a glass, and yawned into it. The thin young man hit the counter faintly with his tumbler.

"She does more than just that, though," said the fat

man with a little annoyance in his soft voice. "Perhaps I haven't explained that she is a lover, too, or did you know that she would be? It is hard to make it clear to a man who has never been out to the Palace of Pleasure, but only serves drinks all day behind a bar. You see . . ." And now, lowering his voice a little, he deliberately turned from the young man and would not look at him any more. But the young man looked at him, without lifting his drink—as if there were something hypnotic and irresistible even about his side face with the round, hiding cheek.

"Try to imagine," the fat man was saying gently to the bartender, who looked back at him. "At some point in the evening she always takes off the purple hat. Usually it is very late . . . when it is almost time for her to go. The young man who has come to the rendezvous watches her until she removes it, watches her hungrily. Is it in order to see her hair? Well, most ghosts that are lovers, and lovers that are ghosts, have the long thick black hair that you would expect, and hers is no exception to the rule. It is pinned up, of course—in her straggly vague way. But the young man doesn't look at it after all. He is enamoured of her hat—her ancient, battered, outrageous hat with the awful plush flowers. She lays it down below the level of the table there, on her shabby old lap, and he caresses it. . . . Well, I suppose in this town there are stranger forms of love than that, and who are any of us to say what ways people may not find to love? She herself, you know, seems perfectly satisfied with it. And yet she must not be satisfied, being a ghost. . . . Does it matter how she seeks her desire? I am sure she speaks to him, in a sort of purr, the purr that is used for talking in that room, and the young man does not know what she seeks of him, and she is leading him on, all the time. What does she say? I do not know. But believe me . . . she leads him on. . . ."

The bartender leaned on one hand. He had an oddly cheerful look by this time, as if with strange and sad things to come his way his outlook became more vivacious.

"To look at, she has a large-sized head," said the fat man, pushing his lip with his short finger. "Well, it is more that her face spreads over such a wide area. Like the moon's. . . . Much as I have studied her, I can only say that all her features seem to have moved further apart from each other—expanded, if you see what I mean." He brought his hands together and parted them.

The bartender leaned over closer, staring at the fat man's face interestedly.

"But I can never finish telling you about the hat!" the fat man cried, and there was a little sigh somewhere in the room, very young, like a child's. "Of course, to balance the weight of the attractive little plunger, there is an object to match on the other side of this marvelous old hat—a jeweled hatpin, no less. Of course the pin is there to keep the hat safe! Each time she takes off the hat, she has first to remove the hatpin. You can see her do it every night of the world. It comes out a regular little flashing needle, ten or twelve inches long, and after she has taken the hat off, she sticks the pin back through."

The bartender pursed his lips.

"What about the second time she was murdered? Have you wondered how that was done?" The fat man turned back to face the young fellow, whose feet drove about beneath the stool. "The young lover had learned something, or come to some conclusion, you see," he said. "It was obvious all the time, of course, that by spinning the brim ever so easily as it rested on the lady's not over-sensitive old knees, it would be possible to remove the *opposite* ornament. There was not the slightest fuss or out-cry when the pin entered between the ribs and pierced the heart. No one saw it done . . . except for me, natu-rally—I had been watching for it, more or less. The old creature, who had been winning at that, simply folded all softly in on herself, like a circus tent being taken down after the show, if you've ever seen the sight. I saw her carried out again. It takes three big boys every time, she is so heavy, and one of them always has the presence of mind to cover her piously with her old purple hat for the occasion."

The bartender shut his eyes distastefully.

"If you had ever been to the Palace of Pleasure, you'd know it all went completely as usual—people at the tables never turn around," said the fat man.

The bartender ran his hand down the side of his sad smooth hair.

"The trouble lies, you see," said the fat man, "with the young lover. You are he, let us say. . . ." But he turned from the drinking young man, and it was the bartender who was asked to be the lover for the moment. "After a certain length of time goes by, and love has blossomed, and the hat, the purple hat, is thrilling to the touch of your hand—you can no longer be sure about the little vial. There in privacy you may find it to be empty. It is her coquettishness, you see. She leads you on. You are never to know whether . . ."

The chimes of St. Louis Cathedral went somnambulantly through the air. It was five o'clock. The young man had risen somehow to his feet. He moved out of the bar and disappeared in the rain of the alley. On the floor where his feet had been were old cigarette stubs that had been kicked and raked into a little circle—a rosette, a clock, a game wheel, or something. . . .

The bartender put a cork in the bottle.

"I have to go myself," said the fat man.

Once more the bartender raised his great hooded brows. For a moment their eyes met. The fat man pulled out an enormous roll of worn bills. He paid in full for all drinks and added a nice tip.

"Up on the catwalk you get the feeling now and then that you could put out your finger and make a change in the universe." His great shoulders lifted.

The bartender, with his hands full of cash, leaned confidentially over the bar. "Is she a real ghost?" he asked, in a real whisper.

There was a pause, which the thunder filled.

"I'll let you know tomorrow," said the fat man.

Then he too was gone.

It was a nice house, inside and outside both. In the first place, it had three rooms. The front room was papered in holly paper, with green palmettos from the swamp spaced at careful intervals over the walls. There was fresh newspaper cut with fancy borders on the mantel-shelf, on which were propped photographs of old or very young men printed in faint yellow—Solomon's people. Solomon had a houseful of furniture. There was a double settee, a tall scrolled rocker and an organ in the front room, all around a three-legged table with a pink marble top, on which was set a lamp with three gold feet, besides a jelly glass with pretty hen feathers in it. Behind the front room, the other room had the bright iron bed with the polished knobs like a throne, in which Solomon slept all day. There were snow-white curtains of wiry lace at the window, and a lace bed-spread belonged on the bed. But what old Solomon slept so sound under was a big feather-stitched piece-quilt in the pattern "Trip Around the World," which had twenty-one different colors, four hundred and forty pieces, and a thousand yards of thread, and that was what Solomon's mother made in her life and old age. There was a table holding the Bible, and a trunk with a key. On the wall were two calendars, and a diploma from somewhere in Solomon's family, and under that Livvie's one possession was nailed, a picture of the little white baby of the family she worked for, back in Natchez before she was married. Going through that room and on to the kitchen, there was a big wood stove and a big round table always with a wet top and with the knives and forks in one jelly glass and the spoons in another, and a cutglass vinegar bottle between, and going out from those, many shallow dishes of pickled peaches, fig preserves, watermelon pickles and blackberry jam always sitting there. The churn sat in the sun, the doors of the safe were always both shut, and there were four baited mouse-traps in the kitchen, one in every corner.

The outside of Solomon's house looked nice. It was not painted, but across the porch was an even balance. On each side there was one easy chair with high springs, looking out, and a fern basket hanging over it from the ceiling, and a dishpan of zinnia seedlings growing at its foot on the floor. By the door was a plow-wheel, just a pretty iron circle, nailed up on one wall and a square mirror on the other, a turquoise-blue comb stuck up in the frame, with the wash stand beneath it. On the door was a wooden knob with a pearl in the end, and Solomon's black hat hung on that, if he was in the house.

Out front was a clean dirt yard with every vestige of grass patiently uprooted and the ground scarred in deep whorls from the strike of Livvie's broom. Rose bushes with tiny blood-red roses blooming every month grew in threes on either side of the steps. On one side was a peach tree, on the other a pomegranate. Then coming around up the path from the deep cut of the Natchez Trace below was a line of bare crape-myrtle trees with every branch of them ending in a colored bottle, green or blue. There was no word that fell from Solomon's lips to say what they were for, but Livvie knew that there could be a spell put in trees, and she was familiar from the time she was born with the way bottle trees kept evil spirits from coming into the house—by luring them inside the colored bottles, where they cannot get out again. Solomon had made the bottle trees with his own hands over the nine years, in labor amounting to about a tree a year, and without a sign that he had any uneasiness in his heart, for he took as much pride in his precautions against spirits coming in the house as he took in the house, and sometimes in the sun the bottle trees looked prettier than the house did.

It was a nice house. It was in a place where the days would go by and surprise anyone that they were over. The lamplight and the firelight would shine out the door after dark, over the still and breathing country, lighting the roses and the bottle trees, and all was quiet there.

But there was nobody, nobody at all, not even a white person. And if there had been anybody, Solomon would not have let Livvie look at them, just as he would not let her look at a field hand, or a field hand look at her. There was no house near, except for the cabins of the tenants that were forbidden to her, and there was no house as far as she had been, stealing away down the still, deep Trace. She felt as if she waded a river when she went, for the dead leaves on the ground reached as high as her knees, and when she was all scratched and bleeding she said it was not like a road that went anywhere. One day, climbing up the high bank, she had found a graveyard without a church, with ribbon-grass growing about the foot of an angel (she had climbed up because she thought she saw angel wings), and in the sun, trees shining like burning flames through the great caterpillar nets which enclosed them. Scarey thistles stood looking like the prophets in the Bible in Solomon's house. Indian paint brushes grew over her head, and the mourning dove made the only sound in the world. Oh for a stirring of the leaves, and a breaking of the nets! But not by a ghost, prayed Livvie, jumping down the bank. After Solomon took to his bed, she never went out, except one more time.

Livvie knew she made a nice girl to wait on anybody. She fixed things to eat on a tray like a surprise. She could keep from singing when she ironed, and to sit by a bed and fan away the flies, she could be so still she could not hear herself breathe. She could clean up the house and never drop a thing, and wash the dishes without a sound, and she would step outside to churn, for churning sounded too sad to her, like sobbing, and if it made her home-sick and not Solomon, she did not think of that.

But Solomon scarcely opened his eyes to see her, and scarcely tasted his food. He was not sick or paralyzed or in any pain that he mentioned, but he was surely wearing out in the body, and no matter what nice hot thing Livvie would bring him to taste, he would only look at it now, as if he were past seeing how he could add anything more to himself. Before she could beg him, he would go fast asleep. She could not surprise him any more, if he would not taste, and she was afraid that he was never in the world going to taste another thing she brought him—and so how could he last?

But one morning it was breakfast time and she cooked his eggs and grits, carried them in on a tray, and called his name. He was sound asleep. He lay in a dignified way with his watch beside him, on his back in the middle of the bed. One hand drew the quilt up high, though it was the first day of spring. Through the white lace curtains a little puffy wind was blowing as if it came from round cheeks. All night the frogs had sung out in the swamp, like a commotion in the room, and he had not stirred, though she lay wide awake and saying "Shh, frogs!" for fear he would mind them.

He looked as if he would like to sleep a little longer, and so she put back the tray and waited a little. When she tiptoed and stayed so quiet, she surrounded herself with a little reverie, and sometimes it seemed to her when she was so stealthy that the quiet she kept was for a sleeping baby, and that she had a baby and was its mother. When she stood at Solomon's bed and looked down at him, she would be thinking, "He sleeps so well," and she would hate to wake him up. And in some other way, too, she was afraid to wake him up because even in his sleep he seemed to be such a strict man.

Of course, nailed to the wall over the bed—only she would forget who it was—there was a picture of him when he was young. Then he had a fan of hair over his forehead like a king's crown. Now his hair lay down on his head, the spring had gone out of it. Solomon had a lightish face, with eyebrows scattered but rugged, the way privet grows, strong eyes, with second sight, a strict mouth, and a little gold smile. This was the way he looked in his clothes, but in bed in the daytime he looked like a different and smaller man, even when he was wide awake, and holding the Bible. He looked like somebody kin to himself. And then sometimes when he lay in sleep and she stood fanning the flies away, and the light came in, his face was like new, so smooth and clear that it was like a glass of jelly held to the window, and she could almost look through his forehead and see what he thought.

She fanned him and at length he opened his eyes and spoke her name, but he would not taste the nice eggs she had kept warm under a pan.

Back in the kitchen she ate heartily, his breakfast and hers, and looked out the open door at what went on. The whole day, and the whole night before, she had felt the stir of spring close to her. It was as present in the house as a young man would be. The moon was in the last quarter and outside they were turning the sod and planting peas and beans. Up and down the red fields, over which smoke from the brush-burning hung showing like a little skirt of sky, a white horse and a white mule pulled the plow. At intervals hoarse shouts came through the air and roused her as if she dozed neglectfully in the shade, and they were telling her, "Jump up!" She could see how over each ribbon of field were moving men and girls, on foot and mounted on mules, with hats set on their heads and bright with tall hoes and forks as if they carried streamers on them and were going to some place on a journey—and how as if at a signal now and then they would all start at once shouting, hollering, cajoling, calling and answering back, running, being leaped on and breaking away, flinging to earth with a shout and lying motionless in the trance of twelve o'clock. The old women came out of the cabins and brought them the food they had ready for them, and then all worked together, spread evenly out. The little children came too, like a bouncing stream overflowing the fields, and set upon the men, the women, the dogs, the rushing birds, and the wave-like rows of earth, their little voices almost too high to be heard. In the middle distance like some white and gold towers were the haystacks, with black cows coming around to eat their edges. High above everything, the wheel of fields, house, and cabins, and the deep road surrounding like a moat to keep them in, was the turning sky, blue with long, far-flung white mare's-tail clouds, serene and still as high flames. And sound asleep while all this went around him that was his, Solomon was like a little still spot in the middle.

Even in the house the earth was sweet to breathe. Solomon had never let Livvie go any farther than the chicken house and the well. But what if she would walk now into the heart of the fields and take a hoe and work until she fell stretched out and drenched with her efforts, like other girls, and laid her cheek against the laid-open earth, and shamed the old man with her humbleness and delight? To shame him! A cruel wish could come in uninvited and so fast while she looked out the back door. She washed the dishes and scrubbed the table. She could hear the cries of the little lambs. Her mother, that she had not seen since her wedding day, had said one time, "I rather a man be anything, than a woman be mean."

So all morning she kept tasting the chicken broth on the stove, and when it was right she poured off a nice cup-ful. She carried it in to Solomon, and there he lay having a dream. Now what did he dream about? For she saw him sigh gently as if not to disturb some whole thing he held round in his mind, like a fresh egg. So even an old man dreamed about something pretty. Did he dream of her, while his eyes were shut and sunken, and his small hand with the wedding ring curled close in sleep around the quilt? He might be dreaming of what time it was, for even through his sleep he kept track of it like a clock, and knew how much of it went by, and waked up knowing where the hands were even before he consulted the silver watch that he never let go. He would sleep with the watch in his palm, and even holding it to his cheek like a child that loves a plaything. Or he might dream of journeys and travels on a steamboat to Natchez. Yet she thought he dreamed of her; but even while she scrutinized him, the rods of the foot of the bed seemed to rise up like a rail fence between them, and she could see that people never could be sure of anything as long as one of them was asleep and the other awake. To look at him dreaming of her when he might be going to die frightened her a little, as if he might carry her with him that way, and she wanted to run out of the room. She took hold of the bed and held on, and Solomon opened his eyes and called her name, but he did not want anything. He would not taste the good broth.

Just a little after that, as she was taking up the ashes in the front room for the last time in the year, she heard a sound. It was somebody coming. She pulled the curtains together and looked through the slit.

Coming up the path under the bottle trees was a white lady. At first she looked young, but then she looked old. Marvelous to see, a little car stood steaming like a kettle out in the field-track—it had come without a road.

Livvie stood listening to the long, repeated knockings at the door, and after a while she opened it just a little. The lady came in through the crack, though she was more than middle-sized and wore a big hat.

"My name is Miss Baby Marie," she said.

Livvie gazed respectfully at the lady and at the little suitcase she was holding close to her by the handle until the proper moment. The lady's eyes were running over the room, from palmetto to palmetto, but she was saying, "I live at home . . . out from Natchez . . . and get out and show these pretty cosmetic things to the white people and the colored people both . . . all around . . . years and years. . . . Both shades of powder and rouge. . . . It's the kind of work a girl can do and not go clear 'way from home . . ." And the harder she looked, the more she talked. Suddenly she turned up her nose and said, "It is not Christian or sanitary to put feathers in a vase," and then she took a gold key out of the front of her dress and began unlocking the locks on her suitcase. Her face drew the light, the way it was covered with intense white and red, with a little patty-cake of white between the wrinkles by her upper lip. Little red tassels of hair bobbed under the rusty wires of her picture-hat, as with an air of triumph and secrecy she now drew open her little suitcase and brought out bottle after bottle and jar after jar, which she put down on the table, the mantel-piece, the settee, and the organ.

"Did you ever see so many cosmetics in your life?" cried Miss Baby Marie.

"No'm," Livvie tried to say, but the cat had her tongue.

"Have you ever applied cosmetics?" asked Miss Baby Marie next.

"No'm," Livvie tried to say.

"Then look!" she said, and pulling out the last thing of all, "Try this!" she said. And in her hand was unclenched a golden lipstick which popped open like magic.

A fragrance came out of it like incense, and Livvie cried out suddenly, "Chinaberry flowers!"

Her hand took the lipstick, and in an instant she was carried away in the air through the spring, and looking down with a half-drowsy smile from a purple cloud she saw from above a chinaberry tree, dark and smooth and neatly leaved, neat as a guinea hen in the dooryard, and there was her home that she had left. On one side of the tree was her mama holding up her heavy apron, and she could see it was loaded with ripe figs, and on the other side was her papa holding a fish-pole over the pond, and she could see it transparently, the little clear fishes swimming up to the brim.

"Oh, no, not chinaberry flowers—secret ingredients," said Miss Baby Marie. "My cosmetics have secret ingredients—not chinaberry flowers."

"It's purple," Livvie breathed, and Miss Baby Marie said, "Use it freely. Rub it on."

Livvie tiptoed out to the wash stand on the front porch and before the mirror put the paint on her mouth. In the wavery surface her face danced before her like a flame. Miss Baby Marie followed her out, took a look at what she had done, and said, "That's it."

Livvie tried to say "Thank you" without moving her parted lips where the paint lay so new.

By now Miss Baby Marie stood behind Livvie and looked in the mirror over her shoulder, twisting up the tassels of her hair. "The lipstick I can let you have for only two dollars," she said, close to her neck.

"Lady, but I don't have no money, never did have," said Livvie.

"Oh, but you don't pay the first time. I make another trip, that's the way I do. I come back again—later."

"Oh," said Livvie, pretending she understood everything so as to please the lady.

"But if you don't take it now, this may be the last time I'll call at your house," said Miss Baby Marie sharply. "It's far away from anywhere, I'll tell you that. You don't live close to anywhere."

"Yes'm. My husband, he keep the *money*," said Livvie, trembling. "He is strict as he can be. He don't know *you* walk in here—Miss Baby Marie!"

"Where is he?"

"Right now, he in yonder sound asleep, an old man. I wouldn't ever ask him for anything."

Miss Baby Marie took back the lipstick and packed it up. She gathered up the jars for both black and white and got them all inside the suitcase, with the same little fuss of triumph with which she had brought them out. She started away.

"Goodbye," she said, making herself look grand from the back, but at the last minute she turned around in the door. Her old hat wobbled as she whispered, "Let me see your husband."

Livvie obediently went on tiptoe and opened the door to the other room. Miss Baby Marie came behind her and rose on her toes and looked in.

"My, what a little tiny old, old man!" she whispered, clasping her hands and shaking her head over them. "What a beautiful quilt! What a tiny old, old man!"

"He can sleep like that all day," whispered Livvie proudly.

They looked at him awhile so fast asleep, and then all at once they looked at each other. Somehow that was as if they had a secret, for he had never stirred. Livvie then politely, but all at once, closed the door.

"Well! I'd certainly like to leave you with a lipstick!" said Miss Baby Marie vivaciously. She smiled in the door.

"Lady, but I told you I don't have no money, and never did have."

"And never will?" In the air and all around, like a bright halo around the white lady's nodding head, it was a true spring day.

"Would you take eggs, lady?" asked Livvie softly.

"No, I have plenty of eggs—plenty," said Miss Baby Marie.

"I still don't have no money," said Livvie," and Miss Baby Marie took her suitcase and went on somewhere else.

Livvie stood watching her go, and all the time she felt her heart beating in her left side. She touched the place with her hand. It seemed as if her heart beat and her whole face flamed from the pulsing color of her lips. She went to sit by Solomon and when he opened his eyes he could not see a change in her. "He's fixin' to die," she said inside. That was the secret. That was when she went out of the house for a little breath of air.

She went down the path and down the Natchez Trace a way, and she did not know how far she had gone, but it was not far, when she saw a sight. It was a man, looking like a vision—she standing on one side of the Old Natchez Trace and he standing on the other.

As soon as this man caught sight of her, he began to

look himself over. Starting at the bottom with his pointed shoes, he began to look up, lifting his peg-top pants the higher to see fully his bright socks. His coat long and wide and leaf-green he opened like doors to see his high-up tawny pants and his pants he smoothed downward from the points of his collar, and he wore a luminous baby-pink satin shirt. At the end, he reached gently above his wide platter-shaped round hat, the color of a plum, and one finger touched at the feather, emerald green, blowing in the spring winds.

No matter how she looked, she could never look so fine as he did, and she was not sorry for that, she was pleased.

He took three jumps, one down and two up, and was by her side.

"My name is Cash," he said.

He had a guinea pig in his pocket. They began to walk along. She stared on and on at him, as if he were doing some daring spectacular things in stead of just walking beside her. It was not simply the city way he was dressed that made her look at him and see hope in its insolence looking back. It was not only the way he moved along kicking the flowers as if he could break through everything in the way and destroy anything in the world, that made her eyes grow bright. It might be, if he had not appeared the way he did appear that day she would never have looked so closely at him, but the time people come makes a difference.

They walked through the still leaves of the Natchez Trace, the light and the shade falling through trees about them, the white irises shining like candles on the banks and the new ferns shining like green stars up in the oak branches. They came out at Solomon's house, bottle trees and all. Livvie stopped and hung her head.

Cash began whistling a little tune. She did not know what it was, but she had heard it before from a distance, and she had a revelation. Cash was a field hand. He was a transformed field hand. Cash belonged to Solomon. But he had stepped out of his overalls into this. There in front of Solomon's house he laughed. He had a round head, a round face, all of him was young, and he flung his head up, rolled it against the mare's-tail sky in his round hat, and he could laugh just to see Solomon's house sitting there. Livvie looked at it, and there was Solomon's black hat hanging on the peg on the front door, the blackest thing in the world.

"I been to Natchez," Cash said, wagging his head around against the sky. "*I* taken a trip, *I* ready for Easter!"

How was it possible to look so fine before the harvest? Cash must have stolen the money, stolen it from Solomon. He stood in the path and lifted his spread hand high and brought it down again and again in his laughter. He kicked up his heels. A little chill went through her. It was as if Cash was bringing that strong hand down to beat a drum or to rain blows upon a man, such an abandon and menace were in his laugh. Frowning, she went closer to him and his swinging arm drew her in at once and the fright was crushed from her body, as a little match-flame might be smothered out by what it lighted. She gathered the folds of his coat behind him and fastened her red lips to his mouth, and she was dazzled by herself then, the way he had been dazzled at himself to begin with.

In that instant she felt something that could not be told—that Solomon's death was at hand, that he was the same to her as if he were dead now. She cried out, and uttering little cries turned and ran for the house.

At once Cash was coming, following after, he was running behind her. He came close, and halfway up the path he laughed and passed her. He even picked up a stone and sailed it into the bottle trees. She put her hands over her head, and sounds clattered through the bottle trees like cries of outrage. Cash stamped and plunged zigzag up the front steps and in at the door.

When she got there, he had stuck his hands in his pockets and was turning slowly about in the front room. The little guinea pig peeped out. Around Cash, the pinned-up palmettos looked as if a lazy green monkey had walked up and down and around the walls leaving green prints of his hands and feet.

She got through the room and his hands were still in his pockets, and she fell upon the closed door to the other room and pushed it open. She ran to Solomon's bed, calling "Solomon! Solomon!" The little shape of the old man never moved at all, wrapped under the quilt as if it were winter still.

"Solomon!" She pulled the quilt away, but there was another one under that, and she fell on her knees beside him. He made no sound except a sigh, and then she could hear in the silence the light springy steps of Cash walking and walking in the front room, and the ticking of Solomon's silver watch, which came from the bed. Old Solomon was far away in his sleep, his face looked small, relentless, and devout, as if he were walking somewhere where she could imagine the snow falling.

Then there was a noise like a hoof pawing the floor, and the door gave a creak, and Cash appeared beside her. When she looked up, Cash's face was so black it was bright, and so bright and bare of pity that it looked sweet to her. She stood up and held up her head. Cash was so powerful that his presence gave her strength even when she did not need any.

Under their eyes Solomon slept. People's faces tell of things and places not known to the one who looks at them while they sleep, and while Solomon slept under the eyes of Livvie and Cash his face told them like a mythical story that all his life he had built, little scrap by little scrap, respect. A beetle could not have been more laborious or more ingenious in the task of its destiny. When Solomon was young, as he was in his picture overhead, it was the infinite thing with him, and he could see no end to the respect he would contrive and keep in a house. He had built a lonely house, the way he would make a cage, but it grew to be the same with him as a great monumental pyramid and sometimes in his absorption of getting it erected he was like the builder-slaves of Egypt who forgot or never knew the origin and meaning of the thing to which they gave all the strength of their bodies and used up all their days. Livvie and Cash could see that as a man might rest from a life-labor he lay in his bed, and they could hear how, wrapped in his quilt, he sighed to himself comfortably in sleep, while in his dreams he might have been an ant, a beetle, a bird, an Egyptian, assembling and carrying on his back and building with his hands, or he might have been an old man of India or a swaddled baby, about to smile and brush all away.

Then without warning old Solomon's eyes flew wide open under the hedge-like brows. He was wide awake.

And instantly Cash raised his quick arm. A radiant sweat stood on his temples. But he did not bring his arm down—it stayed in the air, as if something might have taken hold.

It was not Livvie—she did not move. As if something said "Wait," she stood waiting. Even while her eyes burned under motionless lids, her lips parted in a stiff grimace, and with her arms stiff at her sides she stood above the prone old man and the panting young one, erect and apart.

Movement when it came came in Solomon's face. It was an old and strict face, a frail face, but behind it, like a covered light, came an animation that could play hide and seek, that would dart and escape, had always escaped. The mystery flickered in him, and invited from his eyes. It was that very mystery that Cash with his quick arm would have to strike, and that Livvie could not weep for. But Cash only stood holding his arm in the air, when the gentlest flick of his great strength, almost a puff of his breath, would have been enough, if he had known how to give it, to send the old man over the obstruction that kept him away from death.

If it could not be that the tiny illumination in the fragile and ancient face caused a crisis, a mystery in the room that would not permit a blow to fall, at least it was certain that Cash, throbbing in his Easter clothes, felt a pang of shame that the vigor of a man would come to such an end that he could not be struck without warning. He took down his hand and stepped back behind Livvie, like a round-eyed schoolboy on whose unsuspecting head the dunce cap has been set.

"Young ones can't wait," said Solomon.

Livvie shuddered violently, and then in a gush of tears she stooped for a glass of water and handed it to him, but he did not see her.

"So here come the young man Livvie wait for. Was no prevention. No prevention. Now I lay eyes on young man and it come to be somebody I know all the time, and been knowing since he were born in a cotton patch, and watched grow up year to year, Cash McCord, growed to size, growed up to come in my house in the end—ragged and barefoot."

Solomon gave a cough of distaste. Then he shut his eyes vigorously, and his lips began to move like a chanter's.

"When Livvie married, her husband were already somebody. He had paid great cost for his land. He spread sycamore leaves over the ground from wagon to door, day he brought her home, so her foot would not have to touch ground. He carried her through his door. Then he growed old and could not lift her, and she were still young."

Livvie's sobs followed his words like a soft melody repeating each thing as he stated it. His lips moved for a little without sound, or she cried too fervently, and unheard he might have been telling his whole life, and then he said, "God forgive Solomon for sins great and small. God forgive Solomon for carrying away too young girl for wife and keeping her away from her people and from all the young people would clamor for her back."

Then he lifted up his right hand toward Livvie where she stood by the bed and offered her his silver watch. He dangled it before her eyes, and she hushed crying; her tears stopped. For a moment the watch could be heard ticking as it always did, precisely in his proud hand. She lifted it away. Then he took hold of the quilt; then he was dead.

Livvie left Solomon dead and went out of the room. Stealthily, nearly without noise, Cash went beside her. He was like a shadow, but his shiny shoes moved over the floor in spangles, and the green downy feather shone like a light in his hat. As they reached the front room, he seized her deftly as a long black cat and dragged her hanging by the waist round and round him, while he turned in a circle, his face bent down to hers. The first moment, she kept one arm and its hand stiff and still, the one that held Solomon's watch. Then the fingers softly let go, all of her was limp, and the watch fell somewhere on the floor. It ticked away in the still room, and all at once there began outside the full song of a bird.

They moved around and around the room and into the brightness of the open door, then he stopped and shook her once. She rested in silence in his trembling arms, unprotesting as a bird on a nest. Outside the redbirds were flying and criss-crossing, the sun was in all the bottles on the prisoned trees, and the young peach was shining, in the middle of them with the bursting light of spring.

AT THE
LANDING

———◆———

THE NIGHT that Jenny's grandfather died, he dreamed of
high water.

He came in his dream and stood just outside the door
of her room, his little chin that was like a chicken's clean
breastbone tilting upwards.

"It has come," the old man said, and he made a com-
plaint of it.

Jenny in her bed lay still, waking more still than in the
sleep of a moment before.

"The river has come back. That Floyd came to tell
me. The sun was shining full on the face of the church,
and that Floyd came around it with his wrist hung with a
great long catfish. 'It's coming,' he said. 'It's the river.'
Oh, it came then! Like a head and arm. Like a horse. A
mane of cedar trees tossing over the top. It has borne
down, and it has closed us in. That Floyd was right."

He reached as if to lift an obstacle that he thought
was stretched there—the bar that crossed the door in her
mother's time. It seemed beyond his strength, she tried
to cry out, and he came in through the doorway. The cord

399

and tassel of his brocade robe—for he had put it on—
seemed to weigh upon his fragile walking like a chain, and
yet it could have been by inexorable will that he wore it,
so set were his little steps, in such duty he dragged it.

"Like poor people who have learned to fly at last,"
he said, walking, dragging, the fine deprecation in his
voice, "all the people in The Landing, all kinds and con-
ditions of people are gliding off and upward to darkness.
The little mandolin that my daughter used to play—it's
rising like a bubble, and filling with water."

"Grandpa!" cried Jenny, and then she was up and taking her grandfather by his tiny adamant shoulders. It was
moonlight. She saw his open eyes. "Wake up, Grandpa!"

"That Floyd's catfish has gone loose and free," he
said gently, as if breaking news to someone. "And all of a
sudden, my dear—my dears, it took its river life back,
and shining so brightly swam through the belfry of the
church, and downstream." At that his mouth clamped
tight shut.

She held out both arms and he fell trembling against
her. With beating heart she carried him through the dark
halls to his room and put him down into his bed. He lay
there in the moonlight, which moved and crept across him
as it would a little fallen withered leaf, and he never
moved or spoke any more, but lay softly, as if he were
floating, being carried away, drawn by the passing moon;
and Jenny's heart beat on and on, sharp as birdsong in
the night, under her breast, until day.

Under the shaggy bluff the bottomlands lay in a river of
golden haze. The road dropped like a waterfall from the

ridge to the town at its foot and came to a grassy end there. It was spring. One slowly moving figure that was a man with a fishing pole passed like a dreamer through the empty street and on through the trackless haze toward the river. The town was still called The Landing. The river had gone, three miles away, beyond sight and smell, beyond the dense trees. It came back only in flood, and boats ran over the houses.

Up the light-scattered hill, in the house with the galleries, the old man and his granddaughter had always lived. They were the people least seen in The Landing. The grandfather was too old, and the girl was too shy of the world, and they were both too good—the old ladies said—to come out, and so they stayed inside.

For all her life the shy Jenny could look, if she stayed in the parlor, back and forth between her mother's two paintings, "The Bird Fair" and "The Massacre at Fort Rosalie." Or if she went in the dining room she could walk around the table or sit on one after the other of eight needlepoint pieces, each slightly different, which her mother had worked and sewn to the chairs, or she could count the plates that stood on their rims in the closet. In the library she could circle an entirely bare floor and make up a dance to a song she made up, all silently, or gaze at the backs of the books without titles—books that had been on ships and in oxcarts and through fire and water, and were singed and bleached and swollen and shrunken, and arranged up high and nearly unreachable, like objects of beauty. Wherever she went she almost touched a prism. The house was full of prisms. They hung everywhere in the shadow of the halls and in the sunlight of the rooms, stirring under the hanging lights, dangling and circling where they were strung in the window curtains. They gave off the faintest of musical notes when air stirred in any room or when only herself passed by, and they touched. It was her way not to touch them herself, but to let the touch be magical, a stir of the curtain by the outer air, that would also make them rainbows. Vases with landscapes on them stood in the halls and were reflected endlessly rising in front of her when she passed quickly between the two mirrors. She might stop and touch all things, trace their little pictures with her finger, and put them back again; it was not forbidden; but her touch that dared not break would have been transparent as a spirit's on the objects. She was calm the way a child is calm, with never the calmness of a spirit. But like distant lightning that silently bathes a whole shimmering sky, one awareness was always trembling about her: one day she would be free to come and go. Nothing now held her in her own room, with the great wardrobe in which she had sometimes longed to hide, and the great box-like canopied bed and the little picture on the wall of her mother with upturned eyes. Jenny could go from room to room, and out at the door. But at the door her grandfather would call her back, with his little murmur.

At sunset the old man and his granddaughter would take their supper in the pavilion on the knoll, that had been a gazebo when the river ran before it. There a little breeze came all the way from the river still. All about the pavilion was an ancient circling thorny rose, like the initial letter in a poetry book. The cook came out and served with exaggerated dignity, as though she scolded in the house. A little picture might be preserved then in all their heads. The old man and the young girl looked across the round table leaf-shadowed under the busy black hands, and smiled by long habit at each other. But her grandfather could not look at her without speculation in his eyes, and the gaze that went so fondly between them held and stretched tight the memory of Jenny's mother. It seemed strange that her mother had been dead now for so many years and yet the wild desire that had torn her seemed still fresh and still a small thing. It was a desire to get to Natchez. People said Natchez was a nice little town on Saturdays with a crowd filling it and moving around.

The grandfather stirred his black coffee and smiled at Jenny. He deprecated raving simply as raving, as a force of Nature and so beneath notice or mention. And yet—even now, too late—if Jenny could plead . . . ! In a heat wave one called the cook to bring a fan, and in his daughter's first raving he rang a bell and told the cook to take her off and sit by her until she had done with it, but in the end she died of it. But Jenny could not plead for her.

Her grandfather, frail as a little bird, would say when it was time to go in. He would rise slowly in the brocade gown he wore to study in, and put his weight, which was the terrifying weight of a claw, on Jenny's arm. Jenny was obedient to her grandfather and would have been obedient to anybody, to a stranger in the street if there could be one. She never performed any act, even a small act, for herself, she would not touch the prisms. It might seem that nothing began in her own heart.

Nothing ever happened, to be seen from the gazebo,

except that Billy Floyd went through the town. He was almost unknown, and one to himself. If he came at all, he would come at this time of day. In the long shadows below they could see his figure with the gleaming fish he carried move clear as a candle over the road that he had to himself, and out to the blue distance. In The Landing, every person that moved was watched out of sight, and it made a little pause in every life. And if in each day a moment of hope must come, in Jenny's day the moment was when the rude wild Floyd walked through The Landing carrying the big fish he had caught.

Under the blue sky, skirting the ravine, a half-ring of twenty cedar trees stood leading to the cemetery, their bleached trunks the colors of red and white roses. Jenny, given permission, would walk up there to visit the grave of her mother.

The cemetery was a dark shelf above the town, on the site of the old landing place when the ships docked from across the world a hundred years ago, and its brink was marked by an old table-like grave with its top ajar where the woodbine grew. Everywhere there, the hanging moss and the up-thrust stones were in that strange graveyard shade where, by the light they give, the moss seems made of stone, and the stone of moss.

On one of the days, while she sat there on a stile, Jenny looked across the ravine and there was Floyd, standing still in a sunny pasture. She could watch between the grapevines, which hung and held back like ropes on either side to clear her view. Floyd had a head of straight light-colored hair and it hung over his forehead, for he never was near a comb. He stood facing her in a tall squared posture of silence and rest, while a rusty-red horse that belonged to the Lockharts cropped loudly beside him in the wild-smelling pasture.

It was said by the old ladies that he slept all morning for he fished all night. Stiff and stern, Jenny sat there with her feet planted just so on the step below, in the posture of a child who is appalled at the stillness and unsurrender of the still and unsurrendering world.

At last she sighed, and when she took up her skirt to go, as if she were dreaming she saw Floyd coming across the pasture toward her. When he reached the ravine and leaped down into it with widespread arms as though he jumped into something dangerous, she stood still on the stile to watch. He moved up near to her now, his feet on the broken ferns at the spring. The wind whipped his hair, almost making a noise.

"Go back," she said. She wanted to watch him a while longer first, before he got to her.

He stopped and looked full at her, his strong neck bending to one side as if yielding in pleasure to the wind. His arms went down and his fists opened. But for her, his eyes were as bright and unconsumed as stars up in the sky. Then she wanted to catch him and see him close, but not to touch him. He stood watching her, though, as if to prevent it. They were as still and rigid as two mocking-birds that were about to strike their beaks and dance.

She waited, but he smiled, and then knelt and cupped both hands to his face in the spring water. He drank for a long time, while she stood there with her skirt whipping in the wind, and waited on him to see how long he could drink without lifting his face. When he had drunk that much, he went back to the field and threw himself yawning down into the grass. The grass was so deep there that she could see only the one arm flung out in the torn sleeve, straight, sun-blacked and motionless.

The day she watched him in the woods, she felt it come to her dimly that her innocence had left her, since she could watch his. She could only sink down onto the step of the stile, and lay her heavy forehead in her hand. But if innocence had left, she still did not know what was to come. She would wait and see him come awake.

But he slept and slept like the dead, and defeated her. She went to her grandfather and left Floyd sleeping.

Another day, they walked for a little near together, each picking some berry or leaf to hold in the mouth, on their opposite sides of the little spring. The pasture, the sun and the grazing horse were on his side, the graves on hers, and they each looked across at the other's. The whole world seemed filled with butterflies. At each step they took, two black butterflies over the flowers were whirring just alike, suspended in the air, one circling the other rhythmically, or both moving from side to side in a gentle wave-like way, one above the other. They were blue-black and moving their wings faster than Jenny's eye could follow, always together, like each other's shadows, beautiful each one with the other. Jenny could see to start with that no kiss had ever brought love tenderly enough from mouth to mouth.

Jenny and Floyd stopped and looked for a little while at all the butterflies and they never touched each other. When Jenny did touch Floyd, touch his sleeve, he started.

He went alert in the field like a listening animal. The horse came near and when he touched it, stood with lifted ears beside him, then broke away. But over all The Landing there was not a sound that she could hear. It could only be that Floyd missed nothing in the world, and could hear innumerable outward things. He suddenly flung up his head. She knew he was smiling. And a smile was always a barrier.

She said his name, for she was so close by. It was the first time.

He stayed motionless, and she knew that he lived apart in delight. That could make a strange glow fall over the field where he was, and the world go black for her, left behind. She felt terrified, as if at a pitiless thing.

Floyd lifted his foot and stamped on the ground, and held out his careless arms to catch the horse he had excited. Then he was jumping on its bare back and riding into a gallop, shouting to frighten and amaze whoever listened. She threw herself down into the grass. Never had she known that the Lockhart horse could run like that. Floyd went at a racing speed and he seemed somehow in his tattered shirt—as she watched from beneath her arm— to stream with the wind, and he circled the steep field three times, and with flying yellow hair and a diminishing shout rode up into the woods.

If she could have followed and found him then, she would have started on foot. But she knew what she would find when she would come to him. She would find him equally real with herself—and could not touch him then. As she was living and inviolate, so of course was he, and when that gave him delight, how could she bring a question to him? She walked in the woods and around the graves in it, and knew about love, how it would have a different story in the world if it could lose the moral knowledge of a mystery that is in the other heart. Nothing in Floyd frightened her that drew her near, but at once she had the knowledge come to her that a fragile mystery was in everyone and in herself, since there it was in Floyd, and that whatever she did, she would be bound to ride over and hurt, and the secrecy of life was the terror of it. When Floyd rode the red horse, she lay in the grass. He might even have jumped across her. But the vaunting and prostration of love told her nothing—nothing at all.

The very next day Jenny waited on the stile and she saw Floyd come walking up the road in the morning, with drenched hair. He might have come and found her, but he came to the Lockhart house first.

The Lockhart house stood between two of the empty stretches along the road. It was wide, low, and twisted. Its roof, held up at the corners by the two chimneys, sagged like a hammock, and was mended with bark and small colored signs. The black high-water mark made a belt around the house and that alone seemed to tighten it and hold it together. Floyd stood gazing in at the doorway, as if what might not come out? And it was a beautiful doorway to see, with its fanlight and its sidelights, though they were blind with silt. The door was shut and the squirrels were asleep on the floor of the long cage across the front wall. Under the forward-tilting porch the clay-colored hens were sitting in twos in the old rowboat. And while Floyd looked, out came Mag.

And the next thing, he was playing with Mag Lockhart, that was an albino. Mag's short white hair would stream out from her head when she crouched nodding over her flowers in the yard, tending them with a jack-knife all day, and she would give a splitting laugh to see anyone come. Jenny from the stile watched them wrestle and play. The treadmill ran under the squirrels' quick feet.

Mag's voice came a long distance through the still day. "You are not!" "It is not!" "I am not!" she would scream, and she would jump away.

Floyd would turn on his heel and whirl old Mag off the ground. Mag ran and she snapped at him, she struggled and she crackled like a green wood fire, and he laughed and caught her. She pointed and sent him for the water, and he went and clattered and banged the buckets for her at the well until she begged him to stop. He went straight off and old Mag sat down on her front steps with the hens and rubbed at her flame-pink arms.

And then suddenly Mag was gone.

Jenny put her hands over her forehead, and then rubbed at her own arms. She believed Mag had been there, because she had felt whatever Mag had felt. If this was a vision, it was the first. And it did not frighten her; she knew it only came because she had felt what was in another heart besides her own. But it had been Mag's heart that grew clear to her, while Floyd ran away.

She lay down in the grass, which whispered in her ear. If desperation were only a country, it would be at the bottom of the well. She wanted to get there, to arrive graceful and airy in some strange other country and walk along its level land beneath its secret sky. She thought she

could see herself, fleet as a mirror-image, rising up in a
breath of astonished farewell and walking to the well of old
Mag. It was built so that it had steps like a stile. She saw
herself walk up them, stand on top, look about, and then
go into the dark passage.

But my grandfather, she thought, even while she sank
so deeply, will call me back. I will have to go back. He will
ask me if I have put flowers on my mother's grave. And
she looked over at the stone on the grave of her mother,
with her married name of Lockhart cut into it.

She clutched the thing in her hand, a blade of grass,
and held on. There she was, sitting up in the sun, with the
blade of grass stretched between her thumbs and held to
her mouth, for the calling back that was in the world. She
blew on the grass. It made a thoughtless reedy sound, and
she blew again.

II

The morning after her grandfather's death, Jenny put on a
starched white dress and went down the hill into The
Landing. A little crocheted bag hung by a ribbon over
her wrist, and she had taken a nickel to put in it. Her
good black strapped slippers moved lightly in the dust.
She was going to tell the news of her grandfather, whom
the old ladies had said would die suddenly—like *that*. And
looking about with every step she took, she saw what a
lonesome place it was for all of this to happen in.

She passed a house that only the mice inhabited. She
passed a black boarded-up store where an owl used to live
and maintain its nocturnal habits. And there, a young calf

belonging to the Lockharts used to nose through the grassy rooms, before the walls were carried away by the Negroes and burned in a winter for firewood. In front of the row of Negro cabins was one long fence, made of lumber from old boats, built there to delay the river for one more moment when it came, the same as they would have delayed a giant bent on destruction by some foolish pretext.

Across the end of the road, crumbling under her eyes, was a two-story building with a remnant of gallery, and that was Jenny's destination. The store and the post office were in the one used room. Across the tin awning hung the moss icicles with which the postmaster had decorated for Christmas. Over the door was the shriveled mistletoe, and the gun that had shot it down still standing in the corner. Tipped back against the front wall sat five old men in their chairs, with one holding the white cat. On the step, Son Alford was playing his mandolin that had been Jenny's mother's and given away. He was singing his fast song.

> *"Ain't she cute*
> *Ain't she smart*
> *Don't look twice*
> *It'll break my heart*
> *Everybody loves my gal."*

All nodded to her, but they knew she was not supposed to speak to them.

She went inside, and the first thing she saw was Billy Floyd. He was standing in the back of the room with the postmaster saying to him, "Reckon we're going to have water this year?"

She had never seen the man between walls and under a roof and somehow it made him a different man after the one in the field. He stood in the dim and dingy store with a row of filmy glass lamps and a pair of boots behind his head, and there was something close, gathering-close, and used and worldly about him.

"That slime, that's just as slick! You know how a fish is, I expect," the postmaster was saying affably to them both, just as if they were in any way together. "That's the way a house is, been under water. It's a sight to see those niggers try to clean this place out, falling down to slide from here to the front door and back. You have to get the slime off right away too, or you never can. Sure would make the best paint in the world." He laughed.

There was something handled and used about Floyd, something strong as an odor, the odor of the old playing cards that the old men of The Landing shuffled every day over their table in the street.

"Reckon we're going to have water this year?" the postmaster asked again. He looked from one of them to the other.

Floyd said nothing, he only held a penny. For a moment Jenny thought he was going to drop his high head at being trapped in the confined place, with her between him and the door, which would be the same as telling it out, before a third person, that he could be known in time if he were caught and cornered in a little store.

"What would you like today, Miss Jenny?" asked the postmaster. "Posy seeds?"

But she could not think what she would like. She held her little bag quite still, the strings drawn tight.

All the time, Floyd was giving her a glaring look.

"Well, it makes you think sometimes, to see the water come over all the world," said the postmaster. "I took everything I could out of here last time. Then I come down from the hill and peeked in the door and what did I see? My showcases commencing to float loose. What a sight that did make! I wouldn't have thought I sold some of them things. Carried the showcases out on the hill, but nowhere much to take them. Could you believe I could carry everything out of my store in twenty minutes but my safe? Couldn't lift that. Left the door to it open and went off and left it. So as it wouldn't rust shut, Floyd, Miss Jenny. Took me a long time to scrape the river out of that thing."

All three waited a moment, and then the postmaster spoke again in a softer, intimate voice, smilingly. "Some stranger lost through here says, 'Why don't you all move away?' Move away?" He laughed, and pointed a finger at Jenny. "Did you hear that, Miss Jenny—why don't we move away? Because we live here, don't we, Miss Jenny?"

Then she knew it was a challenge Floyd made with his hard look, and she lost to him. She walked out and left him where he held his solid stand. And when the postmaster had pointed his finger at her, she remembered that she was never to speak to Billy Floyd, by the order of her grandfather.

Outside the door, she stopped still. The weight of the nickel swung in her little bag, and she felt as if she had forgotten Doomsday. She took a step back toward the

challenging Floyd. Then in a kind of haste she whispered
to the five old men, separately, and even to Son Alford,
and each time nearer to tears for her grandfather that died
in the night. Then they gathered round her, and hurried
her to the old women, and so back home.

But Floyd's face glared before her eyes all the way, it
was like something in her vision that kept her from seeing.
It was brighter than the glare of death. He might have
been buying a box of matches with his penny, which was
what his going cost. He would go. The danger of flood
was her grandfather's dream, and the postmaster's store-
keeper wit. These were bright days and clear nights; and
so Floyd would not wait long in The Landing. That was
what the old ladies said, and asked that their words be
marked.

But on a later day, Jenny took a walk and met Floyd by
the little river that came out of the spring and went to the
Mississippi beyond. She sat down and made a clover chain
that would never get long because the cloverheads slipped
out, and while she made it she kept looking with assuring
looks into his illuminated eyes that went over the landscape and searched the sky for clouds. She could hold his
look for a moment and then it would get away. She did not
say a thing to him, for nobody can say, "It is a heavy heart
that makes me clumsy." Nobody can say anything so true
and apologetic. Nobody can say, "Forgive the heavy heart
that loves more than the tongue can say or the hands can
do. Look back at me every time I look at you and never
feel pity, for what my heart holds this minute is better

than what you offer the least bit less." Her eyes were telling him this but if he knew it or felt a threat in it, he never gave a sign. "My heart loves more than I can say or do, but feel no pity, only have a little vision too, of all clumsiness fallen away." She guessed that all grace belongs to the future. But he never had anything to say to her thought or her guess. He stood above her with his feet planted down and looked out over the landscape from within that moment. Level with him now, all The Landing spread under his eyes. Not knowing the world around, she could not know how The Landing looked set down in it. All she knew was that he would leave it when his patience gave out, and that this little staving moment by the river would reach its limit and go first.

Her eyes descended slowly, as if adorned with flowers, from his light blowing hair and his gathering brows down, down him, past his clever hands that caught and trapped so delicately away from her side, softly down to the ground that was a sandy shore. A hidden mussel was blowing bubbles like a spring through the sand where his boot was teasing the water. It was the little pulse of bubbles and not himself or herself that was the moment for her then; and he could have already departed and she could have already wept, and it would have been the same, as she stared at the little fountain rising so gently out of the shimmering sand. A clear love is *in the world*—this came to her as insistently as the mussel's bubbles through the water. There it was, existing there where they came and were beside it now. It is in the bubble in the water in the river, and it has its own changing and its mysteries of

415

days and nights, and it does not care how we come and go.

But when the moment ended, he went. And as soon as he left The Landing, the rain began to fall.

Each day the storm clouds were opening like great purple flowers and pouring out their dark thunder. Each nightfall, the storm was laid down on their houses like a burden the day had carried. The noise of rain, of the gullies filling, of the little river leaping up and running in waves filled all The Landing.

And when at last the river came, it did come like a hand and arm, and pushed black trees before it, but it was at dawn. Jenny went with the others, behind Mag Lockhart, onto the hill and the water followed, whirling and bobbing the young dead animals around on its roaring breast. The clouds lowered and broke again and the rain put out the lanterns. Boat whistles began crying as faint as baby cries in that rainy dark.

Jenny had not spoken for a day and a night on the hill when she told someone that she was sleepy. It was Billy Floyd that she told it to. He put her in his boat, that she had never seen. Jenny looked in Floyd's shining eyes and saw how they held the whole flood, as the flood held its triumph in its whirlpools, and it was a vast and unsuspected thing.

It was on the high hill of the cemetery, when the water was at its peak. They came in Floyd's boat where the river lapped around the dark cedar tops, and monuments like pillars to bear them up scraped their passage, and she knew they rode over the grave of her grandfather and the grave of her mother. Muscadine vines spread under the water rippling their leaves like schools of fishes. It was always the same darkness. Fires burned somewhere, but in the distance, red and blue.

"I . . ." she began, and stopped.

He scowled.

She knew at once that there was nothing in her life past or even now in the flood that would make anything to tell. He already knew that he had saved her life, for that had taken up his time in the time of danger. Yet she might confess it. It came to her lips. He scowled on. Still, it was not any kind of confession that she would finally wish to make. She would like to tell him some strange beautiful thing, if she could speak at all, something to make him speak. Communication would be telling something that is all new, so as to have more of the new told back. The dream of that held her spellbound, with the things possible that hung in the air like clouds over the world, and she smiled in pure belief, for they were beautiful.

"I . . ." She looked softly at him as if from a distance down a little road or a little tether he sent her on.

He took hold of her, put her out of the boat into a little place he made that was dry and green and smelled good, and she went to sleep. After a time that could have been long or short, she thought she heard him say, "Wake up."

When her eyes were open and clear upon him, he violated her and still he was without care or demand and as gay as if he were still clanging the bucket at the well. With the same thoughtlessness of motion, that was a kind of grace, he next speared a side of wild meat from an animal

417

he had killed and had ready in his boat, and cooked it over a fire he had burning on the ground. All the water lapped around. Over its sound she whispered something, but his movement and his task went on firmly about his leaping fire. People who had been there in other floods had put their initials on the tree. Her words came a little louder and in shyness she changed them from words of love to words of wishing, but still he did not look around. "I wish you and I could be far away. I wish for a little house." But ideas of any different thing from what was in his circle of fire might never have reached his ears, for all the attention he paid to her remarks.

He had fishes ready too, wrapped and cooking in a hole scooped in the ground. When she ate it was in obedience to him, though he did not say "Eat" or say anything, he only smiled at the fire, and for him it was all a taking freely of what was free. She knew from him nevertheless that what people ate in the world was earth, river, wildness and litheness, fire and ashes. People took the fresh death and the hot fire into their mouths and got their own life. She ate greedily as long as he ate, and took what he took. She ate eagerly, looking up at him while her teeth bit, to show him herself, her proud hunger, as if to please and flatter him with her original and now lost starvation. But she could make him neither sorry nor proud. When she was sick afterwards, he walked away and waited apart from her shame, as he had left her in his delight.

The dream of love, that made her hold as still in her life as if she heard music, had never carried her yet to the first country of which it told. But there was a country, as

surely as there was herself. When she saw the moon come
up that night and grow bright as it went above the flood
and the boats in it, she was not as sorrowful as she might
have been, now that they floated so high, that no threads
hung down from the moon, no tender ladder all at once
caught light and drifted down. There was a need in all
dreams for something to stay far, far away, never to tor-
ment with the rest, and the bright moon now was that.

III

When the water was down, Jenny went back below and
Floyd went down the river in his boat. They parted with
the clumsiest of touches. Down through the exhausted
and still dripping trees she made her way, again behind
Mag, following the tracks and signs of others, and the
mud sticking to her. Ashes sifted through the air and she
saw them touch her skin but did not feel them. She came
to the stile where she could look at the world below. The
sun was going down and a wind blew following after the
river, and the little town had turned the color of river
water and the trees in their shame of refuse rattled like yellow pebbles and the houses sank below them scuffed and
small. The smoky band of woods that lay in the distance
toward the retreating river still seemed to waver and slide.

In The Landing the houses had turned a little, like
people whose skirts are pulled. Where the front of the
Lockhart house had been pulled away, the furniture, that
had been carried out of the corners by the river and rocked
about, stood in the middle of the floor and showed down
its back the curly yellow grain, like its long hair. One old

store had been carried clean away, after it was closed so long, and in its foundations were the old men standing around poking for money with little sticks. Money could have fallen through the cracks for many years. Fifteen cents and twenty cents and a Spanish piece were found, and the old fellows poking with their sticks were laughing like women.

Jenny came to her house. It stood as before, except that in the yellow and windy light it seemed to draw its galleries to itself, to return to its cave of night and trees, crouched like a child going backwards to the womb.

But once inside, she took one step and was into a whole-new ecstasy, an ecstasy of cleaning, to wash the river out. She ran as if driven, carrying buckets and mops. She scrubbed and pried and shook the river away. Even the pages of books seemed to have been opened and written on again by muddy fingers. In the long days when she stretched and dried white curtains and sheets, rubbed the rust off knives and made them shine, and wiped the dark river from all the prisms, she forgot even love, to clean.

But the shock of love had brought a trembling to her fingers that made her drop what she touched, and made her stumble on the stair, though all the time she was driven on. And when the house was clean again she felt that there was no place to hide in it, not one room. She even opened the small door of her mother's last room, but when she looked in she thought of her mother who was kept guard on there, who struggled unweariedly and all in loneliness, and it was not a hiding place.

If in all The Landing she could have found a place

to feel alone and out of sight, she would have gone there.
One old lady or another would always call to her when she
went by, to tell her something, and if she walked out in
the road she brushed up against the old men sitting at
their cards, and they spoke to her. She did not like to see
faces, which were ugly, or flowers, which were beautiful
and smelled sweet.

But at last the trembling left and dull strength came
back, as if a wound had ceased to flow its blood. And
then one day in summer she could look at a bird flying in
the air, its tiny body like a fist opening and closing, and
did not feel daze or pain, and then she was healed of the
shock of love.

Then whenever she thought that Floyd was in the
world, that his life lived and had this night and day, it was
like discovery once more and again fresh to her, and if it
was night and she lay stretched on her bed looking out at
the dark, a great radiant energy spread intent upon her
whole body and fastened her heart beneath its breath, and
she would wonder almost aloud, "Ought I to sleep?" For
it was love that might always be coming, and she must
watch for it this time and clasp it back while it clasped,
and while it held her never let it go.

Then the radiance touched at her heart and her brain,
moving within her. Maybe some day she could become
bright and shining all at once, as though at the very touch
of another with herself. But now she was like a house with
all its rooms dark from the beginning, and someone would
have to go slowly from room to room, slowly and darkly,
leaving each one lighted behind, before going to the next.
It was not caution or distrust that was in herself, it was

only a sense of journey, of something that might happen. She herself did not know what might lie ahead, she had never seen herself. She looked outward with the sense of rightful space and time within her, which must be traversed before she could be known at all. And what she would reveal in the end was not herself, but the way of the traveler.

In The Landing much was known about all kinds of love that had happened there, and wisdom traveled, when it left the porches, in the persons of three old women. The day the old women would come to see Jenny, it would be to celebrate her ruin that they trudged through the sun in their bonnets. They would come up the hill to say, "Why don't you run after him?" and to say, "Now you won't love him any more," for they always did pay a visit to say those words.

Now only Mag came sidling up, and brought a bouquet of amaryllis to present with blushes to Jenny. Jenny blushed too.

"Some people that don't speak to other people don't grow the prettiest flowers!" Mag cried victoriously as Jenny took them. Her baby hair blew down and her sharp smile cut back into her long dry cheek.

"I speak to you, Mag," said Jenny.

When she walked she heard them talk—the three old ladies. About her they said, "She'll follow her mother to her mother's grave." About Floyd they had more to say. They called him "the wild man" because they had never been told quite who he was or where he had come from. The sun had burned his skin dark and his hair light, till he

was golden in the road, and they freely considered his
walking by again, as if they could take his life up into
their fingers with their sewing and sew it or snip it on
their laps. They always went back to saying that at any
rate he caught enormous fish wherever he fished in the
river, and always had a long wet thing slung over his wrist
when he went by, ugh! One old lady thought he was a
Gipsy and had called "Gipsy!" after him when he went
by her front porch once too often. One lady said she did
not care what he was or if she ever knew what he was,
and whether he lived or died it was all the same to her.
But the third old lady had books, though she was the one
that was a little crazy, and she waited till the others had
done and then explained that Floyd had the blood of a
Natchez Indian, though the Natchez might be supposed to
be all gone, massacred. The Natchez, she said—and she
nodded toward her books, "The Queen's Library," high
on the shelf—were the people from the lost Atlantis, had
they heard of that? and took their pride in the escape from
that flood, when the island went under. And there was
something all Indians knew, about never letting the last
spark of fire go out. What did the other ladies think of
that?

They were shocked. They had thought all the time
he was really the bastard of one of the old checker-players,
that had been let grow up away in the woods until he got
big enough to come back and make trouble. They said he
was half-wild like one family they could name, and half
of the time he did not know what he was doing, like
another family. All in his own right he could scent coming
things like an animal and in some of his ways, just like

all men, he was something of an animal. But they said it was the way he was.

"Why don't you run after him?"—"Now you won't love him any more."

Jenny wondered what more love would be like. Then of course she knew. More love would be quiet. She would never be so quiet as she wished until she was quiet with her love. In the center of everything, in the center of thunder, there was a precious piece of quiet, and into quiet her love would go. The Landing was filled with clangor, it seemed to her, until her love was filled with quiet. It seemed to her that she had been the same as in many places in the world, traveling and traveling, always with quiet to give. It had been enough to make her desperate in her heart, the long search for Billy Floyd to give quiet to.

But if Floyd had a search, what was it?

She was holding the amber beads they used to give her mother to play with. She looked at the lump of amber, and looked through to its core. Nobody could ever know about the difference between the radiance that was the surface and the radiance that was inside. There were the two worlds. There was no way at all to put a finger on the center of light. And if there were a mountain, the cloud over it could not touch its heart when it traveled over, and if there were an island out in the sea, the waves at its shore would never come over the place in the middle of the island. She looked in her very dreams at Floyd who had such clear eyes shining at her, and knew his heart lay clearer still, safe and deep in his innocence, safe and away from the outside, deeper than quiet. What she remembered was that when her hand started out to touch him in delight, he smiled and turned away—not from her, but toward something. . . .

Was it toward one thing, toward some one thing alone?

But it was when love was of the one for the one, that it seemed to hold all that was multitudinous and nothing was single any more. She had one love and that was all, but she dreamed that she lined up on both sides of the road to see her love come by in a procession. She herself was more people than there were people in The Landing, and her love was enough to pass through the whole night, never lifting the same face.

It was July when Jenny left The Landing. The grass was tall and gently ticking between the tracks of the road. The stupor of air, the quiet of the river that now went behind a veil, the sheen of heat and the gray sheen of summering trees, and the silence of day and night seemed all to touch, to bathe and administer to The Landing. The little town took a languor and a kind of beauty from the treatment of time and place. It stretched and swooned, and when two growing boys knelt in the road and caught the sun rays in a bit of glass and got fire, they seemed to tease a sleeper, and when they said "Hooray!" they sounded like adventurers in a dream.

Pears lying on the ground warmed and soured, bees gathered at the figs, birds put their little holes of possession in each single fruit in the world that they could fly to. The scent of lilies rolled sweetly from their heavy cornucopias and trickled down by shady paths to fill the golden air of the valley. The mourning dove called its three notes, kept its short silence—which was its mourning?—and called three more.

Jenny had known the most when she knew Floyd rode the horse in the field of butterflies while she was still; and she had known something when she watched him cook the meat and had eaten it for him under his eye; and now once more, in the dream of July, she knew very little, she was lost in wonder again. If she could find him now, or even find the place where he had last passed through, she would gain the next wisdom. It was a following after, now—it was too late to find any way alone.

The sun was going down when she went. The red eyes of the altheas were closing, and the lizards ran on the wall. The last lily buds hung green and glittering, pendulant in the heat. The crape-myrtle trees were beginning to fill with light for they drank the last of it every day, and gave off their white and flame in the evening that filled with the throb of cicadas. There was an old mimosa closing in the ravine—the ancient fern, as old as life, the tree that shrank from the touch, grotesque in its tenderness. All nearness and darkness affected it, even clouds going by, but for Jenny that left it no tree ever gave such allurement of fragrance anywhere.

She looked behind her for the last time as she went down under the trees. As if it were made of shells and pearls and treasures from the sea, the house glinted in the sunset, tinted with the drops of light that seemed to fall slowly through the vaguely stirring leaves. Tenderly as seaweed the long moss swayed. The chimney branched like coral in the upper blue.

Then green branches closed it over, and with her next step trumpet and muscadine vines and the great big-leaved vines made pillars about the trunks of the trees and arches and buttresses all among them. Passion flowers bloomed with their white and purple rays about her shoulders and under her feet. She walked on into the streaming hot shade of the wilderness, and put out her hands between the hanging vines. She feared the snakes in the sudden cool. Like thousands of silver bells the frogs rang her through the swamp, which then closed behind her.

All at once the whole open sky could be seen—she had come to the river. A quiet fire burned on the bluff and moving as far outward as she could see was the cold blur of water. A great spiraled net lay on its side and its circles twinkled faintly on the sky. Veil behind veil of long drying nets hung on all sides, dropping softly and blue-colored in the low wind and the place was folded in by them. All things, river, sky, fire, and air, seemed the same color, the color that is seen behind the closed eyelids, the color of day when vision and despair are the same thing.

Some fishermen came around her and when she named Billy Floyd they nodded their heads. They said, what with the rains, they waited for the racing of the waters to slow down, but that he went out on them. They said he was out on them now, but would come back to the camp, if he did not turn over and drown first. She asked the fishermen to let her wait there with them, since it was to them that he would return. They said it did not matter to them how long she waited, or where.

She stood by the nets. A little distance away men and women were cooking and eating and she smelled the fish and the wild meat. The river went by immeasurable under the sky, moving and dimly catching and snagging itself, freeing itself without effort, heavy with its great waves of drift, deep with stirring fish.

But after a certain length of time, the men that had been throwing knives at the tree by the last light put her inside a grounded houseboat on the plank of which chickens were standing. The willow branches hung down over and dragged softly back and forth across the roof. There were noises and fires all around. There were pigs in the wood.

One by one the men came in to her. She actually spoke to the first one that entered between the dozing chickens, for now she could speak to everyone, in a vague stir of welcome or in the humility that moved now deep in her spirit. About them all and closer to them than their own breath was the smell of trees that had bled to the knives they wore.

When she called out, she did not call any name; it was a cry with a rising sound, as if she said "Go back," or asked a question, and then at the last protested. A rude laugh covered her cry, and somehow both the harsh human sounds could easily have been heard as rejoicing, going out over the river in the dark night. By the fire, little boys were slapped crossly by their mothers—as if they knew that the original smile now crossed Jenny's face, and hung there no matter what was done to her, like a bit of color that kindles in the sky after the light has gone.

"Is she asleep? Is she in a spell? Or is she dead?" asked a little old bright-eyed woman who went and looked in the door, and crept up to the now meditating men outside. She was so precise in her question that she even held up three rheumatic fingers when she asked.

"She's waiting for Billy Floyd," they said.

The old woman nodded, and nodded out to the flowing river, with the firelight following her face and showing its dignity. The younger boys separated and took their turns throwing knives with a dull *pit* at the tree.

A NOTE ON THE TYPE

The principal text of this Modern Library edition
was composed in a digitized version of
Horley Old Style, a typeface issued by
the English type foundry Monotype in 1925.
It has such distinctive features
as lightly cupped serifs and an oblique horizontal bar
on the lowercase "e."